Copyright © 2018 by Valerie Parente

In Touch

Valerie Parente

To my loving family.

Through every tribulation and blessing that this mental disorder has unearthed, you have stood with me. The reason that I am able to manifest my mind into written word is because of your unconditional support and endless love.

In Touch

Part I

Chapter 1

It is a scientific fact that human brains are permeated with a concept of self. They relay our bodily senses to conscious awareness. You consciously *feel* touched upon your skin because your brain is decoding neural messages of the stimulus from your sensory receptors. Every sense works like that – sight, taste, smell, sound, and touch – and all of those building blocks construct your perception of self. So it is more than an illogical stretch to say that a sense of self is anything beyond a slew of electrical and chemical messages lighting up your brain.

This argument is precisely why I was not going to let the student librarian, my most intellectually competitive friend Natalie, tell me that out-of-body experiences are legitimate.

"I'm serious Jef, I had an out-of-body experience last night!" Natalie shouted down to my comfortable seat on the school library's carpeted floor.

"Mhm…" I dismissed while packing textbooks back into my backpack, preparing to leave the community college campus and start yet another shift reading on the job as a convenience store cashier.

"Just say what you're thinking," Natalie dared. "You always do."

"Well," I took a deep inhale of the stuffy library air, "if you really want me to believe that you were not on mind-altering drugs, hallucinating in the early NREM-1 stage of sleep, or simply dreaming, then I am forced to believe that you are nothing but mentally ill," I declared unapologetically, taking deep pleasure in outwitting somebody as erudite as a fellow scholar.

Natalie's narrow eyes resisted from glaring.

"You know," she deflated with an exasperated sigh, "Someday, somebody is going to challenge you and they are going be on a totally different mental wavelength than you, and that is going to confuse the hell out of you."

"Sure," I scoffed while leaping to a stand and swinging the heavy backpack along my vertebrate, "maybe in a year when I'm at an actual university."

Natalie just rolled her eyes and returned to restocking books from her library cart. I abandoned the scene and made a beeline outside.

"Hey! Sterling!" a voice from the courtyard ahead called out my last name.

Sure enough my childhood friend Gabe was skipping class to toss a Frisbee with the horrible influence that is Carson Monopoulous.

Gabe didn't hesitate to slice the autumn air with his bright orange disc. With impressive centripetal acceleration, the Frisbee hurled right into my hands.

After winning that little debate with Natalie in the library, I admittedly felt the leftover high of arrogance. I decided to show off by throwing the Frisbee from behind my back. With a tricky bend of my arm and the flick of my wrist the orange saucer propelled into motion. The intricate tribal design on the disc's surface morphed into an ambiguous blend of oranges and yellows as it revolved like a cyclone around its center.

Gabe launched himself in the air and caught the soaring disc. "Nice!" he commended the smooth pass, only to whip it back in the most erratic of throws.

The Frisbee displaced a few yards out of my reach, only a few feet away from a girl who was sitting crisscross in the grass.

She had dark, almost black hair, and the type of pallid skin that looked more like a result of dietary deficiency than genetics. Her frame was petite, hunched forward with her legs bent into a pretzel. Odder than her voluntary lonely demeanor was her unbreakable focus on the spiral notebook in her lap.

She scribbled and scribbled onto lined paper, lost in her own world. I found it hard to believe that she didn't notice that a bright orange Frisbee nearly hit her.

"Excuse me!" I called out.

Not a movement from the girl, so I jogged a few feet closer to her.

"Hey!" I yelled in her direction and pointed towards the Frisbee just inches away from her knee, "Can you pass that?"

The young woman tilted her chin upwards, locking her large brown eyes on mine. Charcoal makeup lined the bottom halves of her doe-like corneas which were bordered by unusually long eyelashes.

I felt melancholy radiate off her stare. She had a rare set of emotive eyes, deer-in-headlights eyes, that could communicate words a mouth could not.

My nervous stutter kicked in, "Can you, uh, can you pass the Frisbee over here?"

Biting down on her rosy pink lip, apologetically, she shook her head in refusal.

Confused, I glanced around me to see if she was responding to somebody else. There was nobody in my vicinity though. "Um…"

"Sorry," the lonely girl mouthed, then quickly turned her attention back to her frenzied collection of scribbles.

Awkwardly I paced to the orange disc, still a few feet away from the girl with the notebook. As I picked it up off the grass I tried to get a good look at the girl's face, you know, to make eye contact and say "sorry my friend almost clocked you in the head".

But the dark haired girl refused to look up at me.

Bothered, I retrieved the Frisbee, jogged a few yards away, and then whipped the recreational plate in Gabe's direction. As he caught the disc against his stomach he chuckled, "That was awkward as hell. What was her deal?"

"Who knows," I shrugged off, "I guess she's just a snob."

Eager to give the peculiar snob one last glance, I spun around, only to see that the girl with the notebook was gone.

Only a packet of paper rested in the same patch of fresh autumn grass.

I looked around the proximity, expecting so see the dark haired girl scurrying away. I couldn't spot her though.

After quickly scanning the surroundings again, this time to make sure nobody was staring at me, I jogged over to the abandoned packet.

I knelt down to the world's crust and peered close at the packet. On the top of the page was the title "Obsessive Compulsive Disorder". Curiosity got the best of me and before I could stop myself I was already reading the poem.

<u>Obsessive Compulsive Disorder</u> *by Lacey Parker*

Is there something in this brain

which makes it misbehave?

I can feel voices on my skin that try to seep within,

anxious strains thriving off stress designed to oppress

until I scrub them off my flesh.

I can feel this need to perform a ritual I abhor.

Forced to lather, rinse, these invisible prints

until my brain says I am dismissed.

Have I become a slave

of a poorly crafted brain?

I can feel myself confined in this sick mind.

I must ask for permission before any step or revision,

turning my house into a prison.

I can feel the commands of a meticulous plan,

something so insane makes me redo and rearrange,

turning through this anxiety maze.

Is there any reasoning with this brain

when there is no sense of reason in this brain?

I can feel myself try to justify

all of the obsessions and compulsions,

playing over like mental malfunctions.

Still I feel the hope that a new day will show

that the ego I have ached to maintain

will finally be explained.

      An unidentifiable sense of speechlessness suffocated my vocal chords.
      The ability to adequately put your thoughts and emotions into words was not my area of expertise.
      I had never, to my knowledge, met somebody with this disease before.
      From a shallow angle I could see a parallel between Lacey Parker and my schizophrenic older brother, Peter. That being said, if I mapped out the content of this poem with the firsthand observation of my brother's experiences, there would be a major difference. My brother had a psychotic disorder, but this... this was different. This was a disorder of obsession at its most brazen level.
      Needless to say, I snatched the poem and took it home with me.

In a quiet moment when I would normally default to picturing the class I'd be lecturing as a future physics professor, I pictured that dark haired girl with the big brown eyes sitting in the grass, writing in her notebook. That girl possessed such a fascinatingly sick brain. My logical mind craved to understand her disordered mind.
      I felt like I had a lot to learn from the girl with the notebook. It felt like an obligation. I mean how was it possible for a

human brain to function so irrationally? If she had brain damage like Peter then that would make sense, but what if she didn't? I needed to know. I needed to know how Lacey Parker operated.

Before I went to bed that night I made a point to scan a copy of Lacey Parker's poem and put the copy on my desk. I was nowhere near done with this girl. I needed to get in touch with her mind.

I reached to the floor of my closet where there was a pile of unused binders, and grabbed a black one.

Inside my closet were mounted shelves in which I stacked about thirty binders of research. I designated each binder to a different topic. Anything and everything to increase the knowledge in my brain. To be the teacher and the student at the same time. That's also why I bolted a whiteboard to my bedroom wall. Technically it was just a very large oblong white tile Peter and I found in the basement, but after hosing it down and doodling on it with Expo markers we found it functioned the exact same as your typical whiteboard.

Since we didn't have a lot of money I had to help my mom pay the bills (particularly to pay for Peter's absurdly expensive schizophrenia medication), so I was forced to work full time at the local convenience store straight out of high school.

I hated it. I wanted nothing more than to be at school, using my brain, keeping up my stamina in learning. I was painstakingly depressed during those school-less semesters. I wouldn't socialize. I just worked. Worked, worked, and worked. The only times I was happy, truly happy, was when I would go to the public library and study book after book about whatever the heck I wanted. So I turned learning and studying into a hobby. I'd come home, lock myself in my room, and do one of two things: sleep or research a random topic.

Often I'd relay what I read to Peter at the dinner table. Mom would get mad, say something about how I was confusing him, which just made me try harder to explain the information in the most comprehensive yet thorough way possible. Teaching was important, teaching was everything. It was the obligation that drove me and the obsession that calmed me.

I can't adequately describe how high I get when I learn something new. Reading. Taking notes. Creating an outline. It sets off all sorts of neurotransmitters in my brain. I would study everything if I could, aside from psychology and right-brained oriented subjects like English and philosophy (a class I naively signed up for during my first semester of college). Don't get me wrong, philosophy was interesting, but it drove me crazy. It was so damn wishy-washy and oblique. Just a surplus of questions, hardly ever any definitive answers. I don't think I ever walked away from a philosophy class feeling enlightened. The only comfort in such a lack of knowledge can come from the Renaissance-era astronomer and mathematician Nicolaus Copernicus himself when he declared, "To know that we know what we know, and to know that we do not know what we do not know, that is true knowledge." This is the phrase I repeat to myself when I'm finding difficulty grappling with a concept in fields, typically the less concrete liberal arts.

To this day I think the only thing that kept me from going crazy was these binders.

Without hesitation I grabbed a permanent silver marker from my desk and scrawled "Obsessive Compulsive Disorder" onto the front and side of the black binder then slid the copy of Lacey Parker's poem into the front pocket.

Immobile in my bed, I thought about how I would approach this study, a study more unconventional than my past binder topics.

When it came to finding facts there were options: descriptive studies, correlational studies, and the most manipulative approach of all, the experiment. But for some reason I didn't want to manipulate Lacey Parker, which was odd considering I hadn't even officially met her. Maybe it was her sublime poem- something that both humanized Lacey, the subject, and elicited emotions out of me, the observer. Maybe it was because her cognitive impairments reminded me of my disabled brother and I knew better than to judge her peculiarities so harshly.

For once, I didn't know. I didn't have a definitive answer to why I felt a connection with this stranger, but I did. Regardless of a reason, experimenting on Lacey Parker to learn about the obsessive compulsive brain was out of the question.

To discover the facts of this mental illness from a personal standpoint, a selfish standpoint that involved inserting myself in the study, there was only one option: a descriptive study.

Meticulous observation. Detailed recordings. Verbal surveys that I'd have to initiate under the friendly disguise of casual conversation, a skill that required a smooth stealth I knew I didn't have. I'd be implementing a potpourri of research methods in an attempt to uncover the elusive mental illness, obsessive compulsive disorder and appease my ravenous brain. But nonetheless, this was a stratagem worth pursuing since my final semester of community college required less classes than I was used to and I was anxious to keep my brain sharp, especially if I wanted to excel at a university and become the physics professor I always yearned to be.

When I return that poem to Lacey Parker tomorrow, I will have new and significant information for my precious binder and, more precious, my ever-evolving brain.

Chapter 2

"Obsessive compulsive disorder is characterized by unreasonable thoughts and fears, otherwise known as obsessions, which lead to compulsive behaviors."

I read the definition of obsessive compulsive disorder on the dim smartphone screen, shielding the device behind the desk during this afternoon's programming lesson.

The split second that class ended I pulled the original copy of Lacey Parker's "Obsessive Compulsive Disorder" poem out of my backpack and scoured the courtyard for the girl with the notebook.

Discouraged, I decided I'd head home early before my 5:00 PM work shift.

I was on my way to my jeep when all of a sudden I saw a short little brunette on the metal bench beside the parking lot.

It was no surprise that Lacey was glued to her notebook. Her mouth was very tight. Stressed. And she was deep in her own zone again.

"Um… Lacey Parker?" I fished through the air between us.

She looked up from her notebook and hesitated, "Hi?"

I reached out to shake her hand as I introduced myself, "Jef, Jef Sterling."

"Hi "

She didn't move a muscle. Why was she so stiff?

Dumfounded, my stare transferred from her immobile body to her eyes. They were fear stricken. Quickly I realized aloud, "Oh, uh, er, right, you probably don't like to shake hands."

Now she looked substantially more scared. "How do you-"

Stupid Jef! I hurried to explain myself, "Oh, I, uh" the rambling dribbled from my bumbling mouth, "I just, you see, I found…" I unzipped my backpack and shuffled through, found her poem, then pulled the packet of paper out for her to retrieve. "I think this belongs to you. I, uh, I found it after playing Frisbee yesterday and…"

Immediately Lacey flushed to a paste-like color and the pitch of her voice plummeted, "Oh God." As if struck by a bolt of lightning she sprang into action, catapulting off the bench and snatching the poem from me, "Sorry!"

The natural response to an apology was typically "it's okay," but before the words could make their way out I realized how unnecessary her apology was.

"Sorry?" I raised an eyebrow, "You don't need to apologize for losing-"

"You read it, didn't you?" Lacey pried with more fear than anger.

"Well yeah."

"Then I need to apologize."

She quickly tried to break away.

"Wait!" I reached out, again forgetting her acute fear of germs. At once she threw her arms up in a surrender motion to avoid being touched. As quickly as possible I retracted my arm, "I'm sorry!"

"Don't worry about it," she spit out while taking a step back.

The panic-stricken girl hugged her poem close to her racing heartbeat then scurried away.

I was thoroughly baffled.

I nervously pulled off my backwards Red Sox cap, and raked a hand through the tall nest of dark brown, almost black hair that my mom had been nagging was overdue for a trim. That's a major downside to being a millennial who still lives at home at 23 years old: moms nagging about haircuts.

Day unfurled to night and I kept playing the interaction with Lacey Parker through my head. I lied in bed reflecting while staring at the glow in the dark stars that I never took off my bedroom ceiling.

    Why had Lacey apologized to me? And why did I have to be so awkward? She was the weirdo, not me.

    Recollection of the encounter graduated to making mental revisions of how I could have better handled the situation so that it could have lasted longer. I don't know what it was about Lacey that fascinated me so much. Yes, she was a skilled poet, but I wasn't even a fan of poetry. I was fascinated by her alleged mental condition, but even that didn't feel like the source of my enthrallment today. I felt this unrecognizable dissatisfaction with how speedily she fled off. I don't even know what I wanted from her; all I know is that I was wildly discontented. That poem was a glimpse into Lacey's mind and for some unknown reason I wanted a closer, more intimate look. But there was no way I was going to get that if the girl couldn't do as little as shake my hand.

    Ugh.

    I just... I wanted to know how her disordered mind worked.

The next few days at school were intruded with the thought of that Lacey Parker. I anxiously searched for the girl with the notebook every day. It wasn't until a week after I returned the poem that I finally saw her.

    Lacey was hustling through the crowds of kids on the concrete sidewalk, hugging her notebook close to her heart, seemingly trying to dodge the brush of any strangers' shoulder.

    I wasn't about to let this chance sneak away, so I snuck up on her from the side, "Hey!"

    "What the-" Lacey jolted as she swung her long brown hair out of her face. "Oh, you again. Why do you keep doing that?"

    "Doing what?" I was genuinely unsure of what she meant. This was only our third interaction. Well, second if you don't count the one where she avoided returning the Frisbee then ran off.

Lacey clarified what seemed so flagrantly obvious in her mind, "You've been popping up all over campus! Don't you ever have class?"

"I take seven classes, so yes."

"Yikes," she loosened up, lowering her notebook to her stomach. "And I thought three was bad."

"You only take three classes?" I resented the blatant judgment in my tone. Why did I have to be so bad at talking to girls outside of an academic debate scene?

With a shrug, Lacey cocked her head at an angle and resorted her eye contact to the concrete sidewalk, "I get tired fast."

"Oh, is that a side effect of the OCD?" I forwardly asked, only to quickly realize by the glint of surprise in her doe eyes that my question was inappropriate. "I mean, the, uh, sorry, you don't like to talk about that, do you?"

"I'm fine talking about it. It's usually other people who aren't."

I was way too eager to prove to this girl that I wasn't like "other people".

Unfiltered words fumbled out of my mouth again, "Hey, do you think you have OCD from a shortage of oxygen flowing to your brain at birth?"

Lacey's appalled jaw dropped, "What the hell kind of a question is that? I'll have you know my birth went perfectly fine! Smoothest, fastest, easiest birth my mother ever had! My dad says I was born with my eyes wide open and- ah!" Lacey suddenly realized she was spilling an overabundance of personal information, squeezed her eyes shut and shook her head neurotically as if to rattle away everything she had just shared, "Why am I telling you all of this?"

"Cause I asked a question. That's what people do when they're asked a question, they answer. Hey, speaking of questions, you're afraid of germs and stuff, right? What's the official terminology for that fear? Germaphobia?"

"What is wrong with you?" she blurted out, but not with aggression. There was a strange pity polluting her abhorrence, as if it was a sad mystery to her as to why I would want to know more about her obsessive disorder.

"First of all," her tone upgraded from disgusted to confident and she stood up straighter, pointing her chin up to my six foot two inches stature, "The official term is mysophobia, not germaphobia. And second of all, did you seriously pay that much attention to the poem?"

"Well yeah," I genuinely didn't understand why she was so surprised. "It was interesting that a brain could operate so differently."

"Oh so that's it," Lacey remarked like she finally reached a long awaited conclusion. "You're not used to talking to *different* people with *different* brains."

Now it was my turn to get defensive. "For your information I have an older brother with cerebral palsy and a psychotic disorder."

Lacey's tight lips softened while she took a gentle gulp. "I'm sorry, but I don't know what that means."

I opted to be blunt, "He's mentally retarded."

I couldn't help but take note of how the initial shock of information made Lacey's pupils dilate, but almost instantaneously they constricted, as if it took her a fleeting moment to accept. Usually when people found out about Peter's retardation they got stuck in that dilated pupil stage.

Lacey replied, "Well that's interesting. But I still don't know what you want from me. Unless you need an English tutor or something, I have nothing to offer you."

"Why, are you an English major?"

She nodded somewhat reluctantly, "Yes."

That was it! That was my in! I excelled in school, for the most part, but my greatest weakness was English. I hated that subject. I was the type of person who liked hard facts. Questions and answers. Not that abstract storm of bullshit writing.

Lacey, growing more comfortable with my presence, elaborated, "I also just like English. I write whenever I get the chance."

The initial fascination with her obsessive compulsive disorder unexpectedly took a backseat to the personal direction this conversation had gone. I felt myself veer off the track from my case study.

"Wait, what do you do for fun? For leisure?"

"Write."

I felt the dent of a dimple carve itself beside a newfound smile, "You write for fun?"

Suddenly, her eyes were glowing. Lacey transformed from tired to passionate. "I love writing. So much. It's what I was born to do."

Despite my opposition to literature and liberal arts, I felt like I could relate. I was always reading up on anything and everything educational, experimenting with whatever I could in my spare time, and watching scientific or historic documentaries, all for fun. Not many people my age found pleasure beyond getting blackout drunk and frying their brain.

There was something very rare about this girl.

Lacey continued raving about her favorite activity, "I love writing. I have to write, I need to. It's my therapy. Believe it or not it keeps me sane. Well, as sane as a crazy person can be. But at the same time I also can't over-immerse myself in my writing or else I'll lose all touch with the real world. And it's a really hard balance because sentences and idealized conversations in hypothetical scenarios are swirling around my brain all the time and I need to get them out on paper or else…" Lacey's statement lingered, for she, herself, did not know the consequence.

"Or else what?" I pressed, officially spellbound.

"Or else… I'm not sure. It all feels like a waste. The thoughts. The emotions. The experiences, real and make-believe, all would seem like a waste. I, I would seem like a waste."

As soon as Lacey shut her rosy mouth her face blushed to match her lips. She must have realized she spilled far more information than intended. Before I could touch upon anything she said, her phone started to buzz.

"Excuse me," she hastily whipped out her smartphone, tapped the touch screen a couple of times to activate speaker mode, then took a step to the side of the walkway and held the phone a good twelve inches away from her mouth. "Hello?"

Rather than eavesdrop on her conversation I stood there, focusing on the fact that she put the phone on speaker. It was an odd thing to do, but she did it without hesitation like this was part of her routine.

The more I thought about it, the more it made sense. She must have been deliberately trying not to hold the cell phone to her ear or cheek because she was afraid of the germs. Interesting. Definitely a note for the OCD research binder.

Lacey hung up. "I've gotta go. My dad's here."

"You don't drive yourself?" I pondered curiously.

"Sometimes I do. Today I wasn't feeling up to it."

"Oh."

I wanted to elongate the conversation. I wanted to observe Lacey and her warped brain a little longer, but she was too quick for me.

"Bye," she spit out and sped down the concrete sidewalk to the parking lot.

She was gone. I stood by my lonesome wondering why I was still so unsatisfied.

Chapter 3

Behind the wheel of a worn out jeep I drove home from school.

As I rounded the familiar corner, the driveway came into view, and my sour stomach churned.

My dad's rusty old maroon Chevy truck was parked in the straw-like grass beside our shed. Why Dad couldn't just park on the asphalt driveway was a mystery to me. I swear he just liked to piss my mom off.

I don't know what a pleasant divorce looks like, but it certainly isn't my parents'. Ever since I was 3-months-old they separated, but I didn't find out until I was 6-years-old that my dad left my mom because he couldn't deal with raising a special needs child, my older brother Peter.

Living in the same house as Peter definitely bolstered my willingness to go to the community college a mere fifteen minutes away from home. I wasn't my dad. I don't quit.

Being around for Peter wasn't just about aiding him as he combatted the physical symptoms of his handicaps. I was more worried about his mental state. I know it sounds contradictory, but I swear to God Peter is more independent when I'm around. Don't get me wrong, my mom is a saint, but sometimes she treats Peter like a kid, coddling him even as a 26-year-old adult.

Mom and Peter relied on each other equally. Their symbiotic relationship centered on Peter being the "special" child. My role in the household interrupted their unhealthy behavior.

I'd be lying if I didn't say I went out of my way to break Mom and Peter apart. I'd usually force Peter to do his own laundry or make his own bed. He needed to be self-sufficient. Sometimes I'm convinced when my mom's frantic eyes lock onto him that her brain is still conditioned to perceive her 8-year-old son wobbling on his forearm crutches, getting sad looks from the other parents in the neighborhood.

Dad made a point to make a guest appearance every so often. He'd show up, toothpick lodged between his yellow smoker's teeth, and persuade my mom to let him take Peter and I out to play catch. The activity often resulted in just Dad and me playing catch and my brother pathetically sitting in the grass poking the soil with some stick he found, because his weak muscles left him poor at aiming. My impatient father would then belittle Peter by telling him to "sit this one out". No surprise it was finally Peter's turn when the sun was setting and it was "too late". Just thinking about all those visits made me want to punch my dad in his raspy throat, right on the vein bulge where his ugly brownish purple birth mark resided like a target.

Since I was a little kid Mom seemed ambivalent about dad's random guest appearances. I think part of her wanted him to stop coming by and reminding us of the scars he'd inflicted on the broken family unit. A greater part of Mom wanted Peter and me to have our father in our life though. That was obvious since Mom kept my father's last name, "Sterling", for Peter and me. If I were her I definitely would have changed it. To be honest, I was kind of mad that she didn't change all of our last names. I didn't want to be associated with that disgrace of a human, but if I changed my last name now then it would break Mom's (and Peter's) heart.

After a few irregular breaths in the car, I worked up the courage to go inside the house.

While I shut the rickety door behind me, Peter excitedly hobbled his husky frame into the room, "Dad's home!"

"I can see that," I groaned with a glare on my father. Sitting beyond the doorframe at the kitchen table, he smoked a cigarette. If Mom was home she'd be throwing a tantrum over the smoke.

"How long ago did he get here?" I whispered.

"3:16 PM," Peter answered with his absurdly accurate memory. That was about a half hour ago. I could only imagine what kind of bickering went on between Peter and Dad in those tense thirty minutes. "I asked him if we could play cards but he said we had to wait for you to get home."

Shocker.

As much as I wanted to lock myself in my bedroom and research obsessive compulsive disorder, I wanted more to please Peter. If that meant playing cards with Peter and my loser father then I guess that's what I had to do.

The three of us sat around the kitchen table playing the card game, Bullshit. Peter would interrupt every so often to try and tell my dad a dull story about his day of work as a custodian at my Mom's office building.

"Daddy," Peter nagged.

My dad grunted, "Don't call me that boy."

"Today when I was mopping the conference room floor…"

I zoned out, too busy thinking about Lacey Parker and her beloved notebook. What in the world did she write in that thing? Did she write more poems? Stories?

"Son, it's your turn," the rough sound of Dad's throaty smoke-damaged vibrato broke through my wondering about Lacey.

"Oh, uh, what number are we on?"

"Six," Peter spit out.

I was about to put down a six of clubs when Peter started up again.

"Daddy," he was insistent upon calling him that. Peter was smart enough to know better, he was just doing it to troll with my dad. "Daddy!" he yelled again.

My dad was turning a vibrant shade of red. The vein in his neck protruded. He was losing whatever thin layer of patience he possessed. I tried not to laugh.

"Hellooo? Daddy?"

"Dammit, boy!" Dad snapped and threw his cards on the oak table. "I said don't call me that! Can't you hear? Or is your hearing screwy too?"

My heart fell into the pits of my gut.

Here we go again.

"You don't like it when I call you 'Daddy'?" Peter provoked.

"That's what I said, isn't it, boy?"

My brother whined, "But you never get mad when Jef calls you that."

"Jef hasn't called me 'Daddy' since he was as tall as my knee!"

Sitting there, hearing my dad pick on Peter, gave me plenty of time to sharpen my tongue like a sword. Having finally heard enough I drew my verbal sword and relentlessly cut my father off, "So what's your excuse for calling Peter 'boy'? He hasn't been a boy since, well, since he was as tall as your knee."

My father was dumbfounded. He hadn't equipped himself from the retaliation of his favorite son.

I affirmed with absolute certainty, "Peter's a man now."

There would have been silence, tense silence with my glare fixed to Dad's fear-stricken pupils. But Peter was too eager to invoke a bonding experience that would never work out.

"Jef it's your turn!" Peter nagged.

As much as I wanted to quit, I consented to a few more insufferable rounds of Bullshit. Peter kept losing the card game, since this game required fibbing and he was the worst liar ever.

Dad antagonized my brother as Peter collected over half the deck, "You're not trying, are you?"

"No I am! I really am! I'm doing my best!"

"Well your best isn't good enough!" Dad shouted at Peter.

Ouch.

Whether my dad meant it or not, he was no longer only referring to Peter's card playing.

Chapter 4

The roar of Dad's Chevy truck zoomed off of the grass, leaving behind a cloud of dirt.

"Come on," I urged Peter to look away from the window. I couldn't stand to see him so pathetic, watching Dad storm off after a pitiful hour long visit.

Peter and I went on a nature walk on a trail in the woodland by the convenience store I worked at, the perfect location for Peter's wobbly legs because there were little to no hills. I made a point to take Peter on the walk every so often, typically after a disastrous day like today. If I left my brother cooped up inside then he would watch TV, potentially a program as miserable as the news, and that was not a good situation. Since Peter became paranoid easily, it was best to keep him away from the news at all costs. Sometimes he would have delusions where he'd involve himself with catastrophic current events.

Peter and I, along with our overly hyper dog, York, embarked through the colorful fall forest. Peter talked most of the time. I had difficulty listening to him though. I was too busy trying to figure out how I could effectively get inside Lacey Parker's head.

Every so often Peter would catch me daydreaming and he'd do what he routinely did when somebody didn't respond to him for all of three seconds. "Helloooo? Jef? Jef are you listening to me?"

"Yes, yes, I'm listening."

Peter held up the red dog leash that I refused to put on York. "York is gonna get lost if we don't use the leash!"

"He's fine, Pete," I assured him, as I did about five times per walk.

Peter continued to ramble and I continued to zone out.

"Lean on me," I interrupted Peter as we descended a subtle hill in the ground. This was the hardest part of the walk, but thanks to a routine which had Peter holding my shoulders for support, we were always able to conquer it. The slant was anything but steep, but its abrasive surface made it difficult for a man with cerebral palsy to maneuver.

York was already ahead, dashing into the lake, splashing. The rugged and rolling contour of the softening dirt made my worn out sneakers bend in ways they weren't cut out to bend.

After successfully descending the hill Peter threw his arm over me as if I were the passenger, in the car he would never drive, as we came to a volatile stop.

"Shhhhhhhh Jef!" Peter hissed so that spit catapulted from his lips.

"Peter I'm pretty sure your shushing is a lot louder than my footsteps," I hissed back.

"Shhhhh!" he insisted and pointed ahead into the brush.

After a tired eye roll I looked ahead.

A slender deer stood under an orange and yellow canopy of leaves. Her doe eyes were locked on me. Directly on me.

"Jef don't move or it might attack!"

"It's not gonna attack, Pete," I assured Peter at a low volume. "I can guarantee that deer is more afraid of you than you are of her."

"How can you tell? How do you know?"

"Because," I scoffed haughtily while soaking in the sight of the timid deer, "Just look at her eyes. You can see the fear."

"Oh. Okay."

I shoved down my turkey and cheese sandwich in the crowded cafeteria.

Rather than hanging around I paced out of the building and into the courtyard. I scanned the ground with the utmost vigilance.

"Hey, Jef," some stoner named Jamison patted me on the back.

Jamison Lawson was the type of kid who always had the odor of smoke stuck in the threads of his clothing. He was kind of gross. You couldn't really tell if he had freckles or just a bad case of acne. And he'd do this weird thing where he'd stroke his jawline as if he had a beard, but he didn't have a beard.

Maybe Jamison wouldn't get on my nerves so much if he didn't try to turn every conversation into a political dispute. He was the kind of guy that loved to argue with people for the mere sake of arguing. He'd bring up good points, but his delivery was so aggressive, loud, and obnoxious. And he'd drag out what should have been a fifteen minute discussion into a heated hour and a half long debate. And I had no time for that, especially since my tenacious mind was fixed on finding Lacey Parker.

"Not now," I dismissed Jamison without any bit of explanation and paced onward.

I was neurotically focused on finding the girl with the notebook.

My eyes darted to and fro, left and right, until finally they spotted a long haired brunette sitting at the picnic table under a birch tree.

Lacey was writing diligently in her notebook.

In a hurry I sprinted to the picnic table, tripping two feet in front of Lacey Parker and nearly falling flat on my face.

I sprung upright, hoping she didn't see the blunder, and greeted her with a hasty breath, "Lacey!"

"Hm?" The big doe eyes glanced up from the notebook. The furrowed brow on her forehead quickly smoothed out as she registered who was standing in front of her. "Oh, it's you. You know, for someone who has good reflexes when playing Frisbee you really need to work on your basic coordination skills."

Crap.

She saw me trip.

In my embarrassment I retaliated, "Well you have pretty good peripheral vision for somebody who's always got their nose in the same damn notebook."

A smirk emerged on Lacey's face as her already large eyes widened. Each eyelash a black twig extending from her round eyes like a cute cartoon character.

I consciously had to force myself to remember why I was here.

"I'm going to take you up on your offer," I blurted out while clutching the straps of my backpack a little tighter.

She looked extremely confused. "What offer?"

Her pupils were so intuitive that I almost forgot she couldn't read my mind, "Oh, uh, the English tutoring! I want to take you up on the English tutoring!"

"Seriously?" she almost scoffed. "You're that desperate?"

"Oh no," I was fast to debunk. God forbid anybody think I was stupid. "I'll have you know I graduated high school with a 3.9 GPA."
Immediately I loathed myself for sounding pretentious.

Lacey shrugged. "And you're at community college because...?"

"Financial reasons." I deliberately left out the fact that I wanted to live at home for Peter's sake.

"Ah," she replied, then reverted her attention back to her notebook.

There was no way Lacey would let getting to know her be easy. I had to capture her focus. So I slid in the seat across from her at the chipping red picnic table.

Lacey's eyes transferred away from her writing back to me. Like rapid fire I let my mouth run, "I'm at community college for financial reasons and also because I'm not the biggest fan of the college lifestyle. It's a little too stupid for me. Don't get me wrong, I'm all for education, I'm just not for frying my brain on miscellaneous drugs or drowning in shallow party conversations." I don't know why I was so compelled to share that with her. I just really wanted her to know I wasn't like most college kids. I guess, in some small part of me, I wanted to impress her.

"Say no more," Lacey reciprocated my feelings, "I don't see the appeal of the party scene. Or hooking up with random strangers."

Holy shit, that threw me off. I didn't know how to respond to that. I resorted to dumb stuttering, "Oh, uh, no me neither. I don't, er…"

I swear, it was like she knew I was the *one guy* on campus who wouldn't be capable of talking about hookup culture without becoming a nervous wreck. Damn her intuition.

"Sorry," she revoked apologetically, "I shouldn't have said that. It's just, I can't stand anything that requires one person to touch another person."

Having figured she successfully scared me off, Lacey delved back into writing in that notebook.

So that's how it's gonna be, huh? I knew her game, and I was going to prevail. I was never one to bail on a study. Lacey might have had pinpoint intuition when it came to reading my weakness in addressing intimacy, but she underestimated my persistence when it came to learning.

I sighed a compliant breath and shook my head up and down while wiping off the nervous beads of sweat from the back of my neck, "You're not wrong about that. This is usually the time when males peak in their sex drive."

Her dark eyes flicked up at mine, away from her notebook, as the gentle breeze made her long brown hair sway. I think she was surprised I was still there. She narrowed her mascara covered eyes with skepticism.

"What's your deal Jef?"

"I'm not sure what you mean."

"Why do you want to talk to me so bad? Why haven't you run the other way?"

I was transfixed on her big brown eyes. Damn were they big.

A lightbulb went off in my head as I recalled the deer Peter and I had stumbled across in the woods.

I took a harder look at Lacey. Glazed over her eyes was an artificial mask of coldness. Underneath I could see the fear brewing. Blatant fear. Just like the deer.

All of a sudden I had the confidence to challenge Lacey.

"Why are you trying to scare me away?"

Suddenly her doe eyes lost their hard exterior and revealed only vulnerability. I got her.

"2:30. Tuesdays. I can tutor you at 2:30 on Tuesdays in the library. If you're not there, I'm not going to wait around," Lacey rose from the picnic table and gathered her notebook and pen.

I was overcome with excitement. The type of excitement I get when I know I'm about to be endowed with new knowledge. "I'll be there!"

"Good," she speedily twirled around, effectively flipping her long brown hair over her shoulders without the use of her hands, then began to pace away.

I called out after her. "Why are you always in such a hurry?"

After a brief pause Lacey twisted her torso and made eye contact with me. "Because I hate school and I wanna go home and shower."

Chapter 5

I'm fairly confident that I might be the only person in the history of academia to feel eager about getting tutored.

There were a few moments in my sprint from the academic building to the library that I almost tripped on my long legs.

Upon entering I didn't have to search around for Lacey. Oddly enough my eyes darted straight to her, like eagerness rewired my brain to automatically spot her without hesitation.

It wasn't much of a shock that Lacey was sitting alone at a table. She had a very repellant aura about her. Her posture was stiff. Uncomfortable, really. Come to think of it, I don't think Lacey ever looked fully comfortable.

With her pin straight hair falling over half of her stoic expression, she was staring down at that same spiral notebook residing on the table.

Instead of a proper greeting, I commented on her intensive affinity for that particular notebook, "You really like to write in that notebook, don't you?"

Abruptly, Lacey transferred her focus from the notebook onto me. I was quickly captivated by her wild eyes and felt my throat swell.

Speechless, I took the initiative to sit myself beside her at the table.

Slowly and carefully, as if handling a precious jewel, Lacey sealed her notebook shut. Then, and only then, did she decide to respond to the personalized greeting I had offered. "This notebook," I could feel her voice drawing me forth as she let me in her mind, "is a key to another world. I live in a mental landscape. A realm of daydreams. I use my mental illness and melancholy to create other worlds, alternate universes, make-believe dimensions, whatever you wanna call it. In those other worlds I thrive. And thanks to this notebook I can record what I see, think, and feel in those worlds. Those worlds are special places, and it would be a sin not to write about them."

I was deeply intrigued by the bulk of information she just provided me with, and the eloquent nature in which she delivered that information. I don't know what it was about her, but for some reason she was very well spoken. I think it was this concoction of isolation and creativity that gave her time to perfect the articulation of her every thought.

Everything about her response was overwhelming, so I struggled to sort through it all out loud, "So, are you saying that you like your mental illness because it helps you write?"

"I'm saying I like it to an extent. Believe me, it's caused a lot of problems, you already know that from the poem though," she lowered her voice playfully as she called me out. I hope I wasn't turning red. Lacey went on, "but I'd be lying if I said it wasn't somewhat beneficial. What I've learned is when you combine a creative mind with a mental illness you get pure magic. And for that reason, I wouldn't trade who I am."

I knew she meant it.

But I still couldn't help but recall the anguish expressed in that poem. "But all the unnecessary pain-"

"I can take the pain," she assured. With eyes locked onto me she insisted, "And I like to believe the pain is necessary."

I felt the confusion in my inflection, "How?" I couldn't wrap my mind around a justification for what she had to go through.

"I want to believe there's a reason for my OCD. I, I-" she corrected herself, "I *need* to believe there's a reason."

"So what's the reason you have OCD?"

"I'm still trying to figure that out, but..." She dug her top teeth into her lower lip, contemplating whether or not she should share further, "the best answer I've come up with is that the OCD brings out emotions and an extreme thought process that I can incorporate in my daydreams. The pain, the darkness, it fuels me to write. This mental illness, my demise, is the birth of my art."

The part of me that saw Lacey Parker as "the girl with the notebook", the writer, was in awe of the brilliant depth of her mind. But the part of me that saw Lacey Parker as the poor prisoner narrating that poem was compelled to help her break out. So, using her analogy, I stealthily snuck into her mind.

"But what if that notebook, your 'key', isn't a key that lets you into *another* world? What if it's a key that locks you out of *this* world?"

Stunned, Lacey went mute. There was a mix of shock and bewilderment intensifying the strength of her pupils. She looked at me like she had finally met her match.

Having disarmed her, I continued with my point. "Sure it may help you be a better artist, but what happens when you run out of ways to express your illness through art? What happens when you don't just want to be an artist anymore? And you want to be, I don't know, a wife? Or a mother? One of these days you're going to say that you've had enough."

I think I was starting to scare her. In fact, I know I was starting to scare her. I could see it in her unsettled stupor. This wasn't the type of reaction she wanted to hear.

Having felt satisfied, like I had successfully asserted my intelligence, I changed the subject. "Anyways, I'm sure with all the writing you do you must have aced honors English in high school."

Realizing I was done invading her mind, Lacey sat up straighter and returned to a more casual demeanor. "No, not at all," she allowed the sound of her scoff to ease her out of her seriousness, "I took honors English my freshmen year and barely got by. My teacher demoted me to regular English when I was a sophomore and I stayed in regular through junior and senior year."

That baffled me. "Wait, really? Why? You can write. You can write really well! You're definitely good at English. That doesn't make any sense."

"Let's just say I didn't really listen to the teachers. I wrote what I wanted, how I wanted, regardless of what the teacher said. Whenever they told me to revise or change something I wouldn't listen. I'd leave it. Because what I wrote was perfect the way it was. You know why? Because it was what I felt in the moment. And I wasn't going to censor or degrade those feelings by editing them. One time I swore in an essay. That lost me some points. But whatever," she waved her hand in the air to dismiss the incident as if it had just happened yesterday, "the bottom line is I just didn't like being told what to do. I get enough of that from my sickness."

Her explanation cast me to a reflective silence. I found it interesting how my compliment wound up, in the end, touching upon her obsessive compulsive disorder. I didn't actually have to ask this time for her to talk about OCD, she did it on her own, naturally. And from what I could gather from her little story about high school English classes, this disease has been prevalent in her life longer than I initially thought.

Lacey got down to business. "How are you doing in your English class, Jef?"

"Oh yeah, uh," I almost forgot I was there to be tutored. "I'm getting by with an 89 average, but I don't feel like I'm really retaining anything."

"Are you kidding me? You have a good grade but you *want* a tutor?"

I shrugged, "I have more to learn."

She squinted at me, trying to figure me out. I wanted to tell her I'm not that complicated. But she still tried. In a way, I kind of liked it. Lacey made me feel like there was more to me than I knew.

"What's up with you and learning?" she eventually asked with suspicion.

"I don't know. I guess I just figure why wouldn't you want to know as much as you can about the world you live in?"

Lacey became unusually quiet.

I think my answer inadvertently struck a chord within her.

Feeling I made her uncomfortable, I became uncomfortable, which catalyzed what I do best when I'm uncomfortable: ramble. "I don't love learning to get good grades or ace a test. I just love teaching myself new things, advancing my brain, building my intellect with more and more layers. It's exhilarating like nothing else. I feel like a better version of myself when I know more. Taking things from the outside and storing them in my brain. Comprehending. Interpreting. Evaluating. Analyzing-"

Thankfully, Lacey cut me off, "We should probably start the tutoring session."

"Oh, yeah. Right, right. Of course."

Lacey forced her mind to move on by taking a folder out of her leopard print backpack, only to get upset as soon as she read the label, "Philosophy" on it.

"Fuck," she muttered, "stupid law."

Did I hear her correctly? Law? What was that supposed to mean? "I'm sorry?"

Lacey's pale skin became a rosy shade. She seemed distraught. I could tell she was embarrassed.

"Nothing. Whatever. I didn't mean to say that out loud," she blushed.

"Did you say 'law'?" I wasn't letting up.

"No! Well yes. But it- it's really stupid. You'll laugh at me."

"No I won't," I insisted, aching to fill the cavity of ignorance in me.

She was reluctant, but I caught her glance down at her notebook. It was then that she gave in and explained herself. "I have these laws. Sort of like a set of rules I have to follow. Like 'Don't touch the Philosophy Folder unless you're in Philosophy class'. That's what I just broke. Laws like that protect me from all of my OCD triggers. All the irrational bullshit, trivial fears, blaring sirens, vibrant danger signs. You name the fear and I've got some warning or alarm set up in my brain to go off as soon as I feel like I'm about to break a law."

That was utterly ridiculous. I raised my hand, "Question, do these laws have to go through parliament or something?"

Lacey was not amused. She rose to standing position and agitatedly started to gather her things off of the library table.

"Hey!" I almost fell over in my chair but clung to the table on the way down, "Don't go! I was kidding!"

"I know you were kidding. That's why I'm leaving."

"No, wait, I'm sorry," I stood up and repeated myself, "Lacey, I'm sorry."

Glancing back and forth between me and the table she made her conflicting feelings known. Hesitantly she decided to sit back down. I followed her lead and carefully returned to my seat. This was like trying not to scare away the pure and innocent doe in the forest.

"If I don't follow a law then I'm convinced there will be a consequence. Sometimes the consequence has absolutely no relation to the broken law. Sometimes there's a connection. Sometimes far-fetched, but nonetheless a connection. I'm sure it's all very unreasonable from the outside perspective. But inside, for me, I believe those laws. I don't know why. I just believe them."

"But if the consequences are make-believe then can't you just break the law and see that there are no actual repercussions? Nothing bad actually happens!"

"Oh, no," she laughed, "something bad happens."

"What!" I was getting frustrated with the illogic in her thought process. "What horrible thing happens if you don't obey a 'law'?" I put air quotes around the term accompanied by a mocking tone.

Lacey didn't break her seriousness, though. She arched her back so that she was hovering over the table, closer to me. She carefully enunciated the coveted answer, "I will have a nervous breakdown."

Oh.

"Why do you care anyways?" she flat out asked.

"Oh- uh, wait. I just- uh," I faltered on articulating any word in the English language.

Lacey had the upper hand again in this tug-of-war between our wildly different minds, and she wasn't about to let go. "You ask an awful lot of questions about OCD, Jef. I don't understand why you care so much."

"Honestly," I took a deep breath to collect my thoughts, then released the truth, "I don't either."

"Then why don't you stop caring?"

"Because," my gaze inadvertently dove into her large eyes, "I can't."

I saw her try to fight it, but her smile prevailed

All of a sudden I felt myself sweating with self-consciousness. I quickly tried to take back what I said. "I mean, I-uh, because…" when I couldn't find an alternate response I gave up and just said what I already knew she must have been thinking, "I'm sorry. I'm a real weirdo."

I expected her to laugh at me in agreement. To take advantage of the upper hand. But she didn't. Instead she gave me a break, fixed her compassionate eyes on mine, and spoke kindly, "That's okay. So am I."

Chapter 6

The feeling that I got leaving that first tutoring session was exhilarating. Talking to Lacey gave me the type of rejuvenating feeling you get after a good workout.

The next tutoring session wasn't going exactly how I wanted it to. Lacey focused on my actual English homework most of the time. I tried every now and then to integrate an OCD question into the discussion, particularly about her germ fear because I kept catching her doing weird things like squirting a mound of hand sanitizer on her hand, but she was actively dodging the subject.

Every break that Lacey got she would return to her notebook and write whatever it is that she wrote. Just as curious as ever, I still wanted to know what exactly she was writing.

I was in the middle of scrounging up a paragraph, responding to a short story from my English textbook, when I finally asked Lacey, "What are you writing?"

"Random thoughts, current feelings, snapshots of my brain, what are *you* writing?" she pointed to my homework.

Instead of answering that question I decided to just go for it and heckle her. "So you're writing, like, diary entries?"

In contrast to the stiffness of her posture, Lacey laughed, "When you say it like that it sounds really lame. I'm actually working on a story."

"But I thought you said you were writing about your current feelings and-"

"Yeah, I am. That's how I create a story. My writing is very emotion based. I usually dwell on my feelings and attribute them to a character in some alternate setting, usually a fantasy setting 'cause that gives the most creative leeway."

"So isn't that kind of limiting?"

"What do you mean?"

"Like if you're writing about your feelings, then how do you write about a feeling you haven't experienced?" I threw out random examples, not knowing if these examples were actually things she had experienced or not. I hoped to find out if she'd interrupt me and elaborate on one of them, "Like losing somebody or being rejected or being in love."

That last example wasn't supposed to come out.

Lacey laughed a tad, "I can still write about being in love without ever having been in love."

"But," I tried to recover from the unexpected example with an awkward gulp, "how?"

"What do you mean 'how'?"

"How can you write about romance if you haven't experienced it? How do you know what it's like, or if you're getting it right?"

Lacey straightened in her chair and answered with confidence, "I'm a very avid daydreamer. I've lived an array of many different romantic scenarios in this head. It's called using your imagination."

"It's called guessing!" I interjected out of frustration, being the type of person who liked hard facts. "Guesses are just as misleading as lies."

Lacey, still so damn stiff in her seat that I just wanted to shake her, cocked her head to the side, smirked, and crossed her arms. I think she was entertained by the challenge that automatically came with conversing with a know-it-all.

"You didn't let me finish," she said sharply, like she was drawing a dagger in the swiftest of motions, "I don't *just* use my imagination. I use my imagination *and* my intuition."

From the very little I knew about her already, I had to admit, her intuition was a standout asset.

"I mean just because I haven't actually experienced an event firsthand doesn't mean I can't at least try and understand it."

The wheels started cranking away in my brain as I realized the parallel between Lacey's words and a past physics lesson. "I guess that's valid. You're making up scenes. Your stories are kind of like theories. Like in physics. Theoretical physics."

"What's that?" Lacey asked, surprisingly interested.

"Oh- uh, theoretical physics is basically the counterpart to experimental physics. It uses mathematical models and the..." I tried to find the right word, "abstract ideas of physics to try and explain or rationalize natural phenomena."

I was about halfway through a lecture about the dual particle theory when I realized her tense demeanor softened and I swear I could almost hear those blaring sirens in her head subdue.

My science rambling, which people so often hated about me, was actually calming her. I couldn't believe it. I must have been superhuman to be able to alleviate this girl's stress.

Eventually when I finished with the theoretical physics lesson Lacey posed a question that I hadn't expected.

"You're of, like, genius level intelligence, aren't you?"

"What? No," I denied modestly. "I mean I like math and science, especially physics."

"Uck," she scowled. "I can't stand math and science."

"How?" my pitch skyrocketed as the bias of so many enlightening physics lessons replayed in my memory.

"I don't know, it's too much. Overwhelming. I can't wrap my brain around it without wanting to puke or something. All those numbers and equations make me anxious."

"Ha," I accidentally laughed out loud.

Lacey raised her eyebrows inquisitively.

"Sorry," I quickly apologized, "I'm not laughing at you, I'm just laughing at how opposite we are."

For the first time ever I saw Lacey lean back so that the lengthy brown hair draping behind her were touching the public chair.

"Because, you know, numbers and equations make you anxious, you're more comfortable with words. Then there's me. Words make me anxious and I'm way more comfortable with numbers and equations."

That aroused the corner of her mouth to pucker into a solo dimpled smile. "That is pretty funny."

I don't know why, but something about her smile was very inviting. It wasn't one of those polite smiles that you force to make the awkward people around you comfortable. It was genuine. Extremely genuine. And more full of life than usual. And *I* caused that invigorated smile. Something that came out of *my* bumbling mouth actually caused that. *Me*! Awkward ol' Jef! And that boosted my mood ten stories high.

Afraid that the ten-story-high feeling would fade along with our conversation, I tried to elaborate on the discussion by asking Lacey and her fascinating brain a question. I didn't want to give this girl an excuse to run off and leave campus early, like she usually did.

"Why do you like writing anyways? What's the point?" Lacey nearly choked on her own laughter. "What's the point? Writing is the most purposeful thing I've ever spent my time doing! What could make you feel more significant? With your own mind you can contrive an alternate universe. You are the creator. Without you, an entire realm wouldn't exist.

"Interweaving snippets of personal thoughts into a story or a poem is an art. Being able to hone the English language, to bend and twist it while effectively translating an idea or emotion against the backdrop of a fictional setting is exhilarating! It's asserting your importance!"

I think Lacey got embarrassed from her passionate spiel, because in the following tense seconds that I thought my ears were malfunctioning she turned bright red and flipped the topic of discussion onto me.

"What, uh, what about you? Why do you like all that number jumble or whatever your major is?"

"Physics," I clarified.

"What's so great about physics?" she pressed, now folding her arms.

Humored didn't begin to cover how I felt from such an ignorant question.

"What's so great about physics? *Physics*? Physics is *everything*! Ernest Rutherford once said that 'All science is either physics or stamp collecting'," I couldn't help but laugh aloud at the quote. One glance at Lacey and I remembered where I was, who I was talking to, and quickly realized I was geeking-out. I clamped my mouth shut, then looked back at Lacey, this time really looked at her beyond a shy glance. She wore a winsome smirk and let out what I think was chuckle, but I wasn't sure because the pounding of my nervous heart was canceling out every soundwave flowing through the vicinity.

Regardless of whether or not Lacey laughed, I knew her smile was genuine. I didn't have to hear a laugh to know that. I just knew Lacey was happy, and our direct eye contact was confirmation that I caused that happiness. If there was any chance of my heartbeat quieting down it was gone. My own happiness made my heart race even faster and somehow louder.

Lacey's smile was a greenlight to go on, and without a fraction of insecurity I naturally eased back into gushing about why physics was superior among all sciences. "Molecular biology would be nothing without physics! Genetic engineering, reconstructing genes and creating pieces of DNA, would never exist without quantum mechanics. Chemistry requires a knowledge of electron clouds interacting with each other. Chemistry was revolutionized by Niels Bohr's model of the atom. He first presented the theory of the periodic table of elements! *The periodic table of elements*, Lacey! The atomic structure of each element! The electrons in each atom! The electron's angular momentum, orbit shape, orientation, spin – all that shit we learned in high school!"

Lacey's smile became shy and more subdued. I knew I got greedy and said too much.

"I don't remember any of that 'shit'," she admitted while avoiding eye contact, "In fact I don't think I ever knew it. I scraped by Chemistry with 60s and a teacher who let me off easy because it was the second time I took the course."

I didn't anticipate this conversation coming back to me, so I stuttered a bit. "Well, uh, that's okay. I'm sure if you didn't have all your mental issues- I mean, uh" I hunched forward and diverted my frantic stare to the table's eraser shaving coated surface. I had no doubt that my face was turning red.

Lacey nodded, as if making an internal decision to let me off the hook, then retraced the conversation back to my comfort zone, "You're really passionate about physics."

The corner of my mouth curled with shyness and the distinct sound of a voice lifted itself up an octave, "I don't know if 'passionate' is the right word."

"It is," Lacey confirmed without a tinge of hesitation.

Weirdly feeling like my brain had been infiltrated, I jumped into defensive mode. "Well I can't help but like it. Physics explains stuff, you know? Chemical reactions, electricity, time, things as miniscule as atomic structure and as massive as the very birth of the universe! It can all be tied back to laws of physics, numeric values, formulas and equations people like Max Planck and James Clerk Maxwell put into place. Physics provides answers to *why* everything is the way that it is."

"A lot of those answers are just theories though. Not facts."

"Well yeah, but in a way theories are the most important part of any science. In a way, they *are* science. Every piece of science is technically a theory that hasn't been disproven by experimental measurements. Think about it Lacey, do you know how many theories out there are the basis for the sciences universally studied today? The string theory, Einstein's theory of relativity, the entire quantum field theory!" suddenly I remembered Lacey's aversion to science and math, "Sorry, er- this is probably really boring to you."

"No, not at all," Lacey Parker speedily declared and jolted upright in her seat. I wanted to tell her to lean her back on the chair's frame again, to go back to being relaxed.

"But I thought you didn't like this kind of stuff."

"No please go! Talk! It's a nice change to have this repetitive mind hear something new."

I was so close to questioning Lacey's comment aloud. I found it peculiar how she referred to her mind like it was a foreign entity. I was so used to having control of my mind. Her mind didn't really work that way, though. But I didn't divert the conversation. I wasn't ready to let go of the high that came from my science rambling finally soothing another human being rather than irking them.

With that high fresh in my brain I went on to explain all sorts of physics theories.

Lacey leaned back in her chair. And just as before, the more I talked, the more relaxed she became.

An hour, which felt like five minutes, went by of me explaining some of my favorite physics topics to Lacey.

It wasn't until the library completely emptied aside from me and Lacey that I remembered my interest in Lacey's obsessive compulsive disorder. Surprised by how much I was enjoying talking to Lacey, I actually forgot to bring up the ulterior topic of OCD that I had secretly scheduled these tutoring sessions for. It completely slipped my mind.

"Holy shit," I looked around at the abandoned library. "What time is it?"

"7:00 PM," a cranky old librarian interrupted from behind her desk.

Lacey, having picked up on the caustic sting of the librarian's voice, straightened upright in her seat and started to gather her things, "We should probably go. 7:00 PM is like 1:00 AM in community college time."

It almost pained me to see Lacey stiffen up again. I fought the compulsion to yell at that librarian to butt out and go back to doing whatever the hell librarians do behind the counter.

Lacey and I exited the building together. Make no mistake, she lagged behind me, an action I inferred to be intentional so that I had to touch the door handle and hold it open for her.

Instead of catching the door with her hand she used her foot, kicking it just enough so that it stayed open for the remainder of her crossing the threshold. Who would have thought that a person could perceive touching a door handle as dangerous? Weird.

We had just separated to start our venture towards different parking lots when Lacey finally confronted my OCD curiosity.

"You wanna know more about the germ fear, huh?" she shouted over the wind.

The sound of her voice calling after me came as a total surprise. I turned around to meet her stare.

There was no room in me to play mind games, so I straight up asked, "Was it that obvious?"

Her head fell as she laughed. Her hair was wiggling with the fall breeze while she nodded, yes. "You gave me that classic inquisitive look when I kicked the door open."

I could feel myself turning a burning shade of red. I didn't know I had an inquisitive look. "Oh."

Retracing my steps on the sidewalk, until I was back by her side, a full foot taller than her even with her wearing heels, I admitted my curiosity. "I just want to understand."

She sneered modestly, "That's not going to happen Jef. The germ fear is way more complicated than you'd expect. You won't understand it, trust me."

I took her reaction as a challenge, translating her lack of faith into a personal insult to my brain. Suddenly retrieving my energy I straightened my posture. "Try me."

"Take a seat," she gestured to the bench a few feet behind us.

"You're not afraid of this seat?" I questioned.

"No, I am. That's why I'll be taking a shower then changing my clothes as soon as I get home," Lacey assured me.

As soon as we both settled she began explaining her complex phobia. "I can't touch anything without feeling the germs festering on me. Every touch on my skin feels like a stain to my flesh. It's like a patch of contamination. When I feel that patch of contamination it's just about all I can think of. I get extremely anxious, and suddenly I can't breathe. That 'germ feeling' suffocates me. It's like there is no air. I can't seem to make the feeling go away until I finally wash the patch of contamination off. And when I wash the patch suddenly I can breathe again."

My voice box was at a loss, so she kept talking.

"I don't constantly wash off the germs in the sink or in the shower because I want to. I do it because I have to, because if I don't then I'll suffocate. And if anybody else felt the same sensation I felt then they'd have to do the same. Because nobody can live without air. Nobody." She affirmed with an unflinching stare. I swear, I could feel her pain.

"What I do may be weird, and ridiculous, and wicked embarrassing, but I do it because it's what I have to do to navigate through this world. I do what I have to do to survive. It doesn't matter if the feeling isn't real to other people. It's real to me."

I was still speechless.

Lacey's intuitive gaze knew I was unable to formulate a sentence. She leaned back, taking ownership of the situation. "I don't expect you to understand my fear of germs. I don't even understand it. It's the one thing I've never been able to find the words to describe."

"Wow," I realized the depth of that statement. If I had to credit Lacey with a sole skill then it was her innate ability to manipulate the English language masterfully. So hearing her say that she can't put into words how the germ fear affected her was extremely telling.

"When exactly…" I felt like I was learning how to talk, "when did this germ fear come about?"

"Well," she sighed, "I think I had OCD since I was little but I didn't know it. I didn't actually know what OCD was, and I think, like most people, I assumed I was normal. I just had a lot of weird obsessions and compulsions. But no fear of germs. It was the germ fear that I randomly got in the beginning of 8th grade. You know, puberty. That's what really destroyed me. And my family. I can't begin to describe the toll this mysophobia has had on every Goddamn aspect of my life."

"So this has been going on for a while," I concluded with unexpected sadness.

As the wind picked up Lacey shook her head, "I can't remember life without OCD. I know it existed, but that seemed like a different life. I'm not that girl. I don't know what happened to me to make me so deathly afraid of germs, but it happened, and I have to live a life not having a clue why such an inconvenient and maddening feeling happens every time I touch anything."

I felt my mandible tense up. I was frustrated on her behalf. Lacey might have accepted no answer, but I hadn't.

I felt a fire light within me, and more than anything, I wanted an answer. For the same reason I was so passionate about physics, I wanted to know *why* Lacey was the way that she was.

I didn't bother to shut the light off that night. I knew I wouldn't be sleeping. My mind was too wound up with the thought of Lacey Parker's brain and all of its wondrous idiosyncrasies.

As I usually did by default whenever my mind was racing, I once again locked my vacant stare onto the top right corner of my bulletin board where I had tacked on a scrap piece of paper with my favorite quote of all time written on it. The quote had always resonated with me when it came to strengthening my knowledge in the institutions like science and mathematics. But now, the quote resonated with me on a different more emotional level.

"I have no special talents. I am only passionately curious." – Albert Einstein

Chapter 7

It was a Wednesday morning, and all I could think about was how much I wanted to be talking to Lacey. Learning from her and debating with her in the name of knowledge. The only problem was that I didn't have tutoring until Tuesday.

I went to my first class that morning, and it was excruciating. I wanted so badly to leave to go to the library, where I knew Lacey would be. So, during the break between my first and second class I made a decision I had never made before.

I decided to skip class.

I hardly ever missed a class. Not when I had a cold. Not when I had the stomach bug. Not when Mom thought I caught the Swine flu during its overrated outbreak during my freshman year of high school. But missing a class to talk to Lacey, that didn't seem like a missed learning opportunity. That felt like I was taking advantage of a learning opportunity. The amount of insight and thought provocation that I get from conversing with her is unparalleled. Her wisdom is alluring and her intuition is its own phenomena worth ogling at. What kind of dim witted bricks had I been associating with before her?

I burst into the library's double doors.

"Sterling!" came a familiar call from behind the checkout counter.

"What?" I snapped in my haste, flashing a meager glance up at Natalie.

"I swear to God if I have to tell you one more time to wipe your dirty sneakers on the damn floor mat when you come in I'm going to ban you from the library! You know I close on Wednesdays and I don't want to be vacuuming your Goddamn footprints all night!"

"Sorry," I sighed heedlessly and hurried on.

I spotted Lacey immediately. She was staring down in her lap. I assumed she had her notebook sitting there.

I was too excited to keep from sprinting to the table she was sitting at.

"Hey," I panted a little. Now that I was standing over her I realized she wasn't writing. She was actually on her phone, which was a very weird sight. Lacey didn't strike me as the texting type. Not gonna lie, but the idea of her sitting at the library table talking to somebody other than me, even if by text, made me jealous.

"Oh, hey! What are you doing here? I thought you had-"

"Who are you texting?" my jealousy snipped the restraint between my brain and my vocal chords.

She faltered a little bit, "Oh, uh," she glanced down at her phone, registering my question, then laughed, "As lame as it sounds, I'm texting my dad. I was hoping he could pick me up early today."

I felt a weird sense of relief hearing that she was just talking to her dad. "Oh," I laughed, more at my own awkwardness than as a response to her answer. "No that's not lame at all."

"Eh," she curled the upper corner of her lip and shoved her phone in her pleather jacket pocket, "most young adults text their friends. Well I guess that's technically what I'm doing." Suddenly my jealousy resurfaced, but this time in a different way. "You're friends with your dad?"

Lacey was beaming, "Definitely. My dad's one of my best friends," her wide grin began to disintegrate, "one of my only friends, really."

I found that perplexing. I didn't think Lacey hated people, but why else would somebody so well spoken and witty be so socially isolated? I refused to believe her lack of social interaction was anything short of her own decision. "Do you not like people?" I asked as I took the seat next to her.

"It's not that I don't like people, it's that I can't relate to them."

I wanted to ask why, but I felt like that would have been too pushy. I think Lacey could read the curiosity in my eyes though, for she tried, with a tinge of bashfulness, to explain further.

"I just- I got out of touch a while ago and I never really made the effort to get back in touch."

"What's that supposed to mean?"

"If you really must know, I missed a year of high school. My sophomore year. My obsessive compulsive disorder was so bad that I was too scared to leave the house because of my germ fear. And I got depressed. Dangerously depressed."

I wanted to say something. Anything. But I couldn't. I had never heard of a situation like that. Being out sick because of obsessive compulsive disorder? And then the fact that her OCD caused severe depression? That never dawned on me. Something stuck with me.

"You missed a year of high school?" I stupidly choked out.

"Yeah," she sighed.

"That sounds awful," I commented, thinking of my two year education hiatus after graduating high school.

"That was the year I got diagnosed with OCD."

"And you never got prescribed medicine?"

"The doctors tried to convince me to go on medication, but I refused."

Before I could comment, Lacey strategically changed the subject from medicine by taking a few back-steps in the conversation.

"I lost all of my friends that year," Lacey stated with eyes lowered to the black screen on her lap.

At this point in the discussion my curious mind took a back seat to my pity. I couldn't believe that OCD had any correlation with friendships. That was a bit of a conundrum to me. I tried to imagine if Gabe came up to me and told me he had OCD. Would I end our friendship? No. I wouldn't even consider ending it. That didn't seem necessary.

I don't know if it was compassion from firsthand experience having a brother with schizophrenia, but I couldn't get myself to comprehend why somebody would stop hanging out with a person because their mind was flawed.

I didn't mean to announce my confusion, but my mouth was already stammering, "How- I don't- why? I don't understand, you lost friends because you had OCD?"

"It was my own fault," she was quick to blame herself, seeming to care more about defending her old friends than defending her integrity. "I didn't make an effort to tell them what was going on with me. I iced them out."

"So?"

My aggression caused Lacey to flinch.

I'll admit, even I was surprised by the anger in my voice. Why was I so damn angry?

"Do you at least keep in touch with your old friends?" I pressed. For whatever reason I found myself sincerely hoping she'd say yes, as if her damaged social life actually impacted me.

She frowned probably the saddest of frowns I've seen from her yet. Her eyes were lost in a distant memory, a memory that probably didn't seem like it belonged to the same life she maintained today. "A couple of girls I was close with through middle school used to text me every so often, during high school, to see how I was doing. Never really asked me to hang out though. But I don't blame them! I probably wouldn't have gone out anyways, I'm sure they knew that. And I think they also had no idea how to react towards a friend who was afraid to leave the house."

I soaked in all the information, letting it marinate my neurons, waiting for a proper response to filter through my lips. The only rejoinder that came forth was the scratchy crack of inactive vocal chords. "That's really lousy."

"Yeah," she exhaled an entire world of unspoken elaborations, "it really is."

I didn't like the sadness behind her voice. I didn't like it at all.

Adamant on alleviating her deeply rooted sadness, I made a point to look on the bright side. "The good thing is that this is college. You can make new friends just like everybody else. We're all in the same boat."

"Oh, I don't think so," she dismissed while nervously picking at her hangnails.

That wasn't what I hoped to hear. "What? Why?"

Now picking her hangnails to a point that trickles of blood were forming, Lacey crinkled her nose and slouched forward. Since her frame was already trim it appeared like she was crumbling before my eyes. "I just don't have the energy Jef. I don't have it in me. I'd rather be alone than hurt myself pretending to have a grand ol' time with a bunch of college kids."

I wanted to get down to the bottom of this. "Why would you have to pretend?"

"Because," Lacey moaned, "I get depressed when I hang out with other college kids."

I didn't understand that. If anything I figured socializing would be a mood booster for somebody as segregated from society as Lacey. "Really? Why?"

Lacey sighed a deep sigh and finally stopped ripping apart her nailbeds. I suppose she was tired of my inquisitive nature. "Cause it's always the same thing with kids our age. Sex and drugs. Sex and drugs. Sex and drugs. It depresses me. I wanna have deep, intelligent conversation. Or really humorous conversations! But I don't wanna talk about who banged who last night. I just have no interest in normal conversations. They depress me. I can't relate. So why bother hanging out with kids my age if I can't relate? Ugh, I don't know what my problem is."

I sat there silently for a moment, taking in everything she had just said. I couldn't believe how much I could relate to her feelings. I had never actually met somebody who felt the same way.

Lacey repeated herself apologetically, "I really don't know what my problem is, I'm sorry."

"No, no, it's fine," my mind trailed off.

The more I thought about it, the more I felt like I was onto something.

I got an idea.

"Hey, if you had to think of one word to describe yourself, what would it be?"

She flashed me a baffled stare, thrown off by my seemingly random question. "What do you mean?"

"Like when I think of who I am, I think 'student.'"

"Oh I definitely don't think that," she laughed.

"What do you think?"

She bit her shimmering scarlet lips. Something was causing her to hold back. Was it shame? Was it embarrassment?

After a moment of reluctance Lacey admitted her word, "Sick."

I leaned back into the wooden frame of the library chair, satisfied with her answer. "I think you found your problem."

Lacey was quiet.

In our silence I couldn't help but think to myself, yet again, how much I liked talking with this girl. It didn't matter that the conversation was depressing. It was insightful. Lacey was getting me thinking. And, as mysterious as it was, she was also getting me feeling. The questions I shot her with were no longer just unbiased third party questions. They were questions that I was attaching my own emotions to. I actually cared what the answers to those questions were. I actually cared how Lacey felt. I placed value on what she felt.

This wasn't how research was supposed to go. This wasn't right. But I couldn't stop. I didn't want to stop. I had to get closer to the mind that belonged to Lacey Parker.

Lacey picked up her pen, about to immerse herself in her notebook.

"Hey!" I shot out, not ready to be done interacting.

Her head tilted to the side, "Yeah?"

I blurted out the first thing to pop in my head. "You should hang out with me and my friends." Wow. Any more blunt and I would have sounded like Peter.

Rapidly I tried to reinforce the random outburst with some relevance, "They're not all about sex and drugs. Not all the time, at least." I made a point to disregard Carson. "Believe me, if they were I wouldn't have fun hanging out with them either. I think you'd like them. Really. You'd like them."

I knew she would revert back to being lonely if I didn't push her. And I wanted to push her. I don't know why. I just wanted to help her.

"I appreciate the invite, I really do, Jef. But I don't make friends easily. It's too hard to explain the OCD. That's why I don't have any friends."

I could believe the part about it being hard to explain the OCD, but I couldn't believe that she had no friends. "Oh come on, you must have some friends, right?"

"I don't have any friends."

"That's... so sad," I realized.

She started to scribble notes in her notebook but spoke to me at the same time. "No it's fine. I've become used to it. I don't need friends."

"Everybody needs friends," I said, thinking of Peter.

To my surprise she put her pen down and folded her hands on the table, locking her brown eyes with mine. "Jef, one thing you're gonna learn about me is that I'm not like everybody else."

I didn't know what to say. "I believe that," I shrugged.

She pointed to her notebook by tapping her pen against the pad, "I don't need friends because I can make up friends with my writing and daydreaming."

"But don't you want real friends?"

"No. Real friends are disappointing. They say the wrong thing. I can't control how people behave in this world, but I can control how they behave in my world." After she finished saying this she seemed slightly insecure and, to my pleasure, asked me for my input. "Is that sick?"

Having a schizophrenic brother, and a scientific mind, I had read up so much about schizophrenia. The main aspect that defined the mental illness was *the inability to separate delusions from reality*. So, I relayed that idea to Lacey. "As long as you can tell the difference between your make-believe story world and the real world then I guess you're good."

She nodded with understanding. "I know the difference between the make-believe world and the real world. The make-believe world is better, with better people who get me. I want- no, I need to vent to people who understand me. And I've learned the hard way that those people only exist in my mind." Lacey pointed at the full notebook. "These imaginary friends are there for me. When I'm upset, I confide in them, and they give me guidance, comfort, everything I need from a friend."

I was mystified by this notion. "They can only say as much as you command them to. If you can't think straight, they can't think straight, right? How can you learn anything from a voice that comes from your own brain?"

"You'd be surprised by how many epiphanies I've come to using solely this brain."

I thought of the poem. She wasn't wrong. She definitely had a deeper mind than the average person. But for her to just learn all sorts of life lessons from people she fabricated in her mind alone? That would be crazy. Remarkable, but crazy. Unbelievable, in fact.

Strangely enough, I couldn't honestly say that I didn't believe her. A part of me felt like she was right, like she was capable of coming to wise epiphanies on her own with that disordered brain of hers. It made me wonder, was Lacey some genius in disguise? Were all "different" people like Lacey and Peter really geniuses? And were normal people, like me, more simple-minded?

I didn't want to view myself that way. So, I selfishly continued to try and disprove that genius hypothesis by questioning Lacey.

"How can you know more than you know?" My question sounded confusing but Lacey understood what I meant.

She leaned forward as if letting me in on a secret, and I was gripped by her voice, "Did you ever think that maybe, just maybe, we all have a sea of epiphanies just waiting to be discovered and only certain people, the people deemed as 'crazy', can access it."

I wanted to hear more. I was intrigued by just about everything that came out of her vibrantly glossed mouth. I wanted to talk to her all day.

Suddenly Lacey started to gather her things, and I freaked out.

"Wait!"

Lacey froze, then slowly placed her pen back down. "Yeah?"

I wouldn't let her go. I couldn't. I had to hear more. So, in my desperation, I blurted something out to keep the conversation going.

"Why don't you just give up daydreaming?"

Lacey's eyes widened. She seemed horrified. "I could never do that!"

"Why not?"

"Daydreams are my natural coping mechanism. They're how I deal with reality and all the emotions that come with it. All of my feelings would boil over if I didn't let them out with daydreams that exaggerate my current mood. When I'm overwhelmed I daydream about throwing up. When I'm sad I daydream about crying. When I'm excited I daydream about frolicking throughout the world. And when I'm really excited, I daydream about, well, affection. Touching."

My awkward mouth almost said something super nerdy and embarrassing about how she must have been coping with her adrenal hormones, hormones secreted by the sympathetic nervous system to increase arousal by using them to generate touchy-feely mental images she called "really exciting" daydreams, all as a method to suit her OCD derived continence. I refrained from the biology lesson though, and instead demoted my response to a pathetic, "Oh."

"Oh?" her voice dropped with disappointment. Call me crazy, but I think she would have preferred it if I lectured her about the chemicals in her nervous system.

"What?" I asked and flashed open palms.

"That's all you have to say? 'Oh'? That was really personal what I just told you!"

Dammit, Jef! Don't screw this up! Immediately I became defensive, infusing stammering words with a few flailing hand gestures, "What? No, I- I- I- I figured you wouldn't want to hear me- I mean, I figure you believe what you want to believe and you wouldn't want to hear what I have to say."

"I want to hear what you have to say," Lacey insisted with some urging head nods.

"Uh, okay," I took a deep inhale, itched the back of my head, and exhaled. "I think that this whole 'daydreaming is my way of dealing with reality' thing is probably just one big fallacy."

"WHAT?" Lacey raised her voice.

"Okay, okay, calm down," I hissed while glancing back and forth at all the eyes Lacey's outraged shout had drawn to us. "All I'm saying is-"

"A fallacy? My reliance on daydreaming is a fallacy? You're calling the trait of my mind that I value above anything else, the trait that both elicits and evokes my creativity, a *fallacy*?"

"Well yeah! You know, a false belief, a logical mistake in rationalizing your behavior."

Lacey's pupils were as dark and as sharp as each goop coated eyelash sprouting from her widened eyelids. "Jef you sure as hell better start talking in regular English otherwise I'm gonna assume you're insulting me."

Something told me this conversation wasn't going to end well. I took another well-needed deep breath and attempted to translate my words into diction just delicate enough that they wouldn't offend, "I'm saying I think you're trying to rationalize your choice to daydream by calling it a necessary function of survival."

"I don't choose to daydream, Jef!" Lacey retaliated without a moment to spare. "I can't help but daydream. I'm telling you, daydreaming is like this inborn coping mechanism that I have no choice but to do in order to deal with the world."

"Well it shouldn't be," I argued.

"Don't tell me how I should or shouldn't be! Daydreaming is necessary for me!"

"I believe that you believe that, but, let's be honest here Lacey. You're not really one to believe in the most rational things. I think it takes you a lot of extra effort to function in the real world and I think you're trying to convince yourself that it's worth the extra effort. And that is actually a phenomena I studied before, it's called the justification of effort and it's a way of avoiding this thing called cognitive dissonance, you know, when you have conflicting thoughts about something!"

"And what are my conflicting thoughts, Jef? I'm pretty sure my thoughts have been rather consistent in believing that daydreaming is necessary. The only inconsistency here is you telling me it's unnecessary!"

"Okay, okay, I hear you," I used my hand to try and wave her volume down a notch, "The inconsistency in your cognitions are that, on one end you think these daydreams are helping you deal with the world, but on the other end you recognize that these daydreams are actually disconnecting you from the world. And you're trying so hard to justify all of the hard work it takes for you to maneuver through the world with this disconnected mindset and these OCD fallacies that you function by telling yourself that the la la land fantasies and thoughts are worth having. It's all in an effort to remain cognitively consistent, something I'm sure you're familiar with being that you have a mental illness centered around consistent rituals and a fear of change."

    Lacey's eyes, reminiscent of a fawn, stared up at me.
    No words.

    Just her big brown eyes. And my bumbling mouth that I have finally managed to shut a minute too late.

    That's it. I really did it this time. Not only did I insult Lacey but I also managed to sound like a self-righteous know-it-all. I ruined this friendship.

After a solid thirty seconds of painful silence Lacey finally blurted out a response.

    "What the fuck are you?"

    There wasn't anger in her voice. There was amazement.

    In a sudden haste Lacey gathered her notebook, hugging it close, and stood up. "I've gotta go."

    "What? No, don't go! It's only been, what, twenty minutes?"

    "I told you I get tired easily," she reiterated.

    She was right. The circles under her eyes seemed heavier.

    I knew I couldn't prolong this conversation anymore, but more importantly, I didn't want to prolong this conversation for her sake. I didn't like seeing her so haggard.

    In a hurry I tried to come up with a reason to meet with her again, before our next scheduled tutoring. I couldn't wait that long.

    My eyes flashed to her coffee cup. "You like coffee," I realized out loud, "How about we meet at the coffee shop down the street tomorrow? After whatever class you have?"

    She crinkled her nose, "I don't really like drinking coffee that I haven't personally made, you know, the contamination fear. And I kind of need to have coffee every afternoon, going out would disrupt that."

    "Ah... caffeine addiction, that's because there's a higher secretion of adrenal hormones in response to all that caffeine in your bloodstream. Your nervous system must be addicted to that afternoon high."

"Oh, uh, yeah, I guess. Sure? But that's not exactly what I meant. I need to have coffee every afternoon because it's part of my routine."

"Oh," was my underwhelming response.

I think Lacey felt awkward, because immediately she started trying to explain herself.

"I know it's stupid. Sometimes I'm not even in the mood for the afternoon coffee, but I get anxious when I don't have it and that anxiety makes me grouchy and nasty and mean. So I kind of have no choice but to make it an essential part of my routine. It's dumb, I know. It's really dumb."

For whatever reason I didn't like hearing Lacey ramble and apologize so uncomfortably. It bothered me, it bothered me from an emotional perspective.

"You can bring your own coffee to the shop," I spit out.

She thought about it for a moment. "Can I meet you there at 1:45?"

"Of course!"

I was supposed to be doing homework but instead I found myself locked in my room, at my desk, rereading the notes I had made up about Lacey up until now.

I couldn't focus on OCD though. No. I could only focus on Lacey Parker.

This study wasn't what I anticipated it to be.

Her OCD surprised me. What surprised me more was the creative nature of her mind. I was no longer just studying "Obsessive Compulsive Disorder" like I intended. No. I was now studying "Lacey Parker" as an individual. I wasn't fascinated by the sole swatch of color that was OCD, I was fascinated by every facet of color on the entire spectrum that was Lacey Parker.

And something was bothering me about my interaction with Lacey Parker today.

I kept replaying what Lacey said in the library.

I need to vent to people who understand me. And I've learned the hard way that those people only exist in my mind.

I was determined to disprove that.

I was going to understand Lacey Parker.
Soon enough Lacey would consider me a friend.

Chapter 8

Lacey waltzed into the quaint coffee shop with her thermal mug of coffee, "Hey," she smiled at me.

"Hey," I was weirdly out of breath when all I had been doing was standing by the glass door waiting. "How was class?"

"Boring," her voice dropped, "but I sit in the back so I got away with recording all of my daydreams in my notebook."

"Sounds like a productive class," I gathered, having learned in the days prior just how important writing was to Lacey.

We made our way to the tables. I scooted in a booth without really thinking. As soon as I caught sight of Lacey and her fear-stricken expression I realized I made an error. "Oh. Are you okay with this booth?

She shook her head, "I'm sorry, I can't sit there. There's crumbs all over the seat and-"

"Do you want me to brush them off?"

She bit her lip, "No, it's already tainted. I'm sorry," she turned extremely apologetic, "I'm really sorry. I know I'm being a freak but I just can't. I can't sit there. I'm sorry."

"It's fine," I grabbed my hot coffee, stood up, and tried let her know it wasn't a big deal, "really, don't worry about it. You pick a booth."

Little Lacey led me past a few tables until she found one that was satisfactory.

We both slid on opposite sides of the booth.

With both hands clasping her pink and black checkerboard printed mug Lacey took a sip. "So," she sighed, "how was your-"

"Excuse me mam," an older woman wearing a *Java Zone* apron interrupted. "You can't bring your own coffee in here. You're gonna have to throw that away or leave."

"Oh," Lacey turned a hot pink, "I'm sorry, um," in a spurt of vulnerability she looked to me helplessly.

I was used to customer service giving Peter a hard time so I knew just what to say. I jumped in without hesitation, "She has a medical condition and she needs this particular beverage."

The woman was about to interject, but I wouldn't give her the chance.

"You're not gonna kick her out because of a handicap, are you?"

That shut the woman up, "Oh, I apologize! If you need anything my name is Tina. Enjoy!"

As soon as the old lady was around the corner Lacey flashed me a wide smile, "I'm impressed."

I jokingly patted myself on the back, "What can I say? You learn a surprising amount about how people operate when you need to accommodate a brother with special needs."

"I bet. Hey, I never really asked you about your brother. What's his name?"

"Oh, uh," I was taken off guard. People rarely cared enough to humanize my brother with a name. "It's Peter. His name is Peter."

"And you said he's older?"

"Yup, by four years. His birthday's actually coming up soon."

"Ah, very nice," she nodded, "And he has... what was that you called it?"

"Cerebral palsy. And schizophrenia. We think both are from a lack of oxygen flowing to his brain at birth."

Lacey allowed herself to frown, but only briefly. She quickly rebounded with a refreshingly casual attitude. "What's that like? I hope you don't mind me asking." She was careful not to overstep her boundaries.

"Oh no, it's cool," I was more than happy to babble on about my life to her. I don't know what it was about her, but she was just so easy to talk to. And not just easy to talk to, but appealing to talk to. I truly wanted to share whatever I could with her.

"The cerebral palsy leaves him with some spastic tendencies and the schizophrenia affects his moods and speech every now and then. I have to make sure he takes his antipsychotic medication at dinner, but other than that I don't really notice Peter's issues. I never really thought of him as different, you know? He's my brother. He's always been this way. Hobbling around. Arms awkwardly tucked in at his sides. Some stiff muscle movements. Really exaggerated reflexes. That's just Peter. Yeah, he needed braces to help him walk up until he was about six years old, but I barely remember that since I was, like, three. And he's never been the most coordinated person, but hey- I could say the same about myself."

That last comment aroused a snort of laughter out of Lacey. "Sorry," she blocked her smile with her thermal mug.

I didn't care that Lacey was laughing at my expense. Just knowing that I caused that laughter incited the right corner of my mouth to raise into a smirk, "It's true. Peter teases me all the time about how clumsy and awkward I am 'cause when I get really worked up or nervous or just plain excited I become a spaz, tripping all over the place and using overly animated hand gestures. He says at least he has a medical excuse for being awkward."

"That's a riot," Lacey snickered. There was something infectious in the way her eyes glowed and the natural bounce of her laughter, and before I knew it I was laughing with her.

My head became light and I felt somewhat high as the music of her charmingly goofy laugh blended with mine. I couldn't believe how genuinely good, just downright *good*, it felt to laugh with her.

As both of our laughter evaporated, the serious nature of the subject matter brought me back down from my high.

I sighed, "Yeah, Peter's a good guy. Sometimes he'll have his paranoid freak-outs, starts to talk really fast and incoherently, gets that crazy look in his eye and people get scared, then I have to tell 'em Peter's harmless. Beause Peter wouldn't hurt a fly. He couldn't. Literally he cried the other week 'cause he accidentally stepped on a bug."

"No shame in that," Lacey casually vouched then chimed along. "Peter and I would get along great. Whenever I see an ant in the house I try and capture it with a plastic cup or napkin and put it outside. That or leave it alone, which pisses my family off. Rightfully so."

"Do you feel bad squishing them or is it like an OCD thing?"

"Probably both. I don't wanna be responsible for killing anything. I don't even eat meat," she tacked on that last detail and took another sip of her coffee.

"So would you be offended if I had meat in front of you?"

As she finished gulping down the coffee she waved her hand with dismissal, "Of course not! Go for it."

I felt myself smirking, because whether Lacey meant to or not she just confirmed that there would be another time we'd meet, outside of tutoring, and it would include a meal.

In a hurry to disguise my smirk I jumped back into talking about my brother, "But yeah, Peter's a great brother. Kind. Trustworthy. Oh and he's got this thing where he's brutally honest. Most of the time it's hilarious. Sometimes it gets him in trouble. And he's smart. So smart. He can spell anything. I mean anything," I had somehow descended into hopelessly bragging about my big brother. I didn't mean to, it just happened. "I keep telling my mom he should go to college. I know he could do it. But she got him a job as a custodian at the place she works at. Peter's too smart for that though, you know?" I lowered my head and shook it while fidgeting with the stirrer in my coffee cup, "People don't realize how smart he is."

My eyes lowered to Lacey's hands, which were cupped around that mug.

I realized how cracked they were. Being my awkward self I accidentally blurted out, "You should moisturize."

"What?"

Unsure of what I was referring to, Lacey's eyes imitated mine and focused on her hands. "Oh, that. Yeah I know," she groaned, as if she was told this way too often, "My hands get really dry because I wash them too much. You know, the germ fear."

"That sucks," I sighed.

She shrugged, "Sometimes my knuckles crack so bad they start bleeding, which sucks even more because bandages don't sit well on knuckles."

"That's, like, a medical issue. You don't want scabless cuts exposed when you're out in public. That's considered an open wound and you could easily contract an infection! If anything it's more dangerous for you to keep washing your hands than to leave them alone if that's what happens," in my awkward rambling I realized it wouldn't help to give Lacey something else to be afraid of, "sorry, er, I don't know why I said that. That was weird, that was a weird thing to say."

"No, it's fine. You're not wrong," she agreed, but went on to change the subject. "So, is your English class going any better?"

"Ugh," I wiped my hand over a disdainful grimace, "I hate my English class. English isn't really my thing. And it doesn't help that my English professor is real old school."

"Oh yeah?"

"Yeah. She's this wicked old lady, I swear like ninety years old."

My exaggeration incited a cute laugh out of her, "She's probably got one of those painfully ugly old lady names. Like Gertrude."

"Or Agnes."

"Bernadette."

"Edna."

"Ruth."

Suddenly the woman in the booth behind Lacey spun around. With glasses and a pointed nose she looked like one of those prissy librarians from school. "Excuse me!" she was appalled. "My name is Ruth."

"Oh, I'm so sorry," Lacey apologized, "We were just kidding around."

When the lady turned back around, away from us, Lacey and I locked eyes. One look at the smile she was biting down and I found myself feeling the intense urge to laugh out loud. Before I knew it we were both sitting there fighting laughter.

Lacey changed her mind about my English professor, "Your professor's definitely an Edna," she decided while pointing behind her and rolling her eyes, mocking the woman who had obviously been eaves dropping on our conversation.

As I stared at Lacey's friendly smile I thought of how badly I had misjudged her. A snob? Not in the least.

Compelled by guilt I felt the necessity to apologize for the discomfort I must have caused her before I knew about the OCD. "Hey... I never told you, but I'm sorry if I made you feel awkward, before we met, when I asked you to pass me the Frisbee."

"Oh you don't need to apologize about that," she assured. "I'm sorry I couldn't just pass it." I could see the confidence in her demeanor chip away as embarrassment took over. "I'm so weird, I'm sorry. I know it must have been wicked annoying and strange and-"

"Hey," I cut her off while leaning closer towards the table, "you definitely don't need to apologize about that."

Her red lips arched with pleasure and she sat up straighter. It made me feel good to see that I could refuel her confidence with a simple sign of acceptance.

Lacey dove back into the conversation, "I had seen you guys playing Frisbee before. I actually thought ahead about where I should sit outside so I wouldn't get hit. I thought I was in the clear to be honest."

"You can thank Gabe for that," I jeered, "He has a horrible throw. Come to think of it he doesn't really have a throw. He's so inconsistent."

I don't know why but she was attentively listening, like I was actually saying something of importance. "You really like Frisbee, don't you?"

"Oh my God, yeah," I exclaimed, getting hyped just thinking about it. "It applies all sorts of physics. Like Newton's Third Law or the Bernoulli Principle!" I was getting excited just thinking about the applicable equations and Lacey was looking at me like I was speaking a different language.

Suddenly I felt shy, so I tried to talk more about the sport and less about the science behind it. "Oh, uh, er- passing a Frisbee is fun but Frisbee golf is the best. It gets pretty exciting."

"I refuse to believe anything with 'golf' in the name is exciting." she joked.

A snort of amusement vibrated my trachea. "I swear it's not nearly as lame as it sounds. Imagine mini golf on a greater scale, but instead of tapping some dinky little ball in a hole you're whipping a specially engineered disc in a net, kind of like a cage."

I don't know why I was telling her all of this. What was more of a mystery to me was the smile expanding on her expression. "What?" I felt abnormally jovial, like her happiness was a contagious virus I caught just upon seeing her sincere smile.

Lacey Parker shook her head, "You're just so excited talking about Frisbee. I don't know, it's nice to see."

Lacey was no fan of Frisbee, yet she wanted to hear about it? And because I liked it? I couldn't believe what I was hearing. Last date I raved about something I found exciting, the girl left early.

Wait, was this a date?

No, shut up, Jef. Don't be stupid.

The surprise of having somebody show an interest in what made me excited must have been causing me to think not so clearly.

Pumped, I wanted to bask in the moment and share more of my interest. "Wanna see a picture of the last Frisbee golf course I went to?"

"Definitely," she invited, pushing her coffee aside and leaning forward further over the table. Upon leaning over, some loose hairs fell in front of her goopy black lined eyes. Reactively she blew upwards, towards her forehead. The hairs lifted up a little bit but fell right back down when the channel of air faded. With a sigh she apologized, "Sorry, hang on," and awkwardly wiped the hairs out of her face with the back of her hand instead of moving it the easy way, with her fingers. I guess she didn't wanna touch her face with her fingers?

Anyways, I showed Lacey the Frisbee course photo that I took on my cell phone.

Not many girls entertain me by acting interested in my own interest. To be honest, I don't even think Lacey was acting or just being nice. Despite not really caring for Frisbee, I think she cared because I cared. Maybe I was being crazy though.

"See that?" I pointed to the cage in the top right corner of the picture. "That's the equivalent of a golf hole."

"That's actually really cool. Could you send me that picture?"

"What, this?" I pointed to the photo on my cell phone. "Yeah, sure."

After a quick exchange of phone numbers, I texted Lacey the picture of the Frisbee golf course and continued raving about the sport.

"I really want a Frisbee golf target, but it's a bit more expensive than I was hoping. I'm saving up to get one though."

Lacey jumped on the conversation topic and asked a follow up question, "What do you do for a job?"

"Oh nothing special. Just a clerk at the convenience store down the street from where I live. Not the most glamorous job. I get discounts on gum though, so there's that."

She entertained me with a laugh.

Suddenly my throat tightened and I started to sweat.

Something powerful overtook me. I don't know how to describe it. I had an unprecedented athirst to be with Lacey. In her vicinity. Talk with her. Laugh with her. Hell, I didn't even have to be included in the act. I'd be content sitting on the sidelines watching her study or write or do something as lackluster as wash a dish. The scientist in me wanted to observe everything about her peculiar brain.

Feeling awkward enough as is, I went out of my way to transfer the focus off of me and onto Lacey. "What about you? Where do you work?"

"Oh," her gleeful smile melted, "I don't work. It's hard enough to get me to go to school."

"Oh," I wasn't sure how to respond to that.

I think she sensed that I felt uncomfortable about asking. "I know somebody my age should have a job," she disclaimed, "but I don't know. I'm just not capable yet. It's pathetic and embarrassing."

"No it's okay. I can't imagine it being easy to get out of the house when you're afraid of germs. Every day must be exhausting."

"It really is," she released a relieved sigh, like somebody finally understood her. But I wasn't satisfied like I anticipated I'd be. Understanding wasn't enough.

It was kind of funny, because the only reason I had a slight level of understanding towards her issue was accredited to her poem. And she knew that, but I could tell just by the sincerity in her gaze that she really appreciated me taking an interest.

That night I felt... changed.

I couldn't get enough of Lacey. Not when she tutored me in English. Not when I studied her obsessive compulsive disorder. Not when I skipped class to talk to her. Not when I met her at a coffee shop.

When I thought of her and her issues I felt upset.
When I thought of her and her laugh I smiled.
When I thought of her in general I got excited.
This wasn't supposed to happen.
You aren't supposed to have feelings towards a test subject.

But you're also not supposed to ask a test subject out for coffee.

What was happening to me?

I thought this was gonna go like a sly interview. I'd slip questions about Lacey's OCD into casual conversation, she'd answer, and I'd jot it all down when I got home. No feelings. Just questions and answers. Rock solid information. No emotions.

That wasn't happening though.

When Lacey shared something with me, I felt something. And what started as asking questions for the sake of learning her thoughts flourished into asking questions because I genuinely cared about her as an individual. How that happened, I have no idea. I was mystified by my feelings.

I wasn't familiar with feelings as much as I was with thoughts. But the more I hung out with Lacey, the more that changed. I felt like I was evolving into a more complex form of human or becoming more alive. Like I was half alive before, but with Lacey I was learning how to be fully alive.

And I swear, the more I spent time with Lacey, the more I felt for her. I felt on her behalf, and I felt on my behalf. She was actually pulling emotions out of me that I didn't know I had. Like that random spurt of anger I got when she mentioned losing friends because she had OCD. I had gotten so worked up when she brought that up. Or the streak of elation she invoked upon me by being so attentive when I blabbed about Frisbee golf. I was feeling all sorts of things. And honestly? I kind of liked it.

In a change of course, I was valuing my time with Lacey not just for her thought provoking behavior, but also for the emotional hold she had on me.

Sitting in my room, staring at the front of the black binder, I let guilt seep into my bloodstream. My eyes were fixed on the title, "Obsessive Compulsive Disorder". Was it wrong to be researching Lacey's mental illness? There was so much more to her than mental illness. She was complex. I couldn't help but feel guilty for all that I had written about her mental disorder. But how could I stop writing notes about her? Her layers of thinking were too complex. Ugh.

To ease the guilt on my conscience I grabbed a silver Sharpie from my desk drawer and wrote on my binder's cover, so that it read "Obsessive Compulsive Disorder & Lacey Parker".

Chapter 9

Lacey's arms were folded as she leaned on the library table. I couldn't help but realize there was a fresh coat of gloss gleaming along the table's surface.

"You wiped this down, didn't you?" I questioned out of the side of my mouth, both somewhat amused and somewhat concerned.

She playfully wafted the air between us to diffuse my inquisition. "Just take a seat, would you?"

"You're the boss," I plopped in the library chair. "Tutor away, English major."

"What is it you have to write this week?" Lacey asked me.

"I have to make up some kind of short story," my voice fumbled out accompanied by equally flustered hand gestures attached to my knobby wrists. Why was I so awkward?

"This is for your professor, Gertrude?"

"I thought we decided on Edna."

"Oh right, right," she sighed an airy breath of laughter that was strangely more uptight than it was carefree. I decided right then that one of these days I was going to trigger an airy breath of laughter out of her that would be predominantly carefree. Just wait.

"Anyways," Lacey nodded, realizing what she needed to do. "I'm going to throw some questions at you. Questions every writer needs to consider. Ready?"

In order to brace myself for the storm of wisdom that I just knew was brewing behind her red lips I went ahead and took a deep breath. "Ready."

"When you write a scene, what is happening? And what is the significance of that event? How does it impact the storyline? How does it enforce the theme? What do you even want the theme to be?"

"I'm not really sure," I managed to choke out through the barrage of inquiries. I was already overwhelmed.

"Well what do you want the reader to take away? What's your reason for even writing what it is that you want to write?" I sat there, silently. I had no idea.

Lacey could tell I was struggling, so she took the initiative to further explain. "There has to be a reason why you're writing what you are writing. Nobody writes for no reason. You have a story to tell, whether you know it or not. Sometimes you know it when you sit down and grab a pen, and sometimes you just gotta scribble away whatever nonsense pops in your head, flushing out your thoughts, your emotions, your very guts, until the writing you have laid out shows you what it wants to be. Believe it or not, sometimes the story finds itself. It's a crazy phenomenon, but it happens. And trust me, when it does, when you realize your mind just inadvertently exposed a hidden tale packed with its own theme, that is a euphoric feeling. That's a feeling that makes you have faith in the power of your own mind, even when you have no blatant proof that there's anything worth praising inside there." Lacey paused for a few seconds, I think processing what she had just said. It almost looked like she was on the brink of an epiphany. Call me crazy, but I think her improvised lesson for me unraveled itself into a lesson that could be applied towards herself, freakishly paralleling the phenomena she was in the midst of explaining. With an enlightened fire behind her eyes, Lacey's voice seeped onwards, "That's a feeling that makes you believe in yourself."

In that moment I understood why Lacey Parker hugged her notebook so close to her heart.

Chapter 10

Though I was a textbook kind of guy, I found myself captivated by Lacey's unconventional tutoring. She was getting me to think in ways I never thought before. Nobody had ever had as powerful a hold on my mind as Lacey Parker did.

Staying in touch with Lacey outside of school was hard. She didn't keep her phone on her all the time like most people because she thought it was ridden with germs. I wasn't bothered by that though, because I didn't wanna have stupid text chit chat anyways. I wanted in depth conversations with her right in front of me so that I could see her reactions, mannerisms, and her in all of her subtleties.

For that reason I valued the limited times I had in Lacey's company. The closer I got to her, the more I really wanted to figure her out. I kept finding that after parting ways I couldn't wait to see her again. Not just to quiz her or heckle her about her illness for the sake of knowledge, but to actually understand her for the sake of, I don't know, getting to know her. To listen to her. To be with her.

I could feel the shifting in my interests and I didn't fight it. I didn't want to. I had already looked forward to school, being a knowledge junkie, but lately it wasn't the classrooms that were quenching my knowledge fix, it was Lacey.

My friends had actually started to pick up on my hanging out with her in the library. Sooner or later it was bound to happen, and I had initially been prepared to answer the "Why are you hanging out with her?" questions with an honest "I'm studying her", but the more I got to know Lacey as a human being and not just a study topic, the less I wanted to admit my initial intentions.

Gabe punched me in the ribcage, "Hey dude, you up for some Frisbee this afternoon?"

I was quick to decline. "Can't, man. I've got English tutoring."

"Oh, the snob?" Gabe referenced with a jaunty chuckle and a nod behind me.

I turned to see that he was signifying Lacey, who was sitting with her legs crossed in the grass underneath the shade of a mammoth tree in the process of losing its gold and yellow leaves. She was writing diligently in that flimsy notebook.

While soaking in the image of Lacey hard at work I corrected Gabe, "She's not a snob."

"But the Frisbee-"

"I was wrong," I shut him down, still unable to take my eyes off of the beautiful girl with her nose in her notebook, "very wrong."

The library was packed when afternoon rolled around. Lacey and I had to sit at the notoriously wobbly square tables in the dark corner of the library. I don't know if the change of scenery triggered Lacey to be more rigid, but she seemed extra quirky. I guess change was hard to cope with when you had a mental disorder that thrived off of rituals and repetition.

Lacey strategically placed her pen down, readjusting it until it was perfectly parallel with her textbook and notepad. She had an unreachable glaze over her stare. Lost in her own obsessive compulsive world.

When Lacey was finally satisfied she put her hand in her lap. I could tell she had no idea I had been watching her.

"You good?" I spoke up.

"Hm? Oh, yeah. Fine. I'm fine."

"Is this another law? Everything on the table has to be parallel?"

"Ha, you wish it was that simple." She scoffed. "I have three things on the table. With an odd bunch of items they all have to be aligned. When there's an even bunch of items there needs to be an outlier that breaks the pattern."

I didn't know what to say. I leaned back and smoothed over the orange cap that fell behind my head, "Wow."

Lacey crinkled her nose in her usual cute way, "I know."

"Nah, it's cool," I dismissed while pulling my latest English assignment out of my folder and sliding it across the rickety table to her. I had to rewrite the ending to some short story that I quite frankly didn't understand.

Lacey sat still, both hands clutching the loose leaf sheet I half assed my English homework on.

I folded my arms and pushed back in my seat so that only the back legs of my chair were on the ground. As I fidgeted in the seat I locked my stare onto Lacey's notebook. The key to her mental landscape. What kind of wonders existed in that world were a mystery to me. Damn did I wanna read what was in there. Or any of her writing for that matter.

"Ugh that drives me crazy," Lacey commented halfway through reading my assignment.

There was a high pitched squeak as I landed back to the library rug and leaned over the table, trying to see what I did wrong. "What?"

"Oh it's just you keep switching tenses."

"Psh," I dropped back to my seat and waved her comment away, "That's no big deal."

She disagreed, "It's a very big deal actually. Having the correct tense is important. For example, 'I have friends' is significantly different than 'I had friends'. Totally different meaning."

"Hm," I mumbled unhappily towards the somber example.

Lacey returned to reading. This time she paid me a compliment, "You know what you do well, Jef? You're good at showing and not telling. You describe."

I was half listening to her because I was mesmerized by the notebook on the table. I couldn't begin to imagine the marvels that lived in there.

"Jef are you listening?"

"I don't want to talk about my writing." I unapologetically admitted.

Lacey loosened her grip on my homework and raised her eyebrows at me, "Well then what writing do you wanna talk about?"

"Yours."

Her face heated up. "You do?"

"I wanna read some of the stuff in your notebook."

"Oh no you don't," she laughed, "That's all a bunch of rough draft material."

"Yeah but I feel like I could learn a lot from it."

She slouched with modest compliance, "Possibly."

"So can I read it?" I didn't hold back my persistence to get my hands on the notebook.

Lacey thought hard while staring up at the ceiling lamp, puckering her lips so that they were compacted in a tight pout. After a solid moment of thinking she compromised. "I'll tell you what, I'll select some pieces to show you and we'll make a day of it."

I was almost too excited to talk. I got to read her work and spend a day with this fascinating person? "Deal!" I managed to cough out.

I guess my eager reaction was a little bit too loud, because all of a sudden the library fell quiet. I could feel other students staring at me. In my self-consciousness I scanned the surroundings only to spot somebody I really didn't want to see.

Carson.

He was staring at Lacey.

That bothered me more than it probably should have. It's just that Lacey seemed like this other worldly figure. She was this ethereal mind that I, and only I, had stumbled upon. And to see anybody from my life prior to meeting Lacey doing so little as glancing at her felt like they were threatening my relevance in her life.

From the corner of my eye I could see Carson's expression was twisted with befuddlement.

I knew why he was confused.

He wanted to know why I was sitting with, just as Gabe referred to her, "the snob".

Before Carson could come over and make a detrimental comment I hurried to get Lacey to scram this crowded joint with me.

I quickly improvised some kind of excuse. "Hey, I don't like this corner. It's kind of stuffy over here, don't you think?"

Lacey agreed, "Yeah it is. But there's no other free tables to-"

"Let's just get outta here," I insisted.

"Okay I guess we could sit in the courtyard."

"No!" I didn't want to risk Carson following us. Again, I improvised with the first thing that hit my mind. "Let's go to the park down the street."

Surprisingly she seemed down with it. "Can I drive?"

"Yeah, yeah, of course," I complied eagerly.

Lacey unlocked her silver car and I slid in the passenger seat.

I imagine it was a pretty big deal for somebody as isolated as Lacey to let another person in her car. I wasn't about to blow it by whining about the heated seat.

I tried to watch Lacey as discretely as possible, facing forward but directing my eyes to the side. She awkwardly pinched the metal buckle of the seatbelt, crossed the strap over her upper body, and then quickly maneuvered her hand off of the metal tip and onto the cloth belt, successfully locking herself in. Even once she was buckled she looked uncomfortable. Her posture was still very stiff, like it usually was in the library. I figured she'd loosen up in her own car, but I guess not.

"Warning," Lacey cautioned, "when the car turns on it'll blast some pretty loud metal music."

"I'm ready, look: I'm strapping in," I announced while buckling the seatbelt.

She laughed, and with the click of a button the car awakened. A guttural voice, belonging to what must have been a very vocally skilled female, blared through the speakers.

Lacey's hand shot out to the volume dial and she turned the music lower. "Do you hate it?" she anticipated with a laugh.

"Not hate," I remarked while taking in the screaming vocals, crashing symbols, and chaotic guitars. "Just a little shaken by how loud that was."

"Yeah I kind of go a little overboard when it comes to music. I like to get totally lost in the sounds," she commented while lifting herself up and peering in the rear window to back the car out of the parking lot, "especially with metal. I just love losing myself in that storm of growls and raging instruments."

"I never really understood the appeal of growling in a song," I admitted.

"Honestly I didn't either at first, but the more I listened to it the more I liked it. In fact I love it now. Growling is so unhinged, so straight from the soul. And it so adequately expresses real, raw pain with the utmost passion. I swear, if the fusion of pain and passion had a sound, that is it."

"Hm," I scratched at my right sideburn and nodded, "I don't know, I never really cared for screams."

Lacey shook her head, blushed, and bit down her lower lip which wanted desperately to form into a grin.

It took me a good five seconds to locate the embarrassing territory where her mind had veered.

"In music!" I clarified. "Screaming in other contexts is fine, I mean, uh, not in fear or anything but-" before I could humiliate myself anymore I clamped my stupid mouth shut.

I would have been happy to crawl into a hole and die in that moment, but one glance at Lacey's blushing pink complexion and I couldn't refrain from smirking. I actually made blood rush to that pale visage. I did that. I caused that.

"So! Is this the only type of music you like?" I tried to change the subject to calm myself down.

"By types do you mean outside of the metal genre?" With great ease Lacey braked at a stop sign. I wasn't used to the lack of whiplash.

"Why, are there, like, subtypes in the metal genre?"

"Oh yeah. There's many types of metal, Jef. There's classic metal, black metal, hair metal, industrial, metalcore, progressive metal, doom metal, thrash, power metal, symphonic metal, alternative metal. My personal favorite is metalcore."

I was impressed by Lacey's evident interest. I didn't realize it until now but this was the first interest Lacey showed towards something that wasn't a manifestation of her own mind like writing. "I'm getting the impression you really like music, don't you?"

She turned her head, away from the road, to steal a quick glance at me. "Of course. How could you not? Music is the greatest source of inspiration. Haven't you ever heard lyrics that tell a story? Or lyrics that almost seem like the synopsis to a story? Like their giving you the bare bones of a tale and you can use your imagination to further sculpt the plot. And then there's the fact that you can accompany those lyrics with an orchestra or a guitar riff. Lyrics are an amazing art alone, but incorporate instruments and it's like a story but with sound." Lacey seemed invigorated just by talking about music. I swear, there was more color in her skin tone and more energy in her voice. She raved onward, "Lyrics and sounds have such a unique way of evoking so many emotions. That's probably why I find music so inspiring, because my writing is usually centered around an emotion, and music is a master at drawing forth emotions or elaborating on emotions. It's just so thrilling when a song can give you a feeling, an emotion, an idea. Damn, when a song touches you its euphoric."

I wanted to sufficiently process everything Lacey had shared with me about her love for music, but I couldn't, because the car suddenly came to a halt.

I looked up to see we were already at the park. There was only a little boy and a little girl playing on the jungle gym.

I must have been in such a trance while listening to Lacey, and watching her rather than out the window, that I had no idea we were so close.

Lacey got out of the car before me.

I think her lengthy explanation for loving music had stunned me somewhat immobile.

Slowly feeling came back to my legs and I was able to scoot myself out of the car.

Lacey paced ahead of me over to a picnic table that was standing in wood chips. She lit up like a little kid, "Awww! Swings! Those are the best!"

"Wanna go on them?" I called out while jogging to the table.

She suddenly crossed her arms, making herself smaller, and stepped back timidly, "Oh no, I can't."

It was kind of sad how Lacey worded her declination with the phrase "can't" rather than "won't", as if there was a force completely out of her power prohibiting her from doing something she so obviously wanted to do.

I watched carefully as Lacey went on to tuck a strand of hair behind her ear with a hand that she purposely covered by her long shirt sleeve. "Who knows what kind of filthy children have been on those swings? And I highly doubt they've ever been sterilized."

Seeing the deep stare of forbidden longing in her eyes, I tried reasoning with her unreasonable fear. "What about the rain? The rain washes the germs off."

"No it doesn't," she shut down with the utmost confidence, "You need soap. Water without soap is useless."

I was taken aback. "I don't think that's entirely true."

"To me it is."

"What if I told you-"

"There's no changing my mind. It's a law, Jef, 'You must wash your hands with soap and water'."

I nodded, making the mental note. Little did she know I was gonna go home this evening and make that law a physical note and stuff it in my OCD/Lacey research binder.

The both of us sat down on opposite sides of the iron picnic table. We didn't really talk. Instead we listened to the playful sounds of the little boy and the little girl laughing and running around on the playset.

Lacey watched the kids with nostalgia. "I had the greatest childhood."

"Oh yeah?" I was intrigued by the genuine twinkle in her eye as she silently reminisced.

"When I'm at places like this, despite all the crap I have to go through with OCD and depression, I remember what it was like as a kid and I can't complain. I lived a very fulfilling childhood."

She flicked her head so that her hair fell on her back. I stared, admiring her profile, as the wind gently blew her long dark hair behind her. Tilting her head up to gaze at the clouds I couldn't help but revel at how attractive she was as she continued to speak.

"I'm so grateful this germ fear waited until puberty to kick in. I never would have been able to go rollerblading or play the fun games at arcades or go to the annual carnival in my town or play dolls with my sister in the middle of the floor or swing on the swings at recess. Thank God I got to do all of that. Seriously, thank God," she shook her head in wonderment. I couldn't believe how sincerely grateful she was for such simple childhood activities.

The fact that these completely normal activities were so precious to her was extremely enlightening, and eye opening. She was right. All those types of things were precious. I didn't realize it until she said it though. I took those things for granted.

And if I'm being honest, I do have a tendency to think I'm better than most people. And you'd think I'd especially be that way around somebody as flawed as Lacey, but that wasn't the case at all. I felt a sense of humility when I was with her.

All of a sudden my heart felt whole.

This was exactly why I liked spending time with Lacey. She made me feel like I was learning something not just about a mental disease, but about life in general. Like being around her made me, I don't know… better. I just felt like I was a better version of myself when I was with her. Nobody had ever made me feel that way before I met her.

I was in the middle of mentally marveling at the impact this girl had on me when suddenly the sound of my name on her lips snapped me out of my daze.

"What about you Jef? Did you have an amazing childhood?"

I quickly recovered from my internal mindset and felt Lacey's direct question catalyze a list of memories. "Oh heck yeah," I immediately started recalling all sorts of events, "Sledding with my cousins down the huge hill in my backyard, sneaking my Pokémon cards into school to trade them with my friends, flashlight tag and capture the flag on the beach during vacation, playing video games with my brother. I had a blast."

"I bet you were the type of kid that seemed way older than you actually were. Like an adult mind in a kid's body."

"Ha!" I snorted at the overwhelming truth in that statement. "I was also really shy."

"Oh yeah?" Call me crazy but I think Lacey wanted me to elaborate. And believe me, I wanted to. I wanted to share whatever I could with her.

I couldn't hold back. "I was so shy when I was little, so shy people thought that something was wrong with me." I soaked in the sight of Lacey before me, who was intently listening to every word that fell out of my mouth. She was so genuine, I couldn't stand it. I had never met anybody that made me feel that important. That got me excited, so excited I was motivated to share more pieces of my life with her. "In fact, I remember my mom bringing me and Peter to her work on 'bring your kid to work day' or whatever the hell it was called and when her boss came up to say hi to me I freaked out, like got stupidly scared, and hid behind my mom's leg. Now Peter, on the other hand, had no problem saying hello. So guess what happens? This lady kneels down to me and goes, 'Oh Lorane, this must be your little special one.' She said that to me! Not Peter!"

"No she didn't!" Truly amused, Lacey threw her hands up, covering her mouth and the brim of her nose.

"Yup, she did, swear to God," I laughed.

Suddenly a burst of laughter rumbled behind Lacey's palms. She wouldn't take her hands off her mouth as the unveiled section of her face turned pink. In no time I was cracking up just from seeing her get such a kick out of the story. "You think that's funny, do you?"

Lacey continued to laugh but shook her head. She was still blocking her mouth, trying to be discrete, which was cute because her hysterical laughing was so obvious.

"I'm sorry," she finally wiped away a tear.

I wasn't the least bit offended. On the contrary, I was flattered that she didn't hold back her laughter just because I was telling a joke at the expense of my intellectually disabled brother. "It's okay, you're allowed to laugh," I was smiling ear to ear as the autumn wind kicked in. "Even Peter finds that story funny."

"Oh that's awesome," she beamed, "That is too great. He sounds like such a cool guy, Jef."

It wasn't until Lacey's laughter subsided that a realization hit me.

Lacey just touched her mouth, her nose, and her eye.

She didn't mask her "germy" hands with her long sleeves.

What was that all about? What had occurred differently? All that happened was I talked to her about when I was a child, and she was interested. Did her genuine interest outside, towards my story, have an effect on this mental disease that attacked her inside? Could it be that, just like Lacey made me feel like a better version of myself, I made Lacey feel like a better version of herself? So much better that she didn't feel the urge to perform a compulsion?

Was just the simple act of Lacey touching her mouth or nose or eye a glimpse of her if she didn't have the germ fear? That made me think about how Lacey had told me earlier, at school, how she didn't have her germ fear until puberty. If little actions like putting her hands over her mouth to disguise laughter were prohibited in the thick of her mysophobia, then what kind of major actions did she perform before 8th grade when she didn't have mysophobia?

"Hey Lacey," it was almost weird hearing my voice, knowing I was about to wonder out loud verses in my head.

Lacey, whose nose was pointed towards the young girl giggling on her way down the corkscrew slide, jolted to move her powerful eyes on me. "Yeah Jef?"

"If, uh," I didn't know how to put this, "If you knew you were going to get OCD, you know, the part with the fear of germs, what would you have done differently?"

Her thin lips tightened. She thought hard. "I would have hugged my family more."

Although I was prepared to be saddened by her answer, I was still shaken by the blow of sorrow her response brought me. Don't get me wrong, I hardly ever hugged my mom or brother, and I certainly didn't hug my dad. But my family was broken. Lacey's wasn't. Unless you could equate a mentally ill child to the dismantling of a mother and father. Then again, it was my brother's mental illness that broke my parents apart.

Regardless of the parallels or, lack of, between my family and Lacey's I still found it hard to accept that somebody as emotional and sensitive as Lacey could go without a hug from a parent every now and then. Especially when your parents are your best friends. "You don't hug your family?" I questioned out of disbelief.

Lacey didn't hesitate to answer, "No, I don't. I'm afraid of touching anybody. You know, germs."

"Oh."

She caught onto my unusual silence. "That's not the answer you were expecting, was it?"

I shook my head no, still taken aback.

"What can I say? I miss hugs," she admitted openly, "That feeling you get when your chest meets with another is just pure comfort. And I didn't realize how powerful comfort was, physical comfort, until I got really ill." She shook her head, as if trying to ward off all turmoil she had been through up until now.

Now would have been a good time for her to have a hug.

Lacey went on, "Value your hugs, Jef. They're important. I should have valued mine while I was still sane enough to have them."

Everything and anything from the day's interactions with Lacey was on my mind when I got home. Thank God I didn't have to work the convenience store that night. I spent all of my free time, up until three in the morning, sifting through my memory and recording observations and quotes from Lacey. By the time I called it quits and scrambled into bed the "Obsessive Compulsive Disorder & Lacey Parker" study binder transformed into a "Lacey Proverb" collection.

She had a very philosophical, spiritual way about her. It was disarming. She wasn't like me. She didn't have statistical formulas, like standard deviation or how to calculate z-scores, memorized. She had a surplus of outlandish concepts memorized. Her deformed yet well-intended ideology was engrained in her psyche, a place equally nonsensical as it was virtuous. Her mind was so tangled. But enchanting. Lacey was so strangely enchanting.

In my need to be as meticulous as possible, I retrieved the ol' silver permanent marker and added the word "Proverbs" so that the metallic ink read "Obsessive Compulsive Disorder & Lacey Parker Proverbs" on the binding and cover of the sacred binder.

There was so much I wanted to know, to understand, that my heart started racing and I actually began to worry that I wouldn't fall asleep tonight. I needed knowledge! I just had to keep telling myself Copernicus's wise words.

"To know that we know what we know, and to know that we do not know what we do not know, that is true knowledge."

Chapter 11

A paper airplane skidded over my open sociology textbook.

"Yo, Sterling," Carson jumped into the cushioned seat next to me inside the student lounge.

I picked up the paper airplane and crumpled it, "Don't you have something better to do than interrupt my studying?" I tossed the crinkled ball at him.

"Nah," he caught the former airplane with a single hand then relayed it into the trash can. "So, that was hilarious the other day."

"What are you talking about?" my voice was monotone while I half listened to him, half read about the Charles Horton Cooley's theory of The Looking-Glass Self.

"I'm talking about you sitting with the weird girl in the library."
I flicked my eyes up from my history textbook, "Weird girl?"

"Yeah, you know, the chick who wouldn't pass the Frisbee back to us. Fricken snob."

Oh fuck, how had I forgotten about Carson seeing Lacey and I in the library? How did my overactive brain become so oblivious?

"What were you doing with that weird chick anyways?"

With pent up frustration my upper teeth clamped down on my bottom teeth. I really didn't like hearing Carson talk about Lacey like that. In fact I kind of wanted to punch him in the jaw. But I was not the confrontational type at all, and let's be honest,

Carson would kick my bony ass in a fight. So I naturally resorted to playing it cool.

"She's actually my tutor."

Suddenly Carson's expression brightened like he heard a hilarious joke. "You need a tutor? Dude, why didn't you tell me they assigned you to her! That's a riot!"

Keep cool, Jef. "Nobody assigned me, Carson. I asked her for help in English."

Carson looked baffled. "Why would you do that? Just for a good laugh?"

"What? No! Carson she's not that weird."

"Pfft," his inflection was snarky, "Sure…"

"Seriously. She's not that weird. She's actually really interest-"

"What are you talking about 'not that weird'? Are we talking about the same girl? Usually sits alone? Wouldn't pass the Frisbee? That chick was-"

"Dude, shut up." I swore to myself that I wouldn't exert any more energy on Carson, so I reverted back to reading my textbook.

Carson wasn't done though. "Come on, Jef, you can't honestly tell me she's not weird."

I had enough. "You know what?" In a rage I dropped my history textbook and slammed my palms on the coffee table, causing the clamorous thuds to silence almost everybody in the lounge, "Yeah, she's weird. Okay? You're right, she is weird. But she's also funny, and nice, and she's really smart. So you know what? I don't care."

With that out of my system, I stormed out of the student center.

I decided to cut through the administration building to get to the D parking lot faster.

When I whipped open the door of the building my stomach spontaneously flipped.

Lacey was standing on the other side of the lobby, seemingly talking to that stoner kid, Jamison. Correction: She was just listening to him talk. There was next to no doubt he was bantering about some liberal agenda that absolutely nobody cared about.

From across what was probably a sixty foot long lobby I could tell Lacey was completely uninterested. And I'm sure she was crawling in her skin having to smell the stench of cigarette smoke emanating off of Jamison.

I hurried over, catching the end of their interaction.

Jamison, who surprisingly wasn't ranting about our country's ineffective congress or broken economy, was hitting on Lacey.

"No, but seriously," the kid with the buzz cut boldly pat her on the back of her shoulder, "I wasn't kidding when I said we should hang out outside of school."

I could see the intense discomfort his pat imprinted in Lacey's fake smile. I swooped into action, standing between them so that Jamison's arm was forced off of her. "Sorry to interrupt," I felt obligated to apologize to him, then turned to her, "Hey Lace, I think campus police just ticketed you."

Her pupils flickered with understanding. "Oh no," her voice spiked to a high pitch, sounding more girly than Lacey naturally sounded.

She seized the opportunity and rushed closer by my side, "I should go then, see ya Jamison," she spit out so fast Jamison didn't have a chance to respond.

Quickly I led the escape through the lobby doors.

As soon as we were a few feet outside, past the doors, Lacey spoke in her more comfortable low pitch, "Should I actually be concerned about a ticket or should I be thanking you for saving me back there?"

I couldn't combat a grin, "I think a thanks is in order."

She laughed, "Thank you. Seriously I didn't know how to get out of that conversation without hurting his feelings."

"I know, despite all that black clothing you're surprisingly too nice."

She scoffed, "Thanks. But for real, you can't just turn down a kid like Jamison. You don't want to be on the bad side of a kid like that when he snaps."

I laughed and called her out, "That is incredibly dramatic."

"I know, I'm an extremist." Lacey claimed while pulling her battery powered car keys out of her jacket pocket.

I reverted back to our conversation about Jamison. "To be honest though, there is definitely something off about that kid."

"Right?" she got excited by my agreeing.

Lacey proceeded to open her car door, uncapped a container of disinfectant hand wipes that she kept in the console's cup holder, ripped a wipe out, then started to rub her shoulder with the wet cloth. It took me a moment to realize she was trying to wipe at the spot that Jamison patted her.

"Wait, he's not out here, is he?" she raised to her tip toes to peer at the administration building's entrance. Despite our jokes about Jamison, it was obvious by her vigilance that she didn't want to hurt his feelings.

"No you're good," I monitored the doors to make sure.

"He may be weird, but I'm obviously not one to talk," she went on while struggling to sanitize her faux leather jacket over the shoulder and laughed at her own expense, "I mean look at me."

I awkwardly fiddled with my cap, making sure it was all the way backwards.

"Fuck," Lacey muttered to herself.

"You okay?"

"I can't reach the spot," she struggled to wipe at her shoulder blade. Her tone was thicker with a strange sense of anger.

Seeing and now hearing how truly bothered this was making her I felt like I should assist, "Need help?"

"Please," she handed me another wipe because for some reason the first was no longer good enough. "Try not to touch the pleather with your hand or else it defeats the whole purpose."

"I've got this," I assured her with a mockingly confident tone.

As I rubbed at her left shoulder blade, watching intently as the fresh coat of soapy water shined against the fake leather before quickly evaporating, I wondered to myself what could have possibly been going through Lacey's head at this exact moment.

I was somewhat mesmerized by her bizarre behavior despite the fact that I already knew about her intense germ fear. Out of curiosity I spoke up, "So what would have happened if you didn't clean your coat and just left it alone?"

Through the wipe I could feel Lacey's body tighten. Just the idea seemed to make her cringe. "Ugh," she shuttered in disgust, "It's still really hard to explain, but basically I wouldn't be able to do anything without thinking about that patch of contamination on my jacket. I'd feel the germs on my back. Then when I sit in driver's seat and lean back I'd imagine them spreading to the car seat. To be honest I'd probably try to hunch forward so that my jacket didn't touch the car seat. To be more honest I'd probably assume, at some point in the drive, that I leaned back all the way so I'd still consider the car seat touched. Then the whole seat is contaminated and I'd feel that germ spot every time I sat there."

"That's what I don't understand," I was blunt, "what is this 'germ feeling' like? How do you feel germs?"

She snorted a breath of laughter, "I knew it! I said you wouldn't be able to understand the germ fear!"

"I know," I hated to admit my inability to grasp what she was telling me.

"I can feel the germs. I don't know how else to describe it. I know it doesn't make sense to anybody, including you. But, but..." she scrambled for a counterargument. For a second I thought she would come up with nothing, but then she said one of the most eerily resonating statements I had ever heard from her. "The innate nature of my mind is not obligated to make sense to you, Jef. It just is."

Nature. If there was one thing I've ever learned from my favorite subject, physics, it was that the universe was mind-boggling and, to the dismay of the human mind, nonsensical. Light particles us science geeks call "photons" are both waves and particles. The electrons in an atom never have a fixed position until viewed. Essentially, nothing exists until it is perceived. Nothing is real. Yet, here we are. Nothing about the universe or nature has to make sense to the human brain. It just is. And maybe Lacey's mind, like the universe, just is. Maybe nobody's mind has to make sense to just be.

The innate nature of my mind is not obligated to make sense to you, Jef. It just is.

The mumble, "Hm," was my sole and incredibly underwhelming response.

Lacey and I had gotten so close, but there was still a separation between my mind and hers. Her world and mine.

I continued gently rubbing the jacket with the wipe, thinking to myself how only a thin layer of cloth and black pleather resided between us.

Chapter 12

Once I finished promoting Lacey's jacket from its "unforgivably germy" level to a safer "germy" status she threw me for a loop and invited me over her house.

"You know, for tutoring," Lacey clarified.

I followed Lacey's silver Volvo behind the wheel of my jeep and attempted to mentally note each and every street I drove on.

Once parked in the driveway of Lacey's house, an excitement stirred inside me. Suddenly it hit me that I was about to witness Lacey Parker, the girl with the notebook, functioning (or at least trying to) in her home setting. From a researcher's perspective, this situation was perfect. It had the potential to present ample information. But, weirdly enough, I felt a slight aversion to witnessing that information. On the contrary, I found myself rooting against the OCD, deeply hoping that Lacey would prove herself to be significantly more relaxed in her home environment.

"Here we are," Lacey commented as she pressed the lock on her battery-charged car keys. "How was the drive?"

"Fine. It was fine," I halfheartedly responded. As I loitered on the pavement with my hands nervously fidgeting with the denim lining in my pockets I lost myself in a daydream of a carefree Lacey touching her face without a second thought and sitting in seats with a relaxed disposition.

"Now I have to warn you, my 'returning home' regiment is not pretty." Lacey disclaimed as she led me through the garage.

"Because of the OCD?" There was a hopeful nature behind my voice, wishing she'd say 'no'. But to my dismay, Lacey gave me a nod, 'yes' as we ascended the garage's wooden stairs.

Instead of pulling the screen door open by the handle, Lacey pinched the protruding keyhole above the handle with her fingers at a certain angle so that they wouldn't slip off the gold metal. I didn't say anything as she pulled the door a few inches off of its frame, then quickly ripped her hand off the keyhole and caught the naturally retracting door with her foot. From there she kicked the entire door open and let us inside her house.

It was nice inside, much nicer than my house. Yellow and cheery. Well decorated. Neat.

I kept my hands lodged inside my jean pockets, afraid if I set them free they'd knock one of the many nice vases or flower pots over.

Lacey bent down, unzipped her boots, then slid them aside on the mat.

I was taken for a loop to see that her socks didn't match. The left was a solid vibrant blue and the right was white with a brand logo on the cuff.

"Nice socks," I commented.

She tilted her head out of confusion, then glanced down. "Oh, yeah. That's the OCD."

"You're kidding?" I remarked out of incredulity. Naturally I would have assumed her OCD would make her want matching socks.

"I'm not," Lacey clarified. "I need them to be different."

I was having difficulty wrapping my brain around this. "What? Why? What's the reason?"

Lacey sighed. I could tell this was going to be downright absurd. "If my socks are different then I feel less trapped. Because each sock represents the left or right side of my body. If the socks are the same then my entire body is in the same condition. So when I hear a word that makes me anxious come from my left side, I don't get caught up in my anxiety because I still have a bunch of words that can override that word coming from my right side, a side that's different thanks to the different sock. When the socks are different that means I have different options. I have an out. I don't have to feel trapped."

I had no response to that.

That load of ridiculousness blew my mind. What kind of person projected their freedom onto their socks? What the hell?

"Okay so you wanna see me perform my normal routine?" Lacey asked, as if she hadn't yet started with her OCD rituals.

"Please," I insisted with a nod, "don't hold back."

"Okay..." her voice sang to a "you asked for it" tune. She then announced, "First we get the gross school germs off our hands."

She walked me over to the kitchen sink. I washed my hands first, in about ten seconds. Lacey took probably sixty seconds to wash her hands. I watched as she used both dishwashing and hand soap, apparently just hand soap wasn't effective enough, then scrubbed and scrubbed at her hands as they drastically changed from a pale olive skin tone to scorching red.

Instead of shutting off the faucet with her now clean hand, she ripped off a fresh paper towel and used it to shut off the water, creating a barrier between her skin and the metal faucet handle. Then, strategically, she opened the cabinet under the sink with her toe pulling at the bottom of the cabinet door. In there was the trash, where she threw the paper towel as if discarding something despicable like a squished spider or a dog turd, then shut the cabinet door closed again with the tap of her big toe.
Wow.

As she proceeded to rummage through the food pantry I stared in horror at her lobster red hands.

"Doesn't that hurt?"

"Doesn't what hurt?" she legitimately had no idea what I was talking about.

"Your hands, I think you burned them."

"Ohhh," she realized, "Nah I'm used to it. I burn my hands a lot."

That certainly reinforced her claim, back at the coffee shop, that sometimes her hands got so dry they would bleed.

It had been, what, three minutes in Lacey's house and she had already obeyed three laws? Don't open the door in the garage by its handle. Wear socks that don't match. Wash your hands with hand soap *and* dishwashing soap for a solid fifty seconds. Shut the sink off by pushing down the handle with a paper towel. Open and close the trash bin's cabinet using that same paper towel, dispose of the towel, then close the cabinet door with your big toe.

This poor girl thought she was dodging a jail sentence by following these laws when in actuality it was her obedience to these laws that acted as the jail. Holy fuck was this disease ironic. How could a brain be wired so perfectly wrong that it almost seemed more exceptional than ridiculous?

Awe didn't begin to cover what I was feeling.

I was amazed and I was horrified.

"You can bring your backpack to the table," Lacey pointed at the kitchen table, "That's where I do homework on the rare occasion that I didn't already finish it at school. You can get started and since I like doing work with music I'm gonna go run upstairs and grab my mp3 player while my hands are clean."

Like a marathon runner Lacey shot up the stairs, grabbed her mp3 player, and then hurried back into the kitchen towards the windowsill where a docking station sat.

"Oh gross," Lacey scowled at the docking station's wire on the ground.

I didn't see the problem. "What's wrong?"

"The plug's on the dirty floor. And I just washed my hands. Uck!"

Rather than take matters into her own hands Lacey decided to take matters into her own feet. She went ahead and used her right foot, struggling to get the cord between her biggest toe and longest toe, which must have been difficult considering she had a sock on. Somehow, though, Lacey managed to get hold of the wire. She lifted the wire, impressively balancing on her left leg, and after a few misses was able to stick the plug into the outlet.

"Wow," I reveled, this time out loud.

"You're judging me hardcore, I know."

"No, no," I disputed, "I'm just surprised by how easily you did that. You do that a lot, don't you?"

"Yeah," she resentfully admitted, "You'd be surprised how much I can do with my feet."

While I racked up all the OCD compulsions in my head Lacey proceeded to play her favorite metal band.

"Oh not this again!" a jovial male's voice erupted from the room next door.

Lacey rolled her eyes and hollered into the double door entryway, "Deal with it, Dad!"

Subsequently her dad came waddling in. I assumed he had a bad hip.

I was overwhelmed by nerves all of a sudden, but her father smiled a friendly smile at me and gestured to the mp3 player, "Tell me that's not noise!"

I nervously huffed a breath of amusement and replied, "It's definitely noisy." I didn't want to disagree with the man of the house.

"You guys suck," Lacey playfully joined in.

Her dad wheezed a laugh then glanced to me again, "Now she's mad at the both of us," then he turned back to Lacey, "this is not music!"

"You're not music!" she spit back the nonsensical retaliation like it was usual father-daughter chitchat.

Before I knew it they were interweaving inside jokes into their banter.

I felt totally out of place. Though it was kind of nice to see Lacey connecting with somebody other than myself. I had never really been on the outside like this before. Not with her. I was feeling mixed about it. Somewhat jealous that it wasn't me and her joking. Somewhat happy that she was so close with her dad, something I definitely couldn't relate towards.

I couldn't follow the conversation, but somehow it wrapped up with Lacey referencing her father during the past weekend. "At least I don't sit on the couch early on a Saturday morning screaming 'FIX!' at the television screen when they air a high school cheerleading competition. What could you possibly know about cheerleading?"

That got a laugh out of me. It was half nervous laughter, half genuine amusement. Was it okay for me to laugh at her dad? When their banter came to an end Lacey introduced me, "Oh yeah, Dad, this is my friend Jef."

Score!

Lacey referred to me as a friend!

I would have been more excited if I wasn't so nervous by Mr. Parker approaching me to shake my hand.

"Nice to meet you Jef," he extended his arm.

I received the handshake with a pretty weak grip, "Nice to meet you too, sir."

"Oh please, you're more than welcome to call me Jim."

Soon after her father left the room Lacey joined me at the kitchen table. Instead of sitting flat on her butt she kneeled in the kitchen chair. My long legs hurt just looking at her in that position.

I pulled my chair from underneath me to scoot in, "Is there a reason you're not sitting down normally?"

"I sat on my butt at school and those chairs are filthy with germs. I don't wanna cross-contaminate onto this chair, it saves me from anxiety and anger later when I sit here in my cleaner clothes," she explained it like it was common knowledge, "Though I still wouldn't dare go into my clean bed in the same pants that I wore when sitting here at the kitchen table because I still consider the seat dirty."

I was having a hard time following this. "Wait, so you're saying that you sit on your knees, now, so that you don't spread germs, yet you still consider it too germy to sit here then go to bed? What's the point of kneeling if it doesn't eliminate your fear?"

"I know," Lacey's tone was understanding, "but it's kind of like there's three levels of cleanliness. There's unforgivably germy, germy, then clean. By kneeling on this chair I'm keeping the chair germy instead of unforgivably germy. Germy is satisfactory for the kitchen chair. Now, if we were talking about my bed then germy is unacceptable. My bed has to be completely clean. Does that make more sense?"

I was floored into silence.

The mouthful of nonsense coming out of such an intelligent person was mind blowing.

"Lacey please tell me you realize how illogical-"

"I know you think it's ridiculous but for me... I don't know, there are just, ugh!" she was frustrated by my inability to understand, "Different rules apply to me."

Honestly I was too overwhelmed by Lacey's previous stream of OCD compulsions to argue with her about the current irrational nature of her thought process.

"Fine. Anyways," I changed the subject back to what was really fresh on my mind, "You weren't kidding back at school when you said your dad was your best friend. You guys seem really close."

"We are." Lacey boasted with true pride.

Just by how much she was beaming in regards to my assumption I could tell how important he was to her.

"That's cool," I tried not to sulk.

For the rest of the afternoon I caught Lacey doing weird things.

There was a point where Lacey needed to get a new pen out of a kitchen drawer, and she kept picking up pens, inspecting them, then putting them down. She would tap them with her index finger, telling me she wanted to make sure her thumb wasn't the last thing to touch any item. I guess she had something against thumbs because they were "the outliers of the hand".

Then there was a point where Lacey got thirsty and got a water bottle.

She held the bottle real close while she unscrewed it, peering at the cap with that unreachable stare. As soon as the crack of the broken plastic seal snapped through the air she leaned back and lost that distant stare.

"I needed to make sure it was properly sealed. I'm kind of paranoid when it comes to what I ingest."

I nodded, remembering how she had to bring her own coffee to the coffee shop.

Still, I ached to understand her warped thought process. Did she think it was deliberately tampered with? Or that there was a mistake when it was packaged? I'm not even sure she knew what the thought process was behind her irrational fear. I think she just felt anxiety and acted on it without question.

I didn't ask Lacey any further questions about her quirky bottle opening examination despite my prevalent curiosity. I cared more about helping her enjoy herself than studying her.

Since Lacey's dad worked from home we had to migrate from the kitchen into the sunroom because he had a phone call to make and the music, along with our talking, was too loud.

There, Lacey pointed to the couch on the far end. Half of the couch was covered with a towel. "I sit there," she pointed with her black polished nail. "If somebody else sits there I just remove the towel and put on a new, clean towel."

Instead of sitting in this spot, Lacey sat next to me on an adjacent sofa. She explained that she didn't want to sit on her usual spot while in her unforgivably germy attire.

It wasn't until Lacey's Dalmatian, Piper, ran into the sunroom that I found out about Lacey's fear of touching her pet. Piper came over to sniff her mysophobic owner and Lacey coiled up on the couch, pulling away from her affectionate Dalmatian to evade being grazed by her fur.

"What's wrong?" I had asked her.

Lacey frowned, "I'm too scared to pet my own dog."

Lacey's mom was extremely friendly when she came home from work. I was somewhat awestruck by how hospitable these people were.

As terrible as it might sound, I was more awestruck by how much Lacey's mother and father so obviously loved her. I could tell she was really close with them. They joked with her. They asked her about her day. They showed a genuine interest in her when she would tell them about her day. They loved her, regardless of her illness.

Since we were on the couch, out of her mother's earshot, I commented, "You're really close with both your parents, aren't you?"

"Of course," Lacey answered. "They're the best. I have the best parents."

She wore that same smile she had at the park when raving to me about her childhood.

Rather than be happy for Lacey like a decent human being I felt a little bit jealous of her. My mom and I had a strained relationship because of the circumstances, and my dad was as estranged as a dad could be.

I fucking hated him.

I was utterly exhausted towards the end of the visit. I had such difficulty comprehending all of Lacey's irrational behavior. If I was this tired by standing by and watching Lacey perform her compulsions, how indescribably worn out must she have been having to perform the compulsions firsthand?

It was no wonder Lacey got so tired so easily. If I had to deal with all the weird quirks she had to deal with on a daily basis, I'd be exhausted too. Too exhausted to do anything above the bare minimum functions like hang out with friends or hold a job. Heck, I probably wouldn't have the energy to go out and make friends if my life was run by all those obsessive compulsive laws.

Lacey's poem was right. She navigated through her own home like it was a mine field. Dodging this, dodging that. Finding unconventional ways to do this or that. It was fascinating, really, because she performed her quirky compulsions so casually. I honestly don't think she realized well over half of the strange OCD behaviors she performed. This was just life for her. And it was a shame, because normal tasks really did take her so much extra effort. Opening a door. Washing her hands. Using her mp3 player. She found a way to do these things, but by tedious and such superfluous means. And the worst part was, she seriously thought that those means were necessary.

It actually made me kind of mad... not at Lacey, but at science for plaguing her brain with this chemical imbalance of a mental disease. Lacey Parker was honest and funny and I could go on and on, so why her? Why did she have to have this mental disorder? Why not that kid on the school bus who used to bully Peter and I? Or that bitch in my history class that talked back to the teacher? Why not people like that? Why somebody like Lacey? It just wasn't fair. It wasn't fair, dammit!

"I like you coming over," Lacey said. "It's refreshing."

"Refreshing?" I questioned. I tried so hard to fight off a smile that my strenuous facial muscles actually throbbed.

"Yeah. It's nice to have somebody in this environment really take an interest in what I have to say. I feel like everybody in this house nullifies my input because they think 'Oh, that's just the crazy girl talking! Don't mind her!' But you don't do that. You value what I say. You make me feel like I matter."

I smiled a dumb smile. She started fidgeting with her nailbeds. Each of us were embarrassed by our apparent vulnerability.

In Lacey's shyness she tacked on a quick-witted joke at her own expense, "And what's better than making an attention-whore feel like she matters?"

My head fell with a consecutive laugh.

"See ya," she started to dismiss as she opened the front door.

I bid my farewell and descended onto the granite stoop.

But I faltered, replaying Lacey's honest confession through my head.

It's nice to have somebody in this environment really take an interest in what I have to say.

I could relate. I could relate because so often people in my life tune me out what I said because it was too nerdy. But I couldn't imagine what it was like to have people in my life negate what I said because they perceived the opposite: that my knowledge wasn't good enough because of some crazy label.

Lacey's comment, on top of all the obsessive compulsive behaviors I had seen her perform in her own home, made me feel like she was living in a prison. And I had an idea to help break Lacey out of this joint.

Before Lacey could close the front door I caught it by the rim, "Hey."

"Yeah?" she stiffened to help hold the door open.

"What do you say next tutoring session we go to my house?"

Lacey turned to stone, "Oh I don't know."

"Come on, it'll be good for you. That way you could meet Peter."

Lacey still seemed afraid. "I'm really not good in new places. I- I don't know how I'm going to handle it."

Damn. Lacey's strong fear of change was so prevalent in her obsessive compulsive world. If I wanted to help her break out of her OCD I had to work harder. I had to be blunt, but not too blunt.

"You shouldn't be afraid of change or new situations."

"Why?" she smirked, like she had absolutely no faith I'd be able to pull off convincing her that change wasn't worth fearing.

"Well," I paused to gather the knowledge my comment had stemmed from, "because. You, yourself, Lacey, are like a scientific theory. You've got all these theories about your identity but don't have any evidence until an experiment. If anything you are more yourself in those unfamiliar situations."

"What do you mean?"

"Well, uh," seeing how invested Lacey was in hearing my input, I knew I had an important point to make. And if I was going to make an important point, I couldn't afford to fumble on my words. Not around somebody as eloquent and perfectionistic as Lacey. I had to be poised in my delivery. I had to talk like I did when I taught Peter or even Lacey herself about science. "It's like this," I recuperated with a confident idea. "You, yourself, Lacey, are like a scientific theory. You've got all these theories about your identity. But like anything in science you don't have any sustaining proof of your theory until you perform an experiment. In your case, those experiments are life experience, new experiences. And when you experience a new experience you weed out any false hypothesis you had of yourself. Like a collapse of the wave-function in quantum theory! You have no certainty of who you really are in a hypothetical situation until you experience that situation and collapse any of the probabilities represented by the wave."

Lacey's eyes were wide, but not in fear or confusion or shock. In bewilderment. Amazement. I felt superhuman.

With a faint crack of her throat she expressed her wonder, "I find it incredibly weird that you can look at this from a scientific standpoint."

I couldn't help but laugh with the raised corner of my mouth, "I find it weird that you can't!"

After a few seconds in which Lacey leaned on the front door frame and smiled up at the sky she finally budged. "Well, I guess it couldn't hurt too much."

"It won't hurt at all," I assured her. "You don't have to stay long and you can come straight home to de-germify."

"De-germify?" she laughed, "That's definitely not a word."

I shrugged, "You would know."

Chapter 13

The next few days I was on overdrive in reading up about anything and everything that might shed light on the root of obsessive compulsive disorder.

When I researched on the computer I got an overabundance of cliché firsthand accounts about being "way too organized". The only factual information was, well, not that informative. The web didn't have the most clear-cut explanations for obsessive compulsive order. Not the onset. Not the way the brain operated. Nothing. It was like philosophy class all over again. A whole lot of assumptions and interpretations but no concrete answers. I needed to find those answers. I needed it like a human needs oxygen or like a plant needs water. Conquering ignorance as well as exercising the nerve cells and their transmissions in my brain was vital.
So, I decided to go old school and use good old textbooks to research the human psyche. Naturally, that brought me to one of my favorite places. The school library. So I drove all the way back to campus and rushed inside the library.

I'm not sure why but I had a really difficult time convincing myself to get out of the car.

I don't know why I felt like I had to be stealthy. I guess I just didn't want anybody to see me or find out about my obsessive compulsive disorder study. Something felt extremely risky about using the campus library, the special place where I was getting to know Lacey. It was dark though, and the library wouldn't be open much longer.

Before I could change my mind, I zipped up my gray sweatshirt, flipped on my hood, then made a frantic break out of the car and into the building.

It was weird being in the library without Lacey. I felt her absence. It was sad, actually. That was all the more motivating to get this library trip done as fast as possible.

I hustled down the psychology aisle and quickly flipped through random textbook after textbook to see if I liked the way that the author presented the information.

Eventually I found the perfect book. What won me over was its section on mental illness. Curiosity had gotten the best of me and I read up about schizophrenia, my brother's psychotic disorder. Since I already knew schizophrenia inside and out, both from firsthand experience with Peter and adamant research in the past, I was able to judge whether or not the psychology textbook's passage seemed accurate, and it certainly did. So I trusted it to give me both correct and satisfying information about obsessive compulsive disorder.

As I predicted, the OCD section was well written, so well written that my initial skimming turned into actual reading and somewhere in between pages I found myself sitting on the floor. What I found to be the most fascinating sentence in the entire passage was the line that read, "Obsessive thoughts reflect impaired ways of reasoning and processing information."

Hm. Reasoning. Processing. Maybe I should divert my focus onto how the human brain operates in perceiving anything, not just phobias. That could certainly shed some light on-

"Hey!"

Natalie popped up from behind the bookshelf, dustpan and brush in hand. I'm almost positive my heart catapulted out of my chest, "Oh my- fuck!" after that modest exclamation trailed off into an obscenity I struggled to catch my breath. I slammed the textbook shut and jumped up off the floor. "What the hell are you sneaking around for?"

"Sneaking around? You know I close the library on Wednesdays," Natalie reprimanded. "Besides, you're the one hiding in the aisle with your hood on! Sterling, you look like a fuckin' drug dealer."

"Lovely," with a quick swipe I flung the sweatshirt hood off my head and tightened my grip around the psychology textbook, "I'm just checking a book out."

Natalie's slender eyes peered down at the maroon title, "*Invitation to Psychology*?"

"It's for a research paper," I half-lied.

"I didn't know you took psych..."

"Yeah, well, I take a lot of classes," I hastily rushed past her and made my way down the corridor of bookshelves, "can I just check this out?"

"Sure," Natalie sighed with what I'm sure was accompanied by a roll of the eyes, then joined me at the checkout counter.

Chapter 14

I saw Lacey on Monday, right after her final class of the day.

It had almost been a week since I last saw her, and since then I had done nothing but read and write notes about the psychology of the human brain in attempts to understand OCD.

"Hey, you hanging around?" I forwardly asked Lacey.

"I'd rather not. I'm not feeling good at all." Usually Lacey would try and disguise her low mood with an apology or change of subject, but not today. No. Today she was giving herself permission to be blatantly upset.

This was such a letdown. "What? Why? Is everything okay?"

"I had a rough night," she disclaimed.

The sadness exuding off of her was almost palpable. I couldn't believe how upset she was. I had never seen her this sad and downright depressed.

For the first time I didn't let myself ask her for any details. I knew better. Something was seriously wrong and I wasn't going to make it any better with my heckling. Curiosity wasn't my concern anymore. Lacey was.

If I had to guess, I'd say the source of Lacey's rough night could be drawn back to her OCD. I swear her emotions were too strong to be related to anything that wasn't as prevalent in her life.

"Are you gonna be okay?" I asked her, hearing the fret in my own voice.

"I don't know," Lacey wouldn't look me in the eye. "I just really wanna go home and wash this horrible mood off of me."

"Okay, yeah. You should go home then."

"I can't," Lacey informed me with frustration. "I didn't drive here and my dad's working until 5:00 so he can't come get me." Exhausted by her own emotions, Lacey dropped her bottom on the courtyard bench, crossed her arms so not to touch anything except her own jacket, and stared down at her feet. Trapped. Tense. Unable to drop her head in her hands or relieve her sadness in any other motion, for her OCD had her paralyzed in a less comfortable state.

It was a pitiful sight.

"I'm sorry Jef. I'm too depressed to think straight."

Right then I remembered what Lacey said about being too depressed to go to school her sophomore year and how that was the year she lost her friends. Suddenly I wanted now, more than ever, to be there for her. To be the friend she never had.

"I'll drive you home," I insisted without thinking further.

"Wha- are you sure? I know how out of the way-"

"It's not a problem. I'll drive you home. My car's in the first lot. Do you wanna go now?"

"Uh, yeah, yeah!" she quickly pulled out her phone, "thanks Jef. Really, I'll be right there. Lemme just call my dad."

"Alright," I started to walk away.

On my way down the concrete path I overheard Lacey on the phone.

"Hey dad. No. You don't need to come later. Jef's gonna drive me home."

I was so glad my back was to Lacey, because hearing her casual mention of my name made me grin like a fool. I couldn't help it.

After crossing through the busy parking lot I hopped in my jeep. I allowed myself to sit there, calm and collected, for about five seconds before it sunk in who I had invited in my car. I glanced to the passenger seat. There was all sorts of crap covering the seat. Spare Frisbees. A deck of cards. A case of *Titanfall* that Gabe lent me. "Fuck!" I reacted.

At rapid speed I dove out of the car, sprinted around to the passenger side, and relentlessly chucked everything off of the seat and floor and into the back of the car. I tossed it all in the backseat like it was worthless junk. I could feel the judgmental eyes of the girl smoking in the Cadillac next to me as she watched my spastic tidying up.

Before I slammed the door shut I took a deep inhale. Did it smell in here?

I was too panicked to trust my nose, so just to be safe I scrambled through the console for something scented. All I had was an old bottle of cologne.

Manically, I sprayed the bottle all throughout the passenger side, hoping it would fill the air with a clean aroma.

I took a whiff.

This fragrance screamed "I'm a douchebag", but it would have to do for now.

I jumped off of the running board of the jeep, ran back around the car, and collapsed in the front seat.
I was just in time, too, because Lacey was just making her way into the parking lot.

Lacey looked so tiny when she climbed up the running board and lifted herself into the jeep.

Before she could finish fastening her seatbelt I blurted out, from pure nervousness and insecurity, "I hope it doesn't seem too dirty." It was safe to say I blew my cover.

"It's fine," she resorted to staring out of the passenger window. No friendly smile. No congenial laugh. Nothing. Damn, she was out of it.

Lacey didn't make a peep for over half the ride. And neither did I. Like I said, something was seriously wrong, and I wasn't about to push her to talk about it.

Just when I had about given up on finding out anything pertaining to her sadness Lacey delivered a simple statement.

"My mom freaked out at me last night."

With slight hesitation I responded. "Is she okay?"

"No, not really. It's my fault though. Entirely my fault. And I'm not just saying that to get you to comfort me. I'm just being honest. It was completely my fault."

I wasn't surprised by her brutal honesty. Lacey's honesty never failed to prevail.

"What happened?" I asked. I wasn't pushing her. I could tell that regardless of whether or not I asked she was going to offer information.

"We ran out of dishwashing soap, which I use along with the other soaps. I had just touched my computer, which gives me the contamination patch feeling, and I desperately needed to wash my hands. Without the dishwashing soap my angry anxiety wouldn't shut up though. I *had* to use that soap. And like I said, we didn't have it. And I had already cleaned myself after a day of school, so I wasn't gonna leave the house and get my germ infested car only to get all germy again. No way. So I asked my mom to go out and buy the soap. I didn't really ask, actually. I demanded that she go out and get it. That if she didn't I was gonna have a nervous breakdown. We got in a huge argument about it. I was freaking out from blaring alarms going off in my brain. She was freaking out because I was telling her I felt like I was gonna die if I couldn't get the germs off me. She was screaming like a lunatic about how I was killing her. It was scary. She's losing it. She can't take me and my OCD or depression anymore."

Lacey's situation sounded eerily like something that happened between Peter and my mom when he was having a schizophrenic spell. Those were scary as fuck. Honestly I remember locking myself in my room to get away from the screaming. I remember wanting so badly to blast music so that I could block them out but being too scared to because I was convinced Peter or my Mom might faint or something and I wouldn't be able to help them. I had no idea how to react then to Peter's meltdowns, and I had no idea how to react now to Lacey's.

Lacey continued venting, "I know I was being selfish. Completely selfish. Heck, if my kid behaved that way I'd kick 'em out on the street. But I couldn't help but be selfish. I didn't care about anything but making that germ feeling go away."

Lacey's selfishness reminded me a lot of the addicts on that show *Intervention*. My mom loved that show. She considered that show her guilty pleasure, only allowing herself to watch it when Peter wasn't in the room because she wanted to shield him from its dark and depressing nature.

Those people in that show were so caught up in their illness of addiction they'd nearly torture the people who loved them if it got them closer to a drug fix. Lacey was kind of like an addict. In fact I wouldn't say kind of. Lacey was an addict. She was addicted to performing compulsions, whether it be washing her hands with dishwashing soap to make the voices in her head go away or avoiding touching her philosophy folder anywhere but her philosophy classroom.

Lacey continued, I think more just talking through her thoughts out loud than actually trying to share information with me. "I know there's no excuse for being so selfish but I swear, sometimes I get so overwhelmed by my own thoughts and emotions that I feel like I have to choose between me and other people because I have no capacity for both. And I always choose me. I have to. I don't know why, but I have to. I don't know, I guess I'm just selfish."

I was overwhelmed, to say the least, by the density in every word that Lacey chose to share with me. I hate to admit it, but there was almost too much complexity to Lacey for me to dissect while multitasking with driving. Between Lacey's idiosyncratic personality and her complicated illness I couldn't keep up unless I allotted a significant frame of time to make sense of it all.

"I don't know what to say," I finally admitted.

"I know, I'm sorry," she rapidly shook her head as if the motion would take back what she had just said, "I don't know why I'm burdening you with this information. I guess I just needed to vent."

"I don't mind you venting," I assured her while rotating the steering wheel on a large turn. "I just wish I could help."

"You are helping. Just by letting me vent." I glanced up just quick enough to see that Lacey allowed her lips to gently smile. Despite the brevity of my glimpse, I was nonetheless able to see that her eyes were still very sad.

"I really appreciate you letting me purge all these thoughts onto you," Lacey thanked.

"No problem," I responded awkwardly fast. I kept my focus straight on the road ahead, afraid if I turned to look at her she'd see the wonderful nervousness her gratitude brought to me.

When we arrived at Lacey's house she didn't get out of the car right away. We both sat in our seats, not talking. Something was on her mind, and I wanted to know what it was.

"Hey Jef…"

"Yeah?" I reacted like a speeding bullet.

Lacey unbuckled her seat belt while her pupils dazed off in some distant thought. "This might sound weird, and it's really hard to describe, but do you ever get this feeling, this feeling in your chest where some unknown entity just sucks all the energy out of you from the inside out? It's like this soul sucking feeling. It literally feels like somebody had a vacuum and was sucking every bit of life out of your chest. And it leaves you empty, but not completely empty, because there's still sadness. Just this pure sadness. That's really what it is. Pure sadness."

"Yes, actually." I didn't have to think about it. I knew exactly what she meant. Whenever I saw Peter's sadness after a visit from my dad I felt it. I felt the sadness brewing in my chest, draining me.

Lacey's eyes were frowning at the glove compartment. She didn't appear any more relieved having heard a confirmation from me. She was still deeply sad. And she seemed to be struggling with that sadness, "What, uh... what do you do? What do normal people do when they feel that sadness sucking the life out of their chest?"

I thought for a moment about that horrible feeling. I resided my stare on the orange horizon while pondering. The answer came straight to me like a Frisbee soaring crisply in my direction. "They hug someone."

Her head flicked up at me in a sudden jolt. There was a scared look widening her big brown eyes, like I was suggesting the most forbidden sin out of her. Touching another person was high on her OCD list of things to avoid.

I watched her neck tighten as a gulp dragged its way down her throat. The only response that came out of her was a meek, "Oh."

Chapter 15

After I bought a bottle of water out of the vending machine in the hallway of the student center I met Lacey in the lounge.

I was alarmed by her antsy behavior. She was talking a mile a minute.

"How much coffee have you had today?" I was half joking, half serious.

She smiled a guilty smile and hugged her thermal mug closer, "Like three mugs. But probably more like six 'cause I put in way more coffee grinds than the average person. And I almost ran out of almond milk so it was basically black, which I'm okay with as long as it's really hot. Black coffee always tastes better hot than cold, in my opinion..."

Lacey went on and on. She was definitely hopped up from the caffeine. It was actually kinda cute. And comical, that's for sure. Interesting how caffeine had such a beneficial effect on her brain.

"Okay well Gabe and his girlfriend Beth are out of class at 1:45 so they should be here soon."

Lacey and I took seats at the big square table. Lacey seemed almost restless, perching herself at the very edge of the chair. I don't know if it was because she was hyper or because she was nervous to meet my friends.

"Lace, are you okay?" I realized she was shaking.

"What? Yeah, why? What's wrong? Is there something in my teeth?"

"You're fine," I laughed, "You're just shivering, that's all. Are you cold?"

"A little, but its fine. I'm fine. I'm great," she took another gulp of her coffee.

"You're nervous aren't you?"

Before she could answer Gabe came running in howling my last name like he did every now and then, "Sterling!" I stood up to receive his fist bump. "Is this Lacey?"

Lacey waved, "Yes, hello."

Gabe knew not to try and shake her hand because I warned him ahead of time.

Apparently he forgot to give Beth the memo, because she reached out to shake Lacey's hand. "I'm Beth, Gabe's girlfriend."

Gabe nudged Beth with his elbow and muttered something like "Stop," under his breath.

Lacey, slightly taken by surprise, stuttered out an apology, "Oh, I'm sorry I don't shake hands. It's a weird germ thing."

Beth scrunched her nose so that the stud pierced in the corner of her nostril flickered under the fluorescent lighting. She flashed Lacey a "you're a weirdo" glare from behind her red framed glasses and barely smiled at Lacey. That pissed me off. Damn, I hated that bitch.

Gabe and Beth settled in the seats adjacent to us. Gabe was quick to try and make Lacey feel comfortable, asking her about her classes and what not. And it wasn't long before Beth found a bone to pick with him. Somehow we had gotten to the topic of theme parks when she called Gabe out for not getting her the teddy bear she wanted at some booth.

And so the bickering began. For the next fifteen minutes Lacey and I sat by while Beth and Gabe fought about anything and everything. Every so often Lacey and I would mouth different reactions to each other regarding Gabe and Beth's pointless arguments or I'd make a face at Lacey and she'd pick her coffee mug up to block her laughing smile.

Honestly I was glad Gabe and Beth weren't getting along. It gave me a chance to bond with Lacey in a different way than I was used to. We weren't talking about English or mental diseases. We were just goofing around. It was fun. A blast, actually.

At some point in their verbal quarrel Beth catapulted out of her seat because she was so mad and stormed out of the lounge. Gabe spun around in his seat and yelled, "Good riddance!"

"Finally," I mouthed at Lacey.

She smirked and raised her eyebrows in agreement.

For the next thirty minutes Gabe, Lacey, and I just had casual conversations about things like annoying teachers and the horrible parking situation at this school. As soon as Beth left, Lacey started to break out of her shell. She made some jokes, referenced some movies, she proved herself to be a natural at communication. And she was naturally personable. To think, this was her challenged after secluding herself from socializing for so long. I couldn't imagine how well at interacting she would have been if she hadn't withdrawn herself like a hermit during her high school years. Honestly if I hadn't read her poem about OCD I probably wouldn't have thought there was anything seriously flawed about her.

After a good forty-five minutes of talking a kid named Zeke, who I was friends with through Gabe, walked into the lounge. Zeke Campbell was hilarious, has seen just about every movie that exists, was somewhat artsy-fartsy, and was super friendly, probably one of the kindest kids I knew, but he was a major druggie. Marijuana. Ecstasy. Bath salts. Cocaine. Opioids. Cigarettes. LSD. And of course, alcohol. You name it, he does it. He was actually starting to look like a stereotypical druggie too. He was gaunt. Often wore his tan hair in a low ponytail or under a worn out beanie. And it didn't help that his once tame stubble was now a scraggly beard. Regardless, Zeke was a really nice guy.

He came up to us asking if anybody had a quarter, but not before introducing himself to Lacey. The first thing out of his mouth after, "Hey I'm Zeke" was "Holy shit I'm wicked baked right now, sorry if I seem a little off."

Lacey let out a light laugh, "Oh don't worry I wouldn't have known if you didn't say anything."

"Do you do any drugs?" Zeke forwardly asked her.

"Yeah, it's called caffeine," she raised her cup of coffee.

I was glad she bounced back with a joke. I was embarrassed, on the other hand, because Lacey literally said she didn't want to wind up talking about sex or drugs.

Desperately I wanted to change the subject. But to what?

Zeke was actually part of a farming program in New Zealand. He was really into agriculture and botany, which made sense since his goal in life was to move to Colorado, grow a shit ton of marijuana, then make a living selling it. Typical stoner aspirations.

"Zeke spent his first year out of high school in New Zealand."

"Oh," Lacey perked up then turned to him, "really?"

"Oh yeah," Zeke sat himself down in the seat across the table, "I worked on a farm. It was great."

"That's so cool!" Lacey said, "But I have to ask, did you visit the hobbit hole while you were there?"

Zeke broke into laughter, "Duh! I gotta say though, it's horribly disappointing."

"Don't stay that!" she reacted with playful ease.

"I swear, it's like, a tiny hole. And I actually paid to see it on some rip-off tour."

"Stop," she laughed.

Alright.

Lacey and Zeke were getting along.

Not sure if I regretted that New Zealand comment.

I got up to recycle my water bottle when Carson came into the lounge. He stopped me halfway to the recycle bin. With a pat on my back he nodded to Lacey in the corner, "Hey it's your tutor."

"Yeah," I sighed an insincere laugh and lowered my head, kind of embarrassed talking about her when she was in the same room. "We were just hanging out before her dad came to pick her up."

I don't think Carson listened to anything I just said because his response was on a different train of thought. "You know... she's kind of a fox."

"Yup," I nodded and clamped my teeth down on my tongue then glared at the dirt caught between the tiles on the floor. I really didn't want to engage in this conversation. Something felt weird, almost derogatory, about calling Lacey a fox. Don't get me wrong, I thought she was an attractive young woman. There was no doubt about that. But the idea of talking to Carson about her, in that way, I don't know, it didn't sit well with me. I don't know why because I had never taken the phrase "fox" as an insult before. It was supposed to be a compliment. But I didn't want it associated with Lacey. Something about having gotten to know who she was made summarizing her with a superficial phrase seem belittling. She was just so much more than that word.

"Is she single?" Carson pushed.

The crunch of my hand involuntarily tightening around the plastic water bottle ripped through the air. In an instant an inexplicable envy coursed through my veins. "I don't think she's interested in dating," I gritted the assumption through my tense teeth, not wanting to give my horny friend the okay to hit on Lacey.

"That sucks. She's a little short but still a fox, right?"

"Mhm," I went along with the blood boiling through my jealous veins, "she's got a really nice smile."

"Smile?" Carson punched me in the shoulder. "Are you shitting me Jef? You should be drooling about her tits or ass, not her smile. What are you, gay?"

"No Carson, I'm not gay," I sighed.

Chapter 16

That afternoon Lacey and I were supposed to get some tutoring done, but we decided to bail on schoolwork. Neither of us wanted to be cooped up in the library because it was unusually warm out. I suggested we go on a walk on the trail in the woods bordering the college campus.

Lacey agreed, not without a disclaimer, "Normally I'd say no because I'm wicked lazy but I think that sounds like a good idea. Just not for too long, though. I don't wanna get so tired that I end up half-asleep in the shower."

"Can't you just take a nap when you get home and then shower?" I stupidly asked.

Lacey burst out in laughter. "No! Jef, I won't be able to relax until I shower."

"Oh."

I tried to find a positive spin. "Well that'll only take you, what, five to ten minutes?"

Apparently that was also a hilarious question, because Lacey laughed even harder. "What, a shower? You're kidding right? Showering takes me a good half hour, and that's on a good day. It's horrible. Just outright horrible. The whole process exhausts me. Just thinking about it exhausts me. And believe me, I think about it almost all the time. It makes going out that much less enjoyable because the whole time I'm just thinking about how I have to go home and perform a tedious shower routine before I can lie down and breathe again. I have to sterilize myself. I have to take off my filthy clothes, lather every square inch of my skin in soap, rinse that germ-binding soap off, lather my hair with shampoo and conditioner, then get out of the shower, change into clean clothes, and throw my filthy clothes in the washer machine. Oh, and then I have to wash my hands again, of course, after touching the germy clothes. And that entire shower routine looms over me whenever I'm out. As if I need another thing to make being in public harder. The last thing I need is another reason to stay out of touch with the world around me."

At the risk of sounding like an idiot for a third time I asked the obvious question itching at my mind. "Have you ever actually tried to resist the urge to shower?"

"Of course I've tried!" Lacey raised her voice, sounding offended in contrast to her humored smile. "The anxiety that comes from resisting a compulsion is unbearable, Jef. You don't get it. With OCD you are a slave to whatever your obsession orders you to do. Resisting brings on a whole new level of anxiety, an anxiety I have no language in my vocabulary to properly explain to you. And not to mention the anger resisting a compulsion brings on. Oh my God, I get so grumpy when I feel germy or after I hear a word that disturbs me. I just lose my cool and turn into this ferocious bitch. Trust me, it's best for everyone if I obey my OCD. There's no ifs, ands, or buts about it."

I shook my head tiredly. I was fatigued just listening to her talk.

"We'll take a quick walk so that you don't tire out," I promised, not sure if I was accommodating Lacey Parker or her obsessive compulsive disorder.

It was a shame Lacey had to take her fatigue into consideration. I blamed the mental illness. After seeing her OCD quirks in her home environment it really put into perspective, for me, just how exhausting this mental disorder was.

"Okay."

We quickly stopped at Lacey's car before the walk, where she put hand sanitizer on. She said she wanted to enjoy the nice weather, and she wouldn't be able to do that until she sanitized her hands from "unforgivably germy" to "germy".

Since Lacey felt like her hands were clean enough she was free to touch or itch or play with her hair.

Right before embarking into the thickly settled patch of tall trees an isolated leaf floated down, brushing up against the back of Lacey's hand before making its home among the powdery dirt path. She flinched out of surprise.

"Germ feeling?" I assumed.

"Actually... no," she was grinning in a way that made me feel like she was about to tell me a hilarious joke. "This is gonna sound really bizarre, but-"

"What?" I urged impatiently.

I really needed to learn how to be more subtle with my curiosity.

"I don't get the germ feeling when anything from nature touches me, like leaves, grass, pine needles. I feel nothing. No angry anxiety is triggered," she elaborated and pointed at the crinkly leaf that had just brushed against her, "now if I saw a *person* touch that leaf before it touched me then I'd get that germ feeling. Or if that leaf was in a place that most likely got touched by a human being then I'd feel a horribly nerve wrecking stain on my hand. But it came from the top of that tree, and I know a human didn't touch that single leaf before it fell."

Suddenly it made sense why Lacey had no problem sitting in the grass at school, like in the courtyard when the Frisbee landed beside her the day I found that sacred "Obsessive Compulsive Disorder" poem that initiated our friendship.

It was fascinating, really. For Lacey, nature was safe. Nature was pure. Literally, dirt itself was safer than a door knob.

"You have a mind boggling mental illness," was the only response I could conjure up.

She raised her eyebrows at a pebble she had been lightly kicking between her feet and replied with exasperation, "I know."

Lacey and I moved on and trekked through the forest. The crackle of decaying leaves played as the soundtrack of our footprints. It was actually really nice to see her do something as simple as tuck her hair behind her ear when the wind picked up. There were little subtleties like that that transformed my perception of Lacey from a slave to her OCD into a fellow human being.

Every so often Lacey would rave about how nice the weather was. She proceeded to apologize for, as she called it, the "lame weather small talk" but explained to me that she wasn't used

to being out in the fresh air because she didn't get out of the house much. When I asked why she said it was probably because she was usually too tired or too depressed to get out.
Lacey and I took a break at a large oak tree. There I raised my arms so that I was gripping a high branch to stretch out my back. My shoulder blades cracked loudly.

Lacey crossed her arms and leaned on the heel of her floral boot and commended the landscape, "This was a good suggestion," she seemed awestricken by the encompassing forest, "The autumn is so beautiful. It's too bad winter follows. Blech."

"Yeah," I responded half listening. To be honest I was busy thinking about earlier today when I set Lacey and Zeke up to hit it off with that New Zealand comment and then Carson showing an interest in Lacey.

Lacey picked up on my distant mental state. "Okay what's up with you?"

My arms fell from the above branch. I was a little frazzled by her calling me out. "Huh? What? Me? What, uh, what do you mean?"

"It's probably been a full fifteen minutes, just me and you, and you haven't asked a single question about... well, anything!"

"Oh," I laughed. "I was just, uh, I don't know, I was just thinking about this morning when you met my friends."

Suddenly her composed expression turned worried. "Shit, what did I do wrong?"

"No, nothing! You were great!" I quickly tried to ease her insecurity, but in my rush I accidentally tacked on a thought that should have stayed inside, "You were a little too great."

Lacey's forehead wrinkled. "What are you talking about?" she laughed as the breeze kicked in, instigating her to slide a strand of hair behind her ear, where it would stay still.

"Oh, er, nothing, nothing."

"Jef," my name dragged out of her and I got kind of excited.

I couldn't fight a response to her saying my name. "It's just, Carson was bugging me earlier in the lounge and I didn't know how to answer him."

"What? About me?"

"Er, yeah," I mumbled. I hated this. "He was asking if you were single."

All of a sudden Lacey burst out laughing, "Did he really?" She nearly snorted then sighed, "What a poor misguided soul."

I felt the corner of my mouth curl at the sound of her laugh. But that hint of happiness contradicted my dissatisfaction with the actual content of her response. Her comment, though charmingly modest, raised a question within me. Why did Lacey find it so ridiculous that a guy would be attracted to her? I tried to find a way to get my question across without sounding like I was being invasive. "You... uh, you find that funny?"

Lacey's fragile shoulders wilted forward and her smile faded, "I don't know, I guess. I mean, if he had half a clue what I was really like he'd run for the hills."

"Because of the OCD?"

"Of course."

Having become emotionally invested, that comment stirred up a kind of sadness in me that I had only ever felt towards my handicapped brother. As a way of coping with the sadness I reverted to fidgeting with my Red Sox cap and tried to convince Lacey otherwise, "You shouldn't think that."

"Oh come on Jef. Let's be realistic," she said and reached out to a branch, pinched a bright orange leaf, and proceeded to gently rub it between her finger and thumb. Damn, was it weird to see Lacey voluntarily reaching out to touch something.

"I am being realistic," I ripped my hands away from my cap.

"Nobody's gonna tolerate me and my issues," Lacey said matter-of-factly, "I've already accepted that."

"I don't think that's true," I argued, thinking about how Mom and I tolerated Peter. In the back of my mind, though, lurked the thought of my unaccommodating father.

"You think any guy would want a girl who can't even hold his hands unless he washes them first? Or-"

"Okay, okay!" I cut Lacey off before she could get explicit. Nervous and bashful, I tried aloud to recover, "Well, oh- okay, wow." She had a point though. What guy would be okay with such limited touching... everywhere? "Well if we're talking Carson, then no, but he's a self-proclaimed player."

Lacey shrugged, then took the liberty to continue down the woodsy trail ahead.

I watched her petite figure walk alone through the woodland. What was it like to be so physically, mentally, and emotionally alone?

"Hey, wait up," I jogged to her side.

"Watch out," Lacey signaled towards a dip in the ground that had collected mud, right where I was about to step.

I dodged the mud.

I didn't want the rest of this walk to go like that. Sauntering in silence, only to talk to the other person about mud puddles. I wanted to go back to our usual banter.

Feeling like I got her upset I changed the subject to the most random, most goofy topic I could think of. My clumsiness.

I told Lacey a funny story about how I did the morning announcements on the intercom in middle school with my friend and how I accidentally kept it on while talk to him about the girl I had a crush on. Lacey seemed to find that hilarious. In turn Lacey told me an embarrassing moment of hers. We kept going back and forth; eventually so enthralled in our conversation we stopped walking and collapsed onto a dry log beside the croaking pond.

Our embarrassing stories gradually transformed into middle school stories.

"I remember in middle school, I don't know, 8th grade? I told a couple of kids in my Latin class that I was afraid of germs so they purposely started coughing on me. And it was flu season! Apparently it was funny to watch me freak out and drown myself with hand sanitizer."

I understood all too well, "Middle school kids are obnoxious. Anybody 'different' is a target. When I was in 6th grade Peter was in 8th grade, and all of the 'cool kids' on the bus would whisper Peter's name just to scare him. They got a kick over watching him get paranoid and eventually flip out. It was cruel."

I started scratching at my knobby wrists, feeling somewhat embarrassed and vulnerable having shared that with somebody. "I've never really talked about that before."

"Ugh," Lacey scowled in disgust towards my story, "that's just horrible, Jef. Middle schoolers disgust me."

"I know. Middle schoolers are awful. What kind of person gets a teaching degree for that age group? Sheesh. That whole timeframe is awful."

"Oh you have no freaking idea," I could hear the intense distress behind Lacey's voice as she stared off at the horizon and reminisced internally. "If you knew me back then, damn you would have been scared of me. You wanna talk about embarrassing…"

I was extremely interested at this point. "Whoa, what?" I knew not to laugh. The look in her eyes were very serious. "What do you mean?"

"Middle school was the transition into the germ fear, when I was starting to go through very obsessive phases."

"That's not so embarrassing."

"No it was. I was starting to go through very obsessive phases about people. You know, crushes. Sometimes it was a celebrity. Sometimes it was a classmate. Naturally, for a while, I figured I was just a normal teenager having crushes on people. But as 6th grade went on I found that I was spending all of my free time daydreaming about my crush, imagining him watching me do every day activities or imagining what he would say or do if he were with me at that moment. And since I loved to write, I would start to keep diary after diary, logging the tiniest interaction with my crush. I never sought out to, but eventually I had diaries dedicated to certain people. It was sick, I know that now. But I didn't then. I didn't know what was happening to me, to be honest. I didn't understand that something was wrong until I realized I was getting really upset, like severely depressed, when I thought about how I didn't have my crush as a partner. I had this one crush who was in a few of my classes, and my entire mood for the day depended on whether or not I had those classes. When I knew I'd have a class with him I'd be really happy, and when I knew I didn't I'd literally be a zombie. Somebody who felt like there was no point in existence for that whole day.

"Word got out about my obsessive attitude towards my crushes. And you know middle school kids. They're cruel. Eventually people found out who I liked because being obsessed I couldn't keep my mouth shut about my feelings and we all know secrets didn't exist among girl friends… or teenagers… or among people in general. But anyways, word would get out who I had a crush on, and I'd get teased about it. I remember when the boy that I had my biggest crush on found out I liked him all of his friends made fun of me and so did he. He would go up and talk to me as a joke. And his friends would laugh on the sides. I was so traumatized. Because I liked him more than I had ever liked anybody else. It was just so scarring. So, so scarring. I'm pretty sure it became this big joke when people thought I had a new crush. Like who was the victim this time?

"Those middle school crushes gone wrong became a serious problem but I never addressed it. I would keep those obsessive crushes a secret because I was so insanely embarrassed that I was obsessing over real people. And keeping that secret only made me more out of touch with reality. It was horrible. And humiliating. And holy crap, I can't believe I'm actually telling you this."

With her elbows perched on her lap she covered her face with both of her hands and refused to look up at me.

Weirdly enough, I didn't feel any bit of judgment towards Lacey. If anything, I liked her more, because I couldn't believe how honest she was being. There was no bullshit with this girl. I had known her for about two months and I already knew that she made a point to live by honesty, sincerity, and dignity. How often do you find that in a person? It was rare, that was for sure.

I just sat on the wooden log, reveling at the vulnerable young woman next to me. Lacey Parker confided in me. And I felt honored.

"You must think I'm some psychotic creep," she wouldn't lift her head up.

"No, I actually don't," I declared.

Slowly and carefully her delicate fingers parted, revealing large brown eyes painted with the darkest of eyelashes. Her fragile hands lowered to reveal the rest of her timid expression. "You don't?" her voice sounded as breakable as fine china.

I was adamant to render a gentle response, soft like a pillow for her to fall back on so that I wouldn't break her. "I really don't care, Lacey. Those actions were part of your sickness. I can't judge you based on your sickness. Even if I wanted to."

I couldn't sleep that night.

The glowing star stickers on the ceiling kept me company as I laid wide awake, hands folded behind my pounding head, and let the course of the day's mixed emotions and thoughts run through me.

I was glad Gabe got to know Lacey in the student lounge.

I was pissed off at Beth for just being Beth.

I was embarrassed by Zeke's mention of drugs around the straight-edged Lacey.

I was frustrated with Carson for his sudden, and glaringly shallow, interest in Lacey.

I was sad about Lacey's disbelief any guy would ever pursue a relationship with her.

But more than anything, I was angry. I was angry about Lacey's middle school experience. The onset of Lacey's obsessive compulsive disorder really got to me in a way that left me clamping my jaw so tight I incited a headache.

I kept picturing innocent Lacey feeling so much pain and anxiety but not knowing why. Why her mind fixated on crushes. Why she got made fun of for having intense feelings that she naturally assumed everybody else had.

Middle school was hard enough for normal teenagers, being that it was the development stage where hormones liked to confuse the crap out of puberty-stricken students. Now throw a mental disorder into the mix and you get an unbelievably complicated situation. I couldn't fully imagine how confusing that must have been for Lacey. To expect her to know the difference between a crush and an obsession during that hormonal time frame would be near impossible.

But kids didn't learn about the complexities of mental disorders tangling with normal brain development. And that was why she got bullied.

That was why she got teased.

And that made me angry.

That kept me and my headache awake until the sun came up.

Chapter 17

The Tuesday I invited Lacey to my house for tutoring had finally come.

I sprinted to the doorbell so fast I nearly tripped on a random dog bone in the middle of the hallway. Nothing new there, though.

In my eagerness I ripped open the front door.

There stood Lacey, hugging her notebook, wearing her leopard print backpack over her left shoulder.

"Hey," I opened the door wider to let Lacey in.

"Should I take off my shoes?" she asked in the entryway.

"Oh no, just leave 'em." I casually waved away, only to quickly snap my fingers and retract my statement when the thought that she might have had an OCD compulsion to take shoes off in the house, like at her house. "Unless you wanna take them off."

"I'm fine," she rejected with a friendly tone.

Suddenly my dog charged at the front door towards Lacey.

"No, York!" I awkwardly lunged forward right before he could get his slobbery tongue on Lacey.

Lacey tightened up, crossing her arms to shrink back.

"Sorry about that," I pulled York away from Lacey.

The twerpy runt of a boxer tried to gnaw at my hand as I yanked him by the collar. He squirmed, trying desperately to get to Lacey.

Though Lacey's body was aloof, the voice that came out of it was friendly. "Hi there," she greeted York as her fingers uncurled from their grip around her arm, like a little wave 'hello'. She couldn't even wave like a normal person because she was so frightened by the dog's germs. "What's his name?"

"York," I responded while the hyper little dog continued using my hand as a chew toy.

"Aw cute," Lacey smiled, "But he's not a Yorkshire terrier, is he?"

"No," I was quick to answer in an irritated tone, "Peter named him after the beach in Maine. I told him it came across completely illogical-"

Lacey laughed, "That really drives you crazy, doesn't it?"

"You know it," I agreed.

With a humored grin she rolled her long lashed eyes.

Dedicated to make York leave Lacey alone I grabbed a treat off of the kitchen counter and tossed it down the hall, "Go boy!" When I released my grip around York's collar he went shooting down the hall.

Quickly, before he came running back, I guided Lacey to the family room. She set her backpack down and laid her folders and pen on the coffee table. Not parallel.

I was hoping she'd take out her sacred notebook as well. I had been aching to see what she so attentively wrote inside that thing. She was so immersed in her own little world when she resorted to writing in it. And I was still waiting to read her work.

I handed Lacey my final copy of the short story my professor assigned.

While she read it, I did my physics homework.

"I'm impressed," Lacey announced when she was done reading.

"Really?" Using Lacey's completion as an excuse to take a break from my physics homework, I inserted my pen behind my ear. Overly excited by her approval, I rushed to emphasize just how much I had been listening to her during tutoring. "See, I even stayed in the same tense throughout."

She giggled, probably at my overexcitement, "Yes, I see that. But you need to touch up the dialogue."

"Pfft," I scoffed and fell back on the couch. "That's not gonna happen. I can barely talk in real life. No thank you."

"But it doesn't feel real."

"That's because it's not. It's made up," I reinforced my refusal.

Lacey flashed me a hard stare, "Sometimes the make-believe can feel more real than reality."

I felt like she was hinting at something, but I didn't know what. So, uncomfortable with my lack of knowledge, I decided to be stubborn. "I'm not changing the dialogue."

"Well you should. It doesn't feel natural."

"How can you make something fake feel natural?" I sounded like I was throwing a fit. But seriously, what was the point of English class anyways?

Lacey wouldn't let up. Instead of arguing with me she shared a little bit about herself, "I used to find dialogue super difficult to write. It helped when I stopped trying so hard to think up the perfect interaction between characters and I just let myself daydream freely. I'd daydream about a conversation, usually using me and an imaginary person as the speakers. You should give that a try. It might feel forced at first, but eventually a back and forth will unravel and the characters take on a life of their own. You won't feel like you're directing the conversation, you'll feel like you're just a third party watching the conversation happen. Your job is to write it all down from the sidelines, like you're no more than a voice telling the story unfolding in front of you. That's what being a narrator is about, isn't it?"

"Can I see your writing?" I pressed.

Lacey was hesitant, "Oh I don't know…"

"What are you worried about?"

"I don't know. I just don't usually show people my writing. A lot of it's really personal."

"What fun is writing if you can't share it with other people?"

"Well I don't just do it for fun. The place that my mind goes to when I write is my sanctuary."

I tinkered with the pen behind my ear. "That's interesting."

"What? What's interesting?"

I slouched forward. "Just that your sanctuary is the same place as your prison."

Lacey nodded confidently. "It's true. That's no surprise to me. Nightmares and dreams come from the same place, don't they?"

She caught me there. Having secured the upper hand in the conversation, Lacey honed her newfound confidence and proceeded to unzip her backpack. Was she actually going to show me her writing?

Lacey reached into the bag and, low and behold, pulled out her notebook.

My heart skipped a beat. It was like I was getting a sneak peak at a rare treasure.

"I have to warn you, I write like a crazy person."

I raised an eyebrow, "What's that supposed to mean?"

"You'll see," she opened the notebook to a random page.

There were arrows and notes here and there, boxes, scribbles, illegible chicken scratch mixed with sloppy cursive. It was all so confusing. Fragmented thoughts were splattered all over the sheet, written in all sorts of directions.

It was weird to me because I had exemplary note-taking skills. The eclectic research I stuffed into binder after binder, whether it regarded the structure of a neuron or the philosophy of Nicomachean ethics, were always neat and organized. Clear. Methodical. Highlighter marks over rudimental topics. Systematically color coded or underlined. A highly legible and comprehensive outline that would make for the best cognitive experience.

I glanced back to the scribbles.

"You weren't lying," I remarked in shock.

"Yeah… I guess I'm just scatter brained. I don't have any clue how people can get their thoughts out neatly. That's a mystery to me."

The more I examined the sheet, the more bewildered I got. It was almost indecipherable. I couldn't follow it. I felt like I was trying to solve some sort of verbal maze. I was beside myself. I wouldn't say I was amazed, but I wasn't appalled either. I just had to ask Lacey, "You can look back at this and understand what you wrote?"

"Of course," she answered casually, like my inquiry was unnecessary.

I continued to search the sheet for the dialogue she said she wrote. When I was finally able to find quotation marks I went ahead and read what Lacey had written.

Something wasn't quite right. I spent probably thirty seconds trying to figure out why the conversation possessed the quality of making sense but also not making sense. Then it hit me. The dialogue wasn't in sequential order.

"You have this conversation written backwards."

Lacey leaned over my shoulder, "Oh, yeah. I know," she claimed, "My thoughts were racing in reverse I guess. On overdrive. That happens sometimes. I usually just try to flush it all out and neaten it up later."

For the remainder of the afternoon Lacey did some creative writing while I tried to daydream a conversation for my short story revision. It was hard for me to focus, though, when York propped himself in the corner of the family room with us and started moaning as he stared at Lacey with the whites of his eyes showing. It was pretty creepy.

"York, stop that!"

Lacey came to his defense, "It's okay. He knows."

I raised an eyebrow at her. "He knows what?"

"He can sense my aversion to touch him. My dog gives me the same look. She knows too. Doesn't expect me to pet her. If she's sitting near my spot on the couch when I walk in she'll get up and move out of the way. She only does it with me. Dogs are smarter than you think. They can sense when there's something off about a person."

"Are you serious?" I found that hard to believe, but I knew the ever so honest Lacey was telling the truth.

She assured me, "Yeah. I swear."

I looked back at York.

That boxer's eyes were still piercing through Lacey. In my confusion I itched the hair tucked under my hat's visor. I had to get up. There was too much weirdness in this room for me. "I'm gonna get a drink, you thirsty?"

"Oh no, I'm good. Thanks though."

After grabbing myself a drink from the kitchen I made my way back to the family room, only to be surprised by the gentle whisper of Lacey talking to my dog. I stopped in the doorway and leaned on the wooden frame. Just listening. Watching from behind so that Lacey had no idea I was standing there.

"I'm sorry York. It's nothing personal. You know that, right?" she pointed towards her temple, "The brain up here won't let me touch you. I still like you though. I hope you know that."

Chapter 18

"Done!" I threw my pen to the coffee table, where it bounced off and landed on the carpet.

Lacey looked up from the rough draft of my essay she just started editing. "You finished your physics homework that fast? Holy shit Jef. I'm only on the first page of your essay!"

"Yeah, well, I'm more of a science guy," I got up and picked the pen off the ground, afraid York would get a hold of it.

"Jef!" Peter hollered from upstairs.

Lacey twisted her torso so that she was looking behind the sofa.

I called back to my brother. "I'm in the family room with a friend, Pete!"

The sound of Peter's footsteps banged the stairs while he shouted out, "Who?"

As soon as he came running into the family room he stopped short and stared at Lacey. "Oh, it's a girl. That's different."

Mortified, I quickly introduced Lacey to Peter to change the subject.

"Peter, this is my friend Lacey."

Lacey stood up from the couch and waved, "Hi. It's nice to meet you." No handshake.

"Yes, yes," Peter nodded to himself, "Nice to meet you."

"Okay, uh, alright," I clapped, just about ready to shoo him away.

"Why are you hanging out with Jef?" Peter asked Lacey in his usual blunt manner.

Lacey pointed to the pile of school supplies on the coffee table, "I'm his English tutor."

That made Peter hoot with joy, "Finally!"

"Ha, ha, very funny," I sounded defensive as I awkwardly scrambled over to the doorway with the intention of pushing Peter out of the room.

"Jef is horrible at spelling," Peter went on, "I'm really good at spelling though."

"So I've heard. Jef told me you're a really good speller," she reacted with no more enthusiasm than usual.

I liked that she was acting like her normal self.

I also liked how Lacey's pitch didn't raise to that phony high pitch, like it did when she was interacting with Jamison. That made me kind of happy. Usually girls would talk in a phony "I pity you" pitch to the retarded guy instead of a full functioning fellow college student hitting on her. Lacey's pitch was the same when she talked to Peter as it was when she talked to me, and because of that consistency I knew she was being genuine with him. Her sincerity was refreshing in a world where everybody flashed fake smiles at my retarded brother.

Feeling more content about this introduction, I decided to return to Lacey's side where I plopped myself back in my spot on the couch.

"Lacey, Jef, I'm going to go in the den. I don't want to invade your privacy," Peter announced.

"Wow you're a lot more polite than Jef," Lacey remarked, "The first few times I met Jef he was pressing me with invasive question after invasive question. He's a bit nosy, isn't he?"

"Oh yeah," Peter laughed his belly laugh.

I flashed Lacey a facetious glare.

"What? You're nosy," she laughed while sinking deeper into the couch. There she picked back up my essay that she had been correcting. "I say that with love," Lacey clarified while continuing to write notes on the margins.

I was about to make a comment when Peter, to my dismay, intervened, "Jef, why are you so happy?"

That was enough to make me force the corners of my mouth downward. "What? I'm not- what are you talking about?"

"But you're smiling. Is it because Lacey said she loves you?"

As Lacey's head shot up my stomach plummeted down. "Oh, I-" she tried to start clarifying, but I jumped in like a neurotic spaz.

"Okay, I think it's time for your shower, Peter," I scampered over to the doorway and took the initiative to push Peter back into the hall, "Come on, let's go, you're running late."

"But I-"

I was so stirred up with humiliation I was breaking a sweat. "No just- just go, it's getting late." I pushed him across the room and up the first few steps of the staircase. When he proceeded on his own I finally allowed myself to breathe again.

I took a deep breath, bracing myself for the awkward explaining that was looming, and then turned around.

As I made my way back to Lacey my mouth was already off and rambling, "Don't mind Peter. Sometimes he just, sometimes he says things without- without thinking. He doesn't know what he's, uh, he doesn't know what he's talking about. He's a- uh, he's a retard." As soon as the degrading label slipped my lips I tried to recant, "Wow, okay, um, that was, wow, that was rude. I didn't mean- did I just say retard? That's not like me. That's not like me at all. I'm usually so, so... I'm usually more considerate than that."

Lacey interrupted me, "Jef, it's okay. It's fine."

All too eager to somehow change the subject and nullify the awkwardness I just caused I scanned the family room for something new to do.

My stare fixed itself on the game controllers scattered on a small oak shelf.

"Hey, uh, do you wanna play a videogame or something?"

"Yes!" Lacey was way more compliant than I expected.

"You choose the game," I opened up a drawer full of videogame cases.

"*Nightfire!*" she squealed and pointed at it.

So, for the remainder of the afternoon, Lacey and I shot the crap out of each other in multiplayer.

I made a point to give Lacey the only wireless controller because it was hardly used since Peter and I liked the feel of the wired controllers anyway. Lacey stayed in her seat on the couch while I was confined to the bean bag on the floor.

When Lacey won the first round I was shocked. "How did you-"

"I hate going out in public. When you hate going out in public you wind up playing a lot of video games."

That was incredibly true. "I'm not gonna argue that," I put the controller next to the bean bag and started reminiscing, "Peter used to destroy me in just about every game we played. *Super Smash, Mario Kart*, that awful racing game with Kirby that was so freaking hard to control."

"*Kirby Airride*!" she exclaimed while beaming with nostalgia.

I snapped, "Yes! That!"

Lacey swiped a wavy lock of hair and tucked it behind her ear by pulling her sleeve over her hand. "Please tell me you played in City Trial mode."

"Is that actually a question?" I joked in agreement, leaning back in the bean bag with my hands folded behind my head, pushing down my cap's brim. My grin felt painfully wide. I was having too much fun talking with Lacey.

Lacey and I must have spent another hour playing round after round of *Nightfire*. I wasn't compelled to stop playing, and she didn't seem compelled to go home.

"Okay, last round," Lacey finally sealed the deal.

"That's probably a good idea," I said, thinking how my mom would be home soon and I didn't feel like going through an introduction that would later result in Mom asking me tons of questions about the first girl I've invited over since my high school girlfriend.

I got a clean shot of Lacey's player right off the bat.

"Oh, you bitch!" she spit out.

"Whoa," I reacted with laughter, "Somebody's already a little too into it."

"I know, I know. I'm a ruthless potty mouth when I play video games. Drives my sister insane."

"Cuss away," I invited.

"Will do. Though, I only really swear when I'm losing."

"Then I guess I'll be hearing an earful," I teased.

Having been the brunt of my insult she stuffed her tongue under her lower lip and shook her head.

Lacey, a computer player named Phoenix Soldier, and I wound up tied. The next shot won.

I checked her screen, only to see that she had a sniper locked on Phoenix Soldier.

I was fully convinced she won the round. She had Phoenix Soldier right in her hand but, uncharacteristically slow, she wouldn't shoot. She took so long that Phoenix Solder sniped her first.

"What was that?" my pitch shot up as did my body off the bean bag. I threw my arm out, pointing my open palm at the screen, "Why'd you just stand there and not shoot?"

Lacey grumbled, "Er, I didn't wanna die with thirteen deaths so I let him kill me to end the round with fourteen deaths."

"Oh," I tried to revoke the judgment in my voice.

She even sacrificed her virtual life for this disease.

It made me kind of mad.

She was such a slave. And she was so deep in, I don't think she realized how bad it was.

Despite the bitter end to our videogame, I was overwhelmingly pleased with how Lacey's visit went.

Lacey gathered her things, threw her leopard print backpack on, and followed me to the front door.

"Peter, Lacey's leaving!" I called upstairs. I knew he'd give me an earful if I let her leave without giving him a chance to say goodbye.

Peter stormed down the staircase like an avalanche.

"Bye Lacey!"

She waved at him, "Bye Peter, it was nice meeting you."

"You too!"

Lacey turned back to me, "Hey so I know we don't have tutoring tomorrow but do you think, I don't know, would you wanna hang out after class? It was kind of nice not rushing home right after school and it's supposed to be really nice out. We could just do homework or something at the quarry in my town. I could drive?"

Holy crap, had we really gotten close enough that Lacey was initiating the plans?

"You bet," I confirmed, feeling the sweat on the back of my neck.

"Alright," she released the tension in her posture, "bye," she bid farewell with an amicable and kind grin. My brain told me to give her a hug goodbye, but I voluntarily stopped myself.

"Bye," I exhaled, disappointed by the lack of a physical embrace.

As soon as I shut the front door Peter spoke up.

"I like her."

I bit my lower lip, conflicted by my advancing feelings towards the girl with the notebook. "I like her too."

Chapter 19

"Pay up, motherfucker," Gabe shouted as he tossed me a bag from the sub shop down the street from the college campus.

"You said no mayo, right?" I quizzed while unwrapping the turkey, cheese, bacon, lettuce, and tomato sub sandwich Gabe said he'd get me in when he picked up his steak and cheese sub in between his linear algebra and ethics class.

"Duh," he dropped in the cafeteria seat next to me. "How could I forget after the fit you made last time?"

"It wasn't a fit," I argued with a mouthful of food.

"Whatever man."

As I chowed down on the sandwich I accidentally eaves dropped on a couple of girls a few seats over at the oblong rectangle-shaped table.
Some bleach blond girl blabbed, "Have you seen Kelsey's notes? They're perfect! She's, like, so OCD with her notes!"

Stay out of it, Jef.

"I know," groaned the other girl, "With notes like that it's no wonder why she aced the last exam. If I were OCD I'd be acing exams too."

Nope, I couldn't stay quiet. Not in my enlightenment. I dropped the sandwich away from my aching-to-interrupt mouth.

"You know, taking neat notes doesn't really qualify as severe obsessive compulsive disorder. Trust me, I know somebody who actually has OCD and she is by far the most unorganized note taker I've ever met. Your friend Kelsey probably just likes being organized."

The blond girl gave me a snotty look like "why is this dork talking to me?"

Usually I'd cower if a girl gave me that look, but I was so unafraid to confront her when I felt like I was defending Lacey's honor that that confident attitude rubbed off on how I stood my ground on my own behalf.

The longer that blatantly fake blond glared at me, the more I felt an incentive to be as condescending as possible. "I take it you're referring to an extreme level of obsessive compulsive disorder when you say 'she's like so OCD', right? Don't beat yourself up, though. Mistaking organization skills with OCD is a common misconception."

After rolling her eyes the girl got up and moved to another cafeteria table.

"Dude…" Gabe shook his head.

When I met Lacey at her car at the end of the school day she was very obviously in a defeated mood.

"Hey."

"Hey," she tiredly exhaled while getting in the car. I followed her lead and scooted into the passenger seat.

"How were your classes?" I asked her once inside the vehicle.

Lacey sighed, "Well my English professor gave me a failing grade on my poetry assignment, so that was a bit of a damper."

I was shocked. "You're kidding?"

"Nope," Lacey flopped back in her car seat. "I'm done. I'm just done. I don't understand school."

I wanted to get to the bottom of this. "I'm not following. Did you do the actual assignment?"

"Yup. Analytical essay on a poem."

"Then I don't get it. What's wrong with your professor?"

"I don't know. She's a 'you have to agree with my opinion' type of teacher, which is straight up ridiculous because literature is supposed to be subjective. One right answer is for concrete subjects like trigonometry or physics, isn't it?"

"Yeah it is."

"I must be a fucking moron, because it's not just the professor who thinks I'm stupid. It's the whole damn class. Like the other day, during a class discussion, I shared my interpretation of a short story. And she made us do this dumb thing where you'd knock on your desk if you agreed with somebody's input. And nobody knocked after I spoke. Instead everybody laughed from the lack of knocks. The awkward silence. A room full of young adults thought I was an idiot. It was humiliating."

Lacey picked up her backpack and aggressively chucked it in the backseat of her car. "I hate school! I don't know why I'm here. I don't have the brains."

"Okay, don't go overboard," I tried to calm her down while checking to see if her victimized backpack was still in one piece. "You know that you're smart."

"I'm not smart, Jef," Lacey declared.

I laughed.

She raised her eyebrows, "Good to know my stupidity is funny to you."

Suddenly I realized we weren't on the same wavelength. "Wait, you're serious?"

"Yeah. I didn't graduate high school with a 3.9 GPA like you."

"But you must have been good at school. I mean, you're you. You're smart. Definitely smart."

She shook her head, "I barely got by in high school."

"What? How? I mean, why?" This was news to me. I couldn't understand how that was the case. She had such an intelligent mind. What would make her do poorly in school? Unless- suddenly it hit me. "It was the OCD, wasn't it?"

Lacey's big brown eyes flashed to her hands and she immediately started itching at her cuticles. She wouldn't look up at me as she answered, "Starting from 8th grade through all of high school I would come home from school and have to shower immediately, to get all the germs from the day off of me. I'd throw my backpack in some corner and would refuse to touch it until I had to go to school again. I didn't do any of my homework or study at home because I was too scared to touch any of it."

Wow. Her OCD impacted her grades too? What didn't it impact?

"So if you never did any work, how'd you pass any classes?"

"I'd find a way. Sometimes doing the upcoming homework during class while the teacher was talking. Sometimes scraping something together during study hall. Oh and I'd end up skipping class whenever I got the chance so that I could do my work then. I'd sit in the guidance office, looking busy with homework, and nobody would question me because my counselor told the staff about my OCD and they were definitely afraid to address it. Or I'd stay in the cafeteria for all four lunch periods. That was actually kind of funny. When the bell rang to mark the end of the period I'd walk out of the cafeteria with the crowd of kids then I'd walk back in with the new crowd. Oh and I snuck in an empty conference room and sealed the door shut so people assumed a meeting was going on. That was probably the riskiest thing I'd done. Looking back I don't know what I was thinking. If the dean caught me doing that I'd be in deep trouble. Actually, he did catch me once, and he literally dragged me back to class. If he caught me doing it again, though, he would have been livid. I don't even wanna imagine it. The dean used to be a parole officer, so you didn't want to mess with him. That didn't stop me from sneaking into empty conference rooms, though. I had to do whatever it took to get that homework done, to pass my classes, even if it meant skipping class to do the homework that I was too scared to touch at home. I'd rarely get caught because I wasn't some notorious druggy or rude student. I was polite. I was cordial. I completely manipulated the system, but I didn't do it because I wanted to be defiant. I did it because it was what I had to do, to survive high school, ya know?"

"Holy crap," I remarked, impressed by her apparent stealth. "Lacey its things like that that prove you're smart. Those are some pretty clever stunts you pulled."

She shrugged, "I just did whatever to get by without feeling anxious. Even if it meant sneaking around."

Before I could comment further Lacey suddenly remembered what sparked that entire spiel. The failing grade she received on her English paper.

"I'm not smart," she glanced into the rear view mirror, at her backpack in the backseat. "I got an 'F' in the one class I'm supposed to be good at."

I countered, "That means nothing. You got an 'F' because you didn't agree with the professor, not because you're not smart."

Lacey returned to picking hangnail after hangnail. "Still, that doesn't make me feel any less stupid. Fuck," she tore a shred of skin away from her nail and jolted her stare up at the front window of the car, "I hate this feeling. It's what I used to feel in high school. I should just quit school, altogether. I can't go through this feeling again. I just can't. Ugh, I hate this feeling. I swear, I have it memorized."

As much as I wanted to reason with Lacey about how she shouldn't quit school, my know-it-all mind was more stuck on the inaccuracy of her last statement. "Technically the brain can't memorize a feeling," I corrected.

"Yeah, well the heart can," Lacey declared with a certainty that contradicted the defeated slouch of her shoulders.

My mouth opened, ready to debunk that statement as well, when suddenly Lacey glanced up and made eye contact with me. Her emotive brown eyes, almost green under the sunlight, had a grip on my heartstrings, and suddenly I forgot everything that my brain was telling me. I had no desire to argue with her. As much as I wanted to, I wasn't going to tell her that it's not possible for a human heart to memorize emotions. For some bizarre reason, I liked her metaphorical, figurative, and less literal approach to life. It was oddly charming. To my own shock, I liked that about her. And that drove my mind a little crazy because it didn't make sense for somebody like me to be attracted to that. What the fuck was happening to me?

Having enough of this conversation, Lacey turned on the car, backed out of her parking spot, and steered us off of campus ground. I remained quiet and just listened to the music playing through the speakers. I didn't know what to say. I didn't even know what to think. My internal thoughts were speechless as well, almost stunned into a mute state by the overwhelming attraction I was feeling towards this peculiar girl beside me.

We were on the main road when Lacey first changed the radio station, complaining that the singer used a word that made her anxious. She called it an OCD "taboo" word.

"What was the word?"

Lacey puckered her shimmering lips.

"What was the word?" I pressed.

"Nothing, it was nothing, Jef." she tried to force the topic away.

I laid in her like a notorious interviewer. "No come on. What was the word?"

"I can't tell you."

"Why?"

"Because I'm too scared to say it out loud!" she admitted, still trying to find a suitable radio station.

I really wanted to know what the word was so I tried to the best of my ability to retrace the lyrics I last heard.

"'Fire'? Was it 'fire'?"

I thought she nodded but I wasn't sure.

I repeated myself, "Was it 'fire'?"

Lacey retracted her hand from the radio dial and snapped, "Yes, Jef! Yes!"

"What's so bad about the word 'fire'?"

"Oh I don't know, they're fucking terrifying and destroy houses and everything you own, no big deal," Lacey responded with sarcastic nonchalance then hastily went back to turning the radio knob, causing the car to veer in unison with her arm extending to the dial.

"Lace," I raised my voice.

Quickly she flashed her glance ahead and jerked the steering wheel back on track. As if that wasn't enough of a wake-up call, Lacey returned to trying to change the radio station.

There was that distant, unreachable, look in her eyes. Completely invested in flipping the radio station, Lacey mumbled to herself, "No not that song." She seemed thoroughly scared of whatever that song was too, so she quickly changed stations again.

She kept doing that, trying to perform the compulsion that would shut up her OCD, by turning the dial back and forth. She did this so fast and manically that she forgot to drive straight with the linear road.

"Lacey!" I called out, more panicked than before, and reached out to swipe her hand away from the radio.

"What are you doing!" she reacted with fear.

"What are *you* doing?"

"I told you, I don't like that song! They say a taboo-"

"Holy shit, Lacey! You should be more afraid of changing the station than leaving it alone."

"I know, I know, I'm sorry," she finally did the sensible thing and pulled over to the side of the road with a stomp on the breaks. Corresponding with the whiplash, Lacey slammed her hands on the wheel, "It's the English grade! It's getting me all worked up!"

I couldn't see the correlation. "What does a grade have to do with a random word in a random song?"

"I know, I know, it's crazy, but it relates. The more stressed or distraught or just plain upset I am the more intense my OCD symptoms get."

This was news to me. It was logical though. Peter's schizophrenia was the same way. The more stress, the worse his delusions during his meltdowns.

"Okay," I let myself register this new information, "if you're going to have a meltdown then-"

"A meltdown?" Lacey emphasized out of anger. "This is not a meltdown! A meltdown isn't in the realm of possibilities for me!"

"You're nearly crashing a car and contemplating quitting school over an essay grade. How is this not a meltdown?"

"It's not Jef, trust me! You have not seen a meltdown, and you won't. A meltdown would be a break for me! Sometimes I just wanna fall to the bathroom floor and cry with my head in my hands, but then I remember, 'fuck, the floor is dirty and covered with germs, I can't sit on it.' I don't get the luxury of letting go and just melting down! I'm actually so trapped that I'm trapped from having a meltdown! I don't get to go and cry it out!"

She crossed her arms, making her already petite figure smaller. She looked so brittle. Like even if I could touch her, just a tap would break her. Just a glance in her sad eyes and I knew she was already broken inside.

There it was again. That feeling I couldn't describe. That feeling where I almost desperately wanted to help her. Usually I'd chalk up the feeling to wanting to challenge myself. But that wasn't it at all. I wanted to fix Lacey Parker because, for whatever reason, I seriously cared about her wellbeing. Right here, right now, I was actually in pain myself seeing her in pain. I had no idea I was capable of feeling that strongly for anyone aside from my brother or my mom.

Right then I made it my mission to fix Lacey.

Chapter 20

I forced Lacey to cancel our plans for the quarry. She was way too out of it from that bad grade to be driving. I was honestly concerned for our safety in the car. So, she drove me home.

As if I wasn't down enough by my failed plans with Lacey, I walked in the house to the sound of my mom raising her usually dainty voice at Peter in the family room. I lagged behind the doorway and eaves dropped.

"I am not paying for your bets anymore! In fact, if I ever catch you making another bet I'm taking away your tablet!" Mom reprimanded.

Knowing something was seriously wrong, I crossed through the doorway and inserted myself in the unpleasant discussion. "What's going on?"

My mom had her hands firmly on her hips, "Your brother here made a bet with your father about some hockey score."

"What?" The reaction shot out of me at faster than a bullet. I was pissed, but not at Peter, at my dad. "Dad gambled with you?"

"Yes he did," Peter meekly whispered as his stare descended at the floor.

My mom was rubbing her temples, trying to cope with what must have been another migraine. "Peter, please, just go to your room."

Peter, sulking in humiliation and shame, dragged himself up to his bedroom. The instant I heard the sound of his door close I went off to my mom. "Please tell me he's not going to pay that bastard!"

"Jef!"

"Who fucking gambles with their retarded son? What kind of person does that?" I hissed as not to let Peter hear me call him 'retarded'.

Mom was distraughtly massaging her forehead, "Oh Jef, I don't know what to say about your father."

I decided to be straightforward. "How much?"

"Jef I don't want to discuss money with you." She sounded so exasperated.

"I'm not a little kid, Mom! I have the right to know! How much does Peter owe?"

"I gave him $300 to give your dad next time he comes by."

"Mom! No! That's insane! You can't-"

"I have to, Jef. Do you want your father shouting at Peter?"

"Ugh," I pressed my fists against the side of my head. I was so opposed to having my mom give dad any money, but I was more opposed to hearing my dad bully my brother. I couldn't deal with the fuck-fest this day had become.

"Fine, whatever!" I gave up and climbed the staircase to my room.

That weekend Lacey and I sought out to give the quarry another try. With school out of mind she was in a better mood. I had high hopes.

Had.

While we were sitting by a fountain some guy with poor aim sought to throw a coin in, but missed horribly. The coin bounced onto the back of Lacey's bare hand.

"Oh, sorry, miss," the man apologized.

Lacey, very cordially, responded with a fake "Don't worry about it."

Little did that guy know the colossal impact of his simple mistake. As soon as he strolled away she allowed her discomfort to surface. Her expression was contorted with sourness as she held out her arm like it was drenched in venom.

The unnatural way that she hovered her stiff hand in the thin air parallel to her waist reminded me of Peter's awkward cerebral palsy hands that were usually writhing along his husky waist.

I observed Lacey in her stiffness, trying with every neuron in my brain to understand what she was experiencing. The idea that she truly felt something that could not be felt began to sink in. I had never seen somebody other than Peter so frightened by something they fabricated in their head. I was overwhelmingly and uncharacteristically more sad than I was intrigued.

Despite already knowing the answer I couldn't help but ask, almost to clarify the hard to grasp truth for myself, "You're really afraid aren't you?"

She nodded meekly while staring at her rigid hand.

I couldn't stand to see Lacey so insanely uncomfortable. I wanted to make the elusive "germ feeling" go away. But I couldn't. If I could I would. I really would. Like I said before, I had begun caring about Lacey on a level that surpassed "research subject". I wasn't lying when I said I wanted to fix her. I would fight for her, but how could I fight something that wasn't real?

"I have to go," Lacey insisted.

"What? Now? Right now?"

"It's the germs," she said. "I have to wash my hands with hand soap, dishwashing soap, and body wash."

"No, Lacey, no you don't."

"Because it's what my brain always tells me I need to do."

"Mhm," I mumbled, remembering something I had read from the psych book I checked out of the school library. This seemed like the perfect opportunity to try and fix Lacey's mind with some good ol' logic.

"What? What's that? '*Mhm*'? What is that?" Lacey pestered in her ignorant spawned insecurity.

"I was just thinking-"

"What?" she raised her voice, more so in panic than in anger, almost as if she thought she was the bud of an inside joke between me and some other party. Like I was making fun of her. Like I was laughing at her the way those former middle school kids used to do when they found out she had a new crush. And I really didn't like that.

Before Lacey could fret any longer I clarified, "I was thinking of this thing called the validity effect."

Her fear-stricken eyes mollified and her head cocked to the side. "What's that?"

"Well when people believe that a statement is true, no matter how nonsensical, simply because it has been repeated over and over many times, that's called the validity effect. The more you hear a statement is true, the more apt you are to believe it. Which I'd imagine is easy to fall into when you have OCD because a significant driving force of your disease is that repetition of thoughts. You know, those 'danger signs' and 'blaring sirens' that get stuck on repeat until you obey whatever distorted compulsion they command. OCD thoughts are prone to being wildly nonsensical," with hands bound by the large pocket of my pullover Red Sox sweatshirt the only movement was the disapproving shake of my head, "It's cruel, really."

Lacey firmed her feet into the asphalt, stunting our casual sauntering. "You know a lot about OCD."

I certainly didn't feel that way. If I knew so much about OCD then why couldn't I figure out how to cure her?

"Pfft," rumbled a modest laugh through my esophagus followed by a discouraged sigh, "I don't know anything about OCD."

Lacey stared at me with frowning eyes. She knew I was saddened. I knew she knew. She should have been sad for herself. But no, she was sad for me. She didn't have to say anything for me to know that. There was a potent empathy fueling those emotive pupils that couldn't be misunderstood.

"OCD couldn't be more of a puzzle to me," I admitted the candid confession with another shake of the head.

With nothing more to say, Lacey and I were left staring at each other. No, into each other. I swear I could feel the emotion in her eyes.

Completely in tune with each other. It was... intimate.
But that didn't last.

In a sudden moment, I think the moment that Lacey realized how intimate our connection was, she reverted to panic.

"I have to go," Lacey reminded me, masking her intimacy-fear panic with more tangible germ-fear panic.

"Hm, what? No," I fumbled, taking a few seconds to recover from the strain of our prior eye contact, then returned to trying to reason with her with logic, "The coin probably isn't that dirty."

"It's *money*, Jef! Money is the filthiest of all filth! And 'probably' isn't good enough. I have to assume the absolute worst, most germ ridden thing, has touched that coin which now touched me! I'm sorry! I know there's no reason in this brain but-"

"No, no, Lacey. Hold up," I reflected on the situation with more heart than I knew I had. I felt horrible seeing Lacey in such a debilitating panic. All I could think about Lacey's poem and its tragic implication that her suffering was unreasonable. I wanted so badly to debunk any notion that Lacey lacked reason. "Lacey, you're thinking in extremes and assuming that coin is filthy because coins are notoriously touched by a whole slew of strangers. That's induction. You're using induction. Taking an example of what you experienced and generalizing it to everything. It's inductive reasoning and it's exactly what all of science is based on. There's actually nothing unreasonable about it-"

"I'm sorry Jef but I still have to wash my hands!" It was like Lacey didn't hear a word I said. Like, like her anxiety was too loud to hear any form of reasoning.

Very rarely did somebody hear my scientific input and flagrantly ignore it, dispelling it with nonsensical thinking. *Now* I was getting frustrated on a personal level. "Lacey can't you wait to clean up?"

"No, I can't. I can still feel the circle of germs on my skin, like a stain that I have to get out urgently. I'm sorry Jef but I- I'm suffocating," she fanned herself with her uncontaminated hand.

Scared she was going to faint or something, I took a good hard look at her. That's when I realized her usually pallid white skin now had a dull tint of purple in pigmentation, almost as if she was literally suffocating.

I couldn't believe what was happening. Her feeling was all in her imagination, but it still aroused a physical reaction of overheating and suffocating. This was complete madness. I had to do something. But what?
I did the only thing I felt like I could do. I tried to talk her out of her madness.

"Lacey the germ feeling isn't real," I made an effort to use my most confident tone.

"Yes it is," she disputed while continuing to fan herself.

"No it's not. If it was real then everybody would be able to feel germs when they touched something."

"I told you, I'm not like other people! I can feel it, Jef! It's real to me!"

Out of frustration I lost my compassion and patience. "Lacey it's all in your head! Can't you just, I don't know, choose not to feel the germs?"

That was probably the most insensitive thing I could have said.

"No I really can't! I hate when people say that!" Suddenly the tempo of Lacey's speaking advanced to an abnormally fast pace, "I can't change the OCD! I can't stop being afraid! I can't make the germ feeling go away! Believe me, if I could, I would! I told you, different rules are applied to me!" Lacey was convinced of this.

I was in a cluster-fuck of aggravation. I wanted to tear my hair out with my hands but they were having a tantrum of their own, flailing wildly as I tried to explain the truth to Lacey. "You can't feel germs, it's scientifically impossible! That's gotta be some delusion in your head!"

I think I saw a tear in her eye. She clenched her jaw, suddenly lowering her stern voice. "I don't believe you."

"But it's true, Lace, you can't-"

"No Jef, you don't get it. You could have graduated with a major in 'germ science' or whatever the fuck studies germs, and I still wouldn't believe you! The difference between people like me and people like you is that you need logical evidence. Some rationale for you to believe something. But for me, I don't need any rational proof to believe anything. I just need a feeling. I know it doesn't make any sense, but that's the point! An irrational disorder like OCD makes no sense! Trust me, I know what I'm talking about!"

She started to walk away and mumbled under her breath, "I was stupid to think you'd understand."

Peter needed me to help him while he glued together a model airplane my uncle bought him. He didn't usually need help when he pieced model airplanes together, but it was a full moon tonight.

My mom and I discovered the hard way that Peter's schizophrenia significantly worsens on a full moon. Ever since he nearly lit the house on fire when he was a little kid, while attempting to "scare away the ghosts" he called Jerry and Henry, we realized he needed to be supervised on certain nights. I made the discovery about the full moon correlation with schizophrenia delusions after choosing to research the mental disorder.

While Peter applied glue to the plane's nose I sat at the table in a daze, leaning my head on my fist.

I couldn't get Lacey's meltdown off my mind. Her mind, her brain, was an absolute enigma. I was stumped by her disorder. And I was mad at myself for being stumped.

The memory of Lacey's voice haunted me. *I was stupid to think you'd understand.*

That statement pierced through me. Not only was it an insult to my intelligence, but it was also a sign of how isolated Lacey must have felt. How could somebody feel so isolated when I was right by her side, close enough to touch?

Maybe it was hard for me to accept that Lacey Parker really had a mental problem as legitimate as my cerebral palsy ridden brother. But it was different with a retarded person. Peter had a mental fault. You could hear it through his speech. You could see it in his stunted retention of information. You could detect the mental faults in Peter, but you couldn't detect any mental faults in this obsessive compulsive girl's eloquent speech and quick wit. Lacey Parker had some kind of mental complication that was, well, complicated.

Apparently Peter had been talking to me while I sat at the table brooding.

"Jef? Jef are you listening? Jef why aren't you listening to me?"

"Yes..." I fibbed through a gravelly moan while leaning my cheek so hard on my fist that my jaw hurt.

"What's wrong Jef?"

Although I knew sharing my thoughts with Peter would be useless, I was too distraught to hold it in.

"I'm just confused, that's all," I rubbed my stinging left eye.

"Well the instructions are right there..." Peter pointed at the airplane model diagram.

"No not that, Pete. I'm just-"

"Is it about Lacey, Jef?"

A jolt of shock made me sit up straight. How did Peter know what I was thinking? Was my interest in her that obvious?

"Uh... yeah..." the surprise behind my timbre was blatant. "How did you-"

"Henry says you're upset about a girl."

I shook off the schizophrenic element of his rejoinder, accrediting Peter's correct assumption about my distress to some sub conscious part of his brain that took the form of "Henry".

"What's wrong?" Peter went on.

"I just want to understand her," I complained.

Peter seemed perplexed by my frustration. "Why do you need to understand her?"

"Because, bec- I- I don't, I don't know," I gave up and sighed. "I like her, you know?"

"Do you like her like a boyfriend likes a girlfriend, or like you like me?"

I didn't want to say it out loud. While itching behind my ear and slightly lifting the airplane instructions off the table I pretended to suddenly have an interest in Peter's model airplane.

"Jef? Jef? Jef are you listening to me?"

"The first," I mumbled my answer into my shoulder.

"What Jef? I can't hear you."

"The first!" I jerked my head back up to face Peter. In an instant I was off vomiting out the truth, "The first thing you said. I like her like a boyfriend likes a girlfriend. Okay? I like her! I like her a lot! I have a crush on Lacey Parker!"

Peter smiled his goofy smile, probably proud of himself for getting that confession out of me.

Suddenly I felt like a burden was lifted off of me. I fell back in my chair and stared out the window at the beaming moon. "I have a crush on Lacey Parker."

I never planned on falling for her. I didn't know what was happening. I didn't know anything, except that I was so glad Lacey didn't pick up the Frisbee that day.

Lacey was the type of person that I least expected to have a crush on. If you asked me my type before I met her I highly doubt I would have said a short brunette with a severe mental illness, a subtle gothic edge, affinity for metal music, and English major. She just wasn't my type. I mean, that is if we're going by my history. My ex from high school was a tall redhead. And then Gabe tried setting me up with a cute blond in his economics class last semester but I blew it on the date. Apparently you aren't supposed to talk about the aerodynamics behind Frisbee golf when you're out with a girl. I learned that the hard way. So no, dating didn't work out well in the past. Besides, most college girls were looking for smooth talking muscular men. I was the polar opposite of that.

My mind, naturally abhorring the thought of shallow hookups, rebounded to the thought of Lacey. At first I figured my mind was trying to compensate for the disgust eliciting hook up thoughts with the sweet thought of Lacey, but then the picture of that charming and ever-so perplexing brown-eyed girl kept popping in my head. Throughout the night, every time my mind strayed, whether it was to a topic as simple as the deodorant I kept forgetting to pick up at the drug store or as complex as my current essay regarding the holographic principle in physics, I kept returning to the butterfly-in-the-stomach-inducing topic of Lacey Parker.
I couldn't believe it, but I was falling for her. I was falling for my research topic.

I especially didn't expect to fall for somebody as abstract as Lacey. I liked hard facts. Evidence. She thrived off of notions and ideas that manifested through the imagination. That's why she was so good at writing. It was her gift of an imagination. Come to think of it she also deteriorated because of notions and ideas derived from her imagination, like the 'germ feeling' and 'patch of contamination'. Her creativity was her greatest strength and her greatest downfall.

Chapter 21

There was a light knock on the front door.

"Jef can you get that?" Mom called from the den.

I didn't know why I had to get the door when I was upstairs and Peter was downstairs, perfectly capable of answering a damn door. I didn't argue though. I was too tired, having spent the majority of my night thinking about my feelings towards Lacey Parker.

I spun out of my swivel chair, sluggishly dragged myself down the stairs, and ripped open the front door.

On the patio, stood Lacey, posture slouched as she hugged a black folder and her trusty notebook. Her pin straight brown hair was half pulled back by a black lace ribbon, different than usual way she styled it.

"Hey Jef," Lacey smiled warmly.

Hearing her say my name brightened my mood.

It's weird. Once you realize you're attracted to somebody little things like them saying your name gives you an incredible high. Them addressing you, singling you out, talking directly to you, reminding you that you are an individual and they chose to spend that moment interacting with you was euphoric. It almost made me nervous. But it was a euphoric kind of nervous. Hearing Lacey say my name strangely made me nervous in the best way.

"What are you doing here?" I tried to find my voice.

"I, uh, know I should have called but I was afraid you might not answer 'cause of my outburst yesterday, at the quarry."

Her freshly coated ruby lips melted into a frown, "I'm really sorry about that by the way."

"No, it's okay," I was quick to try transforming that frown back into a smile. And I did.

"Are you still up for reading some of my work?" she hopefully asked.

Excitement shot through me, "Yeah, definitely!"

Without further hesitation I let Lacey in, briefly introduced her to Mom, and then saved Lacey from Mom and all of her questions by escaping onto the small but secluded back porch. Out there Lacey commented on the yard.

"Aw you have a shed!" she got all excited.

"Yeah, my uncle and Peter built it. Why?"

"I love sheds."

That provoked a laugh out of me, "That's an awfully random thing to love."

She laughed at herself, "I know. But we don't have a shed. I just think they're so private. It's like a little house you could use as a recluse when you wanna feel independent but not on your own 'cause when you go outside your family is right there."

"I guess that's kind of true."

"It is true," she instilled.

That gave me an idea. "Do you... do you wanna do this in the shed? I, uh, I could read your writing and you could do some more writing..."

"Yes!"

So, Lacey and I changed our location to the shed. With my hand gripped on the rusty handle, ready to open the shed door, I forewarned her, "There might be some pretty nasty bugs in here, are you gonna be grossed out?"

"Nah," she lifted her hand off of her supplies to wave away the possibility.

I laughed and shook my head, "I don't understand you."

She laughed along, "Me neither."

We advanced into the shed. I pulled on the ceiling lightbulb to light up the little, as Lacey called it, recluse, and opened up lawn chairs.

The afternoon was amazing. We lounged for hours. We went a good hour and a half not talking because Lacey was in her zone writing in her notebook and I was reading a select portion of her old work inside the black folder. Being together in silence for so long was surprisingly not awkward. It felt comfortable.

Lacey's writing was so insightful. Almost philosophical. So poetic, a quality I was never good at employing. And her work was so dense with emotion. I didn't know somebody so young could be this intuitive. Intuition was an imperative quality, but such a rarity. Then again, Lacey was a rarity.

"Do you ever tell people these thoughts out loud, Lace?" I reveled while flipping through the pages.

She briefly paused in her writing, dropping her pen, and retorted, "Kind of. Not this in depth."

"Have you ever considered sending this stuff to a publisher?"

"Pfft," Lacey snorted. "You have no idea how frustrating the literary industry is. Trust me, I've researched. You have to get a literary agent or else publishing houses won't even glance at your work. And getting an agent kind of scares me. Because then I have to work with somebody on my writing and, I don't know, I don't really like collaborating when it comes to my writing. I want to make something out of purely me. No help."

"That's insane," I spit out unapologetically. I could have been ashamed for being so blunt, but it was more shameful to let Lacey hoard her talent to herself because of her stubbornness.

Lacey was taken a bit aback. "I want to establish something big in this world, Jef. A story of my own, not somebody else's."

"Not just one person establishes something big in this world without a little collaboration," I blurted out. With no intention to let Lacey waste her talent I put my all into convincing her to open her mind to collaboration that could actually make her publishing dreams come true. "Lacey, look at a contribution to the world as profound as quantum theory. The entire subject is a collaborative effort to describe the physical world on an incomprehensibly small level. Look back to J.J. Thomson, he proved that electrons were particles around 1906 and it wasn't until 1913 that Niels Bohr proposed a model of the atom that quantized its structure, you know, came up with the idea that electrons exist in stable orbits and can switch between stable orbits by emission or absorption of a photon. He didn't introduce that atomic model, though, until 1922 at Gottingen in Germany. But the theory was nowhere near complete yet. Not even the atomic model was complete yet. Bohr's atomic model described an electron's angular momentum, orbit shape, orientation, but it wasn't until good ol' Wolfgang Pauli came up with the spin of an electron that we got the fourth quantum number! In fact, quantum physics itself is based on equations that came from classical physics. It never would have been, I guess you could say 'solved', without Isaac Newton's classical equations. Just think about something as revolutionary as Einstein's Theory of Relativity! Newtonian equations were involved in the relativistic equations that laid the foundation of the very theory that would become one of his greatest contributions to the entire institution of science! Forget about relativity though. Even matrix mechanics include Newtonian mechanics! You don't just 'discover' all this knowledge with one brain, one mind! Milikan proved Einstein's equations for the photoelectric effect were correct in 1915, ten years after Einstein's paper introducing photons. Heck, light quantum wasn't even officially called a 'photon' until 1927 during one of those conferences, you know, the ones where a bunch of physicists worked *together* to exchange information. Solvay Congress was it called? Yeah, the Solvay Congress. They would have scientific meetings about things like electrons and photons. I imagine it was incredible to hear all the theories we know today when they were first introduced! Did you know there were two separate equations to explain the blackbody spectrum? Not just one guy came up with the coveted equation! The Rayleigh-Jeans law worked for long wavelengths and Wien's Law for short wavelengths! Then you've got guys like Max Planck who came up with his own constant! A fricken, constant, Lacey! Some scientist who studied thermodynamics, pulled from both blackbody formulas and created one mathematical formula which stumped Planck himself because it had no physical basis! He spent months trying to find laws to support his equations. Then Einstein, as usual, re-entered the picture! He said in 1924 that there were two theories of light, 'both indispensable... without any logical connection.' That's where wave-particle dualty came into play!"

    I didn't realize I went on an out-of-control tangent until I stopped to take a well-needed breath. As soon as I realized how much information poured out of my mouth I knew my face turned red.

That was it. Lacey must have thought I was the biggest freak in the world. No normal person stores all those names and dates and facts and-

"What's that?" Lacey asked, after a few regrouping breaths and curious wide eyes.

Shocked by her interest, I lost my train of thought. "Huh?"

"Wave-particle dualty. Sounds interesting. What is that?"

"Oh, I, uh, it's, um, it's this- this thing, this fundamental idea that light acts as both a particle and a wave. Well, 'either, or' really. It depends whether or not the observer or the experimenter is asking a question whose answer relies on particle characteristics or wave characteristics."

"Okay wow," Lacey remarked. "That's kind of trippy."

"You think that's trippy! You should learn about the collapse of the wave-function! *You* of all people would love it. Talk about crazy…"

Immediately I heard the insensitivity in my comment. Crazy. I went red. I couldn't bring myself to look at her face.

Resenting my own voice, I tried to erase the inadvertent insult I just hurled at Lacey. "It- it's pretty weird actually. Really weird. Kind of hard to explain."

"Well," Lacey interrupted without a sliver of anger or sadness. Intuitive and empathetic as usual, Lacey decisively brushed by my comment and gave me a win, "If anybody could explain this stuff it's you."

I tried not to smile. Why? Why didn't she call me out for my insult? Why was she so damn kind to awkward old Jef? I didn't know, but for once I put my curiosity on the backburner and didn't let the future slip away by trying to understand the past.

"Did, uh, did you want to hear about collapsing waves?" If Lacey had dimples they'd be showing now. "Yes."

"Okay," I laughed shyly and, without further delay, dove into a lecture about the transition between uncertainty and certainty on the quantum level. How electrons are spread out, how wave-functions can only give a probability of where an electron could be found, and how you can never know where an electron is placed until actually viewing it. How nothing is real until perceived.

"Doesn't this stuff overwhelm you?" Lacey asked.

I shrugged. You'd think a field with more philosophical implications than most sciences would bother me, but for the most part, it didn't. Quantum theory was naturally inconclusive, giving relative probabilities rather than concrete certainties, but I didn't resent it. I accepted it. "Sometimes I get overwhelmed," I admitted and tried to piece together thoughts that I had never confronted before, "but then I remember there are quantum mechanical equations or conversions from Hamiltonian equations and new-age technology, actual proof that back all this crazy stuff up and, I don't know, that's comforting. The quantum paradoxes seem unbelievable but they have numbers to back them up. So I believe them."

"You know," I informed Lacey, "My English teacher was talking about this poetry reading in the hall the day after my English final. You should really read some of your work."

She wrinkled her nose with indecision. "You think?"

"Definitely. If there's anybody who should be reading there, it's you."

Lacey made a compromise, "I'll read if you come, you know, for moral support."

"Deal," I reached my hand out to shake on it, only to quickly retract my straightened palm, "Oh, right."

I returned to reading more of Lacey's writing.

I purposely didn't tell Lacey I finished reading until about ten minutes after the fact. I wanted to watch her write. Just watch. Watch while wondering what was being conceived in her extraordinary mind and then transported into that sacred notebook.

I tried to be discrete, leaving the folder on my lap and pretending to look down at it, but in reality I was staring at Lacey and her notebook. In that moment ink was descending from that pen, staining the sheet with a meticulously thought out path of words, and only Lacey knew the message they bestowed. She had an entire world of tales, revelations, and lessons in her very hands. I ached to step inside that world. If I could just get a glimpse. A snippet. Something that could relieve the throbbing pressure of longing in my chest.

Chapter 22

"Ugh, Piper," Lacey groaned after her dog's wagging tail threatened to brush up against her arm.

"I got this," I intervened and handed the Dalmation a cracker from the bowl Lacey had poured me, causing her to move away from Lacey's seat at the kitchen table.

"Thanks," Lacey sighed with a forced smile. I could tell she'd had a long day at school and was aching to sterilize herself in the shower. There were circles under her eyes. Her posture was slouchier than usual. She was enervated, totally depleted of energy.

Suddenly it dawned on me that I should offer to leave. "You know, if you want me to go home-"

"I don't want you to," Lacey interrupted before I could finish, "But I think I need you to."

With a nod I started to gather my stuff up.

"I'm really sorry Jef," her face was red with embarrassment. "I know I promised to help you with your English homework-"

"It's fine," I insisted. As much as I didn't want to enable her OCD tendency to shower, I couldn't stand looking at her in such utter exhaustion. "Seriously, I'm fine. Just do what you need to do."

Right before I was about to stand up and head out to my car Lacey caught me by surprise by randomly blurting out, "Why was I born so screwed up?"

I felt my head jerk to face her.

"Seriously, why? Why would I be created into this world if I was gonna be created incorrectly? I was trapped from the start."

"Don't be so sure of that," I contradicted with a famous psychological argument in mind. "Have you ever taken a psych class?"

"No," she laughed at the idea, "My life is already a psych class."

After a brief laugh I went on to ask, "Have you heard of the 'nature versus nurture' arguments?"

"Sounds familiar…"

"It brings into question whether or not we, as humans, are biologically born with certain mental qualities or, in your case, mental quirks. Or if our minds are molded throughout life as results of the experiences in environments surrounding us."

Lacey scrunched her nose while searching through the filing cabinets stored in her brain. "I feel like we talked about this in my philosophy class last semester…"

"You probably did, Lace. It's something philosophers like Plato, John Locke, and Aristotle have been writing about for ages. John Locke actually wrote a passage in *An Essay Concerning Human Understanding* known as the 'tabula rasa'."

"Blank slate," Lacey knowingly translated. I must have appeared surprised because after mere seconds of looking at my expression and she let out a coy laugh. "I took Latin throughout high school."

"Ah," I wagged my finger while sporting the biggest grin possible. I was way too excited to have intelligent discussion with somebody. Ever so eager to continue, I retrieved the segment of my brain that memorized the majority of whatever I read and recited John Locke's essay verbatim, old English and all.

"The 'tabula rasa' passage, if I remember correctly, read 'Let us then suppose the mind to be, as we say, white paper void of all characters, without any ideas. How comes it to be furnished? Whence comes it by that vast store which the busy and boundless fancy of man has painted on it with an almost endless variety? Whence has it all the materials of reason and knowledge? To this I answer, in one word, from experience.'"

"I don't like that," Lacey declared.

"But I thought you hated the idea that you might have been born 'screwed up'?"

"I didn't say I *hated* that I was screwed up," Lacey corrected, "I just asked *why*. Never said anything about hate."

"Oh come on, Lace," I nagged, not buying her little shtick. "Wouldn't you rather believe that you were born with a blank slated mind just like everybody else? That God or whoever's pulling the strings up there didn't make a mistake when they made you?"

"No!" Lacey hastily denied. "If my mind wasn't made to be this way, at birth, then that's like saying I'm not and never was an individual."

"But it means you, as a human being, have *freedom*," I emphasized with a voice full of life. Freedom is exactly what I would have expected she'd want to hear after fearing she was 'trapped from the start' with OCD. I tried my best to reinforce how wonderful the notion of freedom was. "If your mind is a blank slate open to experiences then that gives individuals everywhere the freedom to define the content of their character. Don't you find that- I don't know, invigorating?"

Lacey shrugged yet, in contrast, nodded. "I mean I can see why that would be invigorating for you, Jef. There's nothing wrong with you. If nurture is the answer then that means you made no mistakes in the way you responded to certain events in your life. For me, for somebody who's screwed up, that means somewhere along the way *I* screwed up. That means my OCD could have been prevented, and I don't think I can take that thought with me throughout life without being devastated or somewhat resentful of myself. I mean what kind of legacy does that leave me with? Where's the dignity in that? At least if I was born with obsessive compulsive disorder that still gives me my sense of dignity." Lacey paused to awkwardly swipe back a piece of her loose brown hair with a stiff hand of jaggedly bent fingers. "I guess I just value my legacy over freedom."

I didn't know what to say to that.

A good five straight minutes of auditory vacancy hung through the air between Lacey and I.

When I finally scrounged up the courage to talk about my English class for the sake of giving Lacey a bit of a win after the depressing turn our nature verses nurture discussion took, Lacey was ahead of me and posed the question, "What do you think Jef? Was I born with OCD or not?"

I was taken off guard. Nobody, other than teachers, ever wanted to hear what that know-it-all young man Jef Sterling thought. "You wanna know what I think?"

"Yeah," she let out a laugh at my state of surprise, "Why wouldn't I?"

I almost asked her why would she, but quickly stopped myself from potentially shooting myself in the foot. "I think," I started to feel myself sweat, because for the first time I didn't know what I thought.

Apparently Lacey wasn't the only one with taboo words, because for me the phrase "I don't know" was a taboo.

I just shook my head with confusion and shrugged my shoulders, afraid to admit my ignorance.

Lacey nodded, her intuition being the tool that led her to read my mind. "I don't have a clue, either."

Feeling discouraged and ashamed by my inability to give Lacey a direct answer, I began my departure from Lacey's house by heading to the front door.

"Wait Jef!" Lacey called from behind at her kitchen table in a peppier version of her current tone. I think she was going out of her way to brighten my mood so that I'd leave on a good note, which I appreciated more than she probably knew. "Guess what I realized?"

"What?" With hands clutching both straps of my backpack, I retraced my steps back into the kitchen.

Lacey excitedly informed me, "When you write your name in cursive it appears symmetrical."

"What?" I laughed. Not only was the statement random, but I also couldn't picture what she was saying. I raised an eyebrow and gave her what must have been that "inquisitive look" she mentioned long ago. "What do you mean?"

"Your first name, 'Jef'. If you cut a vertical line down the middle then both sides reflect each other. Look…" She wrote my name in cursive on a loose sheet of paper then slid the paper to my side of the table. "See?"

She was right, the capital "J" and the lowercase "t" looked like the same double loop character only reflected, while the lowercase "e" was already a symmetrical symbol in itself.

"That's actually pretty cool," I laughed.

Not going to lie, I was leaving on a better note than before. It was kind of ironic, actually, because the conversation that I was so excited about, the one regarding philosophy and psychology in the "nature verses nurture" argument, was the conversation that dampened my mood. Meanwhile, the silly conversation I wouldn't have expected myself to care for, the one regarding how my name looked in cursive, was the conversation that boosted my mood.

After bidding Lacey farewell I was out the door.

Two steps down the patio and suddenly I realized something.

Quickly I hopped up the front stoop, swung Lacey's front door open, and called into the house.

"Hey Lace!"

She spun herself around, halfway up the staircase, "Hm?"

I blurted out what was on my mind with no filter. "Why were you writing my name in cursive in the first place?"

Lacey immediately blushed and seemed like she was pretending she couldn't hear my unexpected question. "What's that?"

"My name. You must have been writing it in cursive to realize it was symmetrical... my question is, why?"

She shook her head, but it was still red. "Wasn't writing it," she claimed, "Just pictured it, that's all. Just pictured it in my head."

That was the first time I ever felt like Lacey was being dishonest with me.

Chapter 23

Carson and I had a sociology class together in the afternoon. Halfway through the lecture our professor gave us a break to stretch. During that break, while I was in the middle of cracking my knuckles, Carson got out of his seat in the back of the classroom and stood by me.

"You're really into her, aren't you?" Carson asked. His forward question about something as mushy as my feelings took me by surprise. That, and the fact that he could tell I liked Lacey. A lot. Was it that obvious?

"What are you talking about?" I put down the sociology textbook, something I'd rarely do to converse with somebody as dim-witted as Carson.

"The snob," he still referred to Lacey as.

"She's not a snob."

"Right, whatever her name is. Lavender?"

"Lacey," I corrected with agitation towards his ignorance. Did he seriously not know her name by now?

Right then Carson smiled a toothy smile, almost as if he tricked me into mentioning her.

I'd bet a good heap of cash that I was a bright shade of pink. As I usually do when I'm uncomfortable I fidgeted with my backwards baseball cap. I didn't know what to say.

Carson's curious voice trailed on, "So are you guys, like-"

"No," I shut him down before he could say what I had no doubt he was going to say. Carson had a tendency to be crude, and

I really didn't wanna hear it. Not right now. Not in this context regarding Lacey.

As I leaned back in the chair I squeezed onto the edge of my desk with an overly tight and frustrated grip.

"You should bring her to Zeke's party," Carson suggested. "You know how sick his house is. It's the perfect party house! Tons of guest rooms…"

Gabe tried to sell me on going to Zeke's party earlier that day too, when we were shaking a faulty vending machine to spit Gabe back his money. "You're so uptight," he had said, "Be a normal college kid for once and drink with us. Smoke a little weed. Flirt with girls. It's gonna be a blast."

"First of all," I had been whacking the vending machine on the side while declining the invite, "there's no such thing as 'a little weed' with Zeke. And second, I have a ton of homework to do this weekend."

"That's the shit I'm talking about, man! Loosen up for once! Put down the textbooks and loosen up!"

Gabe definitely got that impression because I told him, just about every night he asked if I was free, that I was busy studying, which was technically not a lie. I was studying OCD and Lacey. Perfecting my binder. Recording details from whatever conversations Lacey had endowed me with earlier in the day.

I had left the vending machine without giving Gabe a definite answer about whether or not I'd being going to Zeke's party.

Now, here was Carson, and I couldn't just get up and leave class. I mean I could go to the bathroom, but he'd pester me the second I came back. Carson wasn't going to take no for an answer.

"Come on," Carson pushed. "Ask the tutor girl."

"I don't think she's really into that kind of scene," I dismissed. "I'm not even sure if I want to go."

"Oh come on, dude," he slammed his palms on my desk, bent down, and whispered coyly, "It'd be the perfect opportunity to get in her pants."

"Ohhh-kay," I shouted over him, uncomfortable by the suggestion. I neurotically dropped my sociology textbook onto the desk so that it made a loud bang that could overpower my friend's voice, then flipped through it, trying to find the next chapter. "I am not having this conversation now. I need to get a head start on the next unit."

"Pffft," Carson sneered.

I locked my eyes on his green eyes and dismissed him in a snarky tone, "Are you still here?"

He just shook his head in disapproval, like he pitied me. "Don't worry, Sterling. You're not that much of a loser."

"Gee, thanks," I scoffed while shooing him away with a hostile wave of the hand.

I didn't see Lacey until that afternoon, before catching the shuttle to take me to the far parking lot where my jeep sat on the pavement getting doused by an aggressive New England rain. Since it was pouring so hard a lot of students were huddled in the lobby. The clashing ruckus of chatty young women, cursing young men, and squeaky rain boots was ear splitting.

A familiar voice that I had been hoping to hear broke through the variety of noises.

"You taking the shuttle?"

I looked below to see my five foot friend. Lacey's rich brown hair was tumbling from her scalp, wavy from the humidity. I didn't know much about hair but to me it looked like it could pass off for being professionally curled. I don't know why she didn't wear it like that more often.

"Jef?" Lacey pressed with lips bent into a darker smile than usual, having been painted with a deep burgundy. "Jef!"

"Oh," I jolted back to alertness. I forgot to talk because I was so busy staring at her and her wavy locks of hair. "Uh, yeah. Yeah, I'm taking the shuttle. Of course, it's a fricken Nor'easter out there." I didn't question her transportation decision until I caught a glimpse of the umbrella in Lacey's hand. "Please don't tell me you're gonna walk to Lot G in this weather."

Her eyes bugged and she raised her eyebrows playfully, "Possibly..."

"Lace!"

"I know, I know. It's stupid, but I hate sitting in the shuttle. It's so cramped and the seats are cushioned and I swear those cushions act like sponges, collecting every little germ from every person who sits-"

"Nuh-uh, nope," I shook my head and smoothed over my ski hat, declining to entertain her OCD this time, "You're coming in the shuttle with me."

"Ugh," she groaned but didn't argue. Instead she shoved the compacted umbrella into her leopard print backpack. While she was in the midst of zipping her bag closed a really tall, almost yeti-looking guy with long hair that split down the middle, stomped by us.

"Hi Brandon," Lacey waved up at the random guy, looking like a miniature human next to him.

The fact that Lacey went out of her way to say hello to somebody took me by surprise. Puzzled, I glanced back and forth between Lacey and the guy who was already pushing his way through the maroon doors. "Who was that?"

"That's Brandon, he's in my philosophy class."

"Oh."

I might be conceited but I think she was more social when she had me by her side. Don't get me wrong, Lacey had all the skills inside of her to be social. I knew she could do it. I think she just needed somebody like me to help her get outside of herself. We were good for each other.

Not gonna lie, though, I was slightly jealous when she said "hi" to this Brandon dude. I know its ridiculous because all she said was "hi", but I remember a time when I was the only guy on this campus she would say "hi" to. Come to think of it... was she greeting other guys like Gabe and Carson since I introduced her to them?

It must have been that jealousy that instigated me to blurt out what I blurted out next.

"Are you gonna go to Zeke's party?" the question randomly shot out without me planning it. I had no intention of going to the party, anyways. Especially after my talk with Carson. I knew Lacey didn't even like parties. I knew I didn't either. So why the heck did I just blurt that out?

Lacey grimaced, "I don't know," she sounded against it.

I felt like an idiot for asking. I knew she wasn't interested. What was wrong with me! Now I sounded like a moron who didn't-

"Are you gonna be there?" Lacey's question interrupted my internal tirade, immediately transforming my mood from self-loathing to high. Did she just ask me if I was going? Me? My attendance was gonna determine whether or not she went?

I tried to play it cool despite my excitement. "Eh, I'm not sure."

"Oh okay," she lowered her head and stared at her flower printed boots. "I probably won't-"

"Actually, why not!" I spit out, breaking my bluff embarrassingly fast. I couldn't help it. I didn't want to miss a chance to see Lacey outside of school. "Can't be that bad, right?"

"Yeah I guess," she agreed. "As much as I'd rather be home I guess I could give it a try. You know, be a normal 21-year-old."

I didn't know what to say, partly because I didn't know how I felt. On one hand I wanted to encourage her to go just to help her break out of her isolation, on the other hand I didn't want her to hang out with people like Carson. Then there was the factor that I hated the party scene but, like I said, I really wanted to go so that I could hang out with her outside of school.

"I'm just not used to being out late. I don't know if I can drive-"

"I'll pick you up," I jumped on the opportunity to drive her.

Lacey's lips arched back into their burgundy smile, "Are you sure?"

"Yeah, it's no problem. I'll pick you up at nine?"

"Works for me!"

Chapter 24

Lacey yawned in the passenger seat right before getting out of the car in Zeke Campbell's cramped driveway. Seeing her against the backdrop of a night sky was really weird. I was so used to seeing her in the daylight.

"Uh oh," I laughed at her premature yawn, "You're tired already?"
She finished yawning before releasing a gentle laugh, "I'm not used to being out this late."

I didn't ask Lacey if she was nervous about being at a college party. I knew Lacey was nervous. I just wondered if Lacey knew that I was nervous. Parties were way out of my comfort zone. What was more out of my comfort zone? Bringing the girl I had a crush on to a party.

I knew the night was gonna be a struggle. It was gonna be hard to please my friends while simultaneously making a good impression on Lacey. My friends wanted me to get drunk and smoke a ton of weed, which was the opposite I knew Lacey wanted to see. It wasn't just about impressing Lacey though. I also wanted to protect her. I was the only person she really knew here. And I was her ride home. She was relying on me. She was putting her trust in me, something I knew she hadn't done with anybody outside of her family in a long time. I would be the biggest douchebag known to man if I got inebriated out of my mind at this party. I needed to stay sober.

"I don't look like a slut, do I?" Lacey tugged down the bottom of her short black shorts that were covering lace black tights.

"What? No!" I nervously spit out. Personally I thought she looked more provocative than usual, but that wasn't saying much. This was the first time I had ever seen the skin on her legs, even though her legs were concealed by tights. I wasn't used to parties so I honestly had no idea if she was showing too much or too little skin.

Hectically I knocked on the front door, distracting myself by the banging sound of my fist against the vinyl.

Zeke answered with a plastic red cup in his hand, "Heyyy!" he pulled Lacey and I in for a hug. I knew Lacey was averted to hugs, but she received it anyways. She had told me ahead of time, on the car ride over, that she was prepared to get "Unforgivably Germy" if it meant making a good impression tonight.

Immediately upon stepping in the house the potent stench of booze hit my nostrils like a freight train.

Alright.

A hug and the odor of beer.

So far this was the polar opposite of Lacey's ideal night.

Fuck. She was gonna hate me for bringing her here by the end of tonight.

I tried not to get nervous though. I reminded myself that Lacey knew what she was getting into when she agreed to come to a party.

"Drinks are in the kitchen, dope is in the basement. Help yourselves guys," Zeke invited only before quickly running off to mingle with another set of people at the front door.

I looked down to the girl a full foot shorter than me, "How're you doing?"

Lacey's long mascara coated lashes extended as her eyes widened, "This is pretty weird," there was happiness in her tone though.

We strolled into the living room. There I introduced Lacey to the few people I knew.

"You've already met Gabe and Beth," I pointed to my friend and his snot nosed girlfriend who made zero effort to say hello.

"And this is Natalie Wu," I gestured towards the Chinese girl sitting beside Beth.

"Hi," Natalie greeted with a welcoming smile.

"I love your bracelet, did you make it?" Lacey asked.

Natalie glanced down at the braided string woven around her wrist, "Oh yeah! I could make you one if you want."

Lacey shyly shook her head, "Oh no, that's okay. I don't wear bracelets."

When Lacey's face started to turn red I got a hunch that her comment was OCD related. When she started to awkwardly babble, trying to explain her lack-of-bracelet-wearing to Natalie I *knew* for a fact that her comment was OCD related.

"I know that seems weird but, I just, I wash my hands a lot and I wouldn't end up wearing-"

"Hey!" I swooped in, saving Lacey from her own voice, "Fun fact that you might be interested in, Natalie probably has the best handwriting in all of New England."

Lacey tilted her head back and lightly clapped, "Oh you're telling me that because my handwriting is a nightmare to read!"

"You're damn right," I nodded.

In a matter of seconds Lacey sat in the cushioned chair closest to Natalie. And just like that she was off socializing, without me.

So, I decided to leave the room and grab myself a drink. Of soda, of course. My college kid "cool" factor wasn't compromised since the drink was in a red solo cup, so I maintained the illusion that I was drinking an alcoholic beverage.

When I returned to the living room to check on Lacey she was raving about a notepad that Natalie had just written on. "Your handwriting is amazing! Can you please be my scribe?"

I didn't want to be an asshole and interrupt while she was having a good time, so I made my way to the free chair at the other side of the living room. There, I sat alone, sipping my soda, and thinking about my deep aversion to parties.

I would say I spent the majority of the next hour people-watching, but that would be a lie. I was Lacey-watching, and I knew it. I forcibly diverted my eyes to other people in the room every time I caught myself watching her. I didn't wanna be that creepy guy. But I couldn't help it. I was on the other side of the room. I could see Lacey talking. I could see Lacey laughing. And sometimes I could see Lacey frowning. And I wanted way too badly to know what she was saying to the people around her, what she was thinking inside that peculiar brain of hers, and what she was feeling in this strange new environment. Every second that passed with me divided from Lacey by this conglomeration of drunk, stoned, and horny young adults I felt like I was missing out.

In the rare moments that I wasn't wondering about Lacey I was brooding about what a stupid idea it was to come to this party.

This was the epitome of stupid. Parties, in general, were the epitome of stupid. The collective amount of brain cells that were getting obliterated inside this house tonight was enough to make me sick.

Seriously, why was I here? *Why*? Why would I ever suggest this? I so much would have rather been at school, in the library with Lacey. At least there we could be alone and actually talk. Share thoughts. Engage in thought-provoking discussions. Here, even if I was able to get a seat near her in this crowded den, I wouldn't be able to hear her over the thumping bass.

Doubts swirled around my head in the same burning way that my heavily carbonated soda swished through my mouth.

There was a point in the night where Lacey got up with Natalie and they both stood in the kitchen for a little while. Fortunate for me, I could see into the kitchen from my seat in the den.

Before I knew it some short, I think Mexican, guy approached Lacey and talked with her for like a damn half hour. He was only about an inch taller than her. I think he was making up for his lack of height with his ostentatious tattoo sleeve of- what the fuck was that mess of ink anyways? Psh. He looked like a real tool.

From my spot across the room I'd say he was offering her Jell-O-shots. One after the other.

Continuously he loosened the liquor infused gelatin by sliding his index finger around the little plastic cup then held the treat up to Lacey's face. Every time Lacey just shook her head with disapproval, declining the offer. And every time I shook my head as well with a self-righteous kind of disapproval that stemmed from a paradoxical feeling of insecurity yet superiority over this ignorant fool.

A scoffing sound erupted in my throat.
What an imbecile. As if Lacey would ever consume something that a stranger touched with his dirty finger. This guy stood no chance. But I couldn't help but wonder, if she didn't have the germ fear, would she have reciprocated the flirting and slurped up the Jell-O-shot?

With eyes glued on the tatted up tool persistently trying to pick up Lacey I took another sip of soda from my red cup.

When Zeke walked by with a solo cup in each hand I called him forth.

"Yo, dude."

"Sterling!" He drunkenly slurred and leaned in, "What's up?"

As discretely as possible I pointed my index finger in Lacey's direction, at the guy who was hitting on her. "Who, uh, who is that?" I asked, hearing the awkward inflection in my voice as I tried to make myself sound impartial rather than jealous.

Zeke spun around, blatantly extended his arm out, spilled some beer on the carpet, and pointed with the red cup at the Mexican. "That guy right there?"

"Yeah," I muffled and bowed my head, afraid the guy would see me.

"That's Brock. He's in my botany class. Do you want me to introduce you-"

"Nope!" I raised my voice while holding my head down, "I'm all set. I'm good. Thanks man."

Zeke stumbled off, leaving me to contemplate the meaning of life with the fizzing bubbles in my soda filled cup.

When Lacey finally came back in the living room she sat down on the couch.

There was a free spot next to her.

I'm surprised I didn't pull a muscle from jumping out of my chair.

As quick as possible I snagged the seat on the couch.

"Jef!" she beamed.

"Are you, uh, are you having fun?" I wondered.

Her skin crinkled on the bridge of her nose, "I don't know. It's different. It's nice being social but I feel really grimy."

Later on in the night Lacey found her way back with Natalie. I didn't wanna interrupt so I went my separate way into the kitchen to joke around with the guys. We were all huddled around the island table ripping on each other. Especially Carson. Carson and his drunken antics were usually the bud of most jokes. He liked it though. You could tell. He loved being the center of attention.

Suddenly there was a tap on my shoulder, a tap with a gentleness that I couldn't place. When I turned around to see short little Lacey at my side I was so surprised that I started to awkwardly choke on my soda.

"Hey Jef," she sounded like she needed to run something by me.

After a few coughs I caught my breath, "What's up?"

"I'm feeling pretty tired so I called my dad. He's gonna pick me up. I didn't wanna make you leave early."

"What! You can't leave, you're the only reason I came!"

All the guys congregated around the island table fell silent.

I was mortified.

She smirked. "You didn't mean to say that out loud, did you?"

I shook my head and sucked in the awkward air between me and everybody else around the island counter. "Nope."

Lacey, still smiling, walked around the counter and opened her arms out.

"Wha- uh, are you, me?" I stuttered like a damn goon. You never would have known I was a 3.9 high school graduate.

"I know, it's weird, isn't it?" she teased about her hug offer.

Before I could make matters more awkward I bent down to my short friend and wrapped her in my arms.

As soon as the skin on my hands matted against her silky hair and shoulder blades I felt a thrill like no other. Exhilaration catapulted my mood. I was so high. So extremely high. I couldn't find a way to describe it. Lacey probably could. I was higher than high.

Lacey left the party. I lasted about eight minutes, to be exact, before remembering how much I fucking disdained parties, and I left.

This night only confirmed my deepening feelings for the girl with the notebook. What started as an interest, then advanced into a friendship, graduated into a crush, had now escalated into a serious infatuation.

I wanted Lacey to hang out with us more. I wanted it for her because I knew she needed to push herself out of her isolation and be social, and for me because I was significantly happier when Lacey was with me. She was the person in the room that I found myself directing the conversation towards. The person I kept glancing at to make sure I didn't miss her reaction. The person who I was trying to impress or make laugh. The only girl, when it came down to it, who I actually cared about.

Chapter 25

From across the community college courtyard I could see Brock, from Zeke's party the other night, eying Lacey from a picnic table's distance. The blond highlights in his stupid spiky hair stood out underneath the sun.

Even from a distance I could see Brock chomping on his gum like the uncivilized cow he was.

I decided to "accidentally" hit him up the side of the head with the Frisbee. When the disc knocked against his temple he tripped backwards in his baggy pants and flashy red and gold sneakers.

"Oops, my bad!" I hollered at him.

Natalie, who was sitting in the grass painting her nails, burst out laughing. I think I saw her raise an eyebrow at me but I wasn't sure what that was all about. I just brushed it off.

At the end of our Frisbee passing session I fist bumped a few guys goodbye and started to make my way off the field, towards the building where my next class was.

Somebody interrupted me though.

"Wow, Jef. You must really like her."

I spun around to see Natalie standing there with a sly grin. She nodded in Lacey's direction with one hand clinging to the strap of her over-the-shoulder tote bag and the other on her hip.

"What are you talking about?" I played dumb, having no idea how or why Natalie would know about my feelings for Lacey.

"I'm not stupid, Jef. You have the best aim out of all of the guys. I saw you throw that Frisbee about thirty feet away from Kenny. You hit Brock on purpose, didn't you?"

Damn. I had no clue how to respond to that. Playing dumb was no longer an option. Shit, why did girls have to be so observant?

Natalie just smirked, not forcing me to answer her question, then strolled away to class.

On one end there was a thrill in hearing a voice outside of my own mind acknowledge the fact that I liked Lacey, but on the other end I felt violated, like I was just figured out.

I stood there uncomfortably and took a deep breath. Naturally my pupils darted to Lacey, who was still sitting at the picnic table with her long dark hair covering half her focused expression as she diligently scribbled in her notebook.

Before driving to my job at the convenience store I hung out with Lacey, Carson, Gabe, and Beth in the student lounge.

"Guys you better be at my Halloween party this Friday!" Carson ordered.

"Yeah, sure," I laughed sarcastically and fell back in my chair. There was no way I'd ever go to another stupid party.

"Wait, are you really having a costume party?" Lacey lit up. "I've always wanted to go to a costume party! Last time I dressed up for Halloween I was in seventh grade."

Suddenly I jolted upright and abandoned my dismissive attitude.

"You've never been to a costume party as an adult?" Beth scoffed.

"No," Lacey shook her head but kept a smile in spite of Beth's judgmental tone. "Never got invited to one."

"Mmmm," Beth raised both eyebrows.

Quick to distract Lacey from Beth's hostile mumbling I interrupted with a self-depreciating anecdote "Well some of us weren't popular in middle school or high school so I've never been to a costume party, *period*."

"You weren't popular during high school?" Lacey asked, and for whatever reason she actually sounded genuine.

Gabe coughed out a storm of laughter while Beth scoffed.

I laughed too at the ridiculous thought, "Absolutely not." I readjusted my cap. "Though people did know me as the retard's little, scrawny, brother."

"Well doesn't that sound pleasant," Lacey replied mockingly.

"What about you?"

"In high school? No. I lost touch with everybody in high school. I think I was somewhat unknown. Maybe a little notorious. The weird girl who skipped classes and missed a lot of school, but nobody understood why."

"Why'd you skip school?" Beth was quick to suck out that flaw like the leech she was.

"OCD," Lacey simply answered without mentioning the crippling depression. I loved her honesty. I loved that she wasn't ashamed by the stigma of mental illness. Her condition was her condition, and she wasn't going to hide in shame.

"It was really hard to go to school or get any work done, but I graduated high school with some extensions and adjustments on certain assignments."

Beth was quick to whine, "Well that's not fair."

I was about to make a snide remark when Lacey and her quick wit beat me.

"No," Lacey disagreed with the nod of her head, "fair is exactly what it was. I was deprived because of my anxiety. That's what an accommodation is for, it's bringing me at level with the rest of you because I have a disadvantage. If anything it was the quintessence of fairness."

Beth huffed, then puckered her lips and refused to talk until her and Gabe bickered about where they were gonna go out to eat tonight.

As soon as Gabe and Beth left the lounge Lacey laughed, "They need to break up."

Chapter 26

When Lacey finished helping me with my English homework in my den she interwove a reference from Zeke's party into the conversation, "So, about that Pokémon collection you have…"

"What about it?" I laughed while shoving my physics folder into my backpack.

"I wanna see your Pokémon collection," she requested.

"Do you really?"

"Yeah! I used to have a ton of Pokémon cards. Actually I still have them. They're in a binder, stuffed away in my closet somewhere."

Immediately I thought of the binders of research stored in my closet, which led me to think of the initial OCD binder I made in honor of observing Lacey. Suddenly I felt like a scumbag. My nervous gag reflex threatened to kick in.

I managed to return to the conversation, "Oh, uh, okay, my collection's on my bookshelf in my room."

Thankfully I just tidied up my room for the first time in a while.

"Here we are," I pulled out the navy binder I shoved at the bottom of my shelf. There were a bunch of Pokémon stickers, half peeled off, on the front.

I was nervous. So nervous. But why? Nothing physically intimate was about to happen.

I stood up and rested the binder of collector's cards on my desk while Lacey took my desk chair. She insisted I sit down and that she could stand up but I wouldn't let her.

"Wow," she commented on the cork bulletin board above my desk. It was covered with awards and ribbons from science fairs ranging from third grade up until my senior year of high school. In almost an instant I was embarrassed. I mean what kind of loser keeps awards from childhood?

Hastily I rushed over, "Oh don't mind that, it's lame. Most of those are just for showing up. No big deal."

Lacey stated her indifference, "I think showing up is a big deal."

"I suppose," I shrugged, then began to go through the Pokémon binder.

We flipped through the plastic sheets, reminiscing about which cards were more valuable than others.

When we had gone through just about every card, Lacey got up from the swivel chair, only after spinning it into motion and jumping off playfully.

She then meandered around the room, arms crossed looking small and short as she stared up at the walls.

"That's adorable," she commented on the glow in the dark stars stamped on my ceiling.

"Oh yeah," I let out a gentle laugh, "I've thought about taking those down a bunch of times but I never got to it."

Unexpectedly the clamor of rough banging on the front door shook the entire house.

Lacey stiffened up as my bulletin board convulsed to the ongoing rhythm of knocks.

My first assumption was that my mom was home for work and misplaced her house keys. I checked the digital clock on my desk. It was 5:09. Mom came home at 5:30 on the dot. Who else would be knocking at-

My stomach dropped as the realization set in.

My father was here.

Shit.

My father was the last person I wanted Lacey to meet. God forbid Lacey's innocent ears hear what sort of oafish comments were bound to spill out of his unfiltered mouth.

I also didn't want her to see the kind of uncultured, crude, uneducated person I spawned from.

The intense dread in me was making my stomach churn. I swear I was gonna be sick.

"Um, I'm sorry." I didn't know what to do.

"We should go get that," Lacey decided for me.

So, we both paced down the carpeted stairs. With a deep breath I twisted the knob and opened the front door.

Just as I suspected, my dad stood on the other side, pinching a cigarette in his hand just inches away from his scraggly beard.

"Son," he greeted with a nod and took a brief drag of his cigarette.

I couldn't believe it. Of all the random visits, he had to pick when Lacey was over. I was eager to make him feel as unwelcomed as possible. "What do you want?"

He was quick to see the short brunette girl standing behind me.

"Hold on there, son, aren't you gonna introduce me to your lady friend?"

I could feel the combination of anger and mortification heating up my bloodstream.

"This is Lacey," I answered through gritting teeth.

"Nice to meet you," my dad reached his hand out. I could feel Lacey's nerves running haywire. "Oh, I, uh," she hesitated, but forced herself to shake his hand, "Hello."

"Rich," he introduced.

When Lacey broke free from the handshake I noticed how stiff her hand was, splaying beside her leg like an awkward extension on her arm.

My dad shuffled through his denim pocket and pulled out a pack of Marlboro cigarettes. "You smoke, Lacey?"

"Hm?" she seemed taken off guard by the question. "Oh, no. No I don't."

As far as I was concerned my dad's offer was anything but appropriate. "Dad," my nasty tone ripped through the smoke filled air.

Dad hastily tried to recover, "Oh, er, I mean, good for you young lady! Smoking's bad," he took another whiff of the cigarette and finished his contradictory lesson, "Real bad."

I had never been so antsy about getting my father to leave. "Dad we're kind of busy with homework…"

"Oh, right," my dad winked at me, "Homework."

If it was possible for a human being to spontaneously combust from holding in pure rage then I was about to blow. "Dad seriously."

"Are ya home alone? You can tell me, son, if I'm interrupting some-"

"I'm here Daddy!" Peter came sprinting to the front door.

Fuck. This was turning into a disaster.

To make matters worse my dad coughed a smoky laugh and whispered to Lacey behind the back of his hand, "Well that's gotta be a real mood ruiner for you young folks, huh?"

I didn't dare look at what must have been a horrified expression on Lacey. Between his attitude towards Lacey and his disrespect towards Peter I was done.

"That's it," I went ahead and pushed my dad back onto the front stoop, "Goodbye Dad."

"Ho- ho- hold up there Jef," he reached back in his pocket and pulled out a thin stack of Red Sox tickets. "I got me here some tickets to the Red Sox tonight. They're playin' the Yankees!"

Aw shit. My dad knew my weakness.

He resumed focus on Lacey. "Do you like the Red Sox?"

Peter didn't hesitate to jump in. "I like the Red Sox Daddy!"

"I didn't ask you for your opinion, boy!" my dad raised his voice, "Don't you know not to talk when others are talkin'? That's rude. Do you know what 'rude' is?" as usual he talked down to my brother in the most condescending manner possible.

Lacey politely responded to the initial question, I think trying to transfer the negative focus off of Peter. "I like the Red Sox but I don't watch often-"

"Of course you do! I only got three tickets though," Dad only did so much as flick a glance at my older brother, like it was too much of a burden for him to actually make eye contact with his own son, "Looks like you're gonna have to sit this one out, Peter."

What an asshole. He never failed to stun me with new lows.
I was gritting my teeth so aggressively I thought they would disintegrate. This was a livid side of me that I know Lacey had never seen before.

My father handed Lacey and I each a ticket.

"Oh uh," Lacey manically darted her stare down on her phone, lifted it closer to her face, then started reading, "Actually my mom just sent me a text. I've gotta be home tonight. So," she made the bold move of handing Peter her Red Sox ticket, "looks like Peter will get to go, actually."

Peter, as excited as ever, punched a fist through the air, "Aw score!"

Suddenly my agitated jaw began to loosen up.

Lacey then walked over to me and stunned me by patting me on the arm, "I'll see you at school tomorrow?"

I was so shocked that she touched me I almost forgot to answer.

"Jef?"

"Oh- yeah, yeah! Of course!"

She smiled, "Okay, bye," then excused herself, walking past my dad and down the patio to her silver car.

"Alright, then," Dad uncomfortably embraced the change of plans, "Guess we'll be taking my truck?"

"I'm gonna go get my camera!" Peter raced up the stairs. He was so excited to finally spend time with my dad. I was still pissed at my father's rudeness in front of Lacey, but I refused to lash out. There was no way I would ruin this marvelous situation for my brother.

An abrupt text message made my cell phone shiver in my pocket. I reached down and checked my screen to see a message from Lacey Parker.

Have fun you three!

I looked outside, past my dad in the doorway, as Lacey's car shifted out of park and proceeded to drive away.

Out of enamored disbelief I shook my head and attempted to ward off a resilient smile.

This meant so much to Peter.

Chapter 27

The library was quiet on an afternoon as warm and sunny as today. It was the perfect opportunity to spend time with Lacey, really digging into the trenches of her cognitive landscape.

"Your mind is a zealot and your doctrine is a disease. Beyond this threshold is everything you can't appease..." Lacey recited the mess of chicken scratch in her notebook, only because I asked over and over what she had written.

"What next?" I pushed, pointing to the adjacent notebook page where her poem continued.

Lacey blushed while I prodded her with dilated pupils. She took a deep breath. I nodded her onward and-

"Sterling," came a voice from over my shoulder.

The unwelcome interruption had me jolt in my seat. "*What?*" I hissed.

Natalie stood behind me, and I immediately began to sweat.

"I've been meaning to tell you, the library got that new book you were looking for. The one about quantum tunneling."

"Finally!" I exclaimed in relief. I had been eagerly awaiting that book for a good month.

My excitement fleeted onward and I remembered how intrigued I had become in Lacey's poem.

Suddenly I felt as if I were choosing between two loves, science and Lacey.

"Er, thanks. I'll check it out later," I dismissed.

Natalie raised an eyebrow, flickered her squint between Lacey's fawn eyes and my panicked eyes, and then shrugged off her efforts, "You know where to find the book, Sterling. Second aisle, two rows down-"

"Yup, got it!" I barked out and turned back to give Lacey my full, undivided attention.

A meager minute passed of Lacey deciphering her poetic notes when she cut herself off.

"Jef, go look at that book."

"What?" I raised my voice. "No, we're doing something here-"

"I have my interests, you have your interests. You've been patient enough listening to my interests," she affirmed with self-deprecation.

I wanted to argue, but Lacey had already closed her notebook. I wanted Lacey to share her interests with me. Now what was I going to do? Share my interest with her?

My eyes flickered to the second aisle in the library.

That was exactly what I would do.

I'd share my interests with Lacey. I wanted to get closer, didn't I? That went both ways! The possibility of Lacey feeling the same way for me as I felt for her would be more than I could ask for.

"Well I guess it's your turn to listen to my interests," I announced across the library table and rose to my feet.

Lacey's eyes widened and she smiled. "What do you-"

"Come on," I clasped the straps of my backpack and nodded Lacey towards the bookshelves. "Let me show you what I've been waiting all month to read."

Lacey followed along my side as we made our way down the tall walls of books. Right where Natalie indicated I found the book. I snatched if off the shelf and mindlessly planted my butt on the floor of the aisle, leaning my head in its comfortable position upon the bookshelf.

"Let me show you," I peeled the fresh page to the introductory. The book felt new and untouched.

Lacey was tense, with arms crossed protectively, consciously opting not to join me.

"I'm sorry but I, I can't sit on the floor of a public library."

"Oh," I could hear my pathetic disappointment.

Lacey's upper teeth dug down on her lower lip, "Hang on," she compromised.

"Wait, what are you-"

Before I could embarrass myself with any more neediness she scurried those heels outside the corridor of bookshelves.

Antsy, I shuffled a glance back and forth between the crumbs on the rug. This was kind of gross.

I wrung my fingers.

I swear I could feel the dilation of time between my frame of reference and Lacey's. Sitting alone for a measly two seconds felt like an hour.

Lacey hurried back with a sheet of paper towels.

One towel at a time she patched together an oblong perimeter of cheap 1-ply cloth.

Lacey flashed those big brown eyes at me, "Don't judge me."

"I'm not!" I quickly revoked whatever indifferent look I might have been giving her. Then my own anxiety started to kick in and I felt like Lacey might view me as some disgusting troll who sat on unsanitary floors. "Should I get a paper towel, too?"

"Oh gosh, no, you're fine," Lacey laughed.

What a silly thing to ask. Stupid, Jef.

"Pfft," echoed a snort from across the aisle. It didn't take much to realize that the meathead sitting at the nearest library table was scoffing in our direction. The two girls he somehow managed to entice to sit with him followed his lead and began to steal glances over at us, giggling along.

Maybe my question wasn't so silly.

"One sec," I told Lace, almost patting her knee in its pretzel crisscross placement, but instantly remembering she would have a breakdown if I touched her.

"What are-"

"I'll be right back."

As quick as possible I ventured across the library, got myself a couple of sheets worth of paper towel from behind the front desk, then returned to Lacey's side where I placed my own sitting area of paper onto the library floor.

Lacey's eyes lit up and she smiled, "Oh Jef you don't have to do that."

"The floor is filthy," I purposely announced loud enough for my voice to travel down the aisle of bookshelves and reach the laughing group of kids at the nearby library table.

As I bent my long legs into a very uncomfortable pretzel position Lacey bit down on her grin. Her voice was discrete and quiet, "You don't really think that, do you?"

"Not really," I whispered back with a relentless smirk, "But they don't have to know that."

For the next hour, no – two hours, I didn't read the text to Lacey. I explained the context in my own diction, more often than not finding ways to incorporate lanky wrists and hands into a pantomime of pertinent gestures. And all the while Lacey didn't break eye contact with me. Maybe it was the blood rush to the head, but I swear she was gazing at me. With her eyes on me I was thriving, like the professor I always dreamed to be, explaining how electric forces underlie every human sense.

Lacey proved her attention had been undivided when she offered a duly follow up question, "So, the sensory experience of touching another human being… that all stems from electric forces?"

"Well, yes," I stammered briefly, dropping the paperback book in my lap to lift both hands. "Can I- er, can I try something with you?"

The panic in her eyes was dissonant with the willingness in her response, "Okay."

Eager to demonstrate how the warmth emitted from a hand comes from infrared light, I held my hand up, palm facing Lacey.

Lacey intuitively knew to hold her hand up, mirroring mine. She must have been really nervous, because her hand was trembling as it hovered mere centimeters away from my hand.

"Atoms make up all solid matter, including our skin. Every atom within your hand is held together by electric forces. The electrons in the atoms of my hand repel the electrons in your hand if we were to channel these electric forces by applying pressure, AKA touch, between our hands."

I paused, allowing Lacey the initiative to merge her palm with mine.

There was a tremble in her fawn eyes that matched the tremble in her hand.

I didn't intend to, but I was holding my breath.

With a sudden rush of courage, Lacey's small fingers lined up along mine.

Her skin felt like a sheet of ice.

Suddenly I forgot what I was saying, or how to talk for that matter.

Why, why had Lacey agreed to touch my hand despite her intense fear of exchanging germs? Had I disrupted her phobia? Or had I stirred a monstrous discomfort within her?

In collateral panic I ripped my hand away from Lacey's.

Lacey gaped at me with those big brown eyes, "Jef?"

I couldn't just sit there and say nothing at the sound of her voice speaking my name. Without thought I instinctively came out straight with my feelings, "I'm baffled by you."

Being the contradiction that Lacey was, she both smiled and shrugged, "Imagine how I feel."

Chapter 28

Classes were winding down and pretty soon I was going to fulfill my English requirement. Normally I'd be ecstatic that I was this close to being done with English classes, but I wasn't. The end of English meant the end of English tutoring, and these tutoring sessions had become a staple for me. They were automatic plans with Lacey Parker, the physically, mentally, and emotionally fatigued girl who struggled to commit to any plans. So, for that reason, I cherished the next Tuesday tutoring session at Lacey's house more than usual. And oddly enough, for that same reason, I think I was more crabby than usual.

Lacey was going over different literary devices with the company of her usual metal music blasting out of a speaker in the sunroom. She brought up stuff like irony, motifs, and foreshadowing. I hated this kind of stuff. And I didn't hesitate to let Lacey know.

"I'm sorry but this is a bunch of garbage."

"What is?" Lacey asked with an anticipatory smirk as she flicked her eyes off of the bulky English textbook.

Transferring my innate frustration out of the hand raking through my hair and channeling it into words, I answered, "Literary devices. I swear English teachers just invented them to try and turn pointless fictional stories into something more exciting."

Before I knew it Lacey and I were in a heated debate.

I stood by my belief, "English teachers act like there's meaning in little things but there's not."

"Yes there is!"

"There is *not*. Literary devices are bullshit."

"Oh really?" she seemed to be humoring me, which I really didn't like because there was a belittling insinuation that I wasn't smart enough to grasp some bigger concept.

To protect my ego I stuck to my argument, making my view more extreme. "It's a mockery of life."

"Is that what you think literature is, Jef? A mockery of life?"

I stubbornly nodded.

"That's a pretty cynical outlook."

This wasn't the first time I was accused of being cynical. "It's the truth."

"It really isn't," she argued. "Foreshadowing exists in real life, motifs exist in real life, irony exists in real life. You probably haven't picked up on it because you haven't searched for it."

Almost as if Lacey and I switched roles, now I was the one crossing my arms, "I'm not buying that."

Lacey rolled her eyes.

Damn, we really did switch roles.

"*What?*" I pressed, extremely grumpy from the repeating thought that this was one of the last tutoring sessions I'd have with Lacey. That damn thought was stuck on replay and wouldn't let up.

Lacey, seeing that I wasn't in the most mentally lenient mood, closed her textbook, pushed it aside, and proceeded to educate through a less conventional method.

"Let me fill you in on a little phase I went through during middle school."

"What, why? How is that releva-"

"Just listen. I used to be really obsessed with videotaping stuff. I used to video tape entire events and hoard footage. I felt like the events needed to be recorded or else it was like they didn't happen. Like a piece of my life would be missing. And you know what happened when I videotaped? I missed out on the moment."

"That's ironic," I determined without thinking anything of my comment.

"I'm sorry- what is it?" she quizzed, cupping her hand beside her ear.

"Iron-" suddenly a realization made my blood drain from my newly spooked expression. I gasped, "Irony."

Lacey leaned back with her arms folded, satisfied, "Mmmhm."

That freaked me out.

"And if I'm not mistaken, that reoccurring video camera symbolized my disconnect from the moment. which made it..."

"A motif," I finished.

"And, correct me if I'm wrong Jef, I'd say that the obsession to capture all these experiences was overcompensating for the experiences I'd later miss out on because of my developing OCD, almost as if my illness was..."

"Foreshadowed," I hardly uttered, nearly inaudible from shock.

On my way out of the kitchen Lacey reminded me of an assignment.

"You have that prose piece due soon."

"Ugh," I groaned while tugging on the zipper of my backpack, "I have no clue what to write about. Can I write about supersymmetry? Or epistemology?"

"What? I don't even- I don't know. Uh, yeah, I guess? You can write anything, really. That's the beauty of prose. There's no rhyming requirements or metrical structure. But you should try to be a little creative."

"No," I doggedly rejected. "I'm not like you Lacey. I'm not right-brained. The left hemisphere of my brain is far more active. Logic. Mathematical sequences. That's my comfort zone. I can't just be creative and deep and artsy off the cuff. When it comes to creativity my mind is, well, it just doesn't work."

"That's nonsense," Lacey rolled her bulbous eyes. "Anybody can be creative, even a nerd like you. All it takes is some inspiration."

I didn't react. I still had no idea what I was going to write about.

"There's got to be something that inspires you. Something that gets you going. Something that sparks your passion. Something that interests you. Pinpoint something that interests you."

I shook my head and snickered, "I can't. Everything and anything that can be processed by the human brain catches my interest. You know what, I'll just write about the theory of knowledge. Can I do that? Can I just write about the theory of knowledge?"

"No," she argued tenaciously.

"But-"

"Let me put it this way," Lacey raised her voice, "You like educating yourself, enhancing whatever the heck makes up your brain."

"Neurons," I corrected. "Neurons conduct the electrochemical signals that transmit information through your brain."

"Sure, neurons," she repeated with little to no retention, probably because she was too caught up in her own abstract mindset. Lacey went on transferring her epiphany onto me, "You like enhancing the neurons in your brain. If you *really* want to better yourself, if you *really* want to elevate your mind to the next level, if you *really* want to exercise your, what do you call it? 'Right brain hemisphere'? Then you should step outside of yourself and write from your feelings, not reiterate a bunch of theories that some philosophers or professors thought up."

"But, but," I was so moved by the mystique Lacey was able to convey with her dialect that the fear of sounding inferior made me stammer in a bumbling fashion. I had to consciously take a deep breath, regain control of my turbulent tongue, then proceed with a blunt response. "I don't feel any inspiration right now."

"It'll come," Lacey assured, "When it's meant to come, it will come. And it doesn't have to be perfect at first. Just sit down and write whatever your hand wants to write. Flush it out. You can touch it up later."

Without any bit of a warning Lacey's younger sister, Felicity, unapologetically stormed into the kitchen towards the mp3 player docking station that had been playing music. "I can't take it anymore Lacey! As if it wasn't annoying enough that you play the same old songs, over and over, you also play it way too loud; I can hear it from the other room! How am I supposed to study?"

Before Lacey could shoot across the kitchen to stop her, Felicity pressed her index finger onto Lacey's mp3 player and turned the volume lower.

I watched Lacey's kind brown eyes transform into livid pits of fire.

Lacey freaked out. And when I say freaked out, I mean freaked out.

"You did NOT just do that! Tell me you didn't just do that!"

"It was too loud!" Felicity fought back.

Lacey's hands were like claws, hovering in front of her intense scowl, looking like they were supposed to be digging into Felicity's head.

"I told you never to touch my mp3 player!" she screamed at Felicity. Her younger sister, unlike her parents, had no patience for Lacey's irrational germ fear. She insistently defended her action, "It's not my fault you're deaf! The volume was way too loud!"

In that moment Lacey actually could have passed off for deaf. She didn't seem to hear a word her sister was saying. "And look," Lacey aggressively gestured towards the cell phone in Felicity's hand, "You're holding your filthy phone! You take that phone out in public, don't you? When was the last time you cleaned that phone?"

"I don't clean my phone! I'm not a *freak*!"

"Now all those filthy door knob, money, and whatever the fuck else you touch in a public setting germs are spread onto your phone, which you spread onto your hands, and have now spread on my mp3 player! I bring that to bed, Felicity! What am I gonna do now!"

"Stop being such a psycho!"

"I hate you!" Lacey was so far gone and there was no getting her back, "You know to tell me if you have a problem with the music so that I can turn it lower! You know better! Now I have to wipe it down with a wipe then hand sanitizer then wait a day until I use it again then-"

"You're insane!" Felicity shouted.

"Well you're a jerk! You knew better! You fucking knew better!"

Felicity waved away Lacey in a "fuck off" motion and stomped out of the kitchen, back into the room where she was trying to study.

Lacey warned me about her freak-outs. Knowing what I knew and seeing what I've seen I could make a logical inference as to what those freak-outs might have look liked, but this was worse than I imagined.

"I'm so sorry!" Lacey apologized for her potty mouth while scrambling around the kitchen, "You should leave Jef! You should just leave!"

All she could focus on was the germs that she believed just infected her mp3 player.

"I can't deal with this," Lacey muttered to herself as she ran to the corner where a tube of disinfectant wipes sat. She ripped out, I don't know, like six wipes, and scrubbed her mp3 player neurotically. "I can't," she kept mumbling, now running over to the kitchen sink, squirting hand soap and, yes, dish soap onto a wet paper towel and actually rubbing it on her mp3 player.

"Lacey, I don't think you should-"

It was no use.

She didn't hear me.

She was in another world.

She was in an uproar like Peter on a full moon, when his schizophrenia was at its strongest.

Awkwardly combing my hair with my fingers I stayed quiet and let Lacey finish with her compulsion before leaving.

When she had finished scrubbing her mp3 player she walked me outside.

I stopped in the middle of her brick patio, refusing to go any further to my car without addressing what had just happened. "Lacey that was... scary."

"I know," she peeped out, unwilling to look me in the eye.

"I mean that... that was such an extreme reaction. Is that what usually happens when Felicity touches your stuff?"

Lacey covered her face and dropped to the short brick wall lining the pathway.

I slid the backpack off of my shoulder to sit by her side.

"When we were younger Felicity was my best friend and I was her best friend. When I got sick half of that changed. Felicity was still my best friend, but I wasn't hers. She hates seeing me around the house. Says I'm home too much, that I never go away. She resents me so much. And I don't blame her. I don't blame her at all. If the roles were reversed I'd resent her too." Lacey shook her head in disgust, still staring at the ground instead of me, "I've damaged our relationship so much, and as long as I'm sick I really don't think I can repair it."

I thought to myself about my vow to fix her.

I didn't bring it up though. I let Lacey continue talking.

"My sister has to go through such bullshit like that back there. When somebody sits in my seat, or somebody touches my stuff, I become this monster. Like what you just saw. I'm an ugly monster and I can feel myself destroying everything in my path but I can't seem to snap out of it. I just have to finish my compulsion before I can think straight. And because of that I wind up saying hurtful, really hurtful, things to my sister or my parents. And they have to listen to it." Lacey's eyes were turning bloodshot. The stress of having her sister touch her mp3 player and the stress of talking about it was getting her worked up. "That's gotta be the hardest part of all of this, how my family is suffering because of me. They don't deserve the pain. I'd rather take all the pain of this illness. It'd be horrible, but I'd take it. My OCD's ruined family gatherings. Vacations. We used to go to the beach every summer and stay with family friends at their beach house, until I was seventeen. I had a panic attack about all the germs, being that I wasn't in my 'safe' house with *my* shower or *my* bed or *my* clean breathing air. I begged my mom to take me home. I begged and begged, sobbing, until she agreed to take me home. And then when she agreed I sobbed the whole car ride home because I knew I had just ruined a family tradition by being afraid of germs. Then the summer after that I tried again to stay at the beach house, and even quicker than before my anxiety kicked in and my mom had to take me home again. Now I don't even bother going. My sister and parents have vacations without me now. And I know it makes them sad to know I've locked myself at home while they're trying to make family memories." Lacey shook her head in disbelief. "It just blows my mind how much pain one person can cause an entire family."

I could understand that. Peter's condition had a similar impact on the whole family. It put my mom in the position of having to take care of her son past adulthood. Heck, it caused my dad to run away when I was only three months old. And then there was me. It was the main reason I was still living at home and going to community college.

But still, I'd never want Peter to feel like he had "ruined the family". I'd rather take on all the pain of having a retarded brother than him ever feel that kind of guilt.

"It's not you that's causing your family pain, it's the illness you have." I told Lacey, feeling the same obligation to save her from guilt.

She cocked her head to the side and let out a timid, "Yeah, I guess." Crossing her arms, holding her small body tightly, Lacey stressed, "Sometimes I think my parents believe they caused my OCD. I hate that they take some of the blame. They won't admit it, but I know they feel guilty. They just have that look of sadness, like they were bad parents. Like they failed on raising a normal daughter."

I had heard enough agony in Lacey's voice to finally interrupt. "This is nonsense. Your disease is a chemical imbalance, not some character flaw your parents could have inspired or discouraged."

"I know that," she agreed, "but they still give me that look every so often. That look like, like 'Where did we go wrong?'"

In a sudden combustion of sorrow Lacey burst out crying. The thought of her suffering parents threw her over the edge.

My stomach dropped.

I had never seen Lacey cry before.

"Lacey..." I heard my imploring tone crack out of my throat.

Tears streamed out of her bloodshot tear ducts.

I wanted to say the right thing, to bring an end to her remorse, but I had no idea how to do that.

I was at a loss.

Do I rub her back? Do I hug her? Obviously not. She would freak out. But what was there left to do? How do you comfort somebody who refuses to be touched?

I was so inexplicably stumped. It was like there was an invisible force field around Lacey, trapping her in her own world. And I wanted so badly to break through and provide some sort of comfort, but I couldn't without setting her into a deep state of anxiety. If only there were something I could do.

It pained me to be on the other side of that force field.

As the sun was setting Lacey remained sobbing. She didn't wipe her tears. She didn't veil her face. She just wept, feeling completely hopeless. And I, I felt completely hopeless as well.

There we were in the evening air, sitting side by side on the brick wall.

I had hoped so many times to be in a situation where I was mentally, physically, and emotionally close to Lacey. But not like this.

I had known her obsessive compulsive disorder caused her pain since I first read her poem. It was obvious. But to see her cry, to actually see the physical sign of her pain, it was excruciating. I didn't like it at all.

And that's when I realized my assumption was incorrect back when Lacey initially explained her germ fear. I thought Lacey had accepted the fact that she had obsessive compulsive disorder. But now, looking at her cry, it was clear. Lacey hadn't accepted it. If she had then she wouldn't be mourning for herself right now.

It hurt to know that I couldn't make her OCD or depression go away, but I could at least try to alleviate some of the pain that it caused. I sat there, unable to touch her hand or hug her, and I wanted to so badly. All I could do was beg her with my stare to let me help her.

"What can I do?" I was verging on pleading.

Instinctively my hand slid closer to hers, but I stopped myself.

This was so much more complicated of an issue that I expected. Her OCD was literally imprisoning her. Preventing anybody on the outside from sweeping in to save her. I mean, really? She isn't even allowed to hug somebody when she's upset?

This merciless mental disease had her all figured out, inside and out. It knew exactly how to keep her isolated. I had to find a way to break in. I had to. She was too special. I scanned the wet glaze coating Lacey Parker's eyes as she mournfully gazed into the grass.

There was so much pain writhing inside of her.

"Come on, Lace. There has to be something I can do."

Lacey sniffed, trying to suck back the emotional torment. Without breaking her sullen gaze on the ground she made a desperate request using her frail and quivering lips, "Can you just… stay here, beside me, while I cry?"

My heart sank, knowing that this was her thinking she was asking a lot from me.

I had no intention whatsoever of leaving her in this condition.

"Of course."

Chapter 29

I vaguely remember learning about obsessive compulsive disorder during our mental health unit in high school. It didn't go this in depth though. It never covered the damage it had on familial relationships or friendships. The resentment it caused between siblings. The stunt it had in the development of becoming an independent adult. The destruction of a social life. The fatiguing toll it had on a person's energy level. The acute embarrassment that resulted from such misunderstood compulsions. And the misunderstandings caused by OCD. That reality hit me hard.

    I thought Lacey was a snob for not passing me the Frisbee. If I had known that she would have had voices screaming in her head to wash her hand if she touched the Frisbee then I never would have called her a snob around the guys.

    School never taught about any of those effects. These were realizations I probably never would have come to if I hadn't read Lacey's incredibly revealing poem in the first place. Who would have thought a poem could shed more light on the nature of this mental disorder than an actual class? Thanks to Lacey I was a more enlightened member of the human race. And being the natural geek I was, who valued knowledge above all else, that enlightenment was indescribably important to me. Lacey gave me that. Whether she realized it or not, she was making me a better person. And to think, the vast majority of the world whom hadn't read Lacey Parker's writing or bothered to befriend her still had no idea what obsessive compulsive disorder was really like for the individual.

Yesterday afternoon at Lacey's was excruciating. To not be able to hug Lacey as she cried killed me. It was hurting me to be so emotionally and mentally in touch with Lacey but so physically out of touch. Just a hug would be nice. Even a graze of our hands accidentally touching would do. Any contact.

There was an undeniably selfish part of me that longed to touch Lacey because I was attracted to her. But a greater portion of that longing stemmed from a deep-seeded yearning to help her. To comfort her. To remind her that somebody cared about her pain, her happiness, and Lacey in her entirety.

"Are you going to Gabe's house Saturday night?" my friend Kenny wondered after a vigorous Frisbee golf tournament. He was still panting, hands on hips, while he asked.

Using the back of my hand I wiped some of the sweat off of my forehead, "Yeah, you?"

"Yeah, Natalie's gonna be there, so, you know…"

Oh yeah. Kenny had a thing for Natalie.

"Is that Parker girl coming?" Kenny asked, as if Lacey's role in my life was the equivalent to Natalie's role in his life.

"I don't know," I thought about Lacey, and her crying last night. "She's been doing a lot lately and I know she likes to spend her free time at home."

"That's kinda weird."

"It's mostly from her OCD," I referenced it casually, figuring Kenny might have heard by now about her disorder since I already filled most of our mutual friends in on it.

"Oh, right," Kenny laughed. Plastered across his face was this goofy smile that itched me the wrong way. But, since Kenny seemed like a generally nice guy, I gave him the benefit of the doubt and faked a cordial laugh.

After a brief glance to my feet I realized one of my shoelaces was untied, so I bent down to fix it. While kneeling on the ground Kenny put his hands on his hips and elaborated on the conversation.

"O-C-D..." he over-enunciated the acronym in a mocking manner, "Does Lacey also spend weekends searching for Bigfoot and following rainbows to pots of gold?"

I questioned his sarcastic tone while rising to standing position, "Why do I get the feeling that you think this is all a joke?"

"Well," he cooed as if I secretly agreed with him.

Hell no.

I tried hard to keep my cool, took a deep breath, then posed the question blaring in my mind, "I'm just curious, what part of Lacey not being able to hug her own parents, or pet her own dog, or go on a vacation in a hotel, do you find so funny? Or maybe it's the fact that she missed an entire year of high school because she was so petrified of leaving the house? Is that it? Is that what's so funny?"

Kenny's narrow eyes widened so that he was looking at me like I was some kind of mutant creature. "Dude I was just-"

"You're just a moron," I cut him off.

I couldn't tolerate the ignorance any longer.

I had to walk away.

I was transfixed on the award decorated bulletin board above my desk, as I reflected on Kenny's stupid implication about OCD being fake.

I just didn't get it. How could you not believe in somebody's mental state? It's not like a mental state was some kind of zombie or warlock or ghost! Lacey was a person, not a ghost.

But she was mysterious like a ghost...

And she was unable to touch certain objects like a ghost...

And...

As fast as possible I whipped my desk drawer open, pulled out a haggard marble journal, grabbed a pen from the cup on my desk, and flushed out every phrase running through my mind. I just needed to get my thoughts out in writing. Like Lacey said, I could touch it up later.

Chapter 30

I did it. It took me until three in the morning, but I did it. I wrote the prose assignment.

The next morning I reread it. Lacey would be reading this today and I had to make sure it was perfect.

<u>She Is A Ghost</u> by Jef Sterling
She is fascinated by ghosts. That's probably because she might as well be one. There are many uncanny connections between her soul and the spirit of a ghost.
Ghosts are souls that are stuck. They can't move on. There is something holding them back, whether its regret, sadness, rage, envy, or any other emotional state; it seems that they are bound to particular settings.
She gets stuck on certain thoughts. She gets stuck on memories. She gets stuck in ritualistic patterns. She is the poster child for not being able to move on. Both her disordered mind and passionate heart hold her back. As a result, she is bound to her home, which is the particular setting that symbolizes her mental confinement.
Ghosts radiate glum energy.
Being the natural pessimist that she is, she radiates glum energy.
Ghosts do not live. They do not experience life. Instead, they wander around, dead inside, a mere shadow of the human they once were.
She does not embrace life. She does not get out and experience the common joys, trials, and tribulations in this world because she has a mental disease

that prevents her from functioning. It sucks the life out of her, leaving her an exhausted corpse of a human who had great potential.
Ghosts scare people. Whether they mean to or not, they frighten others. Others are frightened because they cannot understand the mysterious phenomena of an apparition that is, strangely, both present and also not in touch with reality.
She scares people. Her twisted methods of thinking disturb others. Others are disturbed because they cannot understand the enigmatic paradox of a human being standing before them while simultaneously trekking through a far off and intangible fantasy world.
Everything spooky, elusive, and intriguing about ghosts can be used to describe her. The truth is, she is a ghost.

"Please tell me you have your prose piece done!" Lacey hounded the moment I approached her in the school library.

I shrugged and shook my head, pretending not to have it.

"Dammit Jef! I even called you to remind you! I told you-"

When just enough people glanced up from their books and computers to see Lacey flipping out at me I whipped out the packet from behind my back and raised my eyebrows at her.

Lacey immediately blushed.

I looked over each of my shoulders and announced to the library, "It's okay everybody, she's alright. Go back to studying."

She crossed her arms, slammed her back against the chair, hissed ever so quietly, "You suck," and grabbed my prose poem out of my hands.

With a wide smile, Lacey proceeded to read my work.
She read.
And read.
And read.
And slowly her smile softened.
And she read.
And read.
And her milder smile morphed into an impartial line.
And- oh shit.

I knew Lacey wouldn't like my writing. I knew it! I knew I shouldn't have written it about her! What did she think? Duh, I knew what she thought. She hated it. Fuck, she hated it. This was humiliating!

I nearly leaped over the library table to snatch the packet from her. "It's not very good, I should just throw it away-"

Lacey swiftly pulled the packet closer to her shoulder to dodge my swipe.

We stared in each other's eyes.

Mine were scared. Hers were serious. I knew this was a bad idea.

Suddenly her voice intervened on the locked stare, and something unexpected happened. "I love it."

I was shocked. "You do?"

With a tear in her eye, she nodded.

Pride seeped its way into my bloodstream. I had rendered the girl with all the words speechless.

Chapter 31

Come the day of the Halloween costume party I was nearly miserable.
Gabe, Beth, and I went to Natalie's apartment so that she could do our hair (and Beth's makeup and nails) before Carson's costume party.

Natalie was some kind of beauty expert. Usually I wouldn't know good makeup or hair from bad, but Natalie's work was something else. She was just so clean and precise. Like a true artist. It was no surprise she pursued cosmetology in technical high school and was trying to become a business major to run her own salon.

Lacey said she'd just meet me at the party because she was gonna do her own makeup with organic brands that she carefully researched the ingredients for. I was disappointed, to say the least, that her discomfort using Natalie's miscellaneous hair or heavy duty makeup products postponed the time I'd have with her.

I felt stupid preparing for a costume party without the one person I was actually attending it for. In my ambivalence I tried to reroute my mind from loathing the oncoming event to forgetting it by playing very mentally challenging games on my phone while Natalie spent an hour transforming my boring face into that of a skeleton with a gloppy paintbrush. I didn't complain though, seeing that an hour was nothing compared to the four hours she claimed to have spent transforming herself into an elf warrior before Gabe, Beth, and I arrived at her apartment.

Gabe was Ash Ketchum from Pokémon which wasn't a far stretch from what he already looked like given the beard Beth forced him to shave off. Beth was supposed to be Misty but she made some inept sexism rant about how Misty was an insulting character because she was "basically the male protagonist's sidekick". Instead she chose to be some random slutty pirate, appropriate with her wrist's ugly lighthouse tattoo and her nose, lip, and multiple ear piercings.

Immediately upon seeing Carson open the front door I regretted ever showing up.

Carson was sweaty, shirtless, and smelled like a cross between cheap beer and body spray. He walked around the entire night calling himself a male stripper which was expected because he took any opportunity to take his shirt off and show off both his abs and the massive tattoo of his Greek last name printed across his shoulder blades. The potent jackass fragrance of his cologne suffocated my pores. I couldn't deal with that kid, or anybody else for that matter. To save my sanity I retreated to the outdoor deck abutting the kitchen. Fortunately Natalie and Kenny shared my abhorrence for costume parties and kept me company while party-goers filtered in and out of the house to do one of two things, smoke or throw up over the railing.

It wasn't until Lacey Parker slid open the gliding door and stepped onto the oak deck that I remembered why I agreed to go to this party.

Lacey was dressed as some kind of gothic tiara-wearing princess, in a gown-reminiscent black skirt that dragged on the floor, some black and maroon floral top with long sleeves woven out of a latticework of netting that stretched out to her fingers, and charcoal black makeup running down her cheeks.

"Some kind of princess?" I pointed to the small crystal tiara perched on top of her long brown tresses of slick straight hair.

"Yup," she gleamed. "And you're a skeleton?"

"Sure," I answered ignorantly. "To be honest I just let Natalie go to town with a paintbrush. Do I look wicked scary?"

"Oh yeah," Lacey laughed with an inflection of sarcasm while nodding to the juice pouch in my hand, "The Capri Sun is a nice touch."

"The only thing scary about this drink is that it's a 21st century knock off of a Capri Sun."

"It is not," she dreaded.

"It is," I turned the pouch to face her so that she could read the mediocre brand name, "Say goodbye to your childhood."

Lacey breathed a breath of laughter then seemed to fall into an unintended seriousness only noticeable by the distance in her stare. "Already did."

As the night trailed on I somehow forgot I was at a stupid costume party. I was so happy to be sitting next to Lacey, not touching, of course, but close, that I didn't seem to notice the *Lord of the Rings* couple, Arwen and Aragorn, blowing rings of smoke in each other's hormone-driven mouths.

"Hey, you," the Arwen dressed chick turned to Lacey.

"Me?" Lacey asked, taken by surprise.

"Yeah. Do you have a-"

Before Arwen's doppelganger could finish her question a slobbery glob of gum, having probably been exchanged back and forth between her and Link's tongue, fell out of her mouth and onto Lacey's nearly bare mesh-covered hand.

"Oh my God," the elven princess giggled while covering her mouth, "My bad!"

Lacey spastically flung her arm out and the gum flew off of the back of her hand. Her skin flushed and, like a switch in her head went off, she turned from eloquent and poised to flustered and manic. "Oh, um," Lacey jumped off of the outdoor recliner and scrambled to the deck's steps, "I uh, I'm sorry but I have to- I just remembered I have to call my mom. Let her know where I am."

The girl's laugh faded. "Are you okay?"

"Yeah, I'm fine," Lacey lied. "I just forgot to tell my mom I got here safe."

"Lacey," I leaned forward, about to jump off out of the seat as well.

"I'm fine, Jef," she lied again, then nearly sprinted out the door.

Everybody was quiet.

Awkwardly quiet.

The Aragorn costumed partier looked to me. "Is she okay?"

"She's fine," I was now lying too.

The second her attention diverted back onto her sword wielding boyfriend me and my juice pouch made a break for it.

I snuck outside, where the music was thankfully muffled, and hurried down the patio until I found Lacey, sitting on a small brick wall.

Since both of her hands were assumed "Unforgivably Germy" she clasped them together, almost as a reminder in one joint bundle of rigid fingers. She silently glared down at those hands, violently wringing them together. Angry. Sad. Anxious. A slave to misconstrued stipulations of the mind.

It was weird to see somebody so thoroughly enthralled by completely illogical fears and fallacies. It was hard for me to wrap my brain around the notion that somebody as smart and down-to-earth as Lacey could believe such an absurd and imaginary set of nonsensical rules.

"Lace," I called out while stepping closer, "Don't worry about what happened in there."

"Worry? Why would I worry? I love watching horny people grope each other in front of me."

Of course, between the germy gum and the overly touchy party behavior she must have been beside herself with disgust.

I felt a rugged exhale rumble out of my nostrils, "Lace..."

"I'm fine," she cut me off, continuing to wring her hands together.

"No you're not," I sighed, tossing my juice pouch in the trash and sitting myself alongside her on the brick wall. "This party wasn't as fun as you'd thought it would be, is it?"

She shrugged, "I don't know. I just have a bit of a headache. And I'm having a hard time thinking straight. It's fine, though, it's fine."

"Sensory overload," I determined, and she locked eyes with me. "You've been exposed to a lot of stimuli tonight. Loud music. Boisterous voices. People grazing up against you and," I referred to what I knew was bothering her, "chewed up gum falling on your hand."

Lacey's averted her eyes back to her mesh cloaked hands.

"Sensory overload happens to everybody when they have a busy day, but I think all of the isolation and limited social activity you've been practicing has conditioned your sensitivity threshold to stimuli to be more easily overwhelmed than most. For you, this is a busy day. You can change that though. Just keep practicing going out in public and interacting with other people."

"I don't think I want to," Lacey rejected.

Instantly I went into panic mode. "What? Why?"

"I was looking forward to tonight. To go to a costume party and just hang out, like normal people. And I actually lowered my expectations so that this exact thing wouldn't be happening. But, I don't know, I'm still disappointed, that's all. No matter how much I try to lower my expectations of reality, I'm almost always underwhelmed."

"Well then you aren't lowering your expectations enough," I argued.

"So what do you suggest Jef? Now the solution is expect reality to be a total crap-fest compared to what's in my mind? Oh yeah, that's definitely gonna increase my satisfaction with life."

This conversation had totally derailed from her germ fear onto her overarching fear of reality. And in my frantic passion I lashed out.

"You daydreamed, again didn't you? You daydreamed that this would be a fantastic night where not one germ bothered you and all your dreams came true and-"

"Shut up Jef!" Lacey barked.

"What, now I'm the bad guy?" I retaliated. "You're the one who went off in la la land again! I'm the one trying to reel you back!"

"How dare you!"

"How dare you make me feel like the bad guy when I came out here to see if you were okay!" hurt and embarrassed, I leaped up and stomped down the patio, rounding the corner of Gabe's house until I was in the driveway.

The moment I touched the handle of my car I froze.

Did I really want to leave on this note?

It only took mere seconds for my anger to diffuse and for rationality to sink in.

I turned around to make my way back to Lacey, preparing to find her on the stone wall, but to my surprise right as I turned the corner we bumped into each other.

The second our bodies collided I was overcome by some kind of protective nature that caused me to awkwardly catch her by the shoulders in an effort to keep her from falling.

As soon as I realized what I had done I flung my hands off of her, tripped backwards, and with burning cheeks and nervous neck sweat started to apologize, "Oh God, I'm sorry- I- I'm sorry. I didn't mean to touch you-"

"*I'm* sorry," Lacey cut me off, not seeming to care in the least that we stumbled into physical contact. "I shouldn't have told you to shut up. You weren't saying anything untrue. I did daydream that this would be an amazing night where I had a ton of laughs established all sorts of lifelong friendships, and I was the center of attention. You were right, you were totally right, and it was completely unfair for me to get mad at you for calling me out."

Lacey shook her head out of disgust with herself. I wanted to say something that would alleviate her self-hate, but she was too fast to profess her feelings for me to step in with my thoughts.

"I do this, I always do this! I daydream about something outlandish. Some narrative where I'm famous and in love with all these different dramatic components that make me feel really high and good, but today I daydreamed about something more realistic, I daydreamed about a normal night with friends and I thought that I was lowering my expectations because I was picturing an actual event with an actual person – you, Jef. But having a daydream involving you was anything but lowering my expectations! That was as high of an expectation as anything else! And all day, all damn day, my fame-centered daydreams veered into fantasies about tonight because you kept showing up and I had no damn choice but to daydream about something current. Because you're currently in my life. And that's what's been happening lately! You've infiltrated my daydreams and it's throwing me off and you're throwing me off and it's freaking me out and everything's changing and I don't know what to do!" by the end of that apology, which had sidetracked into a revealing confession, Lacey was completely out of breath.

Holy shit.

It hadn't even slightly occurred to me that *I* was the reason for her high expectations. This was the tallest pedestal I had ever been placed on!

Although Lacey was obviously uncomfortable I couldn't fight the proud feeling that came from knowing I was, in her words, infiltrating her daydreams. If you ask me, that meant she was straying away from fantasies with make-believe protagonist characters and closer to reality... with me.

I couldn't take my eyes off of Lacey.

Her own eyes began to twinkle as she chewed on her lower-lip.

"You're scaring me, Jef," Lacey admitted in a way that made me think she was confronting herself, not me.

The sweltering heat on my neck somehow became hotter.

I watched as my own vulnerability registered in her intuitive mind. In a haste Lacey took a step around me, "I'm sorry," and tried to run away to her car.

"No, wait," I freaked out and sidestepped in front of her, "Please, don't- don't apologize."

I kept stern eye contact on Lacey, trying to translate not only with words but also my physique that I'd much rather she hurt my feelings than compromise her own. Anything to preserve her anomaly of a mind.

"I know but I don't want you thinking that I don't like you as a friend, because I do. I really do. I really like being around you, hanging out with you. But I'm afraid I'll like it a little too much and lose sight of who I am. I'm already having a hard time daydreaming the way that I used to. And I'm struggling to see myself in my daydreams."

In my careful attention to her every word I picked up on the peculiar phrasing she had dropped without second thought. "Wait," I immobilized her mouth, "Did you just say you can't 'see' yourself in your daydreams anymore?"

Lacey's lips quivered and out came a timid, "Yes."

Her casual answer was flooring to me.

"Do- do you usually 'see' yourself in daydreams?"

"What are you talking about? Of course I do." she answered with a candidness that indicated this was usually the case.

Flustered and intrigued, I backpedaled. "Whoa, whoa, whoa, hold up! Let me get this straight. When you daydream about yourself do you actually see yourself from an outside perspective, like a third person point of view?"

Lacey laughed, as if that was the most ludicrous question she had ever been asked. "Of course, doesn't everybody?"

Slowly but ever so powerfully I shook my head, "No, Lacey. No, they don't."

In an instant Lacey's expression transformed from amused to utterly shocked. I swear, every swatch of pigmentation in her skin had completely drained from her fear-stricken face.

"So you're telling me that every daydream, in every imaginable situation, and every emotion those daydreams are drawn from, are all in third person?"

"Yes," she peeped.

"No matter what?" I asked for clarification, still finding it hard to believe. "No matter what emotion? Happy?"

"Yes," Lacey confirmed.

"Stressed?"

"Yes"

"Excited?"

"Yes!"

"*Really* excited?"

"Ye- wait what? *Really* excited? What are you- ohhh..." Lacey suddenly caught on. Her pupils shyly flickered to the asphalt, "Oh, you mean, uh, yeah. Yeah, those are third person too."

"Hm."

I'll admit, the latter question was a little less for intellectual discovery and a little more for my own pleasure, but whatever. I was head over heels into this girl and I just found out I had a role in her precious daydreams. Give me a break.

Quickly I pushed my libido to the side and returned back to the topic of discussion. "That's fascinating!"

"Is it?" she raised her voice out of concern then, after elongating her neck to see past the corner of the house and onto the crowded deck to check if any party-goers had heard her outburst, hissed at me, "Or is it fucking insane?"

"Lace, it's nothing to get upset about."

"I'm insane!" she hissed louder. "I direct and watch my daydreams like they're some kind of soap opera! I incorporate the most important people in my life in them like *me* and *you* like we're just actors performing for my own sick delight! This is so fucked up! Oh my God, I'm so fucked up! You're the one who should be scared, Jef. You should run for the hills."

"Not a chance!" I half-laughed, half-worried.

Though Lacey was freaking out, I was pretty attracted to how impassioned she became from the enlightenment of a newfound discovery. But knowing she was octaves away from having a public meltdown I took on the responsibility to calm her down.

Consciously refraining from reaching out to hold Lacey's hand or patting her on the shoulder I beckoned her to the lawn chairs left in the driveway, in front of Gabe's garage doors.

"Listen," I said as we each sunk into the chairs, "I don't know a lot about daydreams, but I do know a thing or two about the psychological aspects of regular dreams. As much as anybody else, that is. You know, dream theories."

"Yeah?" she prompted, desperately in search of some comfort. I couldn't imagine the shock overpowering Lacey to have just discovered that something so second nature to her, daydreaming, was wildly different than it was for the vast majority of people.

"Sigmund Freud posed a dream theory based on psychoanalysis. He said dreams showed us what drove us, what we wanted, and what limited us. But they did so in a way that crept by our conscious mind and into the unconscious mind. One aspect of the theory that I'll always remember had to do with anxiety. He said that dreams are designed in a symbolic way so that they don't blatantly confront our anxiety, otherwise they'd wake the dreamer, and that all of those symbols are unconscious desires and fears to keep our anxiety at bay. Maybe daydreams are designed with a similar frame of mind, to protect you from being overwhelmed by anxiety. That key parts of your daydreams, like me, are there because they keep your anxiety at bay. So maybe it's a good thing that we hang out a lot in real life."

A flicker of energy dilated Lacey's pupils and a smile spawned upon her face.

Chapter 32

The "Obsessive Compulsive Disorder & Lacey Parker" binder was still on my desk.

I stared at it with ambivalence.

This was it. I had to stop writing down observations about Lacey. I had to stop treating her like a case study. I couldn't go on doing this if I wanted to get closer to her.

But alas, every time I reached out to discard the binder into the trash bin I fell back in my chair.

I stared at the mound of paper stuffed inside the binder.

It was so dense. There was so much information in there.

Everything that I knew about Lacey Parker was recorded in that binder. Did I really want to get rid of it?

But how could I ever defend studying a human being, scribbling down quotes and observations about her, and collect it in a binder without her knowledge? Especially a human being that I was hopelessly infatuated by.

The abrupt banging on my wooden bedroom door brought my dilemma to a halt.

I yanked mercilessly on the door knob and impatiently barked, "What!"

Peter's eyes were bugging out like he had just seen a ghost.

Oh shit, it wasn't a full moon, was it?

Quickly I wiped down my face, as if to erase the scowl I was wearing, then put on an amicable façade and readjusted my tone to be more chipper. "What is it, Pete?"

"Jef…"

I didn't like the worry behind his usually jolly voice. "Yeah?"

Overcome by shame, he lowered his stare to his feet and pouted a childish pout.

"What is it, Peter?"

In his overwhelming shame he scrounged up the courage to flash a brief glance away from his feet and uttered, "I lost the money."

"What are you talking about, Pete?" I was so caught up thinking about Lacey I couldn't place what money he was talking about at first.

After a few seconds it hit me.

He was talking about the money my over-nurturing mom lent him. The money that he owed my father from their stupid hockey bet.

"Whoa, whoa, whoa, wait, you did *what*?"

"I lost the-"

"I heard you!" I snapped at him, sending him mixed signals in my amplifying distress.

Of course today was the day that Dad was coming over to visit.

Dad, for the first time in a while, actually called ahead of time to let us know he would be visiting today. And he was probably only coming to collect the money. There was no way in hell he was going to give Peter a break if he didn't get paid.

Peter babbled, "I'm so so so sorry, Jef. I could have sworn I put it in the new wallet Mum gave me for my birthday, but I can't find it!"

"Okay, okay," I tried to cool myself down by pacing back and forth in my room.

Back and forth, back and forth.

How do I help Peter without enabling him to be dependent? How do I keep him out of trouble?

Back and forth, back and forth, I faced that internal struggle.

"Fine!" I eventually burst out, took a wad of six $50 bills out of the drawer where I put money that I had been saving up, and returned to the hallway where I gave it to Peter.

There goes my Frisbee golf net.

Before letting go of the grimy bills I ordered Peter, "You aren't going anywhere out of my sight until I see you hand this to Dad."

"Okay, yes Jef," he obeyed.

Ugh, I hated treating him like this, like a child I had to keep my eye on.

It pained me to do this. But it's what I had to do to protect him from the wrath of my greedy father.

It was moments like this that I felt empathy towards Mom's overprotective treatment towards my special needs brother.

I waited downstairs, in the den, with Peter until my dad showed up.

"You got my money, boy?" was the first thing out of that asshole's tobacco stained mouth.

"Yes Daddy," Peter handed over the wad of cash.
I glared at the scene from the den, resting my mouth covering arm on the armchair.

My dad stood gnawing on his toothpick, reviewing the stack of money to make sure he got his full pay.

"Can I show you my new model airplane Daddy?"

"Eh," Dad threw himself on the sofa, making it obvious he didn't feel like moving, "Only if you bring 'er in here."

"Okay!"

Peter speedily hobbled off to fetch the antique plane Lacey had bought him, leaving me alone with my scum of a father.

My hands turned into claws, digging into the leather armchair.

Stay calm, Jef.

My nails dug deeper. Fuck, Mom was gonna be livid if I ruined this chair with fingernail stab wounds.

My dad lifted up his legs and rested his muddy work boots on my mom's favorite coffee table that was decorated with shells and sea glass, which we had collected from York beach, underneath a sheet of glass.

I *thought* I'd be able to keep my cool.

I thought wrong.

"Are you proud of yourself?" my tone sliced through the thick air.

Dad glanced up from his wad of cash and took the toothpick out of his mouth, "What's that?"

"You heard me."

He just shook his head and let his shoulders bob up in denial.

"Are you proud of taking $300 from your son?"

He rolled his eyes at me, as if I was unreasonably upset. "We were gambling, Jef. I was just bonding with the boy. It's not my fault the boy made a stupid bet. Believe me, I'd love to give him the money back, but what kind of a lesson would that teach him?"

Infuriated didn't begin to cover how I felt after hearing that load of garbage. "Oh so is that why you visit? To teach us lessons?"

He shoved the money in his wallet and made a weak defense, "I visit because I wanna support my boys! You know that!"

Immediately I thought of Lacey's parents. How supportive they were of her. How they were always there for her, no matter what.

Before I could get any angrier I dismissed my father. "Maybe you should go home, or back to whatever cheap motel you're staying at tonight," I suggested. "In fact you probably shouldn't visit again."

"Jef." Dad actually lifted his dirty boots off of the coffee table, stamped them on the wooden floorboards, and hunched over so that his dungaree coated elbows were perched on his knees. "I'm trying to do you a favor."

"A favor?" I spit out, almost laughing but too angry to actually do so. "Since when was visiting your own son a favor?"

I could see Dad was disoriented. I probably should have shut up there but I was already going off and I found that I couldn't stop myself. "And I say 'son', not 'sons', on purpose. You haven't been all that blunt about your feelings towards him!"

"Who?"

"Peter, you cuck! It would take an idiot not to see how much you hate your retard of a son!"

Crash!
I shot my pupils to the clamor to see none other than Peter at the entryway of the room, empty handed.
Fragments of his model airplane were scattered across the floor.

Chapter 33

I had already told Lacey all about Peter dropping and breaking the model airplane she bought him and she insisted on coming over the next day to help fix it, while Peter was at work with my mom.

And behold, Friday afternoon came, and here I was in the shed, rebuilding the antique plane with Lacey.

"It's not your fault," Lacey tried to comfort me after I told her how I pointed out my dad's hatred for Peter and how I called Peter a retard. Out of embarrassment I opted not to tell her that that outburst unraveled from my cruddy excuse for a father gambling with him.

"I guess," I sighed, trying to lose myself along with my blank stare catatonically fixed onto the crinkled airplane model building instructions.

The disgust in my outburst was still so fresh. It kept playing in my head, over and over. Calling my dad a dirt bag. Pointing out how his disdain for his retarded son. The stomach-churning clamor of Peter dropping the airplane model onto the floor.

Those intrusive thoughts were stuck on repeat and I couldn't, for the life of me, shut them off. Is this how Lacey felt all the time about anything and everything that caused her distress?

It wasn't until a self-loathing hour later that I was able to divert my attention onto something new. Something exciting.

Physics.

I had just finished gluing together the formerly segmented horizontal stabilizer of the model plane. Its angled design had the science-junkie segment of my brain mesmerized.

I squinted to the space in the upper right corner of the room and visualized plausible numbers that would give the horizontal stabilizer the best lift to drag ratio, something I often did out of boredom when examining the different curved surfaces of my Frisbees.

"There's the smile that's been missing!" Lacey giddily observed.

Her random comment snapped me out of my physics daydreaming. "What? Huh?"

"I think that's the first time you've smiled since I got here. Not to sound too fairytale-ish but you've got a twinkle in your eye."

Suddenly my face heated up and I didn't know what to say.

"Lemme guess, you're thinking about Frisbees?"

"Wha- how did you," I nervously laughed from the close accuracy of her guess and from slight embarrassment about whatever goofy smile I must have been wearing.

In my bashfulness I tried to play cool, "I was just thinking about air pressure and airfoils. Nothing special."

"Seems awfully special to you," she laughed and raised both eyebrows in what must have been a failed attempt to raise one out of curiosity.

There was that same smile she had when I first rambled about physics to her, in the library. That smile of being happy because I was happy regardless of the fact that she didn't fully understand the content of my happiness. That smile that encouraged me to continue rambling.

"Sometimes I get bored and look at the different designs of Frisbee discs and try to understand the physics behind its curves and details or the effects of how you throw it. Like when you give the disc angular momentum by spinning it! That's called gyroscopic inertia, which gives the disc stability during the lift and trajectory that follows. That's why it's better to spin it faster. It causes more stability."

Lacey's wide baby doll eyes smiled at me, gaping like I had just spoken a different language. She shook her head in genuine wonderment, "You're way too smart for your own good."

Funny, I thought the same about her.

"Hey!" she interrupted herself, suddenly remembering something, "how's the fund for the Frisbee golf net going?"

Suddenly I remembered the afternoon's initial despair.

Dad. Stupid Dad and his gambling with Peter.

"Oh, uh, that's probably not gonna be happening any time soon. Maybe in the spring."

"What? Why? What happened?" Lacey asked and anxiously started screwing and unscrewing the nozzle of the glue bottle.

"Errr," I cringed, struggling to come out with the truth, "It, uh, it turns out my dad was gambling with Peter and Peter owed him $300, which my mom gave him and then Peter lost. I had to give him the money I had been saving up to keep him out of any more trouble with my mom."

Lacey dropped the bottle of glue onto the table and went silent. Probably from disbelief.

There was a hiatus in the conversation for a solid minute while Lacey kept a stagnant stare at eye-level, on her hand which was in a pinching position as if she were imitating a crab's claw. Slowly and silently she watched the ebb and flow of viscous glue stretch between her finger and thumb.

I didn't mean to make her feel bad with that information. I hated to see her so upset. Her posture became exponentially more stiff in that homemade cherry wood chair, like when she was in OCD mode at the library before I went on a physics rant.

Suddenly I had an idea.

"Hey, do you wanna have a little physics lesson?"

Lacey's stare broke and her brown eyes transfixed themselves onto me. They were smiling again.

"Will you be the teacher?" she asked.

"Of course."

"Then absolutely!"

With an inviting wave of the hand I walked Lacey over to the rickety shelf on the other side of the shed, "Come on," then pulled a heavy box of Frisbees off of the top shelf with an unintentional grunt, and dropped it to the floor.

On the very top of the Frisbee pile was my favorite disc painted like the Australian flag. Immediately I picked it up, "This was my favorite when I was a kid," I said excitedly. "I remember it was the first time in my entire life that my mom went on a company outing trip and it was in Brisbane, Australia. I was, like, nine years old and Mom was a nervous wreck about leaving Peter and I under the care of my Uncle Wilfred. My Uncle forced her to go though, since it was a once-in-a-lifetime chance to go to an all-expenses paid trip to Australia. And she brought this back for me."

"Aw," Lacey swooned, "And it's your favorite Frisbee because your mom gave it to you?"

"Psh. You *would* think there was some sentimental meaning behind it, English major," I teased. "Believe it or not I just liked it because it had the best airfoil."

"What is that?"

"You see, the curved rims on a Frisbee act a lot like the curved design of an airplane's horizontal stabilizer," I nodded to the table of model airplane parts, then returned my attention to the Australian decaled Frisbee, "And when you have a curve like this one the air that flows over the Frisbee speeds up and the pressure drops, creating a better lift. That ratio of lift to drag is brought on by the favorable curve, otherwise known as an airfoil. Now this ties into all sorts of other physics laws and principles. Like the Bernoulli Principle." I led Lacey outside of the shed, into the front yard, we threw Frisbees while I explained aero dynamics until nightfall.

Lacey released a sigh, "I wish I could remember this kind of stuff like you do. You know, smart stuff. Not stupid stuff like taboo words or scary numbers or other OCD triggers that I usually can't get out of my head. Important stuff. Stuff that they taught us in high school."

"You remember important stuff," I reminded her, "Like all that literary terminology. Irony? Symbolism?"

"That's true," Lacey smirked, only to create a rare dimple in her right cheek that quickly leveled out with a dispute, "But I only remembered that because it was important to me. I felt like I could relate to it. I never remembered anything that didn't directly strike a chord in me. That's probably why I never remembered anything in Geometry or Statistics or any subject, for that matter. It made school so hard."

"Even English class?"

"Oh, definitely. I never remembered important details in the stories we read. Always struggled on those post-reading quizzes. I was great at vocab tests, though. Loved vocab. That's probably because it was important to me. In increasing my vocabulary I knew I was strengthening my writing. And I paid attention to how literary devices were used, like irony, because that strengthened my writing as well. *My* writing. When it came to other people's writing, you know, actually reading books and retaining information, I struggled big time. Four years of high school English, and I couldn't tell you how irony was incorporated in plays like *Hamlet* or classics like *One Flew Over the Cuckoo's Nest*."

"Hm," was the only sound that came out of my mouth.

I found it extremely interesting that Lacey, a self-professed narcissist, was so self-absorbed that she couldn't even retain outside information if it didn't feel like it resonated with something already in her mind, heart, or soul.

"It wasn't just reading though. I found school work in general too hard."

I tried to give Lacey the benefit of the doubt and chalked up her struggles with school to a more common scapegoat, "That sounds like a learning disability."

"No but it wasn't always like that. I used to be really good at school work. It wasn't until, well, come to think of it it wasn't until puberty that I started having a really hard time reading and understanding what I was reading."

Of course. The exact same time that her anxiety and OCD transpired. Coincidence? Doubtful.

It was like her brain couldn't retain new information because it was so stuffed with the same irrational thoughts and lies playing on repeat. Like anxiety built a barrier around her brain to keep her as knowledge deprived as possible. The very thought inflicted pain in my chest.

It made me wonder, did other kids who needed special help in school, the "intellectually disabled" kids I'd so often pity, just have a mental ailment occupying their brain and no legitimate learning disability?

I just shook my head in distress, utterly devastated on Lacey's behalf.

"Sadly, I've gotta go," Lacey resentfully dismissed herself, "I have a routine muffin I like to eat at 5:30 with coffee and I still gotta get home and shower so that'll add on another forty-five minutes…"

"Oh, yeah. Of course, I don't wanna force you to stick around." I was a little bummed she couldn't stay longer, but I knew better than to try and break her from a ritual.

I strolled with her across the front lawn and onto the driveway.

"Believe me, I'd love to stick around," she claimed apologetically while opening the door of her car, "But I get super anxious when I break my routine. Sometimes anxiety overrides love."

A lump formed in my throat in reaction to that declaration.

"See you on Tuesday," she said and plopped herself, "We'll be talking about juxtaposition."

"Oh, yay," I joked and forced a laugh. Lacey leaving put me out of the laughing mood. "See ya."

Lacey shut the door then unexpectedly rolled down her window, wearing an alluring smile across her face that begged to be addressed.

"Did you forget something?" I asked as I craned my neck to meet her at eye level.

"No. I was just remembering what you said about that Australian Frisbee, how there was no sentimental reason behind it being your favorite."

"Yeah?"

"Well, I was thinking… you loved that Frisbee because of the scientific aspects of it. The airfoil created by its unique curve, how under the Bernoulli Principle the difference in pressure causes the Frisbee to rise or lift. It's all physics. And you have a deep passion for physics. And, well, passion is one of the most sentimental entities this world has to offer."

Before I could make a comment Lacey grabbed the gear stick of the car and yanked it into reverse. "See you later."

"Yeah, see ya," I reacted in a dumbstruck stupor brought on by the whimsical charm of her thought process. And Lacey actually remembered all that information I had just spewed out. Airfoils. Air pressure. The Bernoulli Principle. Aero dynamics.

But Lacey didn't remember information that wasn't important to her.

So, by logic of deductive reasoning, all that physics Frisbee information must have resonated with her on some level.

The information that was important *to me*...

...was important *to her*.

I had a hard time erasing the smile from my face for the remainder of the night.

Chapter 34

The rain was heavy as it came thundering down, pounding the campus's parking lot pavement like bullets.

It would have been nice to have an umbrella as I speed walked through the parking lot.

Why was I out in the rain? I was worried about Lacey.

Gabe had let me know when we crossed paths in the academic building that Lacey was sitting in her car, in the parking lot, before, after, and during his three hour long Monday class. I wanted to believe she didn't come out because the weather was so bad, but I knew something more deeply rooted was bothering her.

When I finally spotted her silver car through the sideways pellets of rain I charged towards it.

The water kicked up, soaking the lower half of my sweatpants, until I stopped beside the Volvo.

Hectically I knocked on the car window, "Hey?"

Lacey, instead of rolling down the window to respond, leaned over the driver's console, unlatched the passenger door, and gave it a push ajar.
I took the signal and hurried to the passenger side of the car then slid my soaked butt into the seat.

Lacey in her usual makeup stared down at the brakes by her feet. Leopard printed rubber rain-boots. She was prepared to go to trek through the rain and go to class, so why hadn't she?

"Hey, what's wrong? Gabe said he saw you in your car for, like, three consecutive hours. What's going on, Lace?"

Lacey wouldn't divert her stare from the brake pedal. "I don't want to complain to you."

"It's okay. I don't mind."

"No, I always bitch and whine and-"

"Lace," my pitch plummeted, "I'm giving you permission."

She lifted her head up, "I guess I was just too depressed to get out of the car. I got myself to drive all the way here, found a good parking spot, but I just couldn't seem to get out of the car. To walk in that building. I couldn't do it. It had very little to do with germs or socializing or… anything! I just couldn't for the life of me budge."

I knew well enough about how depression operated to know that this was definitely a case of depression. "You're in a rut, aren't you?"

Lacey was off venting. "I don't know. The weather's getting colder. It's dark out earlier. School is getting harder. Everything, everything seems harder. I- I-" suddenly she cut herself short and burst out a seemingly random complaint, "What's the point of school, anyways? I can write, can't I? I'll just live at home and write."

I shook my head, letting her know I was not an advocate for that idea, "You know isolating at home only worsens the depression."

"Ugh, so what," she slammed her head against the headrest of the seat so hard that the whole car shook.

How the heck was there so much strength in such a little body?

"I wanna quit school so badly. I don't belong here."

"No, come on," I tried to reason with her. "You can't do that Lace. That's compromising. You'd be compromising your life, again, for OCD. Just like you compromised your social life in high school. Just like those vacations you had to come home early from. Just like having to go to community college, instead of living away at school. You can't do that to yourself. Not again."

I think she knew I was right, but she still didn't want to listen to me. I could understand that. Sometimes when you're in a funk you don't wanna hear encouragement, you just want an ear to listen to you as you mope.

"Come on," I tried to persuade her to get out of the car and just get out in public for a little bit, "Let's go in the library."

"I'm not going Jef," she stubbornly crossed her arms. "I'm sorry but I just need to go home."

"Lacey," I lowered my voice in a stop-being-ridiculous tone.

"I appreciate you caring, Jef, I really do, but this is a lost cause. I'm a lost cause."

Unwilling to listen to her talk about herself in that degrading manner, I retaliated with an unfiltered response, "If you go home what's gonna stop you from missing your next class? Then the next? Then pretty soon you're dropping out of school altogether. And you know your OCD is way too debilitating for you to maintain a job! You're missing out on life Lacey! Just think, there is an entire world of opportunities-"

"No!" she cut me off, "You can't give me that speech!"

I was a bit flustered, "Huh? What- why, what speech?"

"That speech, that speech you're supposed to give any depressed person. 'There's a whole world out there waiting for you', it doesn't work on me, because for me there is no world full of opportunities, there's a world full of danger and germs and there is nowhere in this world that I can go without danger and germs. It's hopeless. This is so much more than depression. This OCD is stronger. You know what, why don't you just leave, Jef? Do yourself a favor. Just go. You don't want to listen to me sulk."

"No. I'm not going anywhere. I'm not leaving you alone, to drive home in the pouring rain, feeling miserable."

Lacey shook her head manically, "You shouldn't have to listen to this, listen to me. You don't deserve this."

"Neither do you!" I leaned forward, physically lowering myself to her level in an attempt to get her to look me in the eyes. I wanted desperately to get through to her.

She lowered her head, almost as if making a vow, and slowly enunciated the response, "Yes, I do."

"No you-"

"You heard about what a bitch I was when I forced my mom to go out and buy dishwashing soap! You saw the monster I became after my sister touched my mp3 player! I'm torturing everybody that I love! Please, Jef, run while you can!"

Lacey sounded like she was a martyr in a movie, but I knew her dramatic stigma was completely valid.

"Lacey all of that isn't you, I promise. That's not who you are. That's your mind tricking you into acting that way!"

"No," she shook her head rapidly again, "I know my mind isn't tricking me about this, Jef. I make everybody miserable, so I deserve to be miserable-"

"Your mind lies to you!" I yelled over her.

Lacey paused.

Something about that remark resonated with her.

Lacey's huge and deeply bloodshot eyes shifted, abruptly fixing themselves onto me. "What do you mean my mind lies to me?"

"I mean," on the spot I tried to piece together what I wanted to say, "Your mind has you convinced of wildly false and spurious information. It makes you do things to make you feel like you're protecting yourself, but you aren't. If anything you're hurting yourself. There has to be some shred of sanity in you that can see how this diseased mind of yours is tricking you."

Her innocent voice became so meek, "Why would my mind do that to me?" It was almost as if I had just accused her best friend of betraying her.

I felt pain in my chest hearing the vulnerability emanating from Lacey's fragile tone. My shoulders fell with defeat as the best answer I could come up with came out, "Because it's sick."

And in that instant, Lacey was an emotional wreck.

I watched as the mascara dense tears spewed from her tear ducts, painting all the skin in its path black.

She actually touched her face, throwing her head in her hands. "I'm so tired," her statement was plagued with defeat.

"I know," I somberly whispered, watching her body tremble with each whimpering breath.

"I'm depleting. I don't have the energy to do this anymore. This illness is draining my spirit out of me. I'm so tired of feeling every little germ on me. I'm tired of the voices in my head screaming at me, 'Soap and water! Soap and water! Soap and water!' I'm tired of being scared of simple things like walking in a room with my left foot first for fear of some random irrational consequence."

"Have you considered medicine, Lacey?"

"No!" she immediately overruled my suggestion. "I can't take medicine. It will change who I am."

"I don't think that's how it works," I said. I wasn't sure though. I hadn't yet researched OCD medication. "You might get some relief-"

"I'm fine, I'm fine," Lacey's words contradicted her eyes which were getting redder and redder.

"You're not though. Look at you, Lace. You only get one life, and yours is so damn difficult for no reason whatsoever."

"It's not for no reason! Why would you even say that to me?" Lacey grimaced at me with the most potent of detest furrowing her brow.

"Because," I urged, "I don't know how else to get through to you that you don't deserve this, this, this *beast* of a disorder."

"Yes I do."

"No you don't!"

Lacey kept saying "yes I do" while I tried to cut her off with a barrage of "no you don't". I couldn't keep up to pace with her hysteria though.

"There has to be a reason!" she cried out over me, the excruciating pain so prevalent that I was unwillingly rendered to silence.

No longer having to compete with my snarky voice, hers lowered as if she were confiding a secret in me rather than laying down an argument. "There *has* to be a reason for the OCD, Jef. Don't you get it? I have to believe that. Otherwise I- I- I, I'll die of a broken heart."

I felt my jaw clench. How could I argue that?

"I'm sorry," Lacey sniffled while wiping her burning eyes, "I probably look like a train wreck."

I soaked in the view of her, black trails down her face like mascara scars of sadness. "If it makes you feel any better you could easily pass for a really theatrical metal singer."

That made her laugh a smidge as she pumped her fist inward in a "yes!" motion. For a moment her eyes lit up with life. My heart became warm knowing I sparked that.

But quickly Lacey remembered why she was so upset.

"What's it like, Jef?" she begged. "What's it like to touch something and not feel afraid?" The sound of her imploring voice yanked at my soul. I swear I could feel her desperation.

Why? Why did she have to have this sickness?

"It feels like," I became stressed in my struggle to find a proper description of how it felt like to do something as basic as touch something. Touch anything that I wanted and not be scared, "To be honest, it doesn't feel like anything. I touch what I want to touch. I don't think twice about it. It doesn't feel like there's anything else to it. It doesn't feel like there's anything to be afraid of. It's just… freedom."

Lacey gazed into me with sad pupils. The veins in her eyes were a striking ruby hue. Before she could say anything her sorrow overtook her, and she descended back into sobbing, now covering her face with her hands.

All I could do was use my voice to try and console her, for the touch of my skin would make her anxious. "Lace…"

She shook her head from behind those hands, rejecting whatever comfort I could offer her, and continued sobbing.

I couldn't take it anymore.

I wasn't going to sit back and do nothing for the girl I loved. Not again.

I sat up straight and leaned closer to the driver's seat. "Let me hug you," I demanded.

Lacey's head flicked up, her stare breaking off of her palms and fixing on me. There was confusion and shock in her brown eyes. "What? No, Jef. I can't…"

"Yes. Yes you can." Before she could say no I grabbed her cold, tear stained hand.

A shiver made Lacey jolt a little, but she didn't pull away. Lacey stayed still, drilling her eyes on me. Her pupils were shivering. She was so afraid, like she had just broken a highly punishable law.

"It's not dangerous," I strained to get through to her, scrounging up every ounce of confidence in my being to sound convincing. "I promise."

We were both as still as could be. Stares delving in each other's. It was just us.

Me.

And her.

And suddenly...

Lacey's chest convulsed, a loud cry shot out, and she lunged at me, over the driver's console between us.

As her body collided onto mine she nearly knocked the wind out of me. At once she threw her desperate arms around me and surrendered to weeping.

I received her in my unwavering grasp as quick as I could.

My arms clung to her with equal desperation.

I longed so intensely to take away her pain.

Lacey and I sat in the car, embracing each other like we were each other's only hope. I held her tightly, never wanting to let her out of my touch.

Oh, the cruel irony. From my perspective, touching her was the safest place for her to be. From Lacey's perspective, touching me was the most dangerous place.

Part II

Chapter 35

"I have something to show you," Lacey led me to the shed in my backyard. She had been bugging me at school about how she needed to come over my house this afternoon, which was a nice change from me bugging her to hang out. But finals were around the corner and I really needed to buckle down and study.

"Lace," I lowered my voice, "I told you, I really have to study for my physics exam."

"You can study after," she insisted, verbally pushing me onward to make up for the fact that she was too scared to physically push me.

I stopped in front of the door, "What could you have possibly-"

"Don't guess!" Lacey ordered. "Just go in!"

With a push on the rusty handle an earsplitting screech of the shed's creaky door ripped through the evening air.

It was dark, so I reached my fortunately long arm up and tugged on the light bulb chain.

With a click the little shed illuminated.

Shining there, in the center of the shed, was a Frisbee golf net. It was identical to the one from the picture I showed Lacey, around a month ago, at the coffee shop.

"No. Fucking. Way," I was in pure shock.

Lacey had a smile that was beaming even brighter than the silver chains of the Frisbee golf's metal net. "Do you like it?"

"Are you kidding?" I found my voice. "It's exactly what I wanted!"

Lacey clapped her hands perkily, "Yay!"

As amazing as the Frisbee golf target was, I was more amazed by Lacey. My original gawking at the net transferred down to her.

She was busy staring at the net, holding her clasped hands to her chest, like it made her day to make my day.

"I can't believe you did this," I choked out.

Her eyes, a darker brown than usual in this poorly lighted shed, raised to look at me, "Well I knew how much you wanted it."

"Still though," my surprise remained fresh, "You really didn't have to do this."

"Well it isn't right. You work so hard in school then go straight to working behind a counter until nightfall. It's not fair that you didn't get the *one* thing you wanted."

This wasn't anywhere near what I wanted in comparison to how much I wanted her.

Lacey remained oblivious to my feelings and spoke on, "It's just not fair that you had to pay your dad."

"It's not fair that you have OCD," I accidentally spit out. She tilted her head and looked to the floor, "No," she timidly sighed in agreement then quickly bounced back with a positive attitude, "But it's okay. I'm okay. There's worse things."

I stared into her.

How? How did she do it? Any of it. How could she maintain a pleasant mood and have a sense of humor and be so generous and caring while being constantly bullied by a terrible mental disorder?

I was in awe of Lacey. Utter, unprecedented, unconditional awe.

The strength drained from my knee caps. My hands throbbed. Each finger coiled and cramped.

It was hurting me not to be able to touch her at all.

The longer she stared at me, the quicker that intuition kicked in and caused her joyous smile to dissipate. "What's wrong?"

My lips split apart, but nothing came out.

"Jef? Are you okay?"

My throat was tight with stress and longing. I didn't know how much longer I could endure holding in the strong urges to touch Lacey. Those urges were only getting stronger and harder to harbor. Anticipating that I was at my breaking point I was compelled more than ever to be honest with her.

I prepared for the worst reaction from Lacey.

With a weak gulp I admitted, "I want to be able to touch you."

I couldn't believe I just said that out loud. My burning face must have been lobster-red.

Lacey stared at me with fear, but also a tinge of enthrallment. "Why would you want to do that?"

"Because you're here, in front of me, right in front of me. But it feels like you're so, so distant. Like you're a world away. And I, I don't know Lacey, I just can't stand it anymore."

"I'm right here, Jef," she didn't sound like she believed the whisper of her own words.

I wanted her words to allow my mind to rest, for mental equanimity, I really did, but between her illness and my feelings I couldn't quiet the urges that made my bones ache. I had to let it out. I had to say something. And before I knew it, my mouth was blabbing, "It's not just now, Lacey. It's everywhere I go with you. I feel your emotions, sometimes I understand your thoughts, and physically I see you next to me but it's like there's this disconnect, like you're not really living in the same dimension as me, and I swear if I could just touch you it would verify that you really are living here. In the real world."

Lacey seemed frozen in an unreadable state.

What was going on inside her mind? What was she thinking? What was she feeling?

I could only hear the nervous rhythm of my breathing.

Lacey finally responded, eyelashes falling as she looked to the ground, "Everything in the real world scares me."

That irrational statement eased me into more comfortable territory where I could be the voice of reason to her unreasonable beliefs.

"But at least everything in the real world can be touched."

"What's so great about that?" Lacey retaliated. Her transition into eye contact was desperate. She genuinely sounded like she wanted an answer, like she truly had no idea what the appeal of a touch was.

"Because," I scoured my brain for some kind of answer that would convert her out of her imaginary solace and into reality, where I resided, "When you touch something, when you feel something, really *feel* something in your grasp, you're reminded that you're alive."

Her shy pupils fell to the floor. "I don't know if I want to be reminded."

"Why?" sincere bewilderment put stress on my vibrato.

"Maybe life scares me."

"Why is life so scary?"

"I don't know. Maybe because there are expectations and disappointments and failures…"

"… and human connections, and emotions."

"Consequences," she challenged.

"Rewards," I fought back.

"Rejections."

"Opportunities."

"Imperfections."

"You."

"*Me!*" she spit out.

As soon as she spoke she realized what she said and started to piece it together out loud. "Life includes me…"

Having heard herself say this she reverted to her defense mechanism of crossing arms, trying to shrink in this new world she was finally discovering at the ripe age of 21 years old.

I could see her discomfort and I tried to provide alleviation using the subject matter she obsessively sought out. "Daydreams are great, but they're not real. What's real is you. And me." I stiffened my usually floppy hand and gestured towards her and me "this is real."

"I don't know about that." She tensed up and stared to the ground, still folding her arms, while refusing to accept reality. Refusing to accept me.

I was more determined than ever to get through to her. "You can't touch a daydream Lacey! You can touch a real human being."

Silence.

Sixty seconds of silence.

"I don't know if I can," she finally confessed with a delicate tremble.

Right then, without intentionally meaning to, I addressed the root of her problem. A lack of faith in her own ability to embrace another living person.

Her big brown eyes were begging me to do something. But what? I don't think she knew either. But something about her longing stare gave the impression that this delicate young woman was crying for a savior. And although the mere thought of being some kind of knight in shining armor was laughable, I wore the metaphorical silver plates with pride and assumed the role that she needed me to take on.

I didn't think. I just acted.

Mindlessly I rolled up my sweatshirt sleeves above the points of my elbows, then proceeded to hold out lonely hands, facing upwards.

We stood there in the intimate silence.

My breath.

And hers.

Caught in each other's gripping stare.

And I didn't feel awkward.

I didn't bail.

I stood my ground.

And that confidence provoked Lacey to join.

Lacey lifted both hands. Her fingers, slightly curled, anticipatory and ravenous for contact, were quivering as they hovered over my open palms.

Out of seemingly nowhere a bundle of nerves shook me to the core. I was overcome by anticipation too. I didn't realize it, but I had been waiting to feel her touch since I retrieved that Frisbee, next to her.

Lacey lowered her trembling forearms, matching her left hand on my right hand and her right hand on my left hand.

Gently the very tips of her fingers tickled the surface of my palms.
Immediately a cold struck my hands. It was like Lacey really was a ghost, having finally found a way to contact the living. I couldn't tell if the chill that her touch emitted was legitimate low temperature or the power of my nerves.

She was fixated down on our hands. I could feel that she was still nervous. Like she was touching another human's flesh for the first time in a life time.

"It's okay," came the crack of my voice.

Lacey's brown eyes flashed up at mine, absorbed my encouragement, and then lowered back to her hands. After a deep, shaky breath, she carefully proceeded to trail her fingers along my wrists and up my forearms. I could feel her anxiety bleed out her fingertips and leave tracks on my skin while she delicately traced the paths of my adrenalized veins.

Having come right below each of my elbows, Lacey paused, wrapping my arms between her fingers and thumbs. Slowly she rubbed my now goosebumpy flesh, then flickered her stare back in line with mine.

The only sound was the miscellaneous creak of the shed.

"What are you thinking?" I asked in a hush tone.

"Not thinking," she whispered back, "Just feeling."

I don't know what came over me, but suddenly I was compelled to let this gentle girl feel more.

Before I could stop myself I backed up. Her arms fell from mine. I slid off my unzipped sweatshirt, tossed it on a lawn chair, and then pulled my t-shirt over my head.

Lacey didn't say a word.

Shirtless, I stood in front of her, exposing my scrawny upper half under a single fluorescent lightbulb.

Lacey's neck muscle tensed. She remained silent.

Carefully, ever so carefully, she rested her now less cold hands on top of my pounding heart.

A rush of energized anxiety ran its course, rendering me dizzy.

I didn't say anything. I decided to seal my mouth shut and let her explore the sensation of human flesh in the most innocent way.

Her touch lowered, gliding over each rib. I felt like slick clay that she was gently smoothing over.

The caress of her hands came to an abrupt stop when they arrived at the scar below ribcage.

"Stitches," I clarified, the distinct sound of my own voice acting as a humble reminder that this moment was really happening.

She cocked her head to the side, like a confused puppy with saucers for eyes.

I went on with the explanation, "During a summer at the beach I tripped on a rock and went flying onto a shard of what I thought was sea glass, but turned out was just broken glass."

Lacey's expression glowed with amusement, "You were even clumsy back then?"

My head fell forward with an embarrassed laugh, "Not much has changed."

We both laughed.

Lacey's laugh faded faster than usual though.

The pads of her hands dropped from my body, and I was washed over by a wave of despair.

One look in Lacey's emotive eyes and I could tell she didn't want to stop feeling my skin either. Her pupils shivered from my eyes back to my sternum. If my intuition was correct, I swear she wanted to fall into a hug.

My throat was scratchy as I talked to the person I had come to know so well, "Go ahead."

I didn't need to be specific. Lacey knew what I was thinking.

In all her gentleness she rested both hands as if they were a pillow atop my chest.

She leaned in. At about a foot shorter than me she placed her right cheek along my chest.

The most pure of highs made me feel light on my feet.

I couldn't believe how close Lacey Parker was to me. That fascinating brain of hers was up against my beating heart. And the small frame of her body that I had so often searched for in the school crowds was right here.

Everything felt so right in that moment. So serene. So natural. So sincere.

Finally I felt like I could give myself permission to enjoy Lacey Parker's presence.

As to protect her and all of her vulnerability I wrapped my arms around her so that my hands met at her upper back. In the slightest of motions my fingertips bent to feel the texture of the long hair falling down her back. Having been overcome with humility I treasured the subtle curl of my hands against her hair.

At first I thought that my craving to hug Lacey was to say thank you for the gift she bought me, but as soon as my arms enclosed around her I realized what I really wanted was to protect her like the real gift she was.

Lacey and I remained embracing in silence.

All I could hear was the steady inhale and exhale of my breath meshing with hers.

Chapter 36

Moments like the hug Lacey and I shared in her car and in my shed were very rare. Just because she broke through her OCD those times didn't, by any means, make it any more likely she'd break through and touch me again.

After our hug inside her car she drove home and showered. After our hug inside my shed she drove home and showered. To actually get her to hug somebody and then hang around afterwards or prolong the time between contact and washing was no less a struggle. So I made that my next goal in my endeavor to fix her.

I had successfully gotten Lacey to socialize outside of her house for extended periods of time. I had successfully gotten her to make physical contact with another person (to my pleasure, that person was me). The next step was to get her to do those things simultaneously without any instant fleeing or washing compulsions.

"Our next reader will be..." the English professor adjusted her rectangle framed glasses higher on the bridge of her nose as she tried to decipher the list of poetry readers gripped by her old lady hands, "... Lacey Parker."

I nudged Lacey's knee with my knee cap, "You've got this."

"I hope so," she nervously sighed and raised from the plastic chair beside me.

After frantically adjusting the wrinkles in her yoga pants she shuffled her short legs to the front of the hall.

Lacey was so petite behind that mediocre block of wood they called a podium.

Lacey had to lower the microphone a good eight inches, causing a chuckle from the majority of students in the audience. Lacey herself smirked then joked into the mic, "That's better."

I was mesmerized by the sight of Lacey Parker, in the limelight, in front of all these strangers, providing vocals to the treasurable words I had read so carefully in the confines of my shed.

The poetry reading chilled me with mixed feelings. I was proud, so proud, that she got up in front of all these random people and read her work. On the other hand, I was experiencing an elusive kind of melancholy.

While Lacey read behind the podium I made a realization.

I looked at Lacey, knowing what I knew about how dark and warped the mind inside of this special person was, and then I looked at other people in the audience who were looking at her. They had no idea who they were looking at. None. They didn't have a clue. They didn't have a clue how hard it was for this young woman to get up and force herself in the car to come to this reading. They had no clue she dodged through an entire minefield of distorted thoughts to get to this very point. They had no idea she was going to go back to that minefield as soon as she finished reading. They only saw a normal girl. A pretty, friendly, normal girl who seemed to have it all together. Somebody who looked like she had no reason to be anxious or depressed.

Before I knew it Lacey was already done reading, and I had missed it because I was too busy thinking.

Gabe got on his feet and clapped, "Wooo! Yeah Lacey!"

Beth whacked him in the knee, "They don't cheer here."

I saw Lacey grinning though.

The rest of the crowd, including me, joined in Gabe's clapping.

"You're right, she's good," Gabe elbowed me as he sat back down. "Sucks that you've already taken all your English classes. Hope you enjoyed your tutoring while it lasted."

I froze mid-clap.

I had been so mentally consumed by my mission to fix Lacey and my high feelings about our recent hugs that I had forgot, until now, that the end of the semester meant the end of my English courses, which meant the end of tutoring, and with premises like that it meant...

I wasn't going to be hanging out with Lacey nearly as much.
How was I ever going to quench my Lacey Parker thirst *and* fix her OCD if I never had an excuse to be with her one on one? Next time I see her it will probably be at some stupid college party where we don't even get time alone to have deep and thought provoking conversations. Just the thought made my stomach flip.

I shuttered just thinking about Zeke's party and how unhappy I was sitting on the couch with my red solo cup, watching Lacey, out of the corner of my eye, socialize and deny shots and get hit on out of my reach. That blew. In no way did I want to be subjected to that every time I wanted to see her. That was miserable. No, more than miserable. That was hell.
Lacey took her seat next to me.
I was so upset by what Gabe said I almost forgot to congratulate her.

"Oh, uh, great job," I muttered out of the side of my mouth.

"Thanks," she was probably smiling, but I was too busy losing my mind with the jagged cracks of the trite floor. This really sucked.

Once the poetry reading was over Gabe and Beth walked off to their cars in the far parking lot. Lacey and I strolled into the courtyard.

With hands in my pockets I stared at the concrete path below my switching feet.

"So you must be happy," Lacey chatted, "No more English class!"

"Yay." There was no inflection of real joy in my monotone cheer.

If I was reading the vibe between Lacey and I correctly then I'd say she was suspicious of my fake happiness, but deliberately chose not to call me out on it.

"Anyways," she moved on, "have any plans now that the semester is over?"

"Just a whole lot of work at the not-so-convenient store."

She snorted, "The job's really that bad?"

"It sucks."

"Oh. Well at least you'll be making money. That's a good thing."

"I guess," I shrugged.

As much as I should have valued my time with Lacey I was so far from being invested in this conversation. I was too upset.

"I'm sure you'll-"

"I'm not gonna be seeing you around much, am I?" I spit out what was on my wandering mind, totally cutting her off.

Lacey's gentle stride came to a halt. "Well now that the semester's done I'll probably be really busy with my writing and pursuing literary agencies."

"Great," I sarcastically mumbled to myself and took out my aggression by kicking a silver tinted rock with a hostile jab of the foot.

With Lacey's heeled black boot she stomped down on the shiny rock. There was a loud thud and an uncomfortable twitch in her expression that gave me reason to believe she dented her shoe, but chose to ignore it. "Okay what's your deal?"

My eyes shot up from the pathway and onto the big eyed girl whom I had a hopeless crush on.

Angrily she whipped her hands out of her jacket pockets and went off at me, "I just shared *my* work in front of all these random strangers and I'm finally gonna start contacting literary agencies with my work. You know how big of a step that is for me! I thought you'd be happy to hear I was finally blooming outside of myself, into the *real* world, and try to start my writing career."

"I am! I, uh, I know I'm just- uh, I am happy for you!" I struggled to redeem myself.

"Then what's with the bitchy attitude?"

Ooh. I did *not* like the sound of that.

"I know, I know. I'm just kind of, um, I mean, I'm, uh, I'm sorry," I was all worked up. "I'm not used to all these- these- these feelings. I'm used to thoughts. Thoughts, I can work with, not feelings. I'm not like you- you can work with feelings. Capturing them through your words, drawing them forth with your personality, understanding them with your incredible mind. Lacey, you're a master with feelings! And it's kind of funny... because I can deal with thoughts, not feelings. And you, you can deal with feelings, not thoughts." A realization was unraveling through my bantering, "You and I, Lacey, we complement each other! Which is probably why we'd be so perfect together."

That last part of my loose-lipped word vomit caught her off guard.

"Wait, what?" She stared up at me with those brown doe eyes.

By accident I officially put my interest for Lacey out there. Reactively, I tried to cover it up. "I- I- I," I took a deep breath, fixing my stare on the girl with the notebook, the girl who tutored me, the girl who I had strengthening feelings for… and finally I gave up, "I can't do this anymore."

The compact seal of Lacey's dark lips separated a little, "You can't do what?"

Nervously I took off my cap and raked my fingers through my hair, "I can't, I can't act all casual on the outside when I really just wanna," I couldn't properly get the words out, "I don't know."

Out of defeat I slammed the backwards cap on my head, threw my arms to my side, and repeated that blasphemous phrase. "I don't know."

Lacey, with her head tilted upward at me, took a step closer to me, "Yes you do," she reassured with an encouraging nod and a stare that peered deep within me. I think she had a clue where my struggling confession was going. "What is it Jef?" her crossed arms quivered along with her voice, giving the impression that she was nervous, yet intrigued. "Jef?"

"I- I- I don't know. I'm losing sleep over the amazing things you say, I'm not hanging around places after you leave, for the first time I'm skipping class so I can see you, I'm anxious around you, but this really weird good anxiety that makes no sense. Dammit, I'm hitting guys upside the head with Frisbees! I think I'm going crazy!"

Lacey's eyes became rich with compassion and intuition. "What are you saying?" she was shaking a little. If only I could hold her.

"I like you a whole lot more than just a friend, I- I love you as more than just a friend," I blurted out, but quickly rejected myself so that she wouldn't have to, "But I know you're not interested in me like that so-"

"No Jef," she jumped to my rescue with a scratchy throat, "I am interested in you like that."

I was in awe. "Wait, really?"

She nodded rapidly, I think unable to talk.

As I began to perspire I laid my feelings out on the line. "I want to be your boyfriend. And I want you to be my girlfriend."

Lacey remained, gazing into me. I knew she felt the same as I did, I could feel it. She didn't have to agree out loud. I could read it in her pupils.

Suddenly she found a spurt of timid energy in her vocal chords, and in no more than a whisper uttered, "I can't."

That was the ultimate punch in the gut.

I was so crushed, I could hardly breathe.

"Why?" I barely choked out.

She started to tear up, "I love you, and I care about you, and that's why I have to be honest with you. I can't be a worthy girlfriend."

"That's ridiculous," I spit out. "You'd be the perfect girlfriend for me."

"You're mistaken," Lacey tried to dismiss me. I could tell she didn't believe her own dismissal though.

"Lacey-"

Before the tears could escape her eyes she turned away and made an attempt to speedily pace down the concrete path.

I chased after her and planted myself in front of her, "Lace!"

She stared down at my feet, "Jef, don't do this to yourself."

She tried to step around me, but I mimicked her sideways step. My lean legs were like sturdy metal poles drilled through the concrete. I wasn't letting her run away from this. I couldn't.

My feelings were completely out there. Lacey knew I loved her as more than just a friend. She knew I wanted to be in a relationship with her. Everything that I wanted was riding on this moment. I wasn't going to let her get away. Like a gravitational pull, I physically couldn't.

"Jef!" she tried again. "I'm serious. Don't do this to yourself."

"Do what to myself? Turn one of the most- no, the most meaningful friendships I've ever had into a relationship? Actually be with somebody that I care about?"

Lacey shook her head disapprovingly and gestured towards herself, "Trust me, you don't want this."

"Trust me, I do. I want this," I goofily pointed at her small figure with flimsy arms, "I want to be with you. I *know* that! I know that for a fact."

Lacey was all sorts of flustered, chewing down on her burgundy lip, darting her stare in a medley of directions, and shaking her head so fast that I could no longer tell if her body was shaking as well, "No, no Jef. You don't want to be my boyfriend."

"Yes I do Lacey!" I couldn't understand why she was trying so hard to push me away. I thought we had a real connection. No, I knew we had a real connection. I knew regardless of the fact that she just admitted to having a romantic interest in me. So why in the world was she so against this?

In my desperation I pried for clarification, "Do you have feelings for me Lace?"

"Of course," she tossed her arms to her sides in defeat, "I'd be lying if I said I didn't."

"Then what's the problem?" I pried.

She didn't answer. Instead her pupils flashed towards her dry hands which she was nervously scratching.

In that instant the real issue dawned on me.

Her OCD was in the way.

Holy shit this mental illness just wouldn't loosen its chains around her.

Suddenly I felt like I was thrown into an arena. Jef Sterling vs. Obsessive Compulsive Disorder. Trapped behind the Obsessive Compulsive Disorder was Lacey, chained around her wrists and ankles in a tiny dungeon, gated by iron prison bars. Locked by a key she called solace, but I called seclusion.

I tried with all of my might to prove to Lacey that I wasn't going to let the OCD win this fight. "I'm willing to be with you no matter what it entails."

"Jef I don't want you to suffer the way that my family suffers." Her response confirmed that my hunch about the OCD was correct.

"Lace, I'm fine. Don't worry about me. "

"Have you forgotten the fact that I'm afraid of touching people? You're not supposed to be interested in somebody like that."

"I'm not supposed to be interested in a lot of things, but I am!"

"Well stop," Lacey ordered unconvincingly while her eyes trailed me up and down, "It's very…" she struggled to finish that sentence with an insult, "endearing."

"Endearing?" I repeated the unexpected adjective then nodded with approval. "I can take that."

"No!" Lacey squeezed her eyes shut and rapidly shook her head, like it was a rattle that could shake away the slip up she had just made. "You're not taking on anything, Jef. You, you need to just focus on yourself, okay? This conversation between us is done."

As Lacey took a step back, I took a step forward, determined to win her over.

"I'm not afraid of the OCD. I can deal with it."

She sighed while staring off into the concrete pathway. "I know you can, but you shouldn't have to."

"It's okay," I threw my arms out submissively, "Life isn't perfect."

"But I'm *deeply* flawed…" Lacey wouldn't budge.

"And *deeply* gifted," I reminded her.

She just shook her head, bit down a smile, and forced her eyes down. So shy.

Hoping to distract Lacey from her shyness I made a fool of myself and began to hastily ramble, "Besides, who isn't flawed? We're all flawed! Look at that kid!" I pointed to some bearded guy who was trying to push through a door stamped with a "Pull" sign, then proceeded to wave my lanky arm to a girl with half of her hair dyed blue and the other half pink, "And look at her! She's obviously indecisive as hell and didn't know which color to dye her hair!" It probably didn't help my argument when the lady turned her multicolored head and shot me an intense glare.

"Jef!" Lacey hissed while veiling her mouth which I knew was smiling.

I hollered to the indecisive girl, "It's fine, keep walking! I'm just trying to make a point!"

"My God, Jef!" Lacey jeered.

Seeing that picking on random strangers wasn't the best approach to convince Lacey that nobody was perfect, I redirected my stance so that I was ridiculing myself, "And look at me! I'm flawed too. Look," without thinking I bunched up the bottom trim of my Bruins sweatshirt to show her the top hem of my boxers, "just this morning I put my boxers on inside out. I could have fixed it, but I was too lazy to do anything about it."

Her lips curled and a laugh fell out, "Jef," she quickly concealed her smile by turning her head away from me and distantly squinted against the rushing wind, "I don't know."

I think part of her looked in that direction so that her hair was flapping behind her, away from her eyes, without having to use her "contaminated" hands to touch her hair. I think a greater part of her was looking in that direction to avoid confronting the offer I was laying out. There was an obvious hesitation in her meandering "I don't know".

Lacey stared back at me and continued with her streak of commendable honesty, "I don't want you suffering Jef, and I know if you're with somebody who has OCD then you will suffer."

Something about that comment really upset me, but not for my sake, for Lacey's sake.

How was she ever going to find happiness if she pushed everybody who cared away?

"So what are you gonna do in life, Lace? Are you gonna deprive yourself of being with the person you're attracted to just to spare them a little bit of extra stress? You've already deprived yourself of enough! Don't push me away, please."

Her lips were quivering in a frown. "I like you too much to make you settle for somebody as screwed up as me. Don't you want a girlfriend that you can take places? Somebody who won't make you ask permission before every little touch? Somebody... *better*?"

"I don't care about all of that," I struggled to convince her, "I want to just spend time with you and the mind that comes with you."

"No Jef," she denied, "You deserve so much better."

"Nonsense," my response was immediate. "I'm not gonna let you do this. I'm not gonna let you slip away."

Lacey backed up, preparing to break away from the discussion, "You're being crazy."

She spun around and frantically started to leave.

Rather than chase after her I stood firm, stretching my arms upward so that my hands were matted on the back of my head, pressing down the orange visor of my cap, and thinking hard about what else I could say to convince her that we should pursue a relationship.

"Lacey wait!" I called out.

Clinging to her backpack strap on one shoulder, she hesitantly rotated around.

Shouting over the wind, I laid it all out on the line, "When I'm with you I feel like I'm with somebody who finally gets it. Who gets me when I don't get me. Somebody who gets my thinking. Somebody who isn't shallow, but is deep, so deep. Somebody with the most fascinating mind I've ever come across. And that's so much more than I could ask for. You are exactly what I need. You're what I want. And when I'm not with you I feel like something's missing. And it's such a lousy feeling, but it's kind of a good thing, because it helped me realize how much you actually mean to me. You aren't just a person I've crossed paths with. You're a person I really, *really* want to spend more time with. Somebody I want to get closer to, because I feel like I've barely begun to experience what it is that is so special about you. And I know you think it's crazy that I'd want to be with some person who has OCD, but I don't see you as just 'some person who has OCD'. I see you as the smartest, most down-to-earth, funniest, realest person I have ever met. And I'd be crazy to let you go, Lacey."

"Wow," there was no fighting her smile this time. Shyly she clicked her heels on the concrete, making her way back to me. "That was... storybook eloquent."

My throat tightened. "Well you know I'm a natural talker." I joked.

As our laughter faded I felt our stares harden.

I gulped. "I'm infatuated by you."

With the brightest of glows beaming through her eyes she stared up at me. Her mouth was bent in the most genuine smile I had ever seen on her. It was unbelievable.

My mind shut off.

My careful-not-to-do-the-wrong-thing mindset was gone.

My insecurity was lost.

And before Lacey could take that genuine smile away from me I craned my neck down and planted my lips on hers, taking a piece of that beautiful smile for myself.

I was caught up in an indescribable state of disbelief and euphoria. I had no idea how deprived I had been, having never felt the true exhilaration that transpires from touching lips with the person I was intensely attracted to until this moment. There must have been a surplus of endorphins firing through my brain.

Slowly Lacey's lips peeled off of mine. "Oh no," she whispered shakily.

Suddenly I remembered Lacey's disdain for physical contact.

"I'm sorry," I breathed, still not raising my head up but simply tilting my mouth down, away from hers. I knew she hated kissing, but I did it anyways.

"No," she adjusted my jaw line back up, nearly touching her lips with mine. "I actually enjoyed that. I- I loved it actually. But I'm not supposed to."

"According to who?" I stupidly gawked.

Lacey didn't answer. She smiled a paradoxically genuine yet uncomfortable smile. What dysfunctional thoughts were rotating through that mind?

Chapter 37

"I just wanna make sure you know what you're getting into Jef," Lacey said while tossing her leopard print backpack into the backseat of her car in the community college parking lot.

I was leaning on the car with my arm stretched out onto the car's hood. "I know what I'm getting into," I assured her without hesitation.

Lacey slammed the door, "It's going to be really hard to have a girlfriend with OCD."

"So is having a brother with cerebral palsy and schizophrenia, but I can handle it."

She returned to the front of the car before taking off, "Can I have a hug?"

I smirked. It was odd but somewhat endearing that she thought she had to ask me.

I bent down to my short girlfriend, still not fully comprehending the new relationship status. I was floating on a high so far above anything else I had ever experienced, I still wasn't totally in touch with reality.

Lacey, with her arms wrapped around me and her head resting on my chest, made a last disclaimer, "I know it kind of sucks but I just have to give you one last heads up, just because I like kissing you doesn't mean I'm going to feel comfortable doing it a lot. I can't guarantee every hello or every goodbye will include a kiss."

"Will today?" I asked hopefully.

"Not today Jef," she pulled out of the hug.

Right before bed I took the "Obsessive Compulsive Disorder & Lacey Parker Proverb" binder off my desk and irritably threw it in my bottom desk drawer, where all the unfinished projects usually went.

      Lacey Parker wasn't a research subject anymore.
      But I sure didn't feel like she was my partner.

Chapter 38

Lacey wasn't lying. Having a girlfriend with OCD was not easy. Not in the least bit. It was more like having a very emotionally close friend but little to no physical contact. I was always incredibly touched on the emotional plane but untouched in the material world. I tried not to dwell on how I was deprived but focus on how unbelievably lucky I was to have a real connection with another person.

I had a Frisbee golf tournament with Kenny. Lacey wanted to come but it was an hour and a half away from her house and she knew she'd get too tired if she was out the whole day. She said the last thing she wanted was to be a burden or damper my mood with her fatigue.

It wasn't all bad, though. We talked on the phone for an hour after I played, while I was driving home. She had me cracking up, giving me a play by play of the "lame" chick-flick her sister had on TV. Basically tearing it to shreds and explaining how undeveloped the characters were and how cliché the plot was.

It was common for Lacey to miss out on different events. She was limited by what she could and couldn't do because her OCD depleted the majority of her energy. I couldn't get over the cruel nature of this illness, because if anybody needed an excess of energy, never mind a normal amount, it was Lacey. Normal activities were hard enough for her since she was afraid of germs.

I was thoroughly enjoying Gabe's hockey game when Lacey had somewhat of a germ induced panic attack. At first I thought she was just really cold, but then I noticed a distant look in her eyes that only came out when she was really anxious. She wasn't flailing around screaming or hyperventilating or anything like that. She froze. In every way. Lacey's mind, body, and soul froze. She couldn't talk or retain what I was saying to her.

"Are you okay?" I asked over the swift sound of a skate blade slicing a trail into the rink. "Can you hear me?"

"No," she said with a blank stare and opted not to talk further. I literally had no idea what to do.

"Can you tell me what's wrong?"

"I don't know how."

Lacey had to go home as soon as possible. There, she took a shower and changed her clothes. I stopped by her house that afternoon to make sure she was okay.

Unfortunately, since Lacey was "clean", she wouldn't hug me. She just sat in her usual safe spot on the couch and gestured me to sit on the "germy" cushion beside her.

Lacey explained herself. Her composed voice in her home setting, when she deemed herself "clean", seemed like it belonged to a completely different person than the Lacey at the ice rink earlier. She was more coherent, more descriptive, more alert. That's when Lacey told me that she was freaking out earlier because the odor at the rink made her feel like she was breathing in all sorts of dangerous germs.

"Why couldn't you just tell me that earlier?" I had asked.

"I couldn't," Lacey declared. "I was in compulsion mode."

Frustrated, Lacey clutched a bunch of damp hair on her scalp and shook her head in distress. "I know I'm supposed to know how to verbalize my feelings and my thoughts and the world around me, but when I'm in the compulsive mode I can't. I just can't. I can't think straight. I don't know the words behind my tongue and- and as a writer, I'm supposed to."

Seeing how upset Lacey was by her inability to verbalize her thoughts, I decided not to make a big deal of how upset I was by her OCD prohibiting me from enjoying Gabe's hockey game or even hugging her after she showered.

Honestly, I just felt bad. I felt bad for me because I liked her so much and I just wanted to be able to spend time with her, to enjoy common pleasures with her, to show her off in public. And then I felt bad for Lacey because, to put quite simply, her mental condition was robbing her of her youth. Her life, actually.

Despite the fact that my binder full of Lacey Parker observations was in the neglected bottom drawer of my desk, I still wrote down these notes and stuffed them in the binder before I went to bed.
    I guess I wasn't done studying Lacey's obsessive compulsive disorder.

Chapter 39

I picked Lacey up on her front walkway the next night. We were gonna go back to my place and literally *watch* a movie.

"How are you?" I cordially asked Lacey while we trudged down the snow packed patio to my jeep.

"Eh," she moaned. "I got in a fight with my parents."

I opened the car door for her and held her gloved hand while she hopped onto the ramp. As much as I hated the cold weather I was enjoying being able to hold Lacey's hands since she was wearing gloves more regularly.

I boosted myself into the driver's seat and followed up on what Lacey said about getting in a fight with her parents. "Are you okay?"

"Yeah I'm fine. Just a little frustrated. They said I write too much and told me I need to do something else like get a job. But I told them they didn't understand, that I treated writing like my job, that my work ethic wasn't the same as most people. I don't need to drive to another building and sit in a cubicle or stand at a cash register to get work done. I can sit at home and type away to get my work done. They don't get that. Probably because I'm not making any money off of my writing yet. I keep telling them, trying to convince them that eventually I will make money off of it, but I need to work hard on my writing now. I've written entire books. Who can say that about their daughter? I don't get it. I know they're not shallow people and they don't only care about money, so why aren't they proud of that?"

"I don't know," I stupidly answered. I wasn't anticipating that lengthy of a response to my "are you okay".

When we got to my house I was surprised that the front door was locked.

"That's weird," I mumbled and shuffled through my pocket until I found the house keys.

I quickly unlocked the door, I pushed it open only to hear Peter yelling at my mom from upstairs about his imaginary friend, Henry.

"Peter you need to bathe!" I heard Mom yell.

"I told you, Henry says 'no'!"

"I don't care what Henry says! It's been too long since you last-"

"No! Henry's the leader! I have to obey Henry!"

"Oh fuck," I groaned.

Lacey worried, "Should we leave?"

Mom trampled the staircase, so preoccupied with her frustration over Peter's schizophrenic breakdown that she didn't realize Lacey was standing at the front door until she got to the bottom step.

"Jef! You made sure Peter took his Aripiprazole at dinner, right?"

"Yes Mom," I groaned. I hated having that responsibility.

"Are you *sure*? Because I didn't want to say it before but you've been very distracted ever since you and-"

The moment she saw that I had Lacey with me she flushed into a pale state. She was mortified.

Mom frantically waved Lacey and I away. "Don't come in," she insisted in her embarrassment, "You and Lacey go out!"

"Can I at least grab a DVD?"

"No, go, go Jef! Please!" Mom physically pushed Lacey and I outside, back into the cold. "I'm sorry Lacey," her humiliated apology was followed by the instantaneous slam of the door.

In the cold night, I looked up.

Yup. Just as I suspected. Full moon.

Lacey tried to help in the only way she could, "We can go to my house, Jef."

"Alright," I sighed.

We scuttled back to the jeep.

"He's really worked up, huh?" Lacey referred to my brother as she buckled herself in.

"It's because it's a full moon. He's always worse on a full moon."

"Seriously?" she was very surprised.

I nodded while staring at the glowing moon in the pitch black sky.

"That's pretty freaky," her voice was submerged in a weird mixture of fear and fascination.

"It is," I agreed, thinking about how fascinating the vast star studded sky could be.

"Hey," Lacey was suddenly excited, "Do you wanna go down to a ball park or field and just, I don't know, sit outside?"

I was surprised how in tune she was with me. "How did you know–"

"You've got that look in your eye while you're staring up at the moon," Lacey laughed.

I drove Lacey to my high school football field. There was a track bordering it, which I used to run being that I was on the track team for three years.

Lacey said she would have sat directly on the grass if it weren't for the fact that this was a football field, and there was no question that "dirty cleats and sneakers" had been pounding the turf. Lucky for me we were able to simulate a picnic blanket with the beach towel Mom had bought me on her Orlando, Florida trip that I had yet to take out of my trunk from the previous summer.

"Ugh," Lacey muttered as she seated herself in her usual cross-legged position.

"What's wrong?"

"Oh, nothing. My arm's just a little sore."

"It is?" I asked out of surprise. Lacey wasn't one for physical activity. "From what?"

A little scoff vibrated up the path of her throat, "Well it's probably, well, I don't know. Nothing. It's nothing."

I didn't like being left in the dark, but judging by the unintentional concern in my voice I'd say I was more worried than curious. "What happened?"

"Nothing Jef! Literally nothing. It's stupid…"

"Why? What did you do?"

She knew me well enough to know that I wasn't going to let up, so after a strenuous sigh she answered. "I may or I may not have spent a good three hours reading the dictionary last night… which, by the way, is also called a lexicon."

"Okay," I didn't see how that explained her physical soreness, "and that made your arm hurt because?"

"Well I was tired at like 8:00 and wanted to lie down. But I was also bored. And then I caught sight of the pocket dictionary on my desk which I hardly ever look at because it's germy, but I figured if I was gonna lie down I might as well do something productive like better my writing and work on my craft. So I grabbed the dictionary, a pen, and stuck some sticky notes on the cover. I didn't want the germy dictionary touching my bedspread so, while I laid down, I browsed through the dictionary and wrote the definitions of random words that I found interesting or handy on the sticky notes. I must have pulled a muscle from holding the dictionary overhead for such a long time."

Great. As if cognitive complications weren't enough of a symptom from a mental disorder like OCD, now physical ailments were a symptom? Frustrated, I wiped a hand down my face, trying to rub off the irritated groove in my forehead and the frown off of my face. "Oh my God, Lace…" I groaned with pity.

"Yeah…" she cringed in her intuition then started apologizing, "It's pathetic and stupid, I know. You know what, let's just talk about something else. I don't feel like talking about germs."

"Oh, uh, yeah. Okay," quickly I scanned the surrounding football field for something that would change the subject, "um, well, hey! See the stars up there?" I pointed to the night sky.

"Oh God Jef," Lacey giggled with a disapproving shake of her head, "Don't do that."

"What? Do what? What did I-"

"Don't do that cliché thing that every guy does in every romantic movie known to man. You know, where you take the girl you like out star gazing and then say," Lacey lowered her voice in a male-mocking tone, "'Wow, look at all those stars up there. We are so small in the big scheme of the universe.'"

My face heated up. I didn't fully know what topic I had been planning on bringing up, but I'd be lying if I said that the "we're so small, the universe is so big" conversation wasn't a looming topic just around the corner of my brain. Despite my embarrassment, I couldn't help myself from laughing at Lacey's goofy impersonation of a male.

"Really Lace? Is that your best 'guy voice'?" I chuckled.

"Oh shut up!" she beamed with a light nudge of her knee against my shin. "I'm right, aren't I? Tell me that conversation hasn't been brought up in almost every movie that has a guy and a girl against the backdrop of a night sky?"

"That's incredibly true," I laughed with a smile so stupidly wide I pretended to itch my mandible in attempt to obstruct Lacey's view of my foolish grin. I couldn't help but smile wide. The amount that I revered every little facet of Lacey's quick wit and spot on cynicism was too much to hold inside the limited confines of a stoic expression.

As my laugh faded so did my love-struck lightheadedness, and gradually the initial thought I had about the starry sky came into clarity.

"Actually," I announced, serious despite my excitement to impress Lacey with a less conventional and more intellectual discussion. "Look back up at the stars, Lace."

"Really?" she smirked skeptically.

"Just humor me."

"Alright," she laughed, flipped her long brown hair behind her back with a stiff jerk of the neck, and stared into the starlight with those large eyes.

"See all those stars up there? There are approximately 100 billion stars up there in our galaxy, nearly the same amount of neurons estimated to be in the human brain."

Lacey didn't break her stare off of the sky. And I didn't break my stare off of Lacey. Her nose, pointed upward, crinkled as she squinted above. "Is that true?"

"Yes," I nodded.

"Wow," she gaped.

I gazed shamelessly at Lacey's divine profile under the glow of the metaphorical neurons lighting up the sky. Her flexible neck remained craned backward. Her eyes softened. And her illuminated mouth opened ever so slightly, "That's so... beautiful."

"I know," I sighed, awestruck by the sublime beauty that molded the face of the girl sitting next to me.

Suddenly Lacey flicked her head down and locked eyes with me.

A jolt of embarrassment surged through my bones and I nervously veered off into an astronomy lesson.

"Did you know that there's a huge number of galaxies up there besides ours? Edwin Hubble discovered that. It was an incredibly revolutionary discovery for its time."

Lacey breathed a gentle laugh, "That guy must feel pretty damn special."

I felt my mouth twitch with discomfort. What an odd response. "What do you mean?"

"I don't know," she hunched forward in her crisscross disposition and folded her arms, almost as to give herself a hug. "Whenever I hear about people like that, people who revolutionize the world with the thoughts inside their mind, I can't help but feel, I guess, jealous. I can't begin to fathom how special those people must feel. Who could be more special than somebody who uses their individual mind, the world inside their head, to touch a world outside of their head?"

Desperate to alleviate the pained longing in Lacey's voice, I reminded her, "Technically you just described yourself."

"No," she shook her head with genuine disbelief. "I haven't touched the world in any special way."

"Yes you have!"

"No, I haven't. Not yet at least."

I couldn't have disagreed more. My adrenaline was pumping and my voice was frantic. "But what about your writing?"

"Well yeah," she admitted coyly, "My writing is special. And one of these days people are going to see that. Someday, I'm going to expose my mind to the world. People are going to read it. People are going to feel it. I'm going to touch people. I'm going to be somebody special *someday*." She vowed with her doll-like eyes peering off to the far away stars dotting the sky, as if her dream resided light years away. "Someday."

"You're somebody special *today*," I reminded her.

With the sudden adjustment of perspectives, Lacey's unsatisfied attitude became overwhelmingly appeased. A light film of tears glazed over her eyes like the fresh dew that would soon be tickling the field of grass we sat in.

Before her vulnerability got the best of her she sucked in a deep sniff and flipped the focus onto me. "Do you want to be like Edwin Hubble, Jef? To make some revolutionary scientific discovery?"

I thought back to before I fell (hard) for Lacey Parker, when my focus was to come up with an answer for obsessive compulsive disorder that might mark psychophysical and scientific magazines. Then, I wanted to make a discovery. Now, now that my focus has shifted from inherent curiosity to impassioned empathy, from the brain to the heart, I didn't care about discovering something new. I just wanted to better understand the disease that was gnawing at my girlfriend's psyche. Love does that. Who would have thought?

"No," I shook my head in a delayed response, "I don't need to discover something new to the world. It's all new to me. I don't need a Nobel Prize in physics like Louis de Broglie or Phillip Lenard. I'm perfectly happy relaying the information they've found. Teaching what's already been discovered."

"Oh," the meager syllable drew a misty breath into the cold air.

A good thirty seconds of pure silence passed.

Lacey's eyes lowered and her finger traced the white "n" in "Orlando" written on the towel. She was sad again.

"Why do you feel like you need to discover something new to be satisfied in life?" I questioned with an unflinching stare locked onto the fascinating girl beside me.

"Not so much discover. More like create. Create something existential from nothing but my own mind, body, and soul."

"Why?"

Lacey remained fixated on the towel's letters. "I guess I'm just scared if I don't create anything then there's no point to my existence. And I'd rather be anything but unimportant. Insignificant. Small in this gigantic universe."

Understanding the seriousness of our deep talk, I held back the snort that stemmed from realizing I didn't even bring on the cliché "we're so small" conversation and it still came up. Maybe the writers of those romantic movies were onto something more profound than Lacey or I realized.

Suddenly a thought popped up in my head.

"You're not small," I tapped her with the back of my hand. "What did you do last night?"

"I told you," a confused laugh fell out of Lacey's candid mouth. "I read the dictionary."

"And why did you do that?"

"I don't know, because I like increasing my vocabulary."

"Why?"

"Because," her brow furrowed and she thought harder, "I felt like learning new words would better my writing. Expand my mind."

"Exactly!" I exclaimed in pure ecstasy, beyond thrilled to share my excitement for learning with the most important person in my world. "As long as you keep learning and embracing the knowledge this world has to offer then your mind is *always* expanding. Vocabulary, psychology, quantum physics, you name it! It all accumulates. You, your very mind is *always* getting bigger. Your mind today is larger than it was yesterday. And that will *always* be the case. Don't you see? Lacey, you never have to worry about being small in this universe."

She was staring at the grass. Were her eyes wet? Her eyes seemed to be glistening along with the starlight.

"Hey," I nudged her lightly with my elbow.

Lacey broke her tear stricken stare off the grass and, with a recuperating sniffle, nodded.

Instead of the usual apology or self-loathing comment in regards to her refusal to touch me in any way, shape, or form, she kept her mouth shut and went ahead, resting her head on my shoulder. Like a person who doesn't dare scare off the skittish deer, I refrained from verbalizing my pleasant surprise.

We spent the next hour under the galaxy's glowing neurons in awe-stricken silence.

Chapter 40

I tried to look up ways to alleviate OCD symptoms or ease depression and found that art therapy might help.

I asked Lacey if she wanted to spend the day painting and she was all for it. I was not artistic at all but my needs were meaningless compared to Lacey's intensifying depression.

So I went out and bought canvases, brushes, and paint, then came back to my house.

We blasted music through the stereo speakers and painted away. Lacey painted a male's dirt stained hand gently placing a rose in a female's bloody hand.

I painted a horrible portrait of my dog York. It was still fun though. And with all of the messy paint Lacey was surprisingly way less OCD about germs and contamination.

I was lost staring at her painting, interpreting it, dissecting it.

"That looks…" I scoured my brain for a euphonious word but simply uttered, "…sad."

Lacey slovenly wiped her soaking wet brush on a paper towel and laughed, "You say that like it's a bad thing."

"Well," I snickered halfheartedly, eyes fixated on the melancholy painting, "why wouldn't 'sad' be a bad thing?"

"You shouldn't pity the tortured artist, you should admire them."

Raising an eyebrow, I transferred my focus from a bloody painting to the indifferent girl beside me, allowing my expression to invite her to elaborate.

Lacey reciprocated, "It's a good thing when you can turn your pain into art. You're taking something negative and finding the beauty in it. And when you do that the pain is no longer debilitating you, it's actually benefiting you, because you were able to put that pain to good use through creative expression. You're taking away that pain's power by morphing it into a new form, a form you chose, and therefore you own it and it doesn't own you."

I stared at her. Awestricken.

Lacey began to blush and immediately recanted, "I don't know," she nervously dabbed her wet and now colorless paintbrush onto the paper towel, "That's just what I think. Maybe I'm just weird."

Suddenly a cold tickle touched my wrist.

"Jef," Lacey had playfully poked me with her paintbrush.

"Hey!" my pitch shot up in reaction to the touch of the cold black paint, "Do I look like a canvas?"

"I've been trying to talk to you," she laughed, "You're in la la land, as you like to call it."

"I was actually in Lacey land," I nodded towards her painting. "Are you almost done?"

"Kind of. I was gonna give it a few touch ups-"

"Don't!" I was oddly opinionated.

Lacey smirked and tilted her head to the side.

"Technically you could. But I think it looks perfect the way it is. I wouldn't touch it."

"Do you know what this painting is about?" she quizzed.

"Uh, yeah. It's..." my voice trailed into an ignorant oblivion.

Lacey spoke up, no louder than a whisper. "I can feel touch linger on my skin, Jef. I can feel germs infecting my pores, the threads of my clothing, everything that touches me! I can feel what nobody else feels."

Saddened by her extremely elusive predicament, I silently nodded.

"I can feel everywhere someone has been, staining me."

I'll admit, part of it was from a selfish point of view, but I researched OCD rehabs for Lacey as soon as we parted ways. My mind, my soul, and yes, my body, needed Lacey Parker.

I printed out a bunch of information about OCD rehabilitation. With my packet of printouts I drove up to Lacey's house and intervened on her while she was in the middle of spending the day writing. She answered to door, "Jef I told you to call before-"

"I know but I have something for you," I handed her a packet of different rehabilitation centers for OCD in New England.

She reached out, "What's this?"

Before I could answer she read the top of the page that read "Inpatient Obsessive Compulsive Disorder Treatment".

"No," Lacey handed me back the packet.

"Just think about it!"

"Jef I can't go away for treatment! I can barely function in my own house. I couldn't even move out to college. There's no way I can function living at a rehab."

I argued, "But there are professionals there who know that, and they can help you learn how to function."

"No Jef," she was persistent. "It won't even help, I know myself, and I know this isn't curable."

"But Lace. If you could just *learn* from these professionals-"

"There's nothing they can teach me Jef!"

I loved Lacey's stubbornness. It was somewhat of a sardonic joke that her steadfast quality was just as prevalent in her OCD as it was in her personality.

"Would you just look at these papers?"

Lacey shocked me when she snatched the packet from my hand.

Lacey glanced down for a split second, pretended to read, then flashed huge eyes back up at me.

"Wow!" Lacey squealed with mocking elation, "This just solved every problem I think I've ever had!" she swiftly glued her eyes back on her notebook before the considerate person in her could catch a glimpse of whatever hurt reaction she had just inflicted upon my face.

The caustic sting of her sarcasm corroded my ego, but I didn't let it scare me off. "Okay, I get it," I bit back. "So I care about you, sue me! What the hell are you getting mad for?"

"Oh come on, Jef! Be smart!" she retorted with scathing disparagement. "OCD is God-awful! Do I cherish it a little more than I should? Yeah, but that's how I cope with it! I have no choice! I try to find the good in this sickness because I have to face it on a daily basis. But you don't have to give OCD a sliver of your time! You don't have to give me and my miserable self a sliver of your time! You don't have to empathize with me. You don't have to feel my pain. You don't have to face this or follow an algorithm to solve this or do whatever it is you scientific people do. You have no reason to voluntarily burden yourself with this tenacious, constant, persistent, steadfast, strenuous-"

"Stop!" I brought a hasty end to the long list of adjectives effortlessly flowing from her euphonious tongue, more preoccupied with striking back against her antecedent "be smart" comment.

She got red. I don't think she was used to somebody disrupting her.

"Empathy has *nothing* to do with intellect."

Lacey's fawn eyes were shy. "Okay. Wait, what? What are we talking about?"

"*Be smart*. You said, just now, to 'be smart' and stop voluntarily caring about you. Stop voluntarily trying to help you. But I'm not voluntarily doing anything! I- I can't help but- but-" I tore a claw-like grip into my scalp to prohibit my unyielding awkward hands from waving around like a damn fool. I knew I was about to say something embarrassingly personal, and personal was primetime to unleash awkward hand gestures. "I can't help but care about you, okay? I didn't choose to care! I didn't choose to care about that poem! I didn't choose to care about every little perfect thing you say, okay? I didn't choose to melt in absolute awe when I listened to you talk to my brother like an equal! I didn't choose to fall for you!"

All that talking got me lightheaded.

Chapter 41

After sculpting what must have been a perfect sphere out of snow, Peter handed me his snowball.

"Row two, Column three!" Peter commanded.

"On it," I wound my arm back then pitched the snowball at the kitchen window.

Peter and I had been doing this every winter, when the snow was just hard enough, ever since we were little kids. We had a system. With his freakish precision he would ball the snow into a flawless orb. Then, treating the crossing of the window panels like a grid, my big brother would tell me exactly which row and column to aim at with the snowball. Whenever I hit the right spot Peter would enthusiastically hoot with laughter and give me an air-five rather than a high-five, something he did because his coordination wasn't the best.

Mom hated the snowball game we made up, but she never told us to stop. She would never tell her precious sons to stop doing something they bonded over.

With a loud splat the snowball hit the correct segment of the window's glass.

"Woo-hoo!" Peter howled and we slapped each other an air-five.

My mom cracked the window open about an inch to keep the flurrying snow out of the house. She scolded, "Honestly, at what age will you stop throwing snowballs? Don't you have something better to do with your Friday night?"

Actually, I did have something better to do.

I was going to a local pond with Lacey, Gabe, Beth, and a bunch of other people Gabe had convinced to come and play a pick-up game of hockey.

As excited as I was for the night I had been dreading telling my mom about the plans. She hated when I had any plans that excluded Peter. But it wasn't my fault he couldn't balance himself in hockey skates.

Mom's condescending reprimand was a reminder that I needed to locate the bag of hockey pucks Gabe accidentally left at my house last winter when we skated on the shallow pond behind my house. I had been meaning to get those back to him but we both forgot, until now, when we actually needed them for the free skate.

"Ma!" I called over the thickening wind. "Do you know where we put Gabe's hockey pucks? They were in a brown duffel bag! They're not in the shed!"

"Why do you need hockey pucks?" she yelled.

"I'm playing hockey tonight with the guys!"

My mom took an extra moment before answering and shook her head.

That!

That was exactly what I was dreading!

She always shook her head, like I was the most disappointing son, when I said that I had plans that didn't include Peter.

"Did you check the garage?" she eventually shouted back.

"Yes," I groaned.

"Check again!"

Right when I was about to respond with another groan our dog came hopping through the three inches of snow. In his tightly clamped mouth was a chewed up hockey puck.

I dropped my head and hollered back to Mom, "Never mind!"

She already shut the window.

"Really York? Really?" I antagonized while trying to yank the dented puck from York's slobbery jaw. I didn't even bother to order him to drop it. I knew he wouldn't listen.

"I didn't know you were going skating tonight," Peter moped.

"It was a last minute thing," I lied, avoiding eye contact by pretending to be overly-concerned with yanking the puck from York.

"I wish I could go skating."

I knew exactly what Peter was doing, and more importantly, Peter knew exactly what he was doing. He was trying to guilt trip me into staying home. I wasn't about to budge, though. Between Lacey's mental illness and his lifelong retardation I didn't have the energy or patience to be a lenient brother and a good boyfriend at the same time. And let's be honest, I spent 23 years being a lenient brother, and in those same 23 years I lived without Lacey Parker. That was long enough.

With a blunt rejection I diverted the guilt trip.

"Sorry, Pete. You're gonna have to sit this one out."

He didn't say anything after that.

Peter and I trudged into the toasty house. Quickly I shut the door behind to keep the blistering cold out.

As usual after maneuvering through snow, Peter's lower back muscles were hurting, so I had to help him unlace his snow boots.

"I need to go to the bathroom," he announced when I finished untying the shoelaces.

"Alright, Pete."

After putting away the coat, scarf, and gloves Peter left splayed on the floor, I waltzed into the kitchen to grab a snack before leaving to pick Lacey up at her house.

"Dinner's ready!" Mom spun around from the sink.

"Mom I'm going out in like five minutes. I'll just bring a granola bar or…" suddenly I caught sight of the fully made kitchen table.

Peter and I each had a plate set up. Peter's plate was obvious because, well, there was his orange Aripiprazole pill bottle perched next to the dish like it was part of the meal. Aside from that, we had the same dinner. One unappealing miscellaneous patty per plate. No bun. And some sludge pile of watered down squash?

"What the hell?" I poked the beige burger with my bare finger. It was as solid as a rock and as dry as a neglected sponge.

"I'm not sure if you misunderstood, Mom, but I was asking for hockey pucks to bring to the pond, not for dinner."

"Don't be ungrateful, Jef," she chastised. "How many 23-year-old boys get a homemade meal from their mother every night?"

"A lot nowadays, actually. The age for moving out and living on your own in America has risen since-"

"Jef, please. Quit whining and enjoy the meal."

"I'm not whining," I dropped my butt to the chair with disgusted eyes fixed on the dry patty, "I'm just... confused. What is this exactly?"

"This is a lean turkey burger. Peter's physical therapist recommended Peter go on a diet."

"Yeah, *Peter* goes on a diet, not me."

Mom bent over the table and whispered so that Peter wouldn't hear her from the bathroom, "You know very well that he gets anxious if he's not eating the same thing as you, Jef. You can grab something else on the way out the door. Please, do this for your brother."

It's true, I did know that, but the usual compliance I practiced with my saint of a mother was harder to access lately. I was too uptight and stressed out to obey my mom. And let's face it, I might be living in her house, but I wasn't a little boy. It was about time I put my foot down.

Just the smell of the garlic emanating off of the burger was powerful enough to make me choke. I had no faith I'd be able to mask such a potent odor with toothpaste, mouthwash, or gum if I ate this. And if that was the case then there was no way Lacey would stay in my odor-marked "contaminated" vicinity for long.

"I'm sorry Mum, but I can't- I'm not eating this..."

"Jef!" Mom sounded overdramatically appalled, like she didn't even recognize her own son.

I wasn't about to give in, though. "I'll stick with a granola bar."

"Jef..."

"What?" I snapped, quickly jumping out of the chair, "Why do I have to eat the same thing as him? I'm not going to enable him and his weird obsessive compulsive need to eat the same thing as me!"

In a hurry to avoid what must have been shame in my mom's eyes I snatched a granola bar from the cabinet and jetted out of that garlic infiltrated kitchen. With a loud crinkle my grip tightened around the syrupy bar, using its gooey malleability to treat it like a stress ball, and ripped open the front door.

Though the sound of the snow-filled gale blasted through my eardrums, the sound of Mom's angry voice yelling from the kitchen proved dominant.

"You have a problem with Peter's rituals, but you have no problem entertaining your girlfriend's obsessive compulsive needs?"

I paused.

Hesitantly my hand dropped from the door knob.

I'd never officially told my mom about Lacey's OCD condition.

Peter must have blabbed. Typical.

Instead of retaliate to my mother I shook my head and made a break from that crazy house.

After being let into Lacey's household by her younger sister, Felicity, I stood awkwardly in the doorway while Lacey finished applying makeup or straightening her hair or whatever.

I kept my hands in my pockets. Felicity kept her hands on her phone.

I tried to make small talk by asking her about school, since it was her first year commuting to a university, but Felicity kept giving me short answers with her zoned out eyes glued to her phone.

"So, you're more of a math-mind?" I concluded.

Unexpectedly, Felicity broke her zombie stare off of her phone and onto me. "How do you put up with her?"

"I, uh- I'm, I'm sorry?"

"How do you put up with Lace?" she forwardly asked.

Apparently I had heard her correctly.

Dumbstruck, I lost access to my larynx.

"Don't you get frustrated? She's impossible to deal with."

"Uh," with a recuperating crack I found my voice, "Well, I wouldn't, I wouldn't say 'impossible'."

"I would," Felicity declared, then returned to tapping away on the rapidly changing phone screen.

Without meaning to, I spoke up.

"You do know she doesn't act the way she does to hurt you, right?"

With a sharp glare Felicity's trim eyebrows pointed inward, like angry daggers.

All of a sudden the sound of Lacey calling from upstairs interrupted our tense interaction.

"I'm ready!" she pitter pattered down the staircase in slippers, something she told me she had to wear in the upstairs portion of the house to avoid leaving the public germ's from outdoor shoes on her bedroom floor.

Lacey slid open the closet door in the hallway and pulled out some snow boots. One at a time she flipped her slippers off, carefully inserting each foot inside a boot without ever touching the floor. While tying her shoelaces she spoke up to her sister, "Felicity, could you do me a favor and give dad a hug, for me?"

"No!" Felicity didn't take a split second of hesitation to answer. "That's the dumbest question ever! Go hug him, yourself!"

Lacey stood upright, "Please!"

"What the heck? No!"

"Felicity, please! He's leaving for a business trip while I'm out and I'm not gonna see him until-"

"Not my fault!" Felicity bit back.

Helplessly I stood in the corner of the kitchen, not sure if it was my place to meddle.

In my own awkward way I tried to defend Lacey.

"Maybe, um, maybe you should give her a break."

Lacey quickly jumped to her sister's defense, "Jef, its fine."

But the damage was already done, and Felicity was irate. Her hard brown eyes nearly pierced through my soul. "Why should I?"

Damn, was she outward about her anger. Lacey was right when she said that Felicity didn't hold back.

"Lacey always gets a break! She doesn't have to get a job! She doesn't have to be a full-time student! She always gets a break! From my mom, from my dad! From everybody! I'm not gonna enable her too!"

"Yeah but-" suddenly her words plucked a painstakingly recent memory out of my conscience. *"I'm not going to enable him"* I had announced to my mother, about Peter and my refusal to eat the same dinner as him tonight.

Chapter 42

Hockey was a blast, for the most part.

What was not a blast was trying to enjoy myself knowing Lacey's small body was shivering from the cold.

She didn't complain though. But I knew she was freezing because of how she hugged herself with trembling arms. That and I could see how bright red her nose was from the other side of the lake. She forced herself to glide along the ice, on the perimeter of the lake with Natalie at her side. I didn't want to interrupt her "girl time" since Natalie was her only female friend aside from her sister (whom often was a little too harsh with Lacey) but I couldn't help but feel like a real jerk while her teeth chattered and her petite body shook.

Fortunately I was much smoother on skates than I was in sneakers, and in one swift motion I skidded to a screeching halt beside Lacey.

"Wanna wear my jacket?" I breathed into the frigid air.

"Oh, no, I'm fine," Lacey fibbed with a mild laugh, "No need to be chivalrous."

"It's okay, I'm warm from moving around," I explained while slipping my arms out of their sleeves.

"I'm fine, Jef."

"No you're not, come on, it's clean," I insisted, holding the snow coat in front of her.

"I'd rather not, Jef. Thanks though. Really, thanks. Go back to playing hockey with the guys."

I didn't want to, though. I felt like a jerk, like all the other guys playing pickup were staring wondering why that asshole wasn't giving his shivering girlfriend his jacket.

"Come on Lacey," I urged and tried to put it on her but she instinctively swiped my arm away. "I'm fine!"

"Okay, okay," I put the coat back on then returned to the game, feeling like crap.

Hockey wasn't so fun after that.

We played for about thirty more minutes. Gabe got way too into it, shouting at his teammates like this was a legitimate professional game in a stadium.

At one point Carson, to no shock, whacked the hockey puck with the most unwarranted aggression a good six yards away from the goal.

Of course, the puck was heading straight for Lacey and Natalie.

In a fraction of a second, before I even had a chance to call out to Lacey, she ducked, smoothly dodging the hockey puck's wrath.

"What the-" quickly I shut my mouth for fear of sounding too surprised.

"What?" Lacey swooped across the ice and skidded to stop just inches before me. "What is it? What'd I do?" she asked insecurely.

"No, nothing. Nothing. You just, you have *really* quick reflexes."

"Yeah well you can thank a phobia of germs for that. There was no way I was going to let that filthy puck touch me."

After a shower so brief it would have made Lacey cringe, I hurried into my bedroom, whipped my closet door open, and with a ravenous forefinger scanned the topic labeled binding of every single binder until I got to the one that read "The Nervous System, Parts of the Brain".

Speedily I flipped through the perfectly color coordinated sheets of plastic laminated pages and raw paper, searching for information about human reflexes. I was so antsy that I nearly ripped the perimeter of each sheet. I couldn't help it though. I couldn't seem to dispel the lingering shock of Lacey's speedy puck dodge at the pond.

It wasn't until stumbling upon the brightly colored illustration of a human brain that my frenetic fingers froze.

According to the brain diagram, which I'm sure my awkward hand traced from a textbook drawing, the section of the brain responsible for reflexes was the cerebellum (a part located at the lower backside of the brain on top of the brain stem).

In handwriting so neat it was almost feminine I had written that the cerebellum was the motor center of the brain.

I wondered, did this section of Lacey's brain adapt, speeding its reaction rate to the stimuli around her, to best serve her mental illness?

In my impatience for further answers I skimmed the following sheets of paper for any more information about motor skills.

Immediately my keen eye glued itself onto the phrase "motor skills" within a pink-highlighted synopsis of the cerebrum, the largest segment of the brain. This cerebral area was physically located at the highest part of the brain and was, fittingly, cognitively responsible for the highest forms of thinking.

Still as impatient as ever, I read onward.

My stomach nearly dropped at the information I had eerily wrote down a mere year or so ago.

"Cerebrum – in charge of most motor skills, cognitive thinking, and sensory processes."

Sensory processes.

That was seriously thought provoking.

The same place responsible for motor skills, an extension of human reflexes, was also responsible for how the human brain senses the environment in which we live.

Indented on note sheet were further classifications of the cerebrum, breaking this region of the brain into the cerebral cortex- which was even further broken down into cortex lobes.

After tense scanning with what must have been bloodshot eyes I was able to figure out which lobe did most of the perceiving for the sense of touch. It was the parietal lobe, also known as the somatosensory cortex. According to my notes, the parietal lobes processed information about pressure, pain, temperature, as well as touch. On the other hand, what was known as the motor cortex, or frontal lobes, of the cerebral cortex (belonging to the rudimental part of the brain labeled the cerebrum) was in charge of *voluntary* movements and, lieu and behold, creativity, something Lacey certainly possessed. Though reflexes were *involuntary* reactions to stimulus, it was still quite telling that all of these bodily functions were part of the mass of the brain scientists named the cerebrum. What was more telling, and actually vomit inducing due to its shock value, was the uncanny footnote I wrote at the bottom of the page in silver ink.

"Some psychologists believe that if a surgeon applied an electrical current in the somatosensory cortex of a patient's brain then said patient might feel a sensation of being touched on the skin."

Holy crap.

Could this false sensation of being touched be what Lacey called "the germ feeling"? Is it possible that, for some unknown reason, natural electrical currents coursed through the somatosensory cortex of the cerebrum in people suffering from obsessive compulsive disorder?

I don't know, but it was safe to postulate that there was a parallel between Lacey's physical feeling of germs touching her and an electrical current induced parietal lobe. Maybe her cerebrum was more active than the cerebrum of a non-mentally ill brain. Or maybe there was a flaw in communication between neurons in the cerebral cortex. I wasn't sure... yet.
Transferring from my closet to the chair at my desk I took out the OCD/Lacey binder and compared and contrasted what I had just relearned.

According to earlier research, back when I first met Lacey, I had written down that scientists found that some people with OCD had "abnormalities in the prefrontal cortex" of their brain, *not* the cerebral cortex.

Hm. That was disappointingly inconsistent.

I quietly groaned and fell back in the chair. My chin perched itself on my fist, appropriately resorting my posture to the classic "thinker position".

Imponderable didn't begin to describe Lacey's obsessive compulsive disorder. This mental disease was a complete mystery.

And the fact that I hadn't solved this mystery was driving me absolutely mad.

It didn't matter that Lacey was my companion and no longer some interesting peer to impartially observe. Well, to be honest, my observing of her was never impartial. I was biased by attraction from the very beginning. And it was that very attraction that made me so unbreakably determined to understand her and her obsessive disease. I was obsessed with the obsessed.

At 1:00 in the morning I manically worked at my desk, rewriting information about the brain that seemed congruent with my obsessive compulsive research onto new sheets of paper to stuff in the OCD/Lacey Parker binder.

I spent a solid hour writing down an abundance of information, from observing Lacey's OCD moment of lightening quick reflexes in dodging the hockey puck, to this rediscovered brain research, and everything in between. Under the low glow of a desk lamp I tried to be as quiet as possible, since both my smothering mom and sensitive brother were light sleepers. If Mom caught me manically writing in a binder like she did a couple of years ago, in my semesters off from school, she'd flip out. She had viewed all that researching-without-college-credit as neurotic, and God forbid her "healthy" son have something remotely wrong with him. Mom had enough on her plate, being a helicopter parent and all.

By the time I crawled into bed my binder had become exponentially thicker.

Sleep didn't come easily. I lay under the warmth of my comforter, reflecting.

When it came to trying to figure out what went on in Lacey's obsessive compulsive head I felt like I was doing research for a philosophy paper in that the more I looked for reasons, the more questions were begged. I should have been frustrated, but I wasn't. I was too allured by her indifferent morals, self-fulfilling cognition, and askew perception of the world to view her faults as anything less than extraordinary and my stumbling upon her rare gem of a brain as anything less than miraculous.

Chapter 43

Lacey wanted to go shopping. She was supposed to go with Natalie, but Natalie had to bail last minute. I went ahead and offered to go with Lacey. She insisted that I didn't have to if I didn't want to, but I insisted that I go. I didn't mind shopping with her. I knew it made her happy.

She actually warned me in the car that she had a lot of weird rituals that screamed "OCD" at the mall, so I should have been prepared.

I wasn't.

Lacey lagged a little behind me so that I'd have to open the door for her.

We waltzed in the CD store. Lacey, almost instantaneously upon entering and with her right foot first of course, spun around and walked out of the store. I don't think she consciously decided to turn around, I think her body's natural response to the OCD trigger caused her to turn around almost automatically. It was like her mind was programmed. Unfortunately she was programmed wrong. Almost as if the wires were all tangled and plugged in the wrong sockets, firing anxiety in all sorts of directions they didn't belong.

"What is it?" I asked her.

"That song, I can't listen to that song. I can't buy anything in a store that plays that song. Whatever item I'd buy, every time I look at it, every time I used it, I'd think of that song. It will be tainted by association with that lyric. Then I'd taint the day with that lyric."

"That's the craziest thing I've ever heard."

"I know. I'm sorry. I can't go in there though. I just can't."

We had to walk in and out of another store, playing a different song. The store had to sell CDs, like the last store. Lacey called it "overriding" the other OCD trigger from the first store.

This was exhausting. Now I know why doing just about anything took extra energy out of her poor little body.

We were on our way out of the mall when Lacey made eye contact with a random auburn haired girl. I could tell just by her obvious confidence and good looks that this girl must have been popular in high school.

"Tara?" Lacey remarked.

"Hey, Lace," the girl seemed too surprised to fully react. "It's been so long!"

"I know, gosh… how, uh, how are you?" Lacey cordially asked the obligated question you ask a person when reuniting while fidgeting with the shopping bag in her hands.

"I'm good," Tara responded quickly, "Spent the last semester in Australia. How are you doing?"

I made a point to recognize she said "how are you doing" instead of just "how are you". I don't know why but there felt like a difference. It made it seem like there was some kind of fallout between the girls. Was this one of the girls that she iced out in the beginning of high school, during the beginning of her severe germ phobia OCD?

Lacey's pitch became higher, as if she was lying, and answered "I'm doing well. I took a few classes last semester. I'm gonna take more next semester, and I'm writing a lot. Oh!" Lacey suddenly remembered I was there. "And this is my boyfriend Jef."

I reached out and shook Tara's hand, "Nice to meet you."

After a few minutes of awkward exchanges the conversation ended.

Then, out of the blue, another girl from Lacey's high school appeared. This time Lacey and the girl didn't talk. The girl didn't even look at Lacey, actually. She just looked at Tara, and soon enough Tara bid Lacey farewell and chatted up the other girl.

As soon as Tara moved on Lacey excused herself from the mall.

It happened so fast. I dumbly watched her speed walk out of the building.

I knew something was wrong. I think seeing her old friend brought back a lot of feelings she had tried to stuff down.

I chased after Lacey.

She stood beside her silver car, in the parking lot. I couldn't tell if she had been crying. She seemed more in that fragile pre-crying stage. Like she was on the verge of tears. She wouldn't let herself cry though. No, that petite young woman stood firm, finding the strength to hold it in. Strength from a place I hypothesized had been visited far too many times for somebody so young.

I tapped, rather than knocked, on the door to that sacred place. "Do you want to talk about it?"

Her response was simple. "There's not much to talk about."

I was quiet. I had never lost a best friend. What she was going through was out of my area of knowledge. What was I supposed to do to help her?

I wasn't sure. So we both stayed quiet for what seemed like five minutes. Just standing in the parking lot, both staring at the pavement.

Seemingly out of the blue Lacey blurted out, "We used to play with our dolls together."

I flicked my head up, realizing she was finally talking about her and Tara. I felt like the best way to react was by staying silent so that she could let out whatever it was she needed to let out. I gave her a reassuring stare, and she found the will to continue sharing.

"We weren't even little kids. We were teenagers. We'd either play with the dolls in my basement or her basement depending on whose house we were at. Down in the basement nobody could eaves drop on us.

I remember getting so excited when we'd make plans, just the two of us, because I knew we'd inevitably wind up playing with our dolls. She'd come over and bring her bag of dolls or I'd go to her house and bring mine. We'd go downstairs, line up all the dolls and go back and forth between each other, choosing which ones we were in charge of being. Then we'd go down the line and name each character, as if it mattered. We usually didn't remember their names, because we played with like over twenty dolls in total. But we were still very committed to our characters when we played with them.

"We would make these really elaborate stories with the dolls. We'd play, making it up as we went along. And I loved it. It almost gave me a high. Because we were creating a story, together. It wasn't just me. The stories were so much more real, more exhilarating, because they were fueled from a real interaction between friends, not just some unspoken daydream fabricated in a solidary mind. Those stories were in this realm. When we played with those dolls it was like a connection was created between fantasy and reality for me. I was living the best of both worlds. I wasn't half alive anymore. I was fully alive. Because finally I didn't have to be isolated to tell a story. Thanks to Tara I was free to let go of my isolation while still doing my favorite thing, using my imagination. And I think that was part of the reason why our friendship was so important to me. Because Tara was more than a friend. She was a human connection who gave my imaginary stories life. And when I see her now, as a distant human that I don't know anymore, I realize those stories are dead. Because our friendship, our connection, is dead."

I was blown away. Lacey's deep explanation for her sadness pulled at my heartstrings. Up until now I had somewhat of an idea how much she valued her old friendships. But that was it, just an idea. Now it was a feeling. I actually felt her pain. I felt the warm nostalgia in the beginning of her reminiscing. I felt the incredible euphoria in the middle. And I felt the agonizing grief in the end.

Chapter 44

I met Lacey at her house the next day.

She wanted to stay at home and write, but I personally saw that as a camouflage for her to sit at home and sulk. I knew she was still down about seeing Tara. So, I insisted if she had to be home that she let me come over. I promised I wouldn't even hug her if she was too tired from the past days of activity to feel anything short of clean. That was what convinced Lacey to let me come over.

I used to find it bizarre that Lacey would never talk much about her old friends, because she seemed to like talking about anything and everything. But after seeing Lacey's reaction to talking about her friend, Tara, I realized why that was.

As we sat on the couch (Lacey on her blanketed cushion and me on the naked cushion beside her) Lacey vented. "I don't know what it's like to lose a lover, but losing a friend, that has to be the saddest feeling I've ever experienced. And it doesn't help that it's my own fault."

I intervened, "Why, because you have OCD? You didn't ask for that."

"But I pushed my friends like Tara away. It was foolish of me to ice her out in high school."

I tried my best to pull Lacey out of her funk. "Lace, you didn't know any better."

She covered her mouth all of a sudden. I think I triggered some untapped emotion she had been inadvertently stowing away.

"Lace..?" I was afraid if I said anymore just the mere sound waves of my timbre would be enough to break her.

"I didn't know what I was doing," she whispered.

I could see in her intense pupils that something was deeply bothering her. And I mean deeply, like to the core of her very spirit.

While sorting through her feelings aloud, Lacey dug down to that deep place and brought back up a handful of pain. "What if I really did make a mistake, Jef? I want to believe what is meant to happen happens and that there's no such thing as a mistake, but what if there is? What if me entertaining my OCD was the biggest mistake of my life? What if I had great things in store that I sabotaged? What if I'm fooling myself to think I could benefit from this phobia through writing and art? I'd basically be living a lie if that was the case."

I knew I couldn't take too long to respond with some kind of practical consolation. I could thank Lacey's natural impatience for that. I tried to speedily sift through the obsessive compulsive disorder research I had stowed away in my brain, aiming to find some kind of fact-based rejoinder that could debunk Lacey's self-blaming theory.

To my dismay, I wasn't fast enough.

"I feel betrayed," Lacey admitted with a timid crack of the throat. "I feel like an enticing legion of voices swooped into my mind with a contract that promised ultimate safety. And I foolishly signed that contract, not realizing I was signing the contract with my blood until it was too late. Until the voices gave me pain and a synthetic sense of safety that has left me..." she didn't know how to finish that sentence.

I took her loss for words as an opportunity to intervene by comforting her with the facts about OCD I was delayed in delivering. "That's just how obsessive compulsive disorder works, Lacey. It appeals to you through scare tactics. It's not your fault you listened."

"But what if it is, Jef? After all, I listened to the sick voices in my head that told me to shut out my friends. That was my choice," suddenly her head fell back on the couch, "I was so stupid."

"No you're not," I assured her without hesitation. "You're smart. Too smart for your own good."

I think Lacey believed me, but that didn't stop her from replying with an argument. "But I made a stupid decision. I chose OCD over friends and family and a future. I'm not saying this for pity, Jef. I'm saying this to be honest. This illness is my fault. When I was younger I wanted so badly to be different that I was willing to have something wrong with me. I vividly remember wanting to contract a mental illness as soon as I found out what a mental illness was. And I got it. I got what I asked for."

"Hey Lace," I caught her attention, "I've got news for you. You can't choose to have a mental illness. That's the chemical imbalance in your brain messing with your head, again. If you felt like you wanted to have a sickness then you were already sick to begin with. Normal kids with normal mindsets don't hope for that."

Lacey gazed at me with grateful eyes. She was quiet for a couple of minutes before finally talking, "Thank you."

"For what?"

"For saying that."

Wow. I don't think I ever heard, until now, Lacey thank me for rationalizing with her.

Lacey curled up tighter on the couch, almost squishing into the corner between the turquoise cushion and arm of the furniture. She had her feet planted on the edge of the sofa so that her knees covered in leopard printed cloth were close to her chest, also where her fidgeting hands were. Lacey peered down at her fingers and picked at the cuticles. She was so rough I thought she was going to rip off her skin and start profusely bleeding.

"Jef," she said while peeling a hangnail off of her pinky.

"Yeah?"

"I'm tired of all the suffering."

"I know Lacey," having seen all the struggles she had to go through, I sympathized with her pain. "You've got a tough mental illness."

By running her clean fingers through her hair, Lacey flipped her curls to the other side of her head. With a hand clutching her flowy brown hair she elaborated, "I'm not just talking about me, Jef. I'm talking about everybody who cares about me. My parents have suffered. My sister has suffered. My brother has suffered. My boyfriend and best friend has suffered. I mean look at us! I can't even hug my own boyfriend! Look at all the people I've hurt! Oh God!" She buried her head in her hands and mourned, "Nobody was supposed to get hurt."

I watched helplessly as a drop of blood descended her pinky finger.

"Lacey you're bleeding-"

"I don't care," she whimpered behind her hands.

I hated this. I hated not being able to touch her in any way, shape, or form, when she was falling captive to depression, leaving me to rely on nothing but my deficient verbal skills to console her.

"Don't be mad at yourself," I said coaxingly, "none of this is your fault. It's the mental illness, not you."

She didn't respond.

I talked softer and leaned forward, "Do you hear me Lacey?"

No response.

"Lacey... what are you thinking?"

"I don't know, Jef," she finally responded as she raised her head out of her hands. She wasn't crying, but the veins in her eyes were a vibrant ruby. "Don't get me wrong, I know my family loves me, but I know that their lives would be so much better without me."

Suddenly I did a complete flip. "Don't say that!" My soft tone became hard as a rock. "Don't you dare say that!" I raised my voice to a level I didn't even know I could reach. I was actually mad at her. I think my anger took her by surprise as well.

Lacey was really tired and wanted to take a nap. She suggested I go home to spare myself the boredom of watching her sleep, but I refused.

After hearing her acutely more depressed attitude through that "my family would be better off without me" statement, there was no way I was leaving her home alone. That was Depression 101. Call me a dork but I actually paid attention in health class.

Chapter 45

With my hands folded behind my head I laid in bed, only accompanied by Lacey's haunting words from earlier in the day.

Don't get me wrong, I know my family loves me, but I know that they're lives would be so much better without me.

I struggled to sleep that entire night. I was too eager to heal my girlfriend of her mental sickness. In any way that I could help, I wanted to. After spending the night awake on and off, trying to come up with methods of helping Lacey feel less depressed, I finally thought of a place that I could take her.

I knew just where we could go. The forest where I brought York for walks. It was beautiful, and it wasn't snowing (one of Lacey's least favorite things) which was a definite bonus.

"Where are you taking me?" Lacey asked.

"You'll see," I ambiguously answered, turning the steering wheel off the main road and onto a bumpy dirt path.

I let the car roll through the rugged terrain until stopping in a familiar section of the forest.

"Here we are," I yanked the lever into park.

"You brought me to the middle of the woods?" Lacey peered through the window at the foreign landscape.

"Damn right."

"Jef what's going on? You said you were taking me somewhere to calm down."

"I know, and I did. Out here you can get as angry, as sad, or as neurotic as you want. You can just scream it out."

"That's not going to happen," Lacey shut down with a low pitch that sounded like she was mocking a male's vocal chords.

"No, I'm serious Lace, Peter does it when he gets really frustrated. Screams in the woods behind our house. The neighbors used to get scared but they eventually got used to it. Now they hear a grown man screaming and go 'Oh, that's just Peter Sterling.'"

"Jef, I'm not so sure that's a good thing," Lacey giggled nervously.

"Whatever, forget about Peter. Now come on," I opened my car door and leaped out of the tall jeep. The subsequent sound of Lacey slamming her door echoed through the vast woodland and she met me in the front of the boxy car.

"I'm not doing this, Jef."

"Yes you are."

"No I'm not."

I pushed, "Yes, Lacey, you are."

Lacey shook her head, as if the sway of her head was evaporating her smile. "I'm not doing this," she crossed her arms defiantly. "I'm not screaming in the middle of the woods."

"Why not?" I challenged.

"Because I don't want to!"

"Because you're embarrassed?"

"Well yeah. It's ridiculous."

"Really? So when Peter does this is he being ridiculous? Is that what you're saying?"

She got angry at me for that. "Don't you dare go putting words in my mouth! Only I can put words in my mouth." She stabbed her pointer finger inward.

I didn't want to give in to Lacey's stubbornness. There was no hiding that her depression was worsening. She needed help, and I had every intention of helping her in any way I could.

"Please Lacey, just do it, I promise you'll feel better-"

"I can't!" she belted out at me.

"That's what I'm talking about!" I encouraged her anger, "Just yell like that! Scream at the wind, pretend the wind is me pestering you."

"Ugh!" she spun around and started to climb upside the jeep.

"Lacey!"

"I told you I'm not doing this! I'm freezing and I'm not in the mood! Please just take me home."

I wanted to hold out longer, but the horizon was getting dark, the temperature was dropping, and the sun was starting to set.

"Fine, let's just go," I gave up and put myself in the driver's seat of the jeep.

I was mad, both for selfish and selfless reasons. I was mad that I literally spent the entire prior night worrying about her and trying to come up with this idea to help her. And I was mad that she wasn't willing to help herself because of a little bit of embarrassment and a whole lot of stubbornness.

Angrily I twisted the key into the ignition.

The engine roared, followed by a high pitched screech, and then shut itself off.

"What was that?" Lacey fretted.

"Nothing, don't worry about it," I tried to play it cool as I turned the key in the ignition a second time.

The engine roared again, screeched a little, then turned off.

"We're not gonna blow up or anything, are we?" she worried.

"What kind of question is that?" I lashed out, "Seriously, Lace, this is a perfect example of why you need to just scream in the middle of the forest. You're way too uptight."

I tried, yet again, to turn the car on.

The car experienced a chain reaction of malfunctions and sputtered.

"Dead," I finally gave up and announced.

Lacey was far from amused. "What do you mean?"

Frustrated by the entire failure of this plan I threw my hands from the wheel and yelled at her, "I mean it's fricken dead! How else can I put it?"

"But you can fix it, right?"

"Probably not!" I ripped my hat off my head and chucked it over the dashboard then clawed an aggressive hand through my hat hair.

"Are you serious Jef? Aren't boys supposed to know cars?"

"Yeah, boys with dads."

That shut her up.

Seeing that I wasn't gonna be able to fix the car on my own, I whipped my cell phone out of my pocket to call my friend, Troy, who was a car mechanic. His family owned their own auto shop, so there was no doubt he'd be able to figure out the problem.

Of course, since the day was already going so great, one click of my unresponsive phone and I realized it was dead. "Shit," I threw the stupid thing over the dashboard to join my hat.

"Whoa calm down!" Lacey reacted. "What are you doing?"

"My phone's dead also."

Her face turned ghost white, "Please tell me you're joking."

"Geez, Lace, you need to calm down. There's no need to worry, I'll just borrow your phone and call Gabe or something."

"No, Jef, you can't."

"What do you mean? Lemme guess, you don't want my grimy hands touching your precious cell phone."

"No! That's ridiculous!"

"*That's* ridiculous? You know what Lacey- I don't think you're qualified to call things ridiculous or not ridiculous. Leave that to dialectical reasoning, reflective judgment, deductive reasoning, anything but your biased intuition!"

"Why are you being so mean?"

"Maybe I wouldn't be so mean if you let me use your phone to call somebody when we're stranded in the middle of the forest."

"Well whose fault is that?" she fought back.

"Yours!" we both yelled at the same time.

With a sigh I slammed my back into the car seat. "Can I please just borrow your phone?"

"Uh..."

"Seriously Lace? Seriously? You'd rather be stranded in the forest then let me-"

"I didn't bring my phone!" she finally admitted.

Now I think I turned ghost white. "What?" My teeth bit the air. "Why?"

Lacey shrunk in her seat, as if she was afraid to answer.

"Why don't you have your phone?" I pressed.

Instead of looking me in the eyes she stared down at her feet and replied, "I left it at home because I just wiped it down and got it all clean."

I was too annoyed to speak. I just glared at her with unfriendly eyes. I wanted to tell her how stupid and irresponsible that was, but I knew that wasn't a good idea. As calm as possible I just let the words slowly enunciate their way out of my gritting teeth, "Well I guess now there is a need to worry."

My plan to stay cool and collected probably lasted all of three minutes. As soon as that time was up I went off at Lacey.

"There is literally no excuse for not bringing your phone with you when you leave the house! We're gonna have to stay the night in this stupid forest in this stupid car all because of your stupid phobia! And that's right, I called it stupid, because it is stupid! It's fucking stupid! And normally alone time like this would be great for a couple, normally I'd dream for something like this, but you're not even gonna let me do as little as hold your hand, are you?"

She just stared at me, with hurt eyes.

"That's what I thought," I slammed back into the seat behind me and turned to look out the window, watching as the landscape got darker and darker.

A good hour passed.

It was dark. Since the car refused to turn on, Lacey and I were left cold. We weren't talking to each other. Neither of us made a sound. She wasn't complaining about what a jerk I was, probably because she knew I was right. And thank God she wasn't crying. I don't know if I would have been able to handle being sympathetic right now. Was I wrong? We wouldn't be in this situation, stranded in the middle of the woods, if she had just brought her phone like a normal person.

As time went on, the less fresh my anger was, and the sicker my stomach felt as I recollected each aggressive word I spit out at her. Especially calling her illness stupid. I knew for a fact that hurt her, remembering how her "Obsessive Compulsive Disorder" poem specifically said that she knew other people saw her illness as stupid. Technically it was stupid, it was an illness that manipulated the receptors in her brain by effectively turning absolutely nothing into something to be afraid of. Come to think of it that sounded far from stupid. It was smart. Too smart. That's why it was able to find all sorts of ways to twist Lacey's thoughts and beliefs into obeying those ridiculous and impractical set of laws. It was horribly sad.

Shit, now I felt like an absolute asshole for blowing up at her like that.

I turned to look at the girl I just verbally tore apart. Lacey tightly scrunched herself in the passenger seat with her arms hugging her shins. She kept trying to rub her legs to warm up.

"Lacey… I'm sorry if I was a little harsh…"

"Don't," she retaliated, not wanting to hear any bit of an apology.

Feeling horrible, I kicked my head back and stared up at the ceiling. It was naked compared to the glow in the dark stars on my bedroom ceiling.

When I glanced back at Lacey she was curled up even tighter and shivering harder.

"There's a blanket in the backseat. If there are Frisbees on the seat just kick 'em to the floor and you can lie back there in the blanket."

"I don't wanna lie back there, when is the last time you cleaned-"

"Do me a favor and don't finish that sentence," I groaned while rubbing my temples with each hand. I was so tired of listening to her irrationally deem things clean and unclean. I had just apologized and I really didn't want to get mad at her again.

Lacey must have been really upset, because she didn't respond. Without a word she whipped the car door open, hopped out, slammed the door shut, then got comfortable in the back. We were both on each other's nerves, so it was probably best I stayed in the front seat while she laid down in the back of the jeep.

As the night went on I took out the notebook that I left in my glove compartment and jotted down notes about Lacey's behavior that night. I was sure to scribble all of my frustration down about her lack of cell phone, something I quickly realized I should have done instead of lashing out at her. Every so often I'd check on Lacey sleeping. She appeared so much less stressed out when she was asleep. I was relieved. It was that sense of relief that made me realize, no matter how mad I got at her, I still cared about her, and I still loved her.

When I was done writing down notes I made sure to put the notebook and pen back in my glove compartment.

Eventually sleep swept me away.

I woke up in the middle of the night to a shrill scream.

Immediately I went into protective mode and turned to check on Lacey in the backseat. I was horrified to see nothing but my plaid blanket.

"Lace?" my stomach dropped.

Another unhinged blood hurdling scream split through the night air. It was female. Definitely female.

Without hesitation I swung my door open, nearly kicking it, and chased after the scream. Using the round moon as my guiding light I tore through thorny bushes and tangles of branches, hurdled slippery crevices of mud, and crunched fragile saplings with heedless sneakers, not feeling any of the pain I probably should have. I was too high on unprecedented fear and adrenaline, racing through the woods, imagining the worst.

"Lacey!" I shouted at the top of my lungs.

The feminine shriek tore through the grim forest again.

My sneakers pounded the rolling terrain, nearly slipping on packed down patches of decaying leaves underneath a thin layer of old sloshy snow. I did track in high school and I'd be willing to bet I was running faster than whatever record speed I might have ran back then.

I raced. I raced after that scream, preparing to find my girlfriend in a pool of her own blood, having been mauled by a rare New England bear. And as much as I knew that was unlikely, I still worried. I guess that's what happens when you're scared. Fear makes you think irrationally. Wait, is that how Lacey's phobia made her feel *all* the time?

With a violent sweep through a tall bush, I found myself in a familiar opening.

There in front of the frozen over lake, under the starry sky, was Lacey. Screaming up at the full moon.

Lacey didn't completely disregard my advice. There she was, in the middle of the forest, screaming her guts out.

Gradually her scream melted into a pitiful wail.

Just as the intensity in her scream descended, so did her body. Lacey's knees buckled, causing her to collapse on the damp shore.

"Lace," I gasped as I ran to her side and knelt down. I didn't care about asking her before I touched her. I was just so glad to see her alive, in one piece, that I held one hand on her lower back, and the other bracing her head. "What are you-"

Before I could finish my question she burst into tears and fell onto me. "Why?" she whimpered.

I didn't know what to say.

"Why was I made like this?" Lacey plead for an answer and fastened her bloodshot eyes onto mine. I had no clue how to respond, how to alleviate each jagged vein that broke her corneas into a web of cracks.

I wrapped my arms around her, in a hug, and let her weep. She cried and cried while nuzzling against my collar bone.

And even though Lacey was upset, I couldn't help but feel a smidge of relief. Because I remembered, so distinctly, Lacey venting to me earlier, "*A meltdown would be a break for me! Sometimes I just wanna fall to the ground and cry with my head in my hands, but then I remember, 'fuck, the ground is dirty with germs, I can't sit on it.' I don't get the luxury of letting go and just melting down!*"

Lacey was actually letting herself kneel in the dirt and lean in another person's arms. She didn't even care that I was stroking my hand through her hair. Finally I could give her the physical comfort she had been so deprived of in the meltdown she had also been deprived of.

I couldn't help but see the breathtaking miracle of the moment. Because for right now, whether short lived or not, Lacey was free.

Chapter 46

I woke up to the sopping wet feeling of a canine's slobbery tongue licking the corner of my mouth.

"What the-" My vision came into focus and I realized there was a golden retriever standing over me.

I looked to my right, and Lacey was lying in my arm, just starting to squirm to wakefulness.

The dog gave me another wet kiss on the face.

"Hey boy," I ruffled his golden fur with my free hand.

Lacey lifted herself off the snow sprinkled floor. There were snarls all throughout her windblown hair.

In her discombobulation she scanned the bizarre surrounding. "Oh my God," she realized where she was, "I did it. I slept in the dirt!" she burst out laughing, "I'm a germy mess!"

Her pure happiness infected me with laughter, "You are," I continued to pet the golden retriever.

Lacey joined in and scratched at his ears, "And who do we have here?"

We were both in the midst of petting the friendly dog when Lacey suddenly caught sight of my forearms.

"Jef," she pointed to my shins. They were covered in tiny cuts and scabs of dry blood. "What happened?"

"Oh dammit, it's nothing, don't mind that-"

"Jef that's not nothing! What happened to you?"

"Er, I don't know. It must have been from the sticks and thorns I plowed through last night," I remembered.

Lacey's pupils were sorrowful. Her lips split apart, like she was about to apologize on the sticks' and thorns' behalf, when suddenly we were interrupted by an older gentleman with a gray beard. He came running over to grab his dog, "I'm sorry, he's very friendly." Immediately he caught sight of my shredded up legs. "Oh my God, are you okay?"

"Oh yeah, I'm fine," I quickly dismissed, then proceeded to tell him how Lacey and I were stuck in the woods in the middle of the night because there was something wrong with my car. The man offered to give it a look. So we left the lakeside and ventured back to my jeep, where the hospitable man discovered I had a low battery. I felt pretty stupid for not knowing that, but I didn't let it bother me. I was too…happy wasn't the right word. I was too… *grateful* that Lacey was able to withstand a night in the dirt without having a meltdown. She certainly had a meltdown last night, but it was before she decided to let go just for that night, and laid down in the dirt with me.

So, after the older man popped open the hood of my car and gave it a jump start with his jump cable, I wound up driving Lacey home then drove myself back to my house.

As soon as I walked in the door my mom hounded me. "Where have you been Jef? Where did you and Lacey go?"

I stood in the doorway, itching my sideburn, and quizzed her in my defense, "How do you know I was out with Lacey?"

"Your brother told me."

I glanced up at the top of the staircase, where Peter stood, and hissed at him. "Do you have to be such a snitch?"

"Leave your brother alone!" my mom scolded.

"Yeah Jef! Leave me alone!" Peter hollered.

My mom continued to go off at me. "Where were you, Jef?"

"Nowhere," I brushed past her with the intent of going upstairs to my room.

"Don't you dare walk away from me when I'm talking to you, mister!" she grabbed my arm and got a whiff of my grainy hair. "What happened to you any ways? You're filthy! You look like you were rolling around in the dirt!" Right when she said that aloud her eyes bugged out as she jumped to an embarrassing conclusion.

I knew what she was thinking, "Mom no-"

"We need to talk," she ordered with the utmost sternness. No, no, no. There was no way this conversation was going to happen. "Mum nothing happened!"

I tried to break away but she stepped in front of me. "Then you wouldn't mind explaining why you're covered in dirt?"

There was really no easy-to-believe explanation. My girlfriend didn't bring her phone because she was afraid of getting germs on it, I yelled at her, then she had a major meltdown, ran through the woods alone, screamed at the top of her lungs by the lake, and we both fell asleep while she cried in my arms. Yeah that would go over real well. Seriously, though, what could I say that wouldn't make my mom judge Lacey in the most negative light?

"What were you doing last night?" my mom prodded.

"Nothing," I put simply. I knew trying to explain was a lost cause. I just stood there in silence.

My mom shook her head in disbelief. I was a good son who rarely ever caused any trouble or did anything sneaky. It kind of pissed me off that my mom thought I had an obligation to be that way, because normal guys my age were way more wild and out of control than not showing up one Goddamn night. Then again a lot of normal guys my age lived at school or in an apartment, not at home with their mother. Of course Mom didn't know any different. I could thank Peter's disabilities for that.

"I just hope you're being smart," Mom lectured.

"Mum!" I was both annoyed, embarrassed, and insulted.

"Excuse me for being concerned when you stay out all night with your girlfriend Jef! Is she-"

"Mom!" I freaked out and slammed my palms over my ears, "How hard is it for you to realize that I'm a 23-year-old man? I don't need you to treat me like I'm a kid! I'm not Peter!" As soon as that exclamation slipped out I recognized my inconsiderate mistake.

"Screw you Jef! You're a jerk!" Peter shouted from the top of the stairs.

"No, Pete, I didn't, I didn't mean tha-"

"I said screw you!" he stormed off to his room.

Shit. What had I done?

"I hope you had fun with your girlfriend last night, because you won't be going out for a while."

Lacey and I spoke on the phone later, in the evening. I let her know I got in trouble for staying out all night with her.

"So… my mom was pissed when I came home."

"Oh no," Lacey's sigh sounded muffled in the phone. "Does she hate me?"

"No, not at all… she was mad at me."

I sat at my desk, contemplating how much trouble I was in with Lacey's parents for keeping her out all night. "What am I gonna need to do to earn your parents' trust back?"

"Believe it or not, nothing. My mom and dad figured I was at your house all night."

"They were okay with that?"

"Jef, it's me we're talking about. I'm a full grown adult with OCD, they knew I wasn't about to get myself in an uncomfortable situation."

"Mmm," I moaned ambivalently.

"They were actually happy I was out on a Friday night without calling them to come pick me up."

I scratched the back of my head and leaned back in my desk chair, "I guess that's a good thing."

"Yeah," she huffed, "I suppose."

Chapter 47

After the woods fiasco Lacey and I were closer than ever. We had never gotten in a heated argument like that. We had debates and disagreements before but nothing where we were that infuriated, and hurt, at each other. And as angry as I was at her that night, it was a good thing, because the genuine fear and concern I felt when I looked in the backseat and didn't see her made me realize that just because her and her OCD was frustrating me didn't mean I stopped caring about her.

There were flurries of snow sprinkling down on the campus on the first day of the spring semester, what would be my last semester in college. I hated this weather. Barely anybody was outside.

Lacey and I joined up in the library at one in the afternoon to do our schoolwork. While I was rigorously writing an essay outline using my psychology notes Lacey seemed totally out of it. I caught her doodling all over her notebook like five times, which was kind of depressing because I remember a time when she used to deviate from her homework to write thought-provoking pieces. Now she was just mindlessly drawing swirls and scribbles all over her paper. I swear Lacey was getting worse with the cold weather.

I was deep in thought in a more modified "thinker pose". One hand clasping my jaw, the other hand scraping the mustard yellow paint off of the pencil perched behind my ear.

Lacey had her eyes fixed on me and her top teeth biting down on her lower lip.

"What?" I breathed out coyly, still itching the writing utensil behind my ear like it was part of my head.

"You're just, you're really cute with that pencil behind your ear."

Oh God, here comes the stupid smirk.

"Really?" I laughed uncomfortably, "Me tucking a pencil behind my ear is cute? That doesn't strike you as 'germy' or 'gross'?"

"Well it is pretty unsanitary, but your cuteness is overshadowing that grossness. The only way I'd be really turned off is if that was some random chewed up pencil you found on the floor."

My hand froze.

Come to think of it, this was a random pencil I found on the floor.

And I could literally feel the molar indents on it.

In one fluid motion I whipped my hand behind my ear and sent the gnawed pencil flying in the distance, back on the dirty floor where it originated.

"Oh gross!" Lacey burst out laughing upon realizing what the abrupt toss of the pencil implied.

"What are you working on anyways?" she wondered innocently.

I froze. For whatever reason I felt like I had to hide that from her.

"What are you working on?"

"Chemistry," I lied.

"Oh. Like pi and stuff?"

I glanced up from the psychology textbook and laughed, "No. Pi is a ratio used mostly in geometry."

"Oh," Lacey's complexion became an adorable shade of pink, "Oops."

Quickly I scratched at the light stubble starting to form on my cheek to keep Lacey from seeing the endeared smile across my face. I couldn't help but feel stupidly giddy. It was cute when she tried to talk math.

"That was dumb," Lacey laughed shyly and shook her head, "That was really dumb."

The sight of Laccy trying to relate to me in spite of embarrassing herself aroused a potent guilt from the pit of my stomach. I owed it to her to do the same, and honesty might be a good start. After all, I still couldn't shake the internal shame that transpired every time I remembered how this relationship formed on the basis of a selfish ploy to entertain and enlighten my bored brain. So I fessed up about my real homework topic, "Actually, I'm doing psych homework."

With an iridescent twinkle of the eyes Lacey smirked, "Psych? Like psychology? You hadn't told me you were taking psychology."

"I know," I responded lamely.

"Can I see your textbook?" Lacey spoke up.

"Hm?" I didn't know how to say no.

"Your psychology textbook," she clarified, "I've never taken a psych class. Can I look at it?"

I gulped.

Sweated.

"Sure."

Resentfully I unzipped my backpack, pulled the textbook out, then placed it on the table. I couldn't even bring myself to slide the book over to her. She had to lean over the library table and grab it herself.

Lacey curiously began flipping through the pages.

In my nervousness I rambled. "Hey!"

"What?" Lacey shifted her focus off of the textbook and onto me. That gave me a tinge of relief.

"You know how I said you were right-brained and I was left-brained?"

"Yeah?" Lacey perked up, adorably curious. I loved it.

"Well, apparently the left prefrontal region, associated with happiness and anger, specializes with the impulse to approach a situation while the right prefrontal region, associated with disgust and fear, specializes with the impulse to withdraw from a situation."

"Oh!" Lacey's eyes widened, "Like 'fight or flight'!"

"Yes! It's exactly like that!"

"That's so interest-" Lacey paused, suddenly realizing what I meant. "Are you saying that I'm more prone to be afraid and disgusted by things than somebody like you?"

"Well, yeah. Maybe. It's possible. It was in the unit about emotions and I just thought it was interesting."

"Hm."

Hm? What was she thinking? What did that mean?

Lacey returned her attention to the textbook, carefully peeling apart each page and carefully perusing the text. So I decided to do the same, returning my attention to homework.

"Emotions, you said?"

"Yeah. Why?" I asked mindlessly while scribbling away at my outline of how different neurotransmitters affect the brain.

"We're only three days into the semester," Lacey commented.

The judgment in Lacey's tone broke my attention away from my outline and up at her. She was squinting into the psychology textbook like it was written in a foreign language. What was she so confused about? What was she getting at?

"What?" I wondered fretfully.

"We're three days into the school semester," Lacey repeated, then in the simplest of motions Lacey flipped the open book so that it was standing upright on the library table, facing me. "'Emotions in the Brain' is Module 38."

I felt the blood drain from my head.

I had no clue what to say.

I couldn't say that I was in an accelerated class. Even accelerated classes wouldn't be on halfway through their textbook within the first week of the semester.

"I read ahead," I admitted.

"I'll say!" Lacey remarked, dropped the book to the table, then slammed it shut. Quickly shoving her notebook in her backpack, she stood to her feet.

"Wait!" I blurted out and threw my arms forward, knocking my open water bottle but somehow catching it before it wobbled over and spilled.

"Are you only taking this class so that you can, can, analyze me? Diagnose me? Evaluate me like I'm some kind of study?!"

Her overwhelming accuracy launched my adrenaline into overdrive.

"No!" I lied, then jumped out of my seat. "Lace, please don't be mad!"

"I'm not mad," Lacey frowned. "I'm just- just uncomfortable, that's all."

"Lace…"

"I don't like this. I don't like you diminishing my individuality to cognitive theories about human emotions and prefrontal regions of the brain."

"Why?" I nervously laughed. "What's wrong with that?"

"I can't just be postulated like some, some, some statistic or science experiment or research topic."

A nervous sweat began to bloom behind my neck. To disguise my own guilt for studying Lacey I made a retaliatory comment. "Why is that? Are you too good for science?"

Wow.

Sound more like an asshole, Jef.

Chapter 48

"But why Dad?" Peter whined into the phone.

I could hear the loud muffle of my father yelling at Peter on the other line.

That afternoon my dad was supposed to take Peter to a Celtic music concert while Lacey and I got the house to ourselves.

Realizing something was wrong I got up, leaving Lacey perched alone on the couch, and stood by Peter's side while he begged my father for an explanation as to what I assumed was a plan cancelation.

I held my hand out to receive the phone and whispered, "Let me talk to him."

Peter shook his head violently, like a little kid who didn't want to share his favorite toy. "Please Daddy!"

There was more incoherent yelling blaring from the telephone.

"Pete," I mouthed.

"But why do you have to cancel?" Peter moaned to my father.

Feeling an urgency to get Peter off of the Goddamn phone before he had a mental breakdown that might graduate into a schizophrenic episode, I whacked my brother's arm with the back of my hand and hissed, "Peter give me the phone!"

I was too late though.

The monotonous beep of a hung up phone indicated that Dad hung up on Peter.

I could see the tears brewing in Peter's green eyes.
"Pete..."
Peter didn't hear me though. He was in his own world of devastation.
"Whatever he said, Peter, don't get upset-"
Completely neglecting me, Peter shoved the telephone back into the receiver so hard that it actually fell out of its stand. He then charged to the other end of the den.
"Peter!" I called out while struggling to lodge the slippery phone back in its stand.
Lacey knew not to interrupt when Peter's emotions were running high, so when I heard her say, "Peter..." as well I knew something horrible was about to happen.
I spun around to see Peter using his spastic hands to shove all of our board games off of their oak shelf.
"Peter!"
In his tantrum Peter grabbed the ceramic lamp off the shelf, ripping out the cord as well.
"Peter!" I hastily ran to stop him.
Peter didn't care though. In his outrageous distress he weakly chucked the lamp across the room, at the telephone.
Reflexes kicked in and I ducked as the earsplitting sound of glass and ceramic shattering exploded against the wall.
Peter, now sobbing, darted out of the den and stormed upstairs, slamming his door. There was no doubt he locked himself in his room by blockading it with his chair, something he learned ever since Mom got the lock removed from the bedroom door.
I was so worked up with anger, sadness, mortification, and a medley of other negative emotions by what just happened. I felt my nausea kick in. I wouldn't be surprised if I turned green.
I proceeded to clean up the mess Peter had made in his devastation. Bending down, I picked up the slivers of lightbulb glass and ceramic shards.
Lacey, covering her gaping mouth with her hand, stood up from the couch to help. She couldn't believe what just happened either.
"Don't," I signaled her back down, "I've got it."

I could see she was conflicted, but Lacey obeyed my request and lowered back into her seat. She barely whispered, "What can I do, Jef?"

I shook my head, attempting to shake the prior scene out of my memory. I was so humiliated on Peter's behalf. He liked Lacey a lot and I know once he cooled down he'd be painstakingly embarrassed.

"Just, just don't judge him," I asked of Lacey.

She nodded a delicate nod, "I won't."

While I gathered the rest of the broken pieces of lamp Lacey sat by silently and stared down at her dry hands.

I was so glad my mom wasn't home for this. She would have been mortified to know Lacey saw Peter in another crazed state like that full moon incident.

Eventually Lacey asked me if she could at least clean up the board games shoved onto the wooden floorboards. I said yes. I appreciated that she was willing to touch items off of the floor. I knew how bad her contamination fear must have been gnawing at her conscience.

After tidying up Lacey went in the kitchen to wash her hands. I followed along and did the same.

"I'm gonna go talk to him," I told Lacey and leaned down, about to kiss her on the forehead, but hesitated.

"It's okay," she peeped out, giving me the saddest okay to touch her skin with my lips.

I kissed her forehead.

She wouldn't look at me.

When I came back downstairs Lacey was exactly where I left her, standing by the windowsill, looking outside.

My mind, on the other hand, was in a different state.

I just spent a good twenty-five minutes listening to Peter rave about how much he loved his father and how he just wants to hang out with him.

"How is he?" Lacey spun around when she realized I had entered the room.

I fell into the kitchen chair and stared off into space. "He's okay. Just really hurt. And he feels really bad about making a scene in front of you. But he's gonna be okay."

All was quiet except the leaky drip of the faucet.

"Are you going to be okay?" she whispered poignantly.

That question snapped me out of my empty stare and caused my retinas to dart at Lacey's. I was transfixed by the long eyelash decorated eyes delving into my soul.

Honestly... I wasn't okay. I was sick to my stomach. I felt bad for my brother. I felt mad at my dad. I felt guilty for being the favored son. I felt selfishly upset that I couldn't be a normal person and love my girlfriend in a physical way. I felt terrible, really. But for some reason I was unable to vocalize that. There were too many thoughts of rage and malaise swirling around my head.

Without conscious permission my mouth took the initiative to grab one of those random thoughts and say it out loud. "My dad isn't a parent. Parents are supposed to love their kids no matter what."

"Yeah, they are," Lacey agreed with me.

Out of distress I perched my elbow on the kitchen table and matted my palm along my forehead. "I don't get it." I whispered to the oak table surface.

Before I could stop myself I was spilling out all of those distraught thoughts spinning around my head.

"I just, I see the way Peter looks at my dad with such yearning for my dad to love him. Just this pure longing for him to show the tiniest bit of affection. And I don't understand how my dad can look at that same guy and not feel anything. No guilt. No sympathy. No love. Nothing. He just, I don't know, I guess he just doesn't care. That's the only conclusion I can come to. There's gotta be something wrong with my dad. Because when I look at Peter looking at my dad it destroys me inside. He's just so innocent. Just tonight I went in his room, anticipating I was gonna have to spew out some bullshit about how my dad really isn't that lousy of a person, but Peter was already in that mindset. He was gloating about how much he loves my dad. Can you believe that? He says he loves my father! And he really means it!" A disheartened laugh rumbled through my scratchy throat, "Peter doesn't say anything he doesn't mean. It just blows my mind that he could still love my dad after all the antagonistic remarks and poor treatment he puts my brother through. Love? I can't even say that I love my dad. And I feel so guilty because here I am feeling no sense of love for my own dad yet I'm the son who gets all of his attention... and it's my brother who wants it more than anything! I feel so, so, I just, I feel like such a terrible person!"

I was in for a shock when Lacey hurried to my side, knelt down to the dirty tile floor, and squeezed my hand. "You are not a terrible person," she tried with all her might to embed her words into me. "And just because your dad doesn't show affection, doesn't mean he doesn't care."

I locked eyes with hers. In that moment I believed her.

She went on reassuring me in her most comforting tone, "You are not responsible for the cold way that your father treats Peter like the family scapegoat. And just because you don't love your dad and Peter does doesn't make you a bad person. You guys are separate people. And you're entitled to feel however it is you feel."

As I stared at Lacey and listened to every word that passed her poised lips, I was overcome with a sense of ease.

But still, one question lingered.

"How could you not love your own son? How is that possible?" I barely got the inquiry out because I was so overloaded with despair.

"Oh Jef," Lacey sighed, but not with pity. It wasn't pity straining her vocal chords. It was empathy. Like she could feel my pain. "He obviously has his own issues."

"Yeah well that's not an excuse for ditching your imperfect family." I unexpectedly lashed out.

Lacey didn't take the aggression personally. "I'm not trying to give him an excuse, Jef. I'm just giving a reason. Some kind of explanation."

"I know, I know. I'm sorry. I just, I just want to understand. I need to understand."

Lacey now joined her hands together so that they were both clasping my sweaty palm. "Sometimes you can't understand everybody," her voice was softer than before.

There was nothing left to say.

I didn't need to say anything else. Lacey didn't need to say anything else.

I was content.

Chapter 49

"This is disgusting," Lacey sighed while touching page after page of her classmates' flash fiction assignments. She was supposed to read through everybody's work and write review after review. "I hate touching all of these pieces of paper. Half of them have God-knows-what stained onto the assignment. Look, look at this!" Lacey held up a lined piece of paper covered in brown splotches. "I don't know how you could ever want to be a teacher, Jef."

I raised a complacent eyebrow as I aggressively flipped to the next page in my calculus textbook, "I don't compromise my future goals for irrational fears."

Lacey didn't respond.

Stunned by her voluntary silence, I replayed that last sentence.

I don't compromise my future goals for irrational fears.

Not only was I trivializing Lacey's malaise, I was also lying. Hell, my entire community college career was a compromise to accommodate my irrational fear of leaving Peter at home alone.

In a sudden fraught spell Lacey catapulted off the couch and bailed on her homework. "I can't focus, I'll do that later."

I couldn't help but feel responsible for her abrupt spike in aggravation.

"Lacey," I wanted to make amends but the waterfall from the kitchen faucet drowned out my efforts. So I got off the couch to approach her, but Lacey was moving a mile a minute in her hypnotic OCD spell, drying off her hands and quickly scurrying to the bottle of Purell on the window sill.

"My hands were extra germy from that stupid assignment, I should use hand-sanitizer too." she quickly squirted the gel onto her hands, thoroughly rubbed it into her skin, then made her way to the pot on the stove.

"I'm gonna reheat coffee, do you want coffee?"

"Uh, er, no," I responded, flustered.

Lacey flicked on an unoccupied burner. Why didn't she turn on the burner underneath her pot?

"Lacey wrong one," I called out.

"Heat kills germs too, right?" Lacey conjectured and, to my pure shock, began to move her sanitized hands towards the flames.

"LACEY!" I sprinted over and swiped her arms away from the stovetop. My rush of adrenaline snapped Lacey out of her trance. Her pupils dilated and the mind behind those eyes returned to reality. "What are you doing!"

"What am I doing? What are *you* doing! Hand sanitizer is 99% rubbing alcohol and you just doused your hands with it! Don't you know that alcohol is highly flammable? You almost lit your hands on fire!"

"Oh my God, I'm so stupid," Lacey squeezed her eyes shut, then, in what I'm sure was an attempt to transfer the attention off of her embarrassing fumble and onto something else, Lacey locked her stare onto the kitchen sink again.

Two seconds after nearly blowing up her hands she was scurrying back over to the sink. What was happening in that brain?

"Aw are you kidding me!" Lacey shouted at the sink.

I followed, "What?"

Lacey started to put on rubber dishwashing gloves, "There's a mountain of dirty dishes. Ugh. I hate doing the dishes."

That actually took me as a bit of a surprise. "Really? I would have expected dish washing to be quite soothing for somebody like you," I referred to her fear of germs.

"You'd think so," Lacey agreed, "But washing dishes is a vigorous process for me."

"Do you want to take turns?" I offered.

"Don't be ridiculous!" Lacey shooed me away, "You do enough for me. Go back to the table and relax."

"I was in the middle of doing calculus homework," I informed her.

"Isn't that relaxing for a geek like you?"

"True," I laughed.

She shook her head and began scrubbing at a dish, "You're so weird, Jef."

I tried to do the rest of my math homework, but kept getting distracted by Lacey's dishwashing which took far longer than it should have.

I watched across the kitchen as Lacey scrubbed at each dish, refueling the sponge with more soap for each piece of kitchenware.

The strong aroma of lemon scented soap was dense in the air.

I couldn't take it anymore. I pushed in my chair and went to her side.

"Do you need to wash your hands?" Lacey asked, about to knock the handle to the "cold" side with the back of her gloved hand.

"No," I informed her.

Immediately she went back to meticulously scrubbing a seemingly washed dish.

"Lace," I tried to snap her out of her irrational spell. But she was so committed to that dish. "I think it's clean."

She scrubbed and scrubbed and scrubbed.

Eventually I had to intervene by reaching into the sink.

"Wait," she cried out and pulled the dish further away from my hands, "I'm almost done."

"It's clean enough, Lace," I reached out and grabbed the china plate.

"No, not yet," she wouldn't let up her grip.

"Lacey!"

"Just let me finish!" She gave one last yank, and the china dish went flying through the lemon scented air and shattered on the hard tile floor.

We both stared at each other.

"Okay, that wasn't supposed to happen," I blurted out.

After we both cleaned up the glass shards Lacey made a point to kick me out.

"You know what, I'm tired. You should go, Jef. I'm sorry. I know it's early but I need a nap and I'm gonna have to shower before I lie in bed…"

"Why don't you just take a nap on the couch or something?" I suggested.

Immediately Lacey freaked out at my suggestion, "Jef, you know I can't relax until I shower. I can't just lie down on the couch with all these 'school germs' on me. That's disgusting! I don't want to be germy. I want to be clean. Pure. Immaculate, really. To touch things without feeling like I'm ruining them with my cross-contamination."

"Cross-contamination?" I asked, unfamiliar with the phrase.

"Yeah, you know, spreading germs."

Oh God. This added a whole new layer to her already complex mental disorder.

"I thought you were afraid of touching germs for the sake of feeling dirty?"

"Well, yeah, that's the primary fear. But I guess an extension of that fear is that- if I'm dirty and I sit on the couch or touch a door knob then I'll make those things dirty. It's disgusting and gross and- and… shameful."

Lacey worried about worrying. Not sanitizing germy hands now meant feeling germy hands in the future. Cross-contaminating everything and anything in their grasp. As if the very essence of her being relied on the purity of her skin. There was anxiety in the now, no question about that, but it was a 'get rid of the anxiety *now* so that you don't have to feel it *later*' phenomena. This ongoing pattern of 'Don't feel! Don't feel! Don't feel!', something puzzling and eerily contradicting for somebody whose virtues, values, and talents were so centered around emotional feelings.

"You are *not* the germs and bacteria that live on you."

She froze. "You really think that?" she begged.

"Yes," I answered unflinchingly, and for a split second she looked afraid. Then I completed my sentence, Yes I do."

She smiled, and for the night, in the now, that was enough to calm her racing mind.

With an exasperated groan I collapsed on the couch as soon as I got home. Amazing how being emotionally exhausted can bring on physical exhaustion.

"Jef, what's wrong sweetie?" Mom coddled.

"I'm just tired," I moaned into the pillow.

"Is it because you've been taking care of Lacey? Jef, I don't like this."

"What?" I lifted my head off of the pillow. Did I hear her correctly?

Taking care of Lacey? That was an odd thing to say, but I chalked up the bizarre wording to Mom being far too used to taking care of her own disabled loved one.

"No, Mom. Just- just stop. Never mind. I'm not tired. I'm fine."

"Jef don't lie to-"

"I'm fine!" I snapped with a simultaneous jump off of the couch then stormed up the stairs, straight into my room, and slammed the door behind me. *This* is why I need to move out.

Chapter 50

After working an evening shift at the convenience store Lacey picked me up to take me straight to Carson's house.

The drive wasn't long. We were almost at Carson's house when Lacey started acting a little weirder than usual.

Instead of having her eyes on the road in front of her she had her eyes on the road behind her. "Do you think that old guy's following us?"

"Yeah, right," I snorted while twirling my key ring around my pointer finger.

Suddenly Lacey made an unexpected turn down a desolate dirt road.

"You're going the wrong way," I told her.

"I know," she flicked a glance in the rearview mirror, "I'm trying to lose this guy."

A sudden spell of queasiness catapulted from the churning pits of my stomach acid up into my esophagus. "You better be kidding..."

Lacey tried to diffuse the judgment from my tone. "I know he's probably not following me, but I needed to turn just to make sure."

Sighing back an acidic burp I asked myself, wasn't that usually the case? Lacey did a lot of unnecessary compulsions *just to make sure*. She'd make an error in placing an item down with the label sitting head on or tapping a puzzle piece with anything but her index finger. She'd do a lot of that checking or redoing *just to make sure* it was done right.

Now, more than ever, I was realizing that with Lacey's OCD there was a right way of doing things and there was a wrong way of doing things. What I couldn't determine was who got to decide which way was right and which way was wrong, Lacey or the monster inside her named OCD.

"Are you feeling well enough to drive?" I asked her, knowing her OCD had a history of interfering with how she operated a motor vehicle.

"Of course!" Lacey combatted while swatting the air between us. "I'm just being extra careful of strangers. It's no big deal, Jef."

But it was a big deal. Lacey was getting paranoid. So often I saw it in Peter when he'd check all of the locks in the house over and over or when he'd disconnect our Wi-Fi because he was convinced "bad guys" were watching us through our internet connection. And now I could see it in Lacey. And she could see it. She could try and rationalize is as being "extra careful", but regardless of what she labeled it, it was paranoia and it was irrational.

I wasn't sure, was her paranoid mindset part of her OCD or was there another mental ailment looming?

A nervous chill cast goosebumps along every square inch of my flesh.

I swear, just the idea of her contracting another mental illness made that burger in my stomach do a somersault. My brain was racing in overdrive, and for the first time in my entire life I actually wanted to rest my brain. If I could just slow down my nervous system and reduce the tension building inside of me, maybe I'd be able to get some sort relief from this overwhelming anxiety.

In a nervous daze I stared out the window, wondering what lied on the unfamiliar road ahead.

I woke up.

I was in my downstairs bathroom. I was in the same clothes as last night except I didn't have a shirt on.

Confusion came over me.

The last thing I remembered was being at Carson's house, playing foosball in his basement. So what was I doing at home?

I lifted myself up off of Lacey, realizing my head had been lying in Lacey's lap. In the same clothes as last night Lacey was sleeping while sitting on the floor, leaning on the cupboard. It was a rare sight.

Questions that I tried to the best of my ability to answer shot through my recuperating brain. In the crossfire of questions and answers the only fact I was sure of was that Lacey and I had spent the night together. And I didn't remember a thing.

Readjusting myself to a sitting position. I combed a hand through my messy hair and tried with all my might to recall the previous night.

With a groggy belch the stench of vodka immediately hit my nostrils, catalyzing a stream of blurry recollections. Foosball. Lacey sitting in a corner faking a smile. Downing a gnarly swig of rancid vodka. Then another. And another.

Lacey stirred into an awake state. "Really Jef?" her tired throat cracked as she waved a diffusing hand in the air. "You still reek?"

I was thoroughly disoriented as I felt my bare chest. "What's going- did you, did I- I mean, did you and I, did we-"

She crossed her arms and flashed me an unamused look, "What do you think?"

"I'm gonna go with no."

"Correct," she uncrossed her arms.

I felt like an idiot for asking. "Sorry... but where's my shir-"

"You threw up on it so I had to take it off and rinse it," she pointed to the sink above her.

"Oh," my pitch dropped. That's embarrassing. A 23-year-old man who can't hold his liquor? Ugh.

Lacey bent her knees and hugged her legs close, "Sorry to disappoint."

"No... no, that's good," while trying to fix the unkempt hair that was standing up in all sorts of directions I grumbled ruggedly, "I'd be more disappointed if we did something and I had no memory of it."

That got a laugh out of her.

Okay so in the mystery of last night, intimacy was ruled out. The only other clue was my pounding head.

"I'm so hungover," the throbbing reality started to sink in. "How drunk did I-"

"Let's just say you were drunker than Carson."

"Oh God," I cringed at the unpleasant comparison. I knew I owed Lacey an overload of apologies.

I spent the rest of the day trying to ignore my headache and apologizing to Lacey. It was hard to sound genuine though, because I still had no idea why I decided to get so drunk.

Lacey forgave me, which actually instilled some skepticism in my outlook. Why in the world would Lacey forgive me for doing something I knew she had no tolerance for? Something must have happened last night that explained her uncharacteristic forgiveness.

For the remainder of the morning Lacey tried to the best of her ability to fill in the blanks in my memory. She told me that we got to Carson's house while Gabe, Beth, Natalie, and Kenny were all there. I immediately got something to drink. She wasn't happy, but in her words, she didn't want to "be a Beth" and tell me what I could and couldn't do. We all went straight to the basement. Down there I played foosball and I drank. And I drank. And I drank vodka. All throughout the night. And then I puked, so Lacey cut me off and forced us to leave. That's when she took me home.

And here I was. My bathroom floor.

After Lacey left, pieces of the night floated in and out of my memory...

Lacey had held me upright as I dragged down the sidewalk to her car, "Somebody drank a little too much, huh?"

"No I'm good, I'm, uh- I'm good. I have a high alcohol tolorol- toler-alcohol tolerance."

"Sure you do. You reek of beer, Jef."

"Please- ple-please don't dumb- don't dump me." I don't know what I had been stumbling on more, my words or my feet.

I'm pretty sure Lacey laughed while helping me hop in her car, "You'd have to do something a lot more stupid than get drunk for me to break up with you."

Whatever came directly next was hazy. I just remember being sprawled in the passenger seat. I was sloppily in the middle of blabbing, probably something embarrassing, when I burped up some beer.

"Oh, Jef," Lacey kept her left hand on the wheel and used her free hand to find a napkin in her console. She patted my mouth with the cardboard textured napkin, "Hold that there, we're almost at your house."

If I'm not mistaken, I held the napkin. Probably the one thing I did right that night.

Next thing I remember I was hunched over my bathroom toilet. A rancid stream of booze cascaded out my mouth while the sound of Lacey's voice comforted me in the background. "It's okay, you're okay... let it out..." she cooed with a gentle hand clasping my shoulder.

After I was done hurling Lacey had rinsed a bath towel then wiped the remnants of barf off the corners of my mouth.

That was it.

That was the night.

Dammit!

At first I was mortified when that memory resurfaced, but then I realized the bigger picture. "Wait. You cleaned my puke?"

Lacey tucked a strand of hair behind her ear as she confirmed my realization with a coy nod. "I was more concerned about you choking on your vomit than getting a few germs on me that I could wash off later."

Feeling kind of special, I had to fight my grin. What kind of weirdo would I look like to be smiling at the fact the girl I liked took care of me when I gagged all over her. I couldn't help but be happy though. Not just for me, but for her. She put my wellbeing at the top of her priorities, above OCD. Not only did that mean she cared about me a lot, but it also meant that she fought through her initial compulsion to leave my drunken mess unattended. That was actually a really big deal.

I had to go to work.

There weren't many people who came into the convenience store that day. I was left to overthink my sloppy actions last night while unboxing new inventory and ringing up the occasional customer from my stagnant place behind the counter.

The monotonous busy work was broken when Carson came into the store.

"Yo man," he laughed while giving me a high five.

"I'm not giving you free gum," I retaliated before he could even make his usual request.

"Just here for carton of smokes," Carson nodded to the encased shelf of cigarettes and lighters against the wall.

"You do realize you could save a good $70 if you bought these in New Hampshire," I ridiculed.

"Or you could give me a discount."

"No," I cut off, remembering the last time I gave him a discount and got written up by my tattle-tale coworker.

"Aw, fuck you Sterling," he grumbled while pulling a fat wallet out of his back pocket.

At last minute Carson grabbed a massive container of whey protein powder from the side shelf, tucked it underneath his bicep, then lifted his shirt up to conspicuously show off his abs, "Gotta take care of this temple."

"Yet you're about to inhale something packed with ammonia, methane, and a shit ton of other toxic chemicals," I commented antagonistically.

Carson, probably too ignorant to know that ammonia was a toilet cleaner ingredient and methane thrived in sewer gas, stuffed his wallet back into his pocket and dismissively scoffed, "Yeah yeah, smoking's bad, don't do drugs, blah blah blah."

I just rolled my eyes.

Maybe I was just bitter towards Carson's opulent cigarette habit because he was voluntarily addicting himself to a smoking compulsion by choice, meanwhile irrational-ideology-addicts like Lacey Parker were hooked on habits without their consent.

While I unlocked the case and took out a carton of Marlboros Carson shuffled through a hefty wad of cash. Suddenly he remembered something as he glided the grimy bills across the counter, "Hey! How did last night go?"

"Fine," I counted the dollars in my hands. "Why?"

"Just *fine*?"

His invasive tone flickered my glance upwards. Carson was smirking and raising his eyebrows, insinuating what must have been a dirty reference.

"You saw me," I said, "I could barely stand up straight, I was a drunken mess. Lacey took me home."

"Dude I know she took you home. I'm talking about what you guys did once you were home-"

"I puked," I spit out. "I puked a lot." I shuffled through the cash register and pretended to be too busy to have a further conversation.

"That was it?"

Pissed by Carson's thickheaded point of view I retaliated with explicit sarcasm, "Yeah, I puked all over her and she thought it was romantic." I aggressively shoved the tray of the cash register shut and recanted, "Of course she didn't, you moron!"

Carson didn't get it. Nobody got it. There were so many complex factors in our relationship, her illness, my nervousness, that made anything beyond a verbal connection a distant fantasy. Obviously somebody as dim-witted and overly confident as Carson couldn't understand that.

"Was it 'cause we were in the basement? 'Cause you could have excused yourself and..." Carson droned on with more personal hypotheticals.

"Carson I'm seriously about to punch you," I bluntly warned him.

"You're so prude," he complained and started to walk away. Right as Carson was exiting the store he muttered, "I don't understand you."

Suddenly the vivid recollection of Lacey staring down at me came to fruition.

I don't understand you.

That spiteful comment, that simple comment, blasted through my fuzzy memory.

"Lacey," I had pathetically called for her on my bathroom floor.

Lacey knelt down on the floor, lifted my head into her lap, and matted down my sweating forehead with some towel. "What is it Jef?"

I remember staring up at her, admiring how beautiful her gentle brown eyes were as they gazed down on me. It didn't matter that the black makeup had fallen like dark circles under her eyes. Had she been crying?

Slurring my words, I vented to those caring pupils.

"I- I d-don't underst- I don't understand you."

"I know," she stroked a hand through my hair.

"But, but I want to."

"I know," she laughed lightly.

"And- and you still like me?"

"Of course. That's part of the reason why I like you so much. I like you because even though you don't totally understand me, you still try."

I remember I was happy when she said that. But something was still itching at my mind. As I kept rambling I revealed that something,
"The- I mean, that, uh... that g-guy on the stree-road... that guy on the r-road... wusn't followowing- following us."

That made Lacey frown. "So that's what's been on your mind all night?"

"I d-d-don't- I don't want you paranara-noid like that. That makes, um, that m-makes me feel kind of sad..."

"I'm so sorry Jef," Lacey apologized to me with overwhelming empathy.

Then she said something I couldn't remember verbatim. Something like "I was afraid this would happen" or "I knew this would happen.

I snapped out of the flashback.

Now it made sense why I chose to get so drunk last night.

Chapter 51

My final paper, the paper revolving around subatomic particles, which I would be presenting to the entire freshman class, was due by the end of the month. I was more stressed than ever.

Since I had been so stressed about Lacey, and now school, it was nice to do some good old Frisbee tossing in the courtyard with Gabe. That was, until he brought up a sore subject.

"So, how's your asexual relationship going?" Gabe teased as he swished the Frisbee through the chilly air.

"Shut up," I moaned, not in the mood to get tooled on, then whipped the Frisbee at Gabe with relentless hostility.

Gabe nearly fell backwards as he caught the Frisbee. After a recuperating shifting of the feet Gabe stabilized himself and dropped his arms to his sides. He lowered his voice in a serious tone, "How, uh, how is she?"

To my overwhelmed mind, that out-of-character caring question about Lacey was no more than a green light to spill how truly frustrated I was. Not so much by the limitations of her mental illness, but more by the puzzling quandary that was this obsessive disorder. "I don't know, Gabe," I sighed. "Mental sicknesses are a whole lot different than physical sicknesses. Nobody gave her this sickness by sneezing on her. She didn't catch it like it was some kind of contagious stomach bug going around. This isn't some kind of rash or inflammation to an allergen. This is a disease of the mind. A disease of the mind that, in retrospect, was probably foreshadowed by obsessive tendencies and unreasonable anxiety from childhood but didn't hit hard until puberty. Which makes sense because the adolescent brain goes through a pruning process to improve its neural transmissions, especially in the prefrontal cortex, which would explain why her ability to think and reason rationally might have been compromised-"

"Jef!" I suddenly heard Gabe yell, tired with aggravation. The exasperation in his voice implied that the shout of my name was just the last in consecutive stream of shouts I failed to hear. "I came to play Frisbee! Not get an anatomy lesson!"

"Well it was more of a psychology lesson than anything else."

"Dude! Stop!"

Chapter 52

"Oh my God!" Lacey hollered from behind her car's steering wheel.

"What!" I reacted with a spastic jolt upright, eyes frantically taking inventory of the road in front of us.

Lacey glanced in my direction briefly. "Did I forget to unplug my hair straightener before I left?"

Good God. *That* was the catastrophic thought on Lacey's mind? Wanting to avoid showing up late for grabbing food with Gabe and Beth, I intervened on her worry, "You probably did. I'm sure it's fine-"

"But I can't remember," she fretted, hung up on the thought of that burning straight iron still plugged into the bathroom outlet. In a violent jerk she twisted the wheel to the left and spun the car around, pulling off an illegal U-turn.

"Lace!" I flew sideways.

"I'm sorry Jef but I have to go back and check," she panted.

"Lace I can almost guarantee I saw you unplug-"

"I know, but I have to see the plug out of the socket for myself. I have to make sure!"

Three soundless minutes went by on our venture back to Lacey's house. No talking. I had nothing to say because I was so irritated. Lacey had nothing to say because all she could think about was that hair straightener burning the house down. And, of course, the radio wasn't on because God forbid Lacey hear a word like "fire" or "cancer" come through the speakers.

The entire situation was ridiculous.

"What are we doing here?" I finally sighed out of exasperation.

"You know what we're doing," Lacey reminded me with her best attempt at a gentle tone, "We're driving back to my house to check if the straightener's still plugged in."

The nerd in me started to come out. "Based on what reliable evidence?"

"I don't know, Jef. I'm just going by my thoughts here."

I stopped itching my sideburn to throw an irritated hand in the air and impatiently blurted out, "Why can't your thought be 'I unplugged the straight iron'?"

An inquisitive look made Lacey wince ahead, out the car window. For a second I thought she saw something peculiar outside, but as soon as her mouth opened I realized she was caught up in her own mind. "Thoughts. Why do they always have to be bad? Why can't I ever have good thoughts? Sometimes I wish I just couldn't think."

"Don't say that," the demand shot out of me faster than a speeding bullet. The notion of not having thoughts? That was my worst nightmare.

"But thoughts always find a way of scaring me," she justified.

"They shouldn't."

"In a mind like yours they shouldn't. In a fucked up mind like mine they should." Lacey declared as she stared off. I hesitate to say her stare was blank. If anything it was full. Full of something only she could see. As she continued staring at that mysterious something, words continued to draw out her mouth. "Thoughts are horribly dangerous for me. Every potential thought that brews in this mind could destroy me. Thoughts... they're gonna be what kills me in the end."

I wanted to argue her morose stance. To say that she was wrong, that thoughts sparked all sorts of new realities. Inventions. Ideas. Theories. They all sprouted from thoughts. To me, thoughts were the birth of anything and everything. To her, they were deadly.

Again, I soaked in the sight of her distant yet intensely dense stare, a stare that was holding the very thoughts she currently claimed to rightfully fear. And just one look and I knew she was right.

To Lacey, thoughts were death.

"That's devastating," I accidentally concluded out loud.

Lacey tried to swipe her hair over her shoulder with her sleeve yanked down to veil whatever germs she *thought* were covering her hand. "I know," she agreed.

After returning to Lacey's house and confirming that, yes, her hair straightener was unplugged, we arrived to the restaurant fifteen minutes late.

As soon as the waiter delivered our meals to the table Lacey tensed up. "I'll be right back."

I knew something was wrong. So, I beseeched Lacey out of her seat and asked her in private, in the corner of the restaurant, what was up.

"I just need some air. I can't deal with the germs in here. All I can smell is fried food and it's making me feel like I'm suffocating."

Knowing Lacey was embarrassed I scurried back to the table with Gabe and Beth and told them that Lacey and I needed to go for a walk and that they should start eating anyways. When Gabe asked why I tried to imply that Lacey was anxious without filling Beth in by saying Lacey was feeling nauseous, a state Gabe was used to me complaining about when I was overwhelmingly nervous.

While walking down the brick patio behind the restaurant Lacey apologized over and over.

"I'm sorry, I know you don't understand."

"Don't worry, I get it," I said, thinking I was coaxing her.

"No," Lacey laughed half-heartedly, "You don't. I know you don't. Nobody does."

I highly resented that statement. Was Lacey belittling the knowledge I was capable of possessing?

"Lacey," I lowered my pitch and stopped in my tracks, locking my insecure brown eyes with hers, "I know what you're going through."

"No," she shook her head, "You don't Jef. You don't know what this feels like."

"Yes I do," I argued, agitated by her implicit lack of faith in my intellect.

"But you don't! You know *information* about what it's like to have OCD because you see it and your weird photographic memory remembers it, but you don't know by *experience* how it feels to have OCD! See, this is why linguistics are so important. Knowing and feeling are not synonymous."

"Okay, okay," I nodded submissively, as if handing over the gold medal for winning the dispute. "There's a difference between the definitions of 'knowing' verses 'feeling'," unexpectedly Peter's "retard" label resurfaced in my mind and I remembered my aversion to labels. "They're just verbs, though. Labels for actions, really. Just words."

"*Just* words?" Lacey repeated, appalled. "Jef, without definitions and labels and everything else that makes up language you wouldn't be able to make sense of the world around you."

"I don't need to see the world through the eyes of a dictionary to make sense of the world around me."

"Why the hell not?" she asked rhetorically, but something about the question sounded like she was genuinely in search for an answer.

"Because," my hand flung out and finger by finger I tallied my answer, "How I perceive the world is based on what I see, hear, smell, taste, and touch! Making sense of the world is left for the senses. Everything else, defining and labeling whatever stimuli you run into is left for further analysis in the brain!"

When Lacey's impassioned voice didn't present itself, I realized the key phrase in my argument. *Brain*. The left and right hemisphere divided structure that somehow separated us from each other but also balanced each other out. Hers somehow immaculate in spite of being dominated by mental illness and mine somehow obsessively neurotic in spite of being *labeled* healthy.

Before I could stop myself, I let my frustration with Lacey's ill brain overpower my social etiquette and inconsiderately spieled onward. "This is probably why you care so much about definitions. Because your distorted brain and its distorted sensory nerves could use all the help they can get to make sense of its highly warped sensory receptors on your sense organs. For God's sake, Lacey, your brain has you thinking you can feel germs on your skin!"

"There it is again! The importance of linguistics. Jef, I don't *think* I feel germs. I *believe* I feel germs. A belief and a thought *do not* have the same definition, but everybody treats them like they do," she paused, sifting through the ruckus in that brain, but in her exasperation sighed and restated the same dictum, "There is a significant difference between beliefs and thoughts."

"Oh, absolutely," I agreed without hesitation, quick to react probably as a way of keeping up with her intelligence. "Thoughts are far superior."

"Pfft," she snorted in her goofy way, "That's a joke, right? You're joking?"

"Uh," I felt my eyebrows furrow inward, "no, uh, not really. I was serious."

"What?" Lacey laughed at me like I had just said the most ridiculous malarkey known to man.

Regardless of how winsome her laugh was, and regardless of how I usually didn't mind that laugh being at my expense (if anything I sort of liked when she laughed at me, it made me feel relevant in her life in a humbling way that I never felt around anybody else) I was glaringly worried she lost respect for my indifferent brainpower. So, with what was probably an over-reactive burst of adrenaline, I fumbled into awkward stammering. "I, uh, well-"

"I'm sorry, but a belief will always be more powerful than a thought. It might be *the most* powerful thing in the world," she proclaimed.
"Whoa, whoa, whoa," now it was my turn to laugh. I couldn't understand how she could overlook something as pivotal as a human thought, the strings of meticulously-constructed information transmitted between nerve cells throughout the central nervous system, and acclaim something as metaphysical and as biased as a belief. "I don't think that's true."

"You mean you don't *believe* that's true," Lacey insisted with a playful smirk.

"No, no no," I laughed, "Don't do that. I meant what I said."

"Give me one good piece of evidence that proves a thought is superior to a belief," she challenged.

"Well first of all," I started, thinking back to what I had learned in my least favorite class, philosophy, "According to philosophers Morris R. Cohen and Ernest Nagel there are four ways of fixing a belief. Tenacity. Authority. Intuition. And, lieu and behold, the scientific method."

"Go on."

"People have a tendency to believe whatever other people believe, typically higher figures ranging from somebody as trivial as a parent to somebody as reputable as a professor. That's fixing a belief based on authority. Then you've got people who just say they believe something because they've always believed it. Its total self-righteous bogusness. Embarrassing, really. That's what Cohen and Nagel like to call 'Tenacity'. And then there's 'Intuition', the most la la land of all the methods. Those are beliefs from an inexplicable *feeling*. And do you know what all of those have in common? They're all fixed without any pragmatic reasoning. The only reasonable way to fix a belief is to use the scientific method. Problem solving! Evidence! Self-corrective propositions! But do people usually fix a belief using the scientific method? No. They don't. Because that takes effort. Instead they fix beliefs based on 'feelings' and 'desires' and all this other uncalculated nonsense."

"What are you saying?"

"I'm saying that just about any belief that wasn't arrived at using the scientific method is bullshit."

"Wow," Lacey's nostrils flared a little, "That's a bold statement."

"Yeah, well, it's true." I held my hands up apologetically, "Sorry, blame Cohen and Nagel."

Lacey flashed me a coy smirk and shook her head.

"What?" I nervously laughed. I thought I proved my point quite well, so why was she smirking like she won the argument? "What? What is it?"

"All you did was tell me why beliefs are inferior, not why thoughts are superior."

"What? No I-" suddenly I stopped myself, realizing she was right.

Having been thrown off, I became mute, and Lacey took the opportunity to make her input.

"Do you believe in anything Jef?"

"Er, I don't- I, I'm not really, uh, I don't-"

"*Anything*?"

"Well," I sighed a long exhale and reflected on my most passionate convictions. "I believe the world would be a much better place if people were more knowledgeable about, well, anything. And I guess everything. It's important to be intellectually well-rounded. You're more tolerant, less judgey," my voice, in congruence with my long-term memory, trailed off to when I misjudged Lacey as a snob in my OCD ignorance.

"Okay, yeah," Lacey got excited, "And you live your life by that belief! It influences the kind of person you are."

"Well you believe in a false set of rules," I retaliated in a childish tone without even meaning to, "A false set of rules that dictate your life!"

"You're right, Jef," Lacey nodded like a mom trying to allay her child's irksome disagreeing, "I do. But you said it right there, it dictates my life. That just goes to show you how much more powerful a belief is over a meager thought. It's the most powerful force in the world."

Lacey flipped her head so that her hair blew behind her rather than in her face, then went on, "Beliefs mysteriously come and go. You don't make a choice to believe in something. You just do. It's like a natural reaction to your morals and principles and a whole slew of other qualities that mold your individuality. And yeah, I agree with you, beliefs are often intuition based- that thing you call 'la la land', but what's wrong with that? They don't need scientific reasoning. They don't need evidence. They don't need experimenting and hypotheses and all that 'thinky' stuff, but isn't that a testament to how sublime and powerful a belief really is? That you can come to it without all this external experimenting and come to it from pure, raw, intuition inside of you? Can you say that about a thought?"

"Uh, um, er," I was thoroughly stumped, taken aback by Lacey's profound statement.

Lacey continued, "You're right, beliefs don't always take effort. Thoughts, thoughts take effort. Rationalizing, evaluating, analyzing, reasoning. A bunch of stuff that, guess what? Mentally ill people don't always possess. Because thoughts take effort that comes from the brain. And some of us have defective brains. Beliefs, well I don't know where beliefs come from, but because of that mysterious unknown *nobody* can say if they're wrong. *Nobody* can say they came from a defective place. *Nobody*. And that's part of what makes beliefs so miraculous. Thoughts are forced. Beliefs *are* a force."

There was the girl I fell in love with. Lacey Parker, the adage dispenser.

But nonetheless, I wanted achingly bad to defend something as incredible as a human thought, so I scrounged up whatever facts I could to support my original stance.

"Well according to my psych book a thought is defined as a 'manipulation of information'. A manipulation, Lacey! You can bend or twist or do whatever the heck you want with a thought! Any thought! You can't do that with a belief, not without scientific proof, that is."

"You're proving my point," Lacey laughed, "That's exactly why a belief is more powerful. It can't be compromised or manipulated. It's innate. It's a force that can't be reckoned with, not intentionally at least. You can't just go ahead and change a belief, no matter how much you want to."

Her perspective threw me for a loop. "What? No!" I argued with a neurotic speediness. "Since when was 'change' such a bad thing?"

Lacey froze and I swear her skin grew paler.

At first I didn't understand her icy transformation.

Then her current eye contact deviated to the floor, and I realized something.

No wonder Lacey preferred beliefs over thoughts. They aren't easily changed. And she had a disease that pronounced *change* as the enemy.

Without stalling I begged the question, "Why are you so scared of change, Lacey?"

The split second that inquisition arrived at her eardrums her line of vision melded with mine.

"What are you talking about?"

"You are *so* thoroughly scared of change. Change in routine. Change in setting. Change in mindset. Why?"

Keeping her hands in her jacket pockets she just shook her head, "I don't know. Ever since I can remember change has made me anxious."

"Yeah, but why?"

Lacey's already brittle frame crumpled forward with a shy hunch of the shoulders, "I guess, well," she hesitated while searching through the vast lingo in her brain, "I think I'm scared that if I change up my routine or the way my mind approaches something, then it will change who I am. That everything I surround myself with is a part of what makes me, me. So, if things stay consistent in my life then I stay consistent. And I won't lose myself. I'll be stable in my own identity. I'll be in touch with who I am. And I never want to lose touch with who I am."

I nodded. "I believe that."

Chapter 53

Having established that Lacey was too exhausted to prolong the dinner any longer I chose to drive her home.

Lacey was so embarrassed about leaving early so I took the initiative to apologize to Gabe about leaving early.

"Sorry guys, we're gonna have to split."

"Well you should at least pay for half of the meal," Beth said with an egregious attitude.

I rolled my eyes, "Fine," then glanced back to Lacey who was shrinking behind me.

Lacey lowered her head to the ground and whispered so that Gabe and Beth wouldn't hear her. "I didn't bring my wallet. I didn't want to touch money tonight."

"What?" I accidentally screeched, then consciously forced myself to whisper, "I guess, uh, I guess I can pay."

"I promise I'll pay you back as soon as you drop me off at my-"

"What a surprise!" without warning Beth facetiously shouted and jumped out of her seat. "You're rude Lacey. You expect people to hold doors open for you. You don't pay for anything. You don't even have a job! You won't hug anybody goodbye or hello for that matter. You're rude, Lacey. You're a rude, self-entitled princess who won't even show affection to your boyfriend."

Before Lacey had a chance to retaliate I flipped out.

A slew of expletives shot out my mouth as my voice spiked in volume, "Are you fucking kidding me Beth! *She's* the rude one? If there was one person to earn the title of 'bitch' tonight you would win it, hands down!"

"Hey!" Gabe intervened and shoved me back a few feet, but I used the traction of my sneakers against the tile to catch myself. "Watch your fucking mouth, Sterling!"

There were no words that could adequately emphasize just how infuriated I was with Gabe. He was the reason Beth made such a rude comment. She never would have known about Lacey and my lack-of-affection without Gabe running his mouth. "I don't want to hear a word out of you, you deceitful fucker! What are you even doing telling Beth about me and Lacey!"

"Oh shut up, Sterling! What did you expect? She's my girlfriend!"

"Yeah, every other day!" I mocked.

Gabe's mouth tightened with his green eyes locked firmly onto mine. I wasn't intimidated in the least, though. My own jaw was clenching.

I was pissed- no, I was beyond pissed. I was straight up enraged. How dare he defend Beth after that wildly insolent verbal assault on Lacey!
In an interval of heavy breathing Gabe and my eye contact didn't break.

Suddenly, in the most uncharacteristic of acts, I threw a hefty fist in Gabe's gut.

The atmosphere went mute.

I'm sure restaurant guests were shouting but I heard nothing.

It all happened so fast. The rage built up rapidly and before I knew it I had my sleeves rolled up and I was throwing merciless punch after punch at Gabe's skull. Just outright wailing on him with nothing but fury packed in my fists. I was by no means a fighter, and I certainly wasn't anywhere close to being jacked, so this probably looked ridiculous. I didn't care though. I was in my own zone. I could have been shouting vulgarities for all I knew.

After the initial shock of being assaulted by his scrawny friend, Gabe had the upper hand. He was already a rowdy hockey player, so it's safe to say I was in for quite a brutal beating.

My supposed friend flipped me over like a ragdoll. My back slammed to the tile floor and he pounded me in the jaw, over and over. I could taste blood. I would have been embarrassed if I wasn't so infuriated by his inconsiderate attitude towards Lacey, not just my girlfriend, but my best friend.

Before I knew it Carson was in the quarrelsome mix, yanking me out from underneath Gabe.

"You're a fuckin' lunatic just like her!" Gabe yelled over the shaken crowd of people.

I swiped the back of my hand along my mouth, allowing the blood trickling from my mouth to smear along my pulverized skin. "Somebody tell this prick to shut the fuck up!" I shouted so antagonistically I was able to see my convoluted blood and spit mixture flying through the air.

To be honest I'm not so sure I would have lost it if I wasn't so frustrated already about Lacey's OCD straining our relationship.

Chapter 54

February arrived, and Lacey's depression was worse than ever. She was definitely right when she said that her depression had a seasonal component. Her mood was exponentially lower, her formerly creative mind was now stagnant, her outlook on life was exponentially darker, and the hope that charged her spirit to get through each day was all but a dull glow. With all of that negativity churning inside of her it made her will to fight through her obsessive compulsive disorder almost non-existent.

    Though Lacey was my partner, seeing her during the day was never a guarantee. We kept in touch mostly by talking on the phone before she went to bed, and her fatigue that had been amplified by the severe OCD and worsened depression caused her to go to bed early. At this point Peter was more high functioning than her.

    As the semester unfolded, Lacey withdrew.

    Lacey couldn't go a week without missing at least one class. And Lacey seemed to never wanna do anything after school, because she was too tired to deal with the "germ feeling" or just plain too depressed to have even the slightest bit of interest in anything outside of sleeping the day away.

    That's what Lacey did mostly. She'd go home, bathe, get in pajamas, try to write, fail at articulating her thoughts (probably because her mind was so clouded), and wind up falling asleep in the middle of the day. She told me she didn't want to sleep, that she couldn't help it. I was a little scared. It was like her body was going into hibernation for the season. I couldn't imagine having to live that way.

On the rare occasion Lacey would do something, it was usually the weekend, and we usually hung out at her house. I think she was getting too attached to her home. I would try to come up with different things we could do but she shut down almost every suggestion.

Lacey didn't tell me upfront, but I knew she was struggling with her grades. After all, she was missing classes. She was missing assignments. She literally had no interest in her education.

She was so sick. And why? For what reason? What did she do to deserve such a heinous mental disorder?

It was a Sunday night. For whatever reason Lacey was home alone. She was in the middle of a mental breakdown when she called me, desperate to talk to somebody.

"I can't do this anymore," Lacey sounded unbelievably defeated.

"Do what, Lacey?"

"Everything. School. Life."

Realizing this was going to be a very serious talk I put the textbook I had been studying from down on my desk and slid it out of the way. I dropped my elbows onto the wooden surface, exerting most of the tension by leaning forward.

"Okay, okay. Just calm down. Take a deep breath. Just relax Lace," I cooed into the phone.

"I'm so done, Jef. I am just so done. I can't do life."

"Wha- why are you talking like that?"

"Because I'm just- I'm tired. I can barely get myself up and out of the house to come to school three days a week. It takes all the mental strength out of me to get up and go to school, nevermind actually do any work while I'm there. And I'm barely passing my classes. I've got a C- in English, and I'm an English major! I have no use in this world!"

"Whoa, whoa, whoa, Lace. You're getting way ahead of yourself."

"I'm really not. I'm just skipping the bullshit and seeing my education for what it is. Useless."

"It's not though," I argued.

Lacey ranted, "I don't need school to learn 'critical thinking' or analytical skills or reading or anything! I don't need to be there! I don't need to be spending all my mom and dad's money on such a pointless system! I don't need an education!"

"You do if you want a job, and a house, and money. You can't live in the real world without an education."

"Well I don't remember saying I wanted to live in the real world!" Lacey professed through the phone.

My stomach crashed down. I felt like I was going to be sick.

That outburst was morbidly telling about her highly depressed state of mind.

"Stop," my voice cracked into the cell phone.

"Come on, Jef," she sulked as if saying something we both knew. "I wasn't meant for this world."

"You're talking crazy," I insisted, trying to get through to her irrational mind.

Lacey tried to find an explanation for the outcast syndrome she was feeling. "You know I can't make it. I can barely make it a day *with* the support from my parents, I'm not gonna be able to make it out there, on my own in the real world. I probably wasn't meant to last this long."

"You're wrong."

It was quiet on the other line. I watched the clock on my touch screen.

"How do you know?" Lacey's timid peep managed to travel the sound waves.

"Because," I let out a pained sigh while pinching the bridge of my nose in distress. This conversation was taking a massive toll on my queasy stomach. "I know you were meant to be in my life."

Quiet again.

"Well maybe this is as far as I was meant to get."

"Don't say that!" I violently slammed my fist on my desk so hard that it shook the entire room.

"What do you want me to say?" Lacey shouted so loud a storm of static buzzed at my eardrum, "Look, I'm sorry! I'm sorry but this is who I am! Depressed! Crazy! Sick! This is the way I was made! And I can't foresee this resolving itself!"

"You're right," I took my volume down a notch, "It's not gonna resolve itself. It's gonna take something extra, like professional help from a therapist and a psychiatrist, and you're gonna have to put in more effort. Like experiment with medication."

"No! They'll just put me on more and more meds until I'm a completely different mind!"

"Lace, medication can't change your identity, I promise you that."

"You're just saying that."

"Of course I'm not! You've seen Peter! You know I wouldn't lie to you Lacey."

"I can't," she denied, "I don't have the will. I just don't care anymore."

"I think you do," I combatted.

Lacey wouldn't cooperate. "I don't."

"Yeah you do," I assured her, "It's your depression that doesn't care."

Emotions were spiking up and plummeting down. It was tiresome, so when the conversation finally came to a plateau I regrouped. I kicked back in my chair so that the front wheels elevated off the ground and I stayed on the line while gathering my packet of rehabilitation centers out of my top desk drawer. This time there was precisely fifty-three seconds of wordless breathing shared between Lacey and I.

"I'm done," her shrill voice was nearly a whimper. "I'm just done."

"No, stop, don't say that. Things can still turn around. You can get help." I flipped through the pages of my rehab research, quickly skimming them. "How about this. How about I come over and we can get on the computer to explore the options you have?"

No response.

"Lacey? Did you hear me?"

Now I was starting to get a little nervous. I leaned forward, grounding the bottom wheels of the chair.

"Lacey? Are you there?"

Nothing.

In the absence of Lacey's voice I replayed what she last said to me.

I'm done. I'm just done.

A haunting flood of snippets from the conversation bombarded me.

I don't remember saying I wanted to live in the real world!
I wasn't meant for this world.
I can't do life.
I don't have the will.
I just don't care anymore.
I can't foresee this resolving itself!

I pulled the phone away from my ear and shouted Lacey's name one last time despite the blatant blood colored words reading "Call Ended".

In a panic-stricken haste I pressed Lacey's name on my contact list and shot her another phone call.

Voicemail.

I tried again.

Voicemail.

This time I left an angry message, "Lacey answer your phone God dammit!" then pounded the "End Call" square on the screen. "Fuck!" I chucked the cell phone across the room.

With my head in my distraught hands I panicked to myself, "What do I do, what do I do…"

In my deliberation my sight fixed itself on the OCD binder sitting at the top of my desk. Suddenly I was fuming mad. Not at Lacey for her issues. Not at me for making that binder. At her OCD. I fucking loathed her OCD. And that stupid binder was the symbol of her OCD.

I didn't care about research anymore. I was no doctor. I was no therapist. I couldn't save Lacey, no matter how thick this binder got. I was done researching. I didn't care about understanding this illness. I just cared about the safety of the person I loved more than anybody else in the world.
I snatched the binder off of my desk and threw it back into the bottom drawer, then violently kicked the drawer shut so hard I felt a bruise blooming on my big toe.

I jumped out of my desk chair, grabbed my phone off of the floor, and called Lacey one last time while pacing back and forth across the room.

Still no answer.

Screw it.

I was officially in adrenaline mode.

I shoved the cell phone in my pocket, snatched the car keys off of my nightstand, and booked it to my car.

When the engine turned on so did the radio, which just so happened to be blasting that damn "fire" song that triggered Lacey's anxiety.

"Shut up!" I bellowed at the car and punched the radio button off.

My hands were sweating as they gripped the steering wheel tightly. I was speeding like a maniac on my way to check on Lacey at her house. I just needed to see her, I needed to make sure she didn't do anything rash, anything dangerous, in her devastating depression.

"Lacey!" I hollered while banging on the front door of her house.

Every second she didn't answer felt like an hour.

Oh God, please answer.

Please, please, answer.

My breaths were choppy. My legs were shaking. Any moment they were about to give out on me.

I knocked again.

Come on, come on, come on

There was a sudden creaking noise in unison with the twist of the golden door knob.

"Jef?"

The moment I saw Lacey the strength returned to my leg muscles.

"I told you not to show up uninvi-"

"Oh thank God," I exclaimed and unapologetically ambushed her with a hug.

"What are you doing!" Lacey shoved me off with her skinny yet strong arms, allowing OCD to control her action, "Now I have to take a shower!"

"Too bad," I was still catching my breath.

Lacey didn't hear me over the screaming of her own thoughts. She stood there scowling, arms stretched away from her body like she was dripping with venom, "I CAN'T BELIEVE THIS! I can't fucking believe this! I am *way* too tired to take another damn shower! I told you never to touch me after I've showered! You ask! You always have to ask! Thanks a lot you fucking asshole! Thanks a-fucking-lot! I can't *believe* you just did that!

"I don't care!" I shouted over her.

Lacey seemed a little taken off guard, stammering around on her words, "Well you- uh, well you should!"

"Well I don't," I stood my ground. I've had enough of this bastard named OCD. "Why the fuck didn't you answer your phone!"

Her surprise to see me was still fresh, causing her to unconvincingly lie at first, "I don't know!" I think she saw that I was about to blow up at her so she quickly revised her answer to be truthful, "I guess I didn't wanna touch my phone anymore. I was tired and wanted to lie down, which now I can't do because I have to take *another* daunting shower!"

"Don't ever do that again!" I barked at her, still pissed about her ignoring her phone. Now that the reality that Lacey was okay, in one piece, had sunk in I gave myself permission to be mad at her.

"Why are you yelling at me?" she shrunk back a step.

"Because you scared me half to death! Who hangs up without saying bye? What kind of inconsiderate-"

"Stop yelling at me!" Tears built up in her eyes.

"No!" I screamed, more out of passion than anger. "How dare you hang up on me and not call me back!"

"Just go away!" she tried to break away by storming up the stairs.

I took a collective breath to cool down. "Lacey I'm only yelling because I care about you."

"Well I don't!" she cried out and ran down into the bathroom.

"Lace!" I chased after her.

I landed directly on the bathroom door right as it slammed shut.

The sink started running. She was going to try and take a shower.

"Lacey!" I screamed over the water and went to turn the knob but it was locked.

"When I get out of this shower you better be gone!" she hollered over the sink.

"Can't you wait five freakin' minutes before washing that Goddamn germ feeling off of you!" I lashed out.

"No, Jef, I can't!" she yelled back. "I told you a thousand times! I can't make these physical feelings go away! They are always there!" Suddenly the sound of the water running turned off. "I *have* to wash it off! What else am I supposed to do?"

"Learn," off the cuff and out loud I recycled the most pragmatic solution I so often resorted to, "You learn to live with it."

"But I can't-"

"Yes you can!" I pressed my entire body against the door and literally, as well as figuratively, tried to get through to her. "You've spent long enough in pain, Lacey. It's time to get help. You deserve it."

"No I can't!" she defended with an unapologetic bark. "My God, why can't you get it, Jef! This germ feeling, this feeling on my skin, in my hair, its insufferable! And it's never going to leave me alone! I can't fucking just learn to live with it! Look, I'm sorry I don't have some equation that can validate all of my craziness for you, but this is real! Why can't you just *believe* me?"

The doorknob rotated, so I took a step backwards. The door cracked open the slightest bit. I went ahead and joined Lacey in the bathroom.

I could see just how beat up she appeared. There were black streaks underneath her wet eyes implying she had been crying on the other side of that door. Her initial shine in her eyes, that luster, had been worn and dulled by mental illness.

This obsessive compulsive disorder was tearing her apart.

With the desperate flash of her wildly vulnerable large eyes I fully forgot the sound of her angry voice.

Disarmed by the brown eyes pleading at me I could do nothing but stammer, "I- I don't, it's not," her stare softened, almost like an empathetic response to my verbal impairment. The aura of her eyes swiftly transitioned from persecuting to encouraging, as if by conditioning to what I selfishly assumed stemmed from her feelings for me. Having felt the inexplicable emission of her love radiate from her eyes, I was able to clear all traces of anxiety from my throat and construct a coherent sentence. "It's not that I don't believe you… it's that I don't *want* to believe you."

Lacey shook her head. Lips trembled uncontrollably. She backed up the towel rack.

"You're missing out on this life," I stated, "And it's not fair to you. You deserve to experience life."

She crossed her arms and her head fell forward. She cried to the tile floor, "But I only have pain to offer this world."

"That's not true!" I couldn't have been more serious. "You are so much more than your illness Lacey. There's so much more that you offer. You have intelligence, and humor, and kindness, and honesty, and you are bright, so bright. And then there's your writing! How could you forget your writing?"

"No," Lacey whispered delicately while shaking her head, "I can't do that anymore."

My heart dropped. I wasn't following. "What do you mean?"

"I can't write," Lacey choked with welled up eyes and a sob refraining heaviness weighed down her voice.

I panicked while hunching forward. "What are you talking about?"

Lacey purged out a tragic response, "I'm afraid to write certain things, certain words, or end a sentence with certain nouns or verbs that might remind me of my biggest fears like my house burning down or developing cancer or going blind, and it's making writing nearly impossible because my phobic mind is on overdrive all the fucking time and I'm able to find a connection between my greatest fears and just about every single noun or verb I can think up because I swear to God this brain of mine is moving at a far more rapid rate than anybody else's and it's always one step ahead of me! And to make matters worse I can't even write down how frustrated I am with how OCD is limiting my writing and creativity because I'm afraid that putting my frustration out on paper will be seen as ungrateful to the universe and then the universe is going to punish me for complaining and-"

"Oh my God," I stretched my hands over my head. I had no idea Lacey Parker's OCD could ever get this bad. So bad that she couldn't even do the one thing she was, in her own words, born to do.

Lacey shook her head and squeezed her ears, as if trying to make the irrational laws spinning around her head go away. She was falling apart, fast. "I can't do this anymore. I'm so sorry, Jef. I'm so so sorry."

It was like she couldn't hear me.

It was heart wrenching to witness.

I was right here, right in Lacey's grasp, right in her earshot, but she couldn't touch or hear me through the clouds of depression.

With a claw-like grip Lacey grabbed the side of her head. There was so much intense frustration in her clutch. I swear animosity was bleeding out her fingertips and seeping into the mind she resented so much.

The rich brown waves of her hair verged on black in the evening's dark lighting. Bunches of curls wove in and out of the fingers she had lodged on her distraught cranium.

She slammed her back against the wall. With a morbid grace she slid down to the floor.

"I'm so tired," she wept.

Slowly her hand lowered, clutching her head through snarls of hair, meeting her other hand over her breaking heart.

"I know as long as I'm alive I'm going to have this illness. I'm going to be in pain," she croaked, "And I don't want to be in pain anymore. I have to live like this, and I can't. I just can't do it anymore."

I didn't dare ask her what the alternative was. I knew what it was. It was my own taboo word that started with "s" and ended with an "e".

"No," I nearly choked as her self-destructive desire became more apparent than ever.

I dropped beside her and engulfed her in the tightest hug I had ever given.

She let out a wail and fell into me.

The sound of her pain pierced straight through my heart.

This was the same person who taught my mind, who captivated my heart. The person who had been on a slow decline into madness long before I had met her. And it was destroying me to watch the latter portion of her painful descent.

It was so hard to comprehend how a person who brings you so much happiness could be experiencing so much sadness.

My chest was throbbing. My eyes were stinging with fresh tears. This was the most excruciating passion I had ever felt.

I didn't know what to do other than convince her I was here for her. In Lacey's darkest hour I was here for her. And the best way I could convey that notion was to touch her. To tightly hold her with an endurance only love could fuel.

If there was any shred of hope that she could live with this mental illness another day then I had to resonate with it. I had to remind her that she deserved to survive. She couldn't give up.

"I love you so much Lacey," a teardrop fell from my eye and landed on the locks of hair draped over her shoulder.

Lacey hugged my forearm like her life depended on it. She was hanging onto me as if the contact of our skin was the only thing keeping her in touch with this life. It felt like there was no blood in her frigid cold hands. Now, more than ever, she was a ghost. Merely existing as a shadow of her past life, a saner life.

I hugged my ghost closer.

Lacey tilted her head up and, with desperation, gazed up at me. She was barely through that agape frown. "I love you," she sounded like she was pleading to me.

I pressed my forehead against hers and choked back a sob, trying to be the strong man she needed me to be. "You're going to be okay," I whispered with my nose nuzzling against hers. She shriveled to the floor. I stood there in a stupor, aching to do something but feeling too immobile from helplessness.

This was out of my hands.

Being into science, I felt like there was an answer to everything. Some equation or formula that explained why anything was the way it was. But with obsessive compulsive disorder, I just didn't know. I couldn't believe how troubled somebody so smart and funny and attractive and kind could be. It made no sense to me. Peter was born without enough oxygen, so his flawed brain made sense. Peter was from a broken home. But Lacey was born healthy. Lacey was raised by good people with morals and values. What went wrong with her? Why was her brain flawed? It didn't make any sense.

    Nothing made sense to me anymore.

Part III

Chapter 55

As if I wasn't stressed enough from my relationship with Lacey, I had to get up in front of an auditorium of first year students of the community college and motivate them to pursue a physics major.

"Are you nervous?" Peter asked me backstage, right before I walked behind a podium, in front of the crowd.

"No, I'm not. Go away." I shooed him then returned the back of my hand to my forehead to wipe off the trickles of sweat budding forth.

"Picture the audience naked," Peter snickered.

"What? No! Why- I don't- I don't understand, why do people even say that? How is picturing a mass of people butt naked supposed to alleviate my anxiety? I guess if anything it'd give me a good laugh if I felt like giggling like some immature 12-year old but why the hell would I want to be laughing when I'm supposed to be delivering a speech to-"

"Jef!" Lacey, uncharacteristically, clasped my spastic wrists. Her cold hands were like handcuffs.

That was… different. Suddenly I felt thankful that Lacey offered to show up tonight.

"Take a breather," she advised.

My mouth shut and a shiver ran across my lower lip.

Peter tried to chime in. "Yeah Jef. You need to-"

"Hold that thought Peter," Lacey, conspicuously assertive for a change, cut my brother off before he had a chance to tell me to "break a leg" and lead me into a tailspin of ranting about bone fractures.

"Jef, you're going to be a teacher someday. You know how to educate people."

"No, no, I can't. I can't think! I've, I've never spoken in- in- in front of an audience!"

"Okay, okay," Lacey cooed, "Calm down."

"I can't do this!" I burst out and clutched the side of my head like I was squeezing the pent up knowledge out of my brain.

"Jef, listen to me-"

"I- I- I can't! I can't talk in front of all those people!" I nearly whimpered.

"Yes you can."

"No I can't! Oh my God, my heart! Can you hear it? Can you hear that?" I tugged at her hand and planted it on my chest. "You feel that, right? Do you feel that? Oh my God, I'm going into cardiac arrest!"

"No you're not Jef," Lacey tore her hand away from my trembling sternum, "You're having anxiety."

"I- I can't talk, I- I know I can't!"

"Jef!" Lacey finally gave into her touching fear and clutched my face in her firm hands. Her strong, no longer timid deer-like eyes, looked me directly in the nervously wiggling pupils, "Yes you can. Just pretend you and I are having some kind of debate, and to get your thesis across you have to teach me about the importance of physics. Pretend you're teaching *me*."

Teaching Lacey?

Teaching Lacey...

"Jef, when you teach you are the most thorough, clear, eloquent person I know! You can do this. I know you can, I- I believe you can."

With my jaw in the safety of Lacey's clasp I felt my chattering teeth begin to calm from sporadic spasms to gentler quivering.

"Okay," I whispered with a jittery nod in her cupped hands. "Okay, okay."

Behind the podium, the sea of eyeballs were an unwelcome reminder of the limelight I had brought upon myself. But as soon as I found my favorite pair of doe eyes a fire was lit inside me. Every rehearsal for this moment fell to the forefront of my conscience, and without a second thought I was teaching the girl with the notebook about my favorite subject.

"Your perceptions construct reality. What you recognize as reality is a result of all of your five senses: sight, sound, smell, taste, and touch. You see infrared light. You hear decibels of sound. You smell and you taste different chemical substances. And you touch any state of matter at your disposal. You would think this would make any kind of experience in reality an objective event. Technically speaking, this is not the case.
Your reality is different than mine because of your different viewpoint, or what Einstein liked to call, frame of reference. Those differences can be measured. In our universe where space and time are interlaced as space-time, every reference frame happens at a specific position and time. The position in one frame is dependent of the time and position in the other frame. The time in one frame is dependent on the time and position in the other frame.

"Take Albert Einstein's general theory of relativity. This is one of the most well-known scientific theories known to man. This theory helps us understand a sole event perceived by different points of view. Different frames of reference do not have to be moving at a constant velocity in respect to one another in Einstein's general theory of relativity. The equivalence principle tells us that it is not possible to differentiate between an accelerating frame of reference and gravity.

"We rely on fundamental theories like this to make sense of so many aspects of the physical universe. But guess what? Even this theory claims that nature and the universe are full of distortions. The space-time fabric throughout the entire cosmos can be distorted by our perception of gravity.

"Hear me out in this little thought experiment. Imagine being enclosed in a box. There are no windows. You have no idea where the box you inhabit resides. It would be impossible to discern if you were in a box on earth or in a box out accelerating through space where there is less gravity but more acceleration propelling you just the right amount to press you against the floor of the box. That force of acceleration mimics the force of gravity on earth. Your reality of where you are could be totally mathematically in line with the gravity on earth, but you very well might be in space. Gravity. Acceleration. They are all very much distortions of reality.

"And since that is the case, this brings into question… what is the definition of real? What is reality at its most – well, *real* level? Who are you to say that when I reach out and touch something, what I feel upon my skin is not real? The universe is full of enigmas and contradictions and miracles and phenomena that you would not believe even if some guy by the name of Albert Einstein showed you the explicit mathematics behind it.

"The best we can do is make observations of the world – and the people –around us. And I know that sounds very subjective and I know how scary it is to think of your world as something as anything but objective, but that's the beauty in physics. There is always a mathematical formula to counterpart the philosophical implications of the physical universe with objective information. Thanks to brilliant physicists like Hendrik Lorentz, and formulas such as Lorentz transformations, our human brains can objectively relate the observations between different points of view into a clearer picture. Physics, and all science for that matter, advances us towards a better understanding of everything and *everyone* in this world. And isn't that what we all want? To *understand*."

Chapter 56

Last night, after my presentation, all of my adrenaline was gone, and Lacey's small amount of daily energy was at its end. We figured the perfect way to conclude the day would be to lie down like blobs and binge-watch a Netflix series.

"When were these sheets last washed?" Lacey asked before transitioning to the bed.

"Uh," I glanced up, and to my surprise, the bed was fully made with fresh sheets. "Actually... they're clean. My mom must have changed them."

"Good enough," she hopped out of my grasp and climbed onto the bed.

"One sec," I said while bent over to get my laptop out of my desk drawer.

I was prepared to discretely lift the old Lacey binder to get to laptop underneath, but, to my shock, there was no binder. Just the silver laptop.

If the binder wasn't there then where was it?

"What's this?" Lacey asked from atop the bed.

My stomach did a full flip.

I spun around.

"Oh my God..."

Lacey had scooped up the bulk of covers and in her hands was my OCD research binder.

Suddenly my lethargy was overturned by overwhelming panic.

"What the..." Lacey rapidly flipped through the binder. I couldn't imagine what was going through her head. "This goes all the way back to the fall, when we first met... and is this... is this my OCD poem?" she ripped out the copy of the poem and threw it onto the floor.

"No!" I hollered while scrambling to catch the amazing poem that marked the first time we met. It slipped out of my hands though, and I resorted back to trying to explain myself. "I mean yes, yeah it is you're poem, but it's nothing. This binder is nothing, Lacey, it's nothing-"

At lightning speed Lacey flipped through the binder. I lunged forward to retrieve it from her, but she held up her hand at once. "Back the hell off!" she demanded.

I squeezed the sides of my head, watching helplessly as Lacey scanned the pages. Reading. Realizing. Scanning.

Lacey transferred her pupils from the binder onto me. I had never seen a more hurt glaze over her large brown eyes. "Was this... were you making fun of me?"

Oh God. I felt like I was going to throw up.

"No! I swear, no! I was never making fun of you. Never! I was fascinated by the inner workings of your brain and-"

"So I was just some, some... some *experiment* for you to study?"

"No! No- no- no- er, it was more like a case study, mere observation! An experiment involves the manipulation of factors to observe the effect-"

"*You* manipulated me, Jef! You manipulated my trust! Don't you dare try to explain this away with research method definitions!"

I was sweating as I awkwardly tried to recover from her reprimand. "At first, yes, I was curious about your mental disorder, but from the first time you tutored me, heck, from the first conversations when I pestered you at the picnic table I started to care! And the more I got to know you the harder and harder I fell for you! I fell for your honesty and-and- and your sense of humor, and your, your intelligence! And my God, Lacey, I fell for you, everything about you!"

I started to reach out to hold her hand, but she swiped at my arm. "Don't touch me!"

Before I could defend myself any further Lacey loosened the three rings of the binder and purposely tossed it into the middle of the room.

Sheets rained down gracelessly, but I didn't care about them. I cared about Lacey, who made a breakaway out of my room.

"Lacey!" I sprinted after her, chasing her down the staircase and out the front door, into the snowy New England air. "Lace!" I lost my footing on a patch of ice but caught myself from falling. I hurried after her until I finally made it by her side. She was standing next to her silver car.

I reached out to her, "Lacey please let me explain!"

She raised her right hand at me, almost as if she was about to slap me, but using whatever restraint she had left in her she quickly clenched her hand into a fist and lowered it, as if she was squeezing a stress ball. "Get away from me before I lose it and hit you!" she begged.

I couldn't leave her though. She was so worked up. I had to explain myself. "Lacey I know you're mad but you have to understand-"

"Back off!" she stomped her foot hard on the moist dirt road. It was taking everything in her not to lash out at me physically. I honestly thought she was going to pass out from all the physical exertion she had pent up.

"Okay, okay," I held my hands up and backed away, "But please, just listen to what I have to say."

Lacey's extreme mood fluctuated between wildly infuriated and heartbreakingly sad. She cried out, without tears, "I let you in! I let you get to know me! I showed you my writing!" Her fists were pressing against the temples of her head, "I- I- I *touched* you!" that last sentence caused her knees to buckle and with shivering legs she crouched to the ground.
The tears made an appearance, causing her black makeup to run like diluted asphalt.

"Lace," I instinctively collapsed to a crouch, kneeling at her eye level. But Lacey wouldn't merge her line of vision with mine.

"How could you do this to me?" her vocal chords were so strained and frail while she glared onto the ground.

"I-I- I didn't do anything to you, Lacey. I was just interested. So interested! I wanted to understand your illness, then I wanted to understand everything about your mind, then I wanted to just be a part of your life! I love you, Lacey!"

"You've been lying to me through this whole relationship!" she screeched through bright red teary eyes that were not piercing through mine. Her glare was so sharp, not with hate, but with pain. Excruciating pain that came from wanting to hate somebody but not being able to.

That pain took my breath away, and as a result, I struggled to deny her assumption.

Maintaining the sharpness in her glare, Lacey carefully articulated through gritting teeth, "You *deceived* me."

"No I didn't!" I burst out, now with anger. "I've been completely committed to you, and only you! The fascination with the OCD was just a side interest..." I continued on babbling, trying to defend myself, but Lacey just bowed her head to the ground and proceeded to weep louder than my voice, "... Lacey please, please understand! OCD is just another part of your fascinating mind that I had to explore! It would be virtually impossible for me to get to know you without getting to know your OCD! Please, think about this rationally!"

That comment seemed to throw her into a tailspin of rage. She jerked her head up from its focus on the dirt and jabbed an angry index finger at me, "Don't fuck with me Jef! Don't play the 'you're crazy' card!"

Deciding she had enough of my company she ripped her car keys out of her pocket and shot up off the ground.

Suddenly the realization that she was about to get behind the wheel of her car set in, and I panicked, "No, no, no!" I frantically cried out as I scrambled up to standing position, not without moronically tripping over my big feet a few times.

Lacey's current fury, along with her severe depression that I knew had hit a dangerous low level, was in no condition to get behind a machine that could easily kill her. I couldn't in my right mind let her operate a vehicle in the extreme mindset she was in.

With feet shuffling nervously against the dirt Lacey reached for the car door handle. I just managed to grab her by the wrists. Immediately her hand lost its grasp on the car keys and they fell to the ground.

"Let go!" she shouted at me while trying to break free from my clutch.

It made me feel sick to my stomach to hear her scream like that at me, like I was some predator attacking her, but no level of misconstrued personal degradation was going to stop me from saving her from herself. "You can't drive like this!" I was desperate for her to understand.

She kept writhing and squirming, "Jef I swear if you don't let go of me-"

"I'll let go if you promise not to drive until you cool down!"

"How fucking dare you! How dare you, Jef! How fucking dare you!" Lacey screamed and, without any hesitation, kneed me in the crotch.

Reactively I lost my grip of her and lunged forward in pain, now clutching my excruciatingly throbbing groin.

I couldn't recover fast enough. In a matter of seconds Lacey was in the front seat of her car. An immediate explosion of music blasted through the speakers in tandem with the twist of the key in the ignition. With the deafening volume blaring Lacey speedily backed up.

As Lacey's car started to fly out of my driveway I neglected the pain in my crotch.

Muscle memories from high school track kicked into gear and I chased after her, banging on the silver vehicle's windows, yelling at her to stop the car. Lacey turned onto the main road, and I didn't let up. I chased her down the neighborhood street, still screaming her name. Then Lacey accelerated and naturally the laws of physics kicked in, leaving me no longer able to keep up with the skidding tires.

"Lacey! Wait!" I called after the car in desperation with hands over my head. "Lace," I tried to holler, but I had lost my breath.

My heart was booming in my eardrums.

My vision became clouded from the black spell of low blood pressure.

My legs buckled, and I dropped to the pavement.

Sitting in the middle of the road, I struggled to catch my breath.

Chapter 57

I called Lacey's cell phone over and over, desperate to make amends. She wouldn't answer though. After twenty-five minutes, when she should have been at her house already, she still didn't answer. But I kept trying to call her.

An hour passed, and she still didn't answer. What started out as worry for my sake turned into worry for her sake.

7:30 in the evening hit and my phone buzzed. I answered it so quick I didn't even check who was calling.

"Lacey?"

"Jef?" sounded a voice that wasn't Lacey's, but closely related.

"Yeah?"

"It's Felicity," Lacey's younger sister explained.

Immediately I knew something was wrong. "Are you with Lacey? Is Lacey with you? She won't answer her phone."

"What? Isn't she with you?"

"No."

"But she left an hour-" dread set in before I could finish that sentence.

Felicity called me back fifteen minutes later and filled me in on the relieving whereabouts of Lacey.

Turns out Lacey veered off the road, onto a curb, blew out her front tire, and rather than do the logical thing by stopping the car and calling for help, she barely managed to force that car on a two mile journey home on three tires. According to Felicity, the front rim of the car was completely ruined after skidding on two miles of asphalt. Also according to Felicity, and to my relief, Lacey lost her car driving privileges.

What bothered me most was how illogical and senseless driving home on three wheels was. There was literally no excuse. And that discord between what the sensible action would have been with the actual action Lacey took was stone cold proof that OCD was behind her unreasonable decision.

Upon hanging up the phone and learning that Lacey was home and safe, I floored it on the gas pedal, using my jeep as if it was a racecar, and sped down the highway.

I was scared. I was mad. I felt guilty. A tornado of emotions were tangling with a mess of thoughts. Did our fight cause Lacey's OCD symptoms to amplify? Did she try to change the radio station and swerve off the road in her obsessive compulsive frenzy? Or was she paranoid again about somebody following her while she was driving? Was Lacey just distracted from her anger with me? And then there was the worst thought, did Lacey crash the car on purpose?

Since Lacey didn't expect me, she had already showered and was cooped up in her room. When Mrs. Parker told Lacey I had come over to see her I could hear, from downstairs, her begging her mother to tell me to go home. Her mom was on my side though, and urged me to go up in her sacred room and have a talk with her.

As soon as I stepped in the room Lacey, lying in her bed like a sick person, refused to make eye contact with me while commanding, "Don't you dare walk in here with your dirty shoes on."

So with a sigh I bent down, unlaced my shoes, and proceeded into the room.

A mixture of dark circles from exhaustion and smudged makeup stained underneath those clouded eyes. Looking at the highly valuable and highly breakable girl that I loved more than anything in such a rough state felt like a punch in the stomach.

"Was it the OCD?" was the first thing out of my mouth. There was a dangerous quality behind my interrogation-like reaction. I sounded like I was asking about another man who hurt her, as if I was going to beat him up.

Lacey's far off stare finally confronted mine.

Lacey didn't have to tell me it was her OCD that made her crash the car. The embarrassed look in her eyes confirmed that the answer was yes.

I was extremely frustrated. I wanted so badly to take her OCD by the throat and strangle it to death. But I couldn't. I couldn't fight something that was hurting Lacey from the inside of her mind, the same place that made me love her so much.

"You know you shouldn't drive when you're upset! Stress makes the OCD worse!"

"Shut up," Lacey spit out.

A muscle in my neck tensed as I opted to keep my mouth shut.

"I am so mad at you." her voice was shrill, its usual strength having been compromised by pain that stemmed from my actions.

"I know," I prepared to apologize, but suddenly a bombardment of memories interrupted that impending apology.

The past months replayed through my mind at rapid fire. Lacey weeping about how awful of a sister she felt after OCD commanded her to lash out at Felicity for touching her mp3 player. Lacey locking herself in her car in the school parking lot, too anxious to attend class. Lacey mourning a friendship lost to OCD after seeing her old friend at the mall. Lacey screaming in the middle of the forest, only to fall onto me while begging for an answer as to why she was made with this mental illness. Lacey's morbid phone call that had me worried she hurt herself, and the resulting breakdown on her bathroom floor as the both of us cried over her debilitating mental disorder. The screaming battle we had in my driveway just hours ago over the OCD research binder I had created. And suddenly I remembered how damn tired I was.

Before I made a decision on what to say I was already talking. "You have such a special life Lacey, and I can't stand by and watch you destroy that life," I told her. "You have to get help. You can't avoid it any longer."

"I told you Jef, I'm never going to do that! I can't!"

"Lacey!" I was mad now, "Please! I don't want to be doing this right now, but I have to. I can't be with you if you're not gonna help yourself. Please, Lace."

"Jef…"

"Please! You can't prolong it anymore! When you get stressed, Lacey, your OCD gets ten times worse, which I didn't even think was possible. You've nearly blown up your hands by trying to kill germs! And now you got in a car accident-"

"I got in a car accident because I just found out my boyfriend had been keeping tabs on all the crazy shit I say!"

"That is not what this is about!"

"Yes it is!" she shouted with vulnerable brown eyes staring up at me. Suddenly I saw the girl with the notebook with the doe eyes staring up at me. The girl that I tried with all my might not to scare off. The girl that I tried to protect.

"Lace, I'm not doing this anymore," I gasped out with painstaking remorse fueling my breath. "You could have killed yourself tonight because you were flipping through stations like an obsessive compulsive maniac and then driving home on a blown tire without calling for help because your OCD told you that you couldn't turn your damn phone on! You need help! You need serious help!"

"No Jef!" Lacey doggedly refused.

I wanted to be by Lacey's side, I really did, but I couldn't be by her side if it meant watching her allow herself to decline into madness. If she sought outside help then I'd be more than willing to stay by her side, but she wasn't willing. That stubborn heartbreaker wasn't willing. And the thought that she didn't care enough about me to get help and save our relationship felt like a knife to my chest. Lacey had a hold of my heart. She had it as soon as I became emotionally invested in her. Before I met Lacey, when I had only read her poem she had touched my heart. Once we became friends she had the entire muscle in her grasp. But I swear, in this moment where she was refusing to save her from herself, she might as well have carved my heart out of my chest and left it bleeding in her small hands.

I couldn't fight it anymore.

As much as I hated to do so, I had to give her an ultimatum.

"You have to make a decision Lacey. What's it going to be? Are you going to go get help for the OCD or not?"

Lacey took a deep inhalation before talking.

The tension was unbearable.

I could hardly breathe.

Finally she responded. "I can't change who I am."

That was the second time today I felt like the wind was knocked out of me.

"What? No," I halfheartedly laughed, not believing her, "You don't know what you're saying."

"I sure as hell do," Lacey bit back.

My heart fluttered, and reality hit. Hard.

"No," I caught my breath. "Please don't do this Lace."

"I have no choice," she argued.

"Yes you do," my legs turned flimsy so I grabbed the rail on her bed to stay upright, "Come on Lacey. Please!"

Was this really happening? Was Lacey choosing OCD over me?

"We both knew this was going to be a challenge."

I saw what was happening in front of me and I couldn't keep my cool. Almost uncontrollably I set free my pent up aggression, "You think I don't know that? I knew this would be a challenge! But that doesn't mean you can just give up!"

"Jef," she shook her head, sounding so exasperated. "Don't make this harder."

"No," I cut her off, "This is supposed to be hard! That's what a challenge is!"

"Well maybe I'm just not cut out for a challenge Jef! I wish I was, I really do, but I'm not! I'm tired! Okay? I'm so damn exhausted! And so are you."

"No!" I raised my voice over hers. I didn't care that I sounded like a crazy person. The incomparable fury gnawing away at me was excruciating and I needed to let it out. "You're wrong! You're just wrong! This is the wrong decision! Lacey, we're great for each other," I stood by what I said.

Lacey shook her tired head, "I can't be free from this disease, but you can."

"Lacey!"

"It's over," Lacey finalized with anticlimactic swiftness.

When she said that, reality finally sank in for me.

Lacey chose OCD over me.

Truthfully, I expected Lacey to pick me over OCD. I don't know why. All of the knowledge I had gathered about the power of her obsessive compulsive disorder would have led me to believe that she'd choose OCD first, but I wasn't basing my expectation on knowledge. For once, I was basing my expectation on feelings. And I felt that Lacey and I belonged together.

I yelled louder than I meant to. "This is a huge mistake!"

"Jef," Lacey's mother inserted herself in the room, "Maybe you should go."

"Wait!" I blurted out while throwing my hands in the air and knelt down at Lacey's bedside, "Please Lacey! Think about what you're-"

"I'm sorry Jef but I really think you should go," Mrs. Parker went on in a coaxing tone that made me feel like I was some lunatic she needed to dispel. But I didn't want to be treated like a lunatic. I wasn't the crazy one here.

"Just, please, hang on," I held up a one second forefinger behind my back and continued to lock my burning eyes onto Lacey's, and she just stared at me like I was pathetic.

"Jef…" Lacey's mom insisted, this time her voice didn't sound like she was telling me I was crazy, it sounded precautionary. Like I should run while I could.

Lacey shook her head and transferred her stare onto the wall ahead.

I had no choice but to leave.

Right as I slammed the door I heard the following sound of Lacey bursting into tears.

Chapter 58

I couldn't go back to my bedroom with the OCD research binder dismantled and sprawled all over my floor. I was too torn up by Lacey dumping me. I was distraught about her car accident. And I couldn't for the life of me tell if I was more sad than I was mad.

Upon parking the car in my driveway I stalled from going inside the house. I spent a good hour walking around my neighborhood, hands in pockets while the stale night air stung my skin.

I strolled empty handed through my neighborhood in the dark night, only accompanied by that full moon. I didn't care how sketchy I probably looked. If a cop came by, whatever. I didn't give a fuck about anything but my broken relationship with my best friend.

Though the moon was bright and full, it provided no vibrancy to the world around me. Everything seemed to be in grayscale, including myself. I could see the white glow of the orb safe in the sky, but I couldn't feel its radiance illuminating the red of my jacket or the navy of my cap.

Moments from throughout my relationship with Lacey Parker were flashing through my head like a rapid strike of lightning. Memories from before we started dating, memories while we were dating, and the brief but bitterly fresh memory of us after we broke up in her bedroom. It didn't matter if the memories were good or bad, they all felt bad because my mind knew that they were over.

I bet a cigarette would be good right about now. I couldn't smoke though. I knew too much about how those sticks of poison would pollute my insides. But oh how nice it would be to take out my frustrations and sorrow with the drag of a cigarette. For once, ignorance sounded a lot better than knowledge.

I was in so much pain. And as far as I was concerned I had no choice but to be in that pain. Because I had to stand my ground with this break up in order to prove a point: that Lacey needed help with handling her obsessive compulsive disorder and depression.

I knew I was doing the right thing by separating myself from Lacey, but there was a little voice in my head trying to convince me that I was no different than my father. That I was a no good rotten excuse for a man who ditched a mentally ill person because I couldn't handle it.

I kept telling myself that wasn't the case though.

I left Lacey because I wanted to save her, not myself.

I needed to believe that. And part of me did. But part of me didn't.

I was so confused.

All I knew was that I wanted Lacey Parker to be able to function in this world. I just wanted Lacey better. And if that meant I couldn't be with her, well, then I'd take all the pain and sorrow that entailed just to know she was healthy and happy. That's what I really wanted. Truthfully. Because going on a life with Lacey Parker, knowing that she was suffering, was not a life I wanted to live.

Lacey would never want to hurt me. I knew those empathetic brown irises so well. They would never look at me with a desire to inflict pain. Like in the driveway. She wanted to hate me, I could see it, but she just couldn't. I knew that. I knew that from the bottom of my broken heart. Lacey would never make a choice to hurt me. No. Lacey would only hurt me if she felt like she had no choice but to do so. She believed that. And the belief that she had no choice but to hurt me was completely distorted. And who caused distorted beliefs in that brain of hers?

Obsessive compulsive disorder.

The flopping of my feet smacking the middle of the empty street morphed into stomping.

Suddenly I didn't question the sadness verses anger in my emotional state. The ratio of anger to sadness was significantly higher.

I was infuriated.

OCD did this. OCD broke Lacey and I up. OCD talked Lacey into ripping my chest cavity open and tearing my bloody heart out.

But no matter how angry I was at the OCD for what it had done to me, I was angrier about what it did to Lacey Parker.

OCD caused her to crash her car. OCD tried to kill her tonight, and OCD has been trying to kill her all along, forcing a smart, kind, and yes, troubled girl, into a slow downward spiral. A downward spiral that could be identified by the morbid thoughts escaping her lips.

I could still hear the pain in her voice.

I just don't care anymore.
I don't have the will.
I wasn't meant for this world.
I don't remember saying I wanted to live in the real world!
I can't do life.
I can't foresee this resolving itself!

Anger did not begin to cover how those auditory recollections made me feel.

My wild eyes fastened onto the full moon. The very symbol of mental illness.

You, I glared at the beautiful spotlight in the dark sky. *You are the culprit.*

There was an ethereal pull drawing me towards that loathsome moon.

My stomps on the damp pavement accelerated. My tense hands balled into fists. Despite the chilly draft in the air I began sweating. I could almost hear the loud pop of my brain snapping.

Like a lunatic I chased the full moon.

It took until a distant siren interrupted my voice that I realized I was talking out loud.

"Why?" I interrogated the full moon.

I took a slamming step onto a sidewalk bench, ascending so that I was closer to the starry sky.

"Why!" I repeated my desperate question with a raised voice and threw my lanky arms to my sides. "Why would you put that kind of pain inside her?"

...

There was no response but the lingering echo of my question which remained unanswered.

Just like I had intellectually drilled Lacey when we first met, I drilled the higher power in the sky whom might be in charge. "What did she do to deserve that?" I pressed.

...

Still, no reply.

I stood in the empty neighborhood underneath the moonlight, feeling taunted by the silence. "I'm waiting for an answer!" I called out. The over the top anger that had rendered inside of me was spilling out of my mouth with a distinct tone now. "The least you could do is give me an answer! After all you've done to her with this mess you named OCD! Or do you have no idea what I'm talking about?"

...

No answer to that question either.

I continued to drill the moon for an answer. "Do you have any idea what you've done to her?"

...

"Or me?"

...

"Do you?" I escalated to full on yelling. It was so loud that I could feel the veins bulge out of my neck. "Is this entertaining to you?"

...

"Is it?"

...

"Or do you find this whole situation sad?"

...

I had never felt short until this night.

I felt so far away from the all-knowing sky.

I got on my tip toes, stretching my calf muscles, trying to get higher, closer. I painstakingly longed to touch the sky.

With whatever strength I had left I fueled my voice box with ripe sound. "Do you even care?" I pled. "Do you even hear me?"

…

"Why did you give Lacey Parker OCD?"

…

"Come on! Tell me!"

…

"Tell me!"

…

"Why'd you give her this mental disorder?"

…

Idle pondering had become asking. Asking had become interrogating. Interrogating became begging. And begging had become silence.

That night my mom answered the front door to a police officer clinging me by my arm after some disturbed neighbors phoned in a noise complaint about a young man they thought was tripping on some psychedelic drug was shouting at the sky.

Chapter 59

It had officially been nine days since Lacey and I separated. And my heart hurt just as much as it did the day we broke up. The pain, it was so fresh, like it just happened. I swear that sadness, loneliness, and devastation was engrained in every heartbeat.

Maybe Lacey was right. Maybe hearts *did* memorize feelings.

School sucked.

I missed Lacey so badly. I just wanted her in my company. I didn't care if she didn't even touch me. I just wanted to be with her. In her vicinity. Talking to her brilliant but ridiculously twisted mind. I barely cared about all the physical aspect of companionship. What seemed so important to an adolescent boy didn't matter here in the dismal adult world, now that Lacey was gone. At age 23 I'd be thankful for my close friend to give a simple glance in my direction. That is, if I actually found myself in the same setting as her. The only opportunity I had to see her was at school and that hadn't happened. She was probably in and out as soon as possible now that she didn't want to lag behind and hang out with me. I was her best friend at school. Anywhere outside of home, really. I was her best friend. Was.

To my own despair I could finally relate to Lacey, on an empathetic level, regarding the pain she had felt having lost friends like Tara. Lacey was right earlier, after she saw Tara at the mall. Losing a friend was probably the saddest feeling I've ever experienced.

As if the sadness of losing a best friend and a girlfriend wasn't aching enough I also had to deal with that horrible post-relationship paranoia of picturing my ex with a new partner.

I knew there was no flipping way Lacey was hooking up with another guy, but me not being attached to her with the "boyfriend" title made it way too easy to worry about her with somebody else. With all of Lacey's problems intimately, emotionally, and mentally, I knew it wasn't anywhere near rational for me to picture her in a relationship. But I wasn't thinking rationally anymore. I think pain does that to you.

Intrusive images kept popping in my head. No matter how hard I tried to resist, I kept imagining her with some other guy. Over and over. It made me utterly sick. Him making her laugh. Him opening doors for her. Him touching her. Oh God. I couldn't go there without the pit of my stomach somehow lowering itself down like the abyss it had become.

After class I sat inside my car and basked in all of my distress, anger, and sorrow. I didn't know what else to do. There was so much pain inside of me. More pain than I felt capable of handling. I had no clue how to deal with it, so I just stayed in the student parking lot and let it do its worst.

At a loss, I examined the messy dump of a vehicle I was sitting inside. There were torn wrappers, empty bottles, Frisbees, loose papers, books in poor shape, wires and cords to stuff like Nintendo GameCube controllers and phone chargers, and lots of other random items scattered throughout the seats, floor, and dashboard. I had definitely let go of my allegiance to keep my car clean now that I didn't have my OCD girlfriend to accommodate.

I wasn't just slacking on my cleanliness towards the jeep. I also let up on my personal hygiene. I haphazardly deodorized. I stopped shaving. My mom hated my brunette stubble. She said I looked careless and dirty, but what did I care? Without an obsessive compulsive mysophobic girlfriend I no longer needed to care about appearing clean.

I continued observing all the junk I had hoarded inside my car. My eyes traced the trail of a cord hooked up to my car and my mp3 player.

Suddenly I had an idea of how I could cope with my overwhelming pain.

Right away I scrolled through my music library and pressed on the playlist I had titled "Lacey". It was a compilation of brooding metal.

I turned the volume knob and blasted the aggressive music so deafeningly loud that the bass made my car tremble. I couldn't care less about the students glaring at me as they walked in and out of their cars in the busy parking lot. They could go fuck themselves.

I was uncharacteristically attracted to the music I initially perceived as chaotic noise. The eruption of thrashing guitars, slamming drums, and smashing cymbals were surprisingly cohesive, building on each other. It was an explosion of sounds that were somehow complimentary and methodical.

When the bridge of the song hit an earsplitting screech of guitar strings exploded through the speakers, followed by a deep bellow that must have spawned from the very pit of the singer's stomach. It was almost unfathomable that a woman could make such an animalistic sound. And rather than deter the sound like I usually did, my pained emotional state took command and I embraced it. In fact, I loved the scream. It was so… expressive.

Lacey was onto something way back when we first started hanging out and she told me that the growling in songs expressed such raw pain. Now that I was listening to it with this distraught mindset I could hear the inexplicable pain in every shrieking vocal and guttural growl.

"Hardcore, man," Gabe commented on the music choice as he tossed a backpack full of video games in the corner of my family room. I had been blaring metal songs through the docking station on the window sill for the past five hours.

Gabe was crashing at my place. He planned it. He decided I needed to have some guy time to get over Lacey. "Shooting the crap out of zombies is the best way to get over a girl," was his reasoning when he invited himself over.

I lasted, I don't know, ten minutes until Gabe chucked his controller at the floor out of frustration.

"Okay this is ridiculous," Gabe struggled to sit up straight in the bean bag chair. "I've seen you defeat an entire legion of zombies with nothing but a pistol before. What the hell is wrong with you?"

"I'm just not in a zombie killing mood, I guess."

"Well get in one!" he punched me in my muscle-less tricep, "Dammit, Jef. You're bringing me down."

"Sorry," the insincerity in my apology was marked by the lack of interest behind my monotone voice.

"Do you wanna play a racing game?"

"Not really."

"Strategy game?"

"No."

"Holy shit man," Gabe exclaimed, probably shocked that I refused to play my favorite game. "You really are hung up on Lacey, aren't you?"

Stressed, I rubbed my temples. "I can't stop thinking about her."

"Dude if you like her so much why did you dump her?"

Instantly I got worked up and tried to defend myself. "I told you, Gabe, I didn't dump her! It's complicated. She has OCD, really bad OCD, like really God awful OCD!" I shouted while jerking my arm to the bean bag cushion so that I was no longer clawing at my scalp, "And she wasn't doing anything about it! No therapy. No rehab. No meds. Yeah, I gave her the ultimatum, but she chose OCD over me! As far as I'm concerned she broke up with me!"

"Fine! She broke up with you!" Gabe agreed tiredly. "Quit thinking about it so much, man! That's what you do, you think and you think and you think. Just chill out, play some mindless video games. Lacey will come around. They always do."

Pissed that I even heard the sound of Lacey's name in Gabe's mouth, I snapped. "Dude, shut up! You're the last person who should be giving relationship advice!" in my acute rage I chucked the controller at the outdated gaming console. "If anybody's relationship was supposed to last, it was mine! Not yours! Your relationship is a joke!"

I expected Gabe to shout at me, to tell me to go fuck myself, but he didn't. Instead his response was, "You think I don't know that, genius?"

Whoa.

Did not see that coming.

Gabe lost his cool and kept shouting, "Me and Beth are a freaking disaster!"

Taken aback to finally hear my oldest friend admit something he'd never fess up to before, I meekly responded, "You actually think that?"

"Hey, man, I never really apologized for spilling to Beth about your weird no-touching relationship."

"If this is an apology then it sucks," I spit out.

"Okay, okay. Let me start over. I just didn't really understand why you'd be with a girl that barely freakin' touched you. I guess I just don't know what it's like to be so mentally in touch with a person to the point that it actually outweighs all the physical downsides. If anything, Lacey was, like, the best thing for you. You guys were always talking and laughing and that's like, I don't know dude," Gabe's head fell forward and he matted a frustrated palm against his forehead, "Shit, I'm actually jealous that your relationship actually came from a mature friendship."

Even though I appreciated the apology, my humiliation overrode my gratitude and I reacted with some good old monotone sarcasm. "Thank you. That was beautifully spoken."

Instead of giving me some uplifting pep talk Gabe opted to stay silent.

The only noise was the blaring guitar riff emanating off my speakers. As soon as the song came to an end Gabe took the opportunity to talk. "You aren't gonna try to get over her, are you?"

"She keeps replaying in my mind," I whispered into my hands.

Chapter 60

Mrs. Lubben, the professor of my psychology class, spent the latter portion of the lecture teaching about perceptions.

"Often people think perceptions only apply to vision. Perceptions are interpretations of any of the five senses: vision, hearing, smell, taste, and touch. Perceptions are not always factual. They can be biased or skewed, influenced by emotions, expectations, and beliefs. When a sensory signal is unclear we resort to what we believe of the world. If you believe that the environment is dangerous, a touch on the shoulder might arouse fear rather than excitement. Many believe this kind of panic and fear stems back to human's primal days when survival was a real struggle."

With Lacey on the brain, I thought of her irrational perception of the world. Everything external was so dangerous in her mind. But why? Was it her wildly impractical fear of everything part of her genetic makeup? Was she one of those people who contracted some bacterial infection or Lyme disease at a young age and then began to exhibit obsessive compulsive symptoms that weren't treated in time to reverse the OCD? I was on my way to my car in the student parking lot when I finally, after fourteen days, caught sight of Lacey Parker. She was coming out of the passenger side of a car. In my jealousy I checked to see if a guy was behind the wheel.

    It was another guy. Thankfully, her dad.

I was too overwhelmed by finally seeing Lacey to go deep into hypothesizing why she wasn't driving herself to school.

Hastily I tried to fix my slouching posture so that I didn't look nearly as pathetic as I was feeling. I didn't want Lacey's first thought when she saw me to be "I'm glad I dumped him".

I scratched at my stubble insecurely. Would she like the facial hair? Probably not. In my insecurity as I stared at Lacey I realized something. I wasn't angry at her, like I thought. There was anger… but it wasn't directed at her.

"Jef?" she spotted me.

The sound of her saying my name was something I had been aching to hear the past two weeks. And the past two weeks were such a fog, but in a matter of seconds the sound of my name on Lacey's tongue cast my feelings into clarity. It was amazingly clear.

I wasn't mad at Lacey. No. I was mad for her. Because I knew her potential. And I couldn't bear to watch her neglect that potential and spend her life walking in and out of stores on different feet or staying at home in that same seat she covered with a towel.

"Jef," Lacey repeated, seeing that I didn't respond, as she advanced a few steps closer to me.

Naturally I became lightheaded. My mouth was suddenly dry. I barely got out a 'hey' before awkwardly dropping my keys out of my hands.

Quickly I scrambled to the pavement, picked up my keys, dropped them again, then picked them up again. When my eyes locked onto Lacey's I blurted out, "I was just thinking about you."

"Oh, I, uh," I could see the strain in her jowls. She was fighting a smile.

"I'm not mad at you."

"Well that's good, because you shouldn't be," she replied.

Interestingly enough, that remark made me mad. Through gritting teeth I asked, "Why shouldn't I be?"

"Because I didn't do anything wrong."

Feeling a confrontational vibe, I subtly retaliated, "And I did?"

Lacey's pleather coated shoulders bobbed up, "Well yeah. You studied me."

I quickly defended myself, "I only did that because you were so interesting-"

"No, you thought my OCD was interesting. Not me."

"That's not true-"

Lacey rambled on, having apparently been rehearsing this altercation in our fourteen days apart, "I thought that you were interested in my OCD because you cared about me. But you were really only interested in me because you cared about the OCD."

Lacey wasn't the only person who might have imagined this altercation. I, too, had imagined this conversation going down way too many times the past few sleepless nights to hold back from letting my thoughts spill out. I didn't hesitate with delivering my side of the argument, "I was interested in you Lacey! At first, yeah, it was the OCD that I was interested in. But as soon as you opened your mouth to me in that first tutoring session I knew there was something more to you than just OCD. Something amazing and captivating and wonderful about you." There were commuters gathering around Lacey and I in the parking lot as I professed my feelings loudly, but they didn't make me hold back. I was off and running my mouth and no stranger was going to stop me from making my verbal strides towards the person I was drawn to, "I was interested in all of you Lacey! And I cared! I cared about all of you! Ever since we first talked, since we exchanged knowledge in a conversation, I cared about you! Why does it have to matter when I started caring?"

"Because it just does!" Lacey stood by her anger and hugged her arms tighter to her chest.

"No it doesn't!" So much for not being mad at her.

"Yes it does!"

"Why!" I leaned closer to her in my desperation for an answer. "Why does it matter that I was interested in your OCD before I was interested in you as a whole!"

"Because!" Lacey's volume lowered like she was embarrassed by what she was about to say. "When people ask me how I met the love of my life I'll say 'he was studying me'! What kind of story is that!" she spit out.

There were too many emotions whirling through my head. First of all, I couldn't begin to explain the euphoria I felt hearing her refer to me as the love of her life. Secondly, I was wicked confused as to why she cared so much about telling the perfect story to-

That was it.

A story.

That was it!

"Oh I get it," I sounded a little cocky having caught onto her mindset, "You want some kind of storybook plot to our relationship. You want a scene that can exceed any of your daydreams. Something of fairytale proportions. That's the author in you. And your perfectionism! You know for somebody who claims to hate chick flicks that's a pretty hypocritical pattern of fantasizing you've got there. But you can fix that. You can condition your psyche out of those patterns, just like you conditioned your psyche into them-"

"Oh here we go again," Lacey threw her head back then looked around, as if there was some kind of invisible crowd that could sympathize with her obvious discord.

I was too eager to enlighten her to clamp my babbling mouth shut. "No, trust me, I know what I'm talking about. My professor just talked about perceptions and perceptual sets! They're these habitual ways of perceiving stimuli in a certain way. You perceive the world as a place you don't fully belong in or want to be part of, and as a result your sense of touch is compromised and-"

"My God, Jef, stop! Just stop! I never conditioned myself into having OCD rituals! Why do you have to pin everything unique about me to some sociological statistic or a philosophical principle or some orthodox scientific definition! Why can't you just accept that I am the way I am because of *my* personality? Not because of some weird physiological malfunction between the- the- the," she paused to confine the incoming examples with finger drawn air quotes, "the 'neurons' in my brain or the some other scientific explanation!"

"Okay, first of all, personality is a science in itself, and second of all, neurons aren't some make-believe thing so I'm not really sure why you put air quotes around-"

"God dammit, Jef! This is exactly what I mean!" Lacey yelled over me, causing more commuters to stop in their tracks and eavesdrop on us. "Just stop! Stop analyzing me like I'm some kind of freakshow!"

I guess that was insensitive.

And I couldn't honestly deny the truth; Lacey had a point. Why hadn't I ever attributed her phobic quirks to her personality? Why was it so hard for me to believe that maybe, just maybe, Lacey was the way she was because of her innate personality? She certainly believed that. And Lacey was the first person who would do anything to preserve her personality. That was blatantly true in everything she did. But once again, the question still lingered... *why*?

Before I could apologize, Lacey ran past me, so unusually close she nearly brushed up against me.

I wasn't going to let her get away from me though. I had been losing sleep over our break up. I had been screaming at the moon and getting dragged home by the police. Shit, I had grown a beard! I wasn't letting Lacey get away after all her absence had put me through in only two weeks.

As Lacey stomped down the sidewalk I made a late attempt to win her over.

"Lacey!" my timbre in that holler cut through the noisy wind. Lacey's five foot body tensed into stillness. Lacey turned around, locked eyes on me, and opted to keep her mouth shut. I inhaled, cleansing my vocal chords with the fresh wind, then exhaled the purest of breath, "You have put so many limitations on yourself."

With the slightest bit of hesitation Lacey opened her mouth to respond, closed it, then opened her mouth again, this time with a shake of the head.

"I'm doing the best with what I've got in here," she pointed to her brain with an overly-conscious forefinger millimeters away from touching her temple. "I'm sorry but that's just how it is."

"But it doesn't have to be that way," I sighed a breath of empathetic exhaustion.

"Yes it does!" she belted out, "You don't get it Jef! I can't take some mind-altering medicine! If I do it could dispel my creativity." Lacey bowed her head to the ground, took a deep breath, and then locked eyes back on mine with unprecedented conviction, "I am uniquely flawed, it's okay to accept it, I know I am. But I'm also uniquely talented. And you know what? I will gladly take that. Because I'd rather have an overabundance of issues and a smidge of talent than have neither. I never want to be ordinary, Jef."

Overwhelmed by her emotive proclamation I stood there, dumbstruck into silence.

"Lace..." I barely uttered.

"I have to go, Jef," Lacey declared in a fear-stricken tone and scurried her tiny frame into the academic building.

I swear she could feel herself veering closer to forgive me, closer to changing her mind about what I had done by studying her. That forgiveness was the greatest threat to her unaccommodating perceptual sets which structured the consistency of her precious personality.

Chapter 61

Being at school continued to suck.

I tried to put dating out of sight, out of mind, but every little reminder of Lacey just reminded me how lonely I was destined to be without her.

I was constantly juggling between accepting my loneliness and downright resenting my life for my loneliness. I knew that I was never going to find somebody else like Lacey. I didn't even want somebody *like* her. I wanted her. There was no alternative. No comparison. I would have bet my life that nobody was more perfect for me than her.

That being said, the overhanging thought of Lacey's absence transformed the college campus from a place I thrived to a place I despised. I'd try to get in and out of there as quickly as possible, ironically the way Lacey used to do before she met me.

When the weather started getting remotely close to warm I pushed myself to go hang around in the community college courtyard and play Frisbee with the guys once I was out of class. I sucked though. My thoughts were far away in self-pity as I remembered playing Frisbee the first time Lacey and I met.

"Come on, Sterling!" Carson crossed the field and slammed into me. Roughly he massaged my shoulders then gave me a whack on the back, "Snap out of it!"

"Sorry," I apologized as the whiplash of his smack wore off of my lanky build. I don't know why I apologized though. I wasn't sorry.

"What's the fuckin' deal, man?"

"Nothing," I lied, "I'm just a little rusty, that's all."

"Nah, that's not it," Carson, for once, was slightly perceptive. "It's Lucy, isn't it?"

"Her name is Lacey."

"Whatever, Lacey," he carelessly corrected himself. "It doesn't matter. She doesn't matter. It's been like a month. You gotta get over her."

"Eighteen days to be exac-"

"You've been keeping track? Sterling you seriously need to get over her!"

I had no interest in arguing so I kept my indifference short. "I don't want to get over her, Carson."

"You know what would do the job? A rebound. Some meaningless fling to get your mind off of Lacey."

"No thanks," I denied and tried to walk away, but Carson snatched my weak shoulder and yanked me back. Completely disregarding my response, he went on to scrounge me up a potential hookup. "There's plenty of girls around here you could get with. Like her!"

I didn't bother looking where he was pointing as I threw my head back and groaned.

"Or her."

"I don't wanna-"

"What about her? She's cute!" Carson literally grabbed my cranium and redirected it down.

I glanced at the blonde who was sitting with a group of guys at a picnic table. She was nothing special.

All of a sudden the young woman jumped out of the bench and let out a high pitched scream. "Bee!" she announced and swiped her flimsy hands in the air at the misunderstood bug.

"No." I flat out rejected, turned around, then made a break away from Carson.

Marching down the sidewalk I muttered to myself, "I swear the world is testing me."

The next school day I decided to linger after class in the lounge and study regardless of how warm it was outside. I wasn't up for another failed attempt at playing Frisbee. And I certainly wasn't about to go to the library, the setting marked in my memory as the place where I gradually fell in love with Lacey Parker.

Right when I was about to finish reading the assigned chapter in my textbook a familiar guy interrupted me.

"Yo Jef."

I glanced up to see Zeke in his red, yellow, and green striped beanie. There was a confused look in his eye.

"Hey," I greeted hesitantly.

Zeke leaned down to me and lowered his volume, "What's, uh, what's wrong with your girlfriend?"

I slammed my textbook shut and retaliated, "Dude what did I say about making fun of her?"

"No, seriously. She hasn't been showing up to my Sociology class."

"Oh I know," Kenny chimed in, which came as a shock to me. I hadn't even realized he was sitting at the table in front of me playing cards with a bunch of other guys.

"I heard she admitted herself to the loony bin," Kenny volunteered the information loud enough for the entire lounge to hear.

Immediately upon hearing that I shoved my textbook in my backpack, zipped it up, then began to pace away. I didn't even bother to reprimand Kenny about his inconsiderate announcement. I was too overcome with emotions to scold some stupid college kid.

Behind me I heard Zeke call out, "Wait where are you going?"

I couldn't talk though. My throat was dry, my mind was racing, and I couldn't differentiate between feelings of relief that Lacey was getting help, excitement that there was a chance she sought out help because she wanted to salvage our relationship, and worry knowing that if she was institutionalized in a program to fight her anxiety then she was certainly suffering.

Without turning back I got to my car and sped out of the school zone.
I had to get to Lacey's house and find out what was going on.

I drove over the speed limit with the eyes of a hawk on the street. What would usually take roughly fifteen to twenty minutes to get to Lacey's house took me exactly twelve.

With an eager index finger I rang the doorbell.

Anticipation made me lightheaded. I had no idea if I was going to see Lacey on the other side of that door.

I didn't have to wait long to find out.

Lacey's mom opened the door, "Hello Jef," she smiled with pleasant surprise. "What brings you here? I'm afraid Lacey's not home."

"Mrs. Parker," having finally used my larynx, for the first time since Zeke asked me what was wrong with Lacey, my parched throat cracked, "I don't mean to be invasive, but can you at least tell me if Lacey's okay?"

Mrs. Parker stared at me with motherly eyes, soft and welcoming. "Jef, why don't you come in?"

I entered the house on that invitation.

"Are you hungry?" Lacey's mother asked as she led me in the kitchen.

"No, I'm all set," I answered.

From there Mrs. Parker and I sat at the kitchen table and she filled me in on Lacey's current situation.

"You are something else, Jef," she laughed. "To come all the way here to find out about Lacey. You didn't text her or 'snap' her or whatever you kids do on your phone?"

"No, ma'am. Lacey isn't the most avid phone user."

Her mom raised her eyebrows, "Oh believe me, I know. She hardly responds to the messages I send her when I'm at work. It drives me crazy."

"Me too," I chuckled nervously as I pictured the girl I loved.

After a brief sigh Mrs. Parker cut to the chase. "Lacey's depression hit hard this winter. She stopped going to class. I don't think she was actually finishing any of her assignments. She was barely getting out of bed. It was like her sophomore year of high school all over again, when she was first diagnosed. So last week we officially withdrew her from the semester."

I was relieved to hear that. I knew Lacey didn't care now about school, but sooner or later she'd start to be thinking straight and I knew she'd beat herself up if she had a failing grade on her transcript.

"We just enrolled her in an outpatient program for people with obsessive compulsive disorder. She's there six hours during the day, until three o'clock. It goes for five days a week for three weeks. In the meantime Jim is searching for a therapist in New England so that she'll have regular therapy once a week. We've already got a psychiatrist in place, so that's good. The hope is that she'll convince Lacey to take some kind of medication for her OCD and depression."

With a cracked throat I responded to that abundance of wonderful information. "That's... that's great."

"Lacey should be home within the next fifteen minutes if you'd like to see her."

"No," I quickly rejected the invite, "It sounds like things are moving in the right direction and I don't wanna stir anything up."

Chapter 62

Gabe was beyond excited for the Frisbee golf tournament we had entered in over the weekend. Gabe figured if there was any chance I could distract myself from Lacey it would be with a Frisbee golf tournament.

And for the most part, the competitive nature of the game actually did loosen my mind from Lacey. Not the whole time, but in random spurts. I faded in and out of thought about her.

By the seventeenth hole I was too busy fighting Kenny for the first place title. Right before we took our turns on round seventeen most of the guys stopped for a water break. Me, wanting to keep myself in the zone, refused to get off the field. I passed the Frisbee with Gabe, trying harder and harder to smoothen my throw.

As the Frisbee came hurling at me, about a foot too high, I leaped up, grabbed the disc, and landed to the ground in a spiral motion that caused me to face a different direction. It was then that I thought my eyes were deceiving me.

The short brunette I had been working tirelessly to block out today was walking in my direction.

"Lacey?" I was shocked to see her here, at my Frisbee golf tournament. She couldn't even come to these when we were dating. I nearly dropped the Frisbee out of my hands. "What are you-"

"We need to talk," she straightened upright and crossed her arms over her black and gray leopard printed shirt that was, to my shock, a three quarter length sleeve. Lacey almost never wore anything but long sleeves since she impulsively used long sleeves to cover her hands.

"Okay, yeah, sure," I was so fast to agree that I scarcely took a chance to breathe. I just couldn't believe she was here. I knew I had on the biggest grin.

"Okay so I was think-" Lacey paused, seemingly distracted by something, "You know, it's really hard for me to yell at you when you keep smiling!" the ends of her mouth were threatening to curl as she stared at my contagious smile. "I came here because I'm still mad at you Jef! You shouldn't be happy. What's the big deal?"

"You showed up," I answered in my brightest mood.

Lacey went mute. Her brown eyes looked almost greenish under the bright sunlight while they delved into mine.

A full fifteen seconds of silence went by of us standing in front of each other, all alone, in the open field.

Well, I thought all alone.

"Jef! Pass me the Frisbee!" Gabe hollered from across the lawn.

I neglected to react to my friend. I didn't dare divert my attention away from Lacey.

"Listen," I began to apologize about my studying of her yet again, "I thought I was being smart by observing you, but it was dumb. Really dumb."

"Yeah, it was," she agreed with agitation. "Do you have any idea how violated that makes me feel? It's hard enough for me to let people in without them keeping record of everything I say and do."

"I know," I moaned, still fresh with anger towards myself. "I know, Lace. I realize that now. You've gotta understand though, that wasn't where my mind was when I made the binder."

"Then where was it Jef? Where was your mind focused on? Here?" she gestured her angry hands at her crotch.

"No!" I burst out. "Why do you have to go there!"

"Because, Jef. I've got news for you! I might not have let you inside," she pointed to the lower half of her body and I tried to keep my eyes glued to her eyes, "But I let you *inside*," she then pointed to her brain. "My mind is the most intimate part of me. We couldn't have been more in touch even if you fucked me."

"I get it!" I resorted to shouting at her. "Okay! I get it! I get it all too well! You can't be in a relationship because it's too hard to please your OCD while being a girlfriend! And you chose OCD over a relationship! Lace, your goals, major and minor, are reprioritized by your fears. Just like mine are reprioritized by my curiosity," I hastily then pointed to my friends far off in the field, "Just like Carson's are reprioritized by his sex drive. And Gabe's are reprioritized by his bizarre need to be in a relationship regardless of whether or not he's happy. Believe me Lacey, I get it."

I'm pretty sure I hit the nail on the head, which, to my dismay agitated her more than it charmed her.

"Don't tell me how my mind works, Jef!" Lacey retaliated. "It's not that simple! I can't be in a relationship with somebody who went behind my back and took notes of my behavior like I was some freak of nature test subject!"

"I just wanted to understand you! That's all I wanted!" I hollered so loud that my shout echoed in the vast field. With the brunt of my frustration pinned on Lacey's stubbornness I disregarded my shyness and admitted the touchy feely parts of me, "I just wanted to understand the girl I was falling in love with! But you know what? It doesn't matter! The research, the journal entries, the notes, none of that matters anymore! Because I'd rather not understand a single thing about you and get to be beside you than understand you completely and have to be apart!"

Suddenly the anger that occupied Lacey's sharp pupils transformed into fear. She tightened up, crossing her arms so that she somehow appeared even smaller. She lowered her frantic stare down at her feet in what I assumed was an attempt to hide the vulnerability emanating from her light brown eyes.

"You don't mean that Jef. You always want to understand things. You… you can't mean that."

"I swear Lacey, I mean that," I implored to drill in her.

"No no no no," she shook her head rapidly, trying to convince herself otherwise. "You're not being yourself. See, you're not being yourself."

"No," I argued, "in a crazy way I feel more like myself than ever. Instead of some computer with all these facts and codes stored away I feel like, like, a human. You make me feel like a human. A human with unanswered questions and all sorts of feelings and it's humbling. I feel humble with you."

"Stop!" Lacey snapped while fighting a smile. "Stop saying really charming things! Just stop!"

Gabe's voice interrupted. "Jef! Just pass me the Frisbee!"

I stayed transfixed on Lacey, whose hard visage was weakened by my romantic outburst. I could tell I disarmed her, but she still fought to seem in control of the situation.

"I can't be with you." she finally said.

"Why, Lace? Why! I said I'm sorry! I know I messed up! I get it! Why can't you just forgive me!"

"Because!" uncharted resentment caused her to raise her voice over mine. "How am I supposed to be with somebody who is tainted by this bad connotation? I'll see you and I'll just see the boy who studied me behind my back! The boy who only talked to me because I had OCD!"

Unwilling to give up, I argued onward. "At first, yeah, I talked to you because you struck me as weird! But what kept me coming back to you was you, not your OCD! I don't even think it started out with little things. I fell fast and hard. And yeah, there were little things I liked about you. I got excited when you texted me. Or said my name. Or just smiled at me. But there were also the more profound elements of you that I loved! Your writing. Your sincerity. Your personality. And yes, your mind! And like it or not, that included your mental disorder! Dammit Lacey, I was falling for you in your entirety. And I- I- I- think I'll go crazy if you don't realize that!"

Lacey was speechless.

"I know I screwed up by making that binder behind your back. But please Lace, can you please forgive me?"

Lacey allowed that binder reference to get her worked up. "Believe me, Jef, I want to! I really do! But I can't, Jef! I can't let it go!"

A realization hit me. She couldn't let go of what I had done, and why was that? Because she had a disease that didn't allow her to let go of things very easily. She was treating me like another element in her "dangerous" reality that she could deem as tainted or not tainted, like her taboo words. Her method of perceiving me was on the same mindset as her OCD. In a way that was kind of uplifting, because if she could just get help with her OCD, then she'd be able to let go of what I had done. I'd be in the clear.

"What is it going to take for you to forgive me?"

"Nothing!" she burst out with a sureness that faded before my eyes. Her hard expression softened with uncertainty as an epiphany sounded into resonance. "There's nothing you can do," a spurt of newfound energy jolted through her like an electric shock. The high voltage revelation caused her to bid farewell abruptly, "I'm sorry, I've gotta go."

Before Lacey could turn around, Gabe heckled me again, "Dude, pass the Frisbee!"

"Sh," I waved him away, "Something's happening!"

"Dude, just pass the Frisbee!"

I guess Lacey had enough of listening to Gabe because she snatched the Frisbee out of my hands, "Fine!" She whipped the disc in Gabe's direction, "Fetch!"

Then, without further notice, Lacey stormed off the grass and towards the road.

I was... there were no words to describe my state. I was dumbfounded. Beside myself. Flabbergasted. Absolutely flabbergasted.

I couldn't take my eyes off of her as she marched away to her car.

Gabe, having retrieved the Frisbee, came running over to me. "What was that about? You guys still fighting?"

I was too mesmerized by Lacey to answer, let alone break my stare off of her. I asked Gabe in my unflinching bewilderment, "Did you see that?"

"No. What?"

"She touched the Frisbee, Gabe. She passed you the Frisbee!"

He snarked, "Yeah, I know, I was there. It was a lousy throw."

I disregarded whatever grumbling comments he continued to make after that as I watched Lacey's silver car pull onto the main road and drive away. The happiness I felt was indescribable.

When her car was out of sight I finally gave Gabe my attention. He raised an eyebrow at me. "What are you so damn happy about? Wait, are you guys back together?"

"No," I exhaled a breath of laughter.

Gabe was confused. "Then shouldn't you be upset? You haven't been doing well, man."

"Yeah, but Lacey has."

Chapter 63

Lacey's improvement fueled me through the next few days. I went from a significantly depressed mood to a moderate depressed mood, which by comparison felt like a high. But that faded as soon as Peter shed some light on a very dark subject.

It was a Thursday night, and I surprisingly didn't have to work.

Peter was hanging out in my room, on the floor reading an old science magazine on aerodynamics that I had on the bookshelf.

"Jef, did you and Lacey break up because of me?"

I was thoroughly perplexed by Peter's random question. "What? No, why? What do you even mean, Pete?"

"Well Mom cleaned your room at 3:25 before we left for the business trip because I told her that Lacey wouldn't want to go in your room if it was messy."

"Peter!"

I was two seconds away from yelling at Peter to stay out of my business, when suddenly the realization hit me like a freight train.

Before Peter could finish talking I stormed down the stairs, found Mom cooking at the stove, and let her have a piece of my mind.

"You planted that binder! You- you- you sabotaged my relationship!"

A few seconds of silence as Mom's eyes slowly fluttered shut.

My heart was palpitating at an enormous rate. My mouth was arid. I could barely breathe, I could barely think.

"Jef," Mom guiltily droned with a sour frown.

Even though my gut knew the truth, my brain wouldn't accept it. "Oh my God, you did, didn't you?"

My mother looked like she was about to burst into tears. Instead of owning up to what I knew she did she pinned the negativity onto me. "Jef you weren't focused when you were dating Lacey. You forgot Peter's medication several times. Instead of spending time with your brother you were going out and-"

I completely disregarded my manners and wailed over Mom, "What were you thinking? 'It's not enough for my son to have one shitty parent, let's make that two!'"

"Jef!" she cried out.

"No!" I yelled at her without remorse, something I had never done before. "Don't! Don't do that! Don't try to make me feel bad for you! I won't!"

I didn't talk to my mom for the next week straight.

I tried to saturate myself with schoolwork, but it was so damn hard. Because of that newfound knowledge about what Mom did, I couldn't stop thinking about what could have been between Lacey and I if mom didn't strategically place that binder onto my bed to destroy what should have been the most romantic night of my life.

The only thinking I did was about Lacey, wondering what exactly she was doing, when I'd see her next, and if she'd ever find it in her to forgive me. I couldn't seem to stop myself from thinking about her. If I'm being honest I'd say I had an idea of what Lacey must have felt, being inadvertently stuck on certain topics, thoughts, obsessing and obsessing without trying to.

For once in my life I wanted to shut my brain up. All I could think of was Lacey and I just needed a Goddamn break from it. I needed to neglect my brain and just let go.

So, I stopped thinking altogether. That must have been where my obsessing was different than Lacey's, because I could stop.

I was as good as a zombie at the convenience store. I actually forgot to do the most basic of tasks before closing, like taking out the trash or manually locking up the outdated cash register.

I wasn't embracing my time at school. I'd go to class, unengaged (probably to the relief of the professors who loathed my frequent hand raising), then rev up the jeep's engine a good twenty-five miles per hour over the speed limit on my eager endeavor home. And my study habits for schoolwork? Next to nonexistent. Study habits in the name of leisure? Completely nonexistent.

I could feel my once sharp brain downgrade to a duller version of itself. But as much as it bothered me, I wasn't gonna do anything about it. I just didn't see the point. Who was I trying to impress with my brain? Not Lacey anymore. And certainly not myself.

It wasn't in my nature to drink to get drunk. I still wasn't fond of the sluggish and dimwitted feeling it gave me but, like I said, lately I just didn't care.

So I thought, why not get drunk? I already wasn't keeping up the strength to think clearly.

I had the perfect opportunity to drink as irresponsibly as possible this weekend because my mom was away with some old friends.

She wanted me to be on top of Peter the way she usually was, but I had no intention of babying him like she did. That wasn't even in the realm of possibilities seeing that I could barely take care of myself the past few weeks. My unshaven face was proof of that.

Since my mom and I weren't much of drinkers and Peter couldn't have alcohol because it would mix with his meds, there was no alcohol aside from two hard lemonades acting more like decorations than edible beverages perched in the fridge in the garage.

I wasn't supposed to leave Peter alone for more than an hour, but I was in such a selfish mood to get drunk that I just had to get out and buy something with alcohol in it. And there was no chance I'd bring Peter along because he would tell my mom when she got back. Hell, he'd probably call her up to tattle on me.

Impatient and dying to drown my brain, I did the bare minimum to prepare Peter's supper. I made sure he took his daily dose of Anipiprazole medication then threw the cardboard pizza box from the night before onto the kitchen table. I didn't even bother to get him a plate. I had no intention of washing dishes tonight. No. Tonight I was getting full on obliterated.

"Jeffff, why do I have to have my pizza cold?" Peter whined while I zipped up my sweatshirt on my way out the door.

"I told you, I have to go run an errand and you know you can't use the oven without me here."

"Why can't you heat my dinner then go after?"

"Because I just can't."

"But-"

"My God, Peter, I said 'no'! Just have your damn pizza and leave me alone!"

I stormed out into the lovely Massachusetts forty-five degree weather, got behind the wheel of my car, and sped to the nearest liquor store.

Two cases of beer, a bottle of rum, and a bottle of vodka replaced Lacey's place in the passenger seat while I rolled the car down the neighborhood street.

It was about 6:45 and moderately dark but there seemed to be a gray fog or something coming from the down the block. The closer I got to my house, the more noticeable the fog became.

"What the-" I leaned over the wheel and squinted as my house came into view.

I didn't even get a chance to pull into my driveway. My gut dropped and the realization of what I was seeing hit me harder than a freight train.

That wasn't fog.

It was smoke.

And it was pouring out of my house.

"Oh God, PETER!"

The fire bled from the corner of the kitchen into the den.

I had never before experienced an adrenaline rush so powerful.

A Jetstream of dark gray smoke flumed out. Flashes of bright orange fire flickered out of the charring windows. Singed panels melted in reverse, curling from the bottom up with an orange glow.

"Peter!" I yelled at an earsplitting volume.

Having no idea where he was and fearing the worst, I assumed Peter was still inside the house.

I looked in that inferno and imagined my brother struggling to hobble out on weak leg muscles.

"PETER!" I screamed and ran at the speed of light, to the den's side door

A blazing flame climbing up the screened door must have been roasting the metal handle, because when I mindlessly clutched my hand around it my skin was instantly burned.

"Shit!" I ripped my singed hand away.

Immediately I felt patches of scorned flesh on my fingers and palm harden. But that didn't stop me from reaching out again and yanking the door open.

I bolted inside, through the dense smoke and flailing flames, and through coughing continued to call out for Peter.

A series of throaty coughs responded to my cries.

"Peter!" I crouched under the stream of smoke and tried to blindly estimate my way to the kitchen.

I made it across the span of the den, gripped the door frame, and peered into the kitchen which was ablaze with vibrant flames.

Slowly, my brother's silhouette limped into view against the fire backdrop.

"What did you do!" a heave followed my scream.

"I'm sor-" Peter coughed, "I'm sorry! Oh no, I'm so sorry! I'm sorry! I just wanted-" out came another cough, "warm pizza so I turned on the oven and- oh no, oh no, I'm sorry! I'm so sorry!" Peter balled his hands into fists and started punching himself in the temples.

"Stop!" I shouted and in my adrenaline rush ripped his fists away from his head regardless of the throbbing it induced on my burnt hand. Through the pain I dragged my older brother through den and outside.

"Quick, run to the Carmichael's next door! I'll meet you there!"

"I'm sorry Jef-"

"Go!" I pushed him in the direction away from the fiery house.

Having watched Peter hurriedly wobble across the lawn, into safe territory, I whipped the cell phone out of my pocket, turned it on (lately I didn't even bother leaving it on), and dialed 9-1-1 with my dominant right hand in spite of the excruciating pain.

Out of breath, I dropped to the snow dusted lawn, and waited for the firetrucks to round the bend. All the while I watched, in breathless awe, as my house burned. The embers floated away carelessly, like little stars leaving behind destruction.

As I came down from the shock of adrenaline I struggled to catch my breath while sprinkling the dirty snow from the ground onto my burnt hand. I could already feel my skin blistering. Damn, it hurt!

Who would have thought that touching a door handle could be so dangerous?

Chapter 64

It was appropriate that spring, the season of rebirth, was right around the corner.

After the fire incident I officially gave up drinking. At least for now, for the sole purpose of getting drunk. It wasn't worth it to begin with, but after I let the craving cause myself to ditch my special needs brother only to come home with him nearly dead and an entire room and a half of the house burnt to a crisp it definitely wasn't worth it. I had no excuse for being so careless with Peter, not even the loss of my relationship with Lacey; because losing the relationship with my girlfriend didn't and couldn't justify losing the one with my brother, no matter how painful.

Not only was I done with alcohol, but I was also done being altogether stupid. It was time to be myself again. Time to be the brother, son, and student I was supposed to be.

I came clean right away and told my mom I had left Peter home alone so that I could pick up booze. I was willing to do anything and everything to make sure Peter didn't feel guilty about the fire. I assured him it was my fault for neglecting his request for a heated dinner then leaving him by himself with the temptation of a stove.

Needless to say Mom was infuriated. She screamed. She screamed a lot. She screamed about how irresponsible I was. She screamed about how if I wasn't a full grown adult she'd ground me. She screamed that she ought to kick me out of the house (though she would never follow through with that) and how if I was going to be a "selfish idiot" I needed to find a place of my own. She screamed about how, regardless of the fact that I was a full grown adult, I was now forbidden from ever bringing alcohol in the house again. Personally I wouldn't pin the blame on the alcohol for what happened, I'd pin it on myself, but I didn't argue. Like I said, I was done drinking for a while.

    I have to say though, out of all the things to come out of me nearly destroying my family and home, the most surprising was how my dad stepped up to the plate and actually lent his hand in repairing the house.

    Dad brought some of his buddies over to knock the den's charred remains down. For the next few months he vowed to build the foundation, frame it, roof it, and then help with the interior of a new den. I didn't even care if he failed to follow through. Just the fact that he was showing up to help was beyond my wildest dreams.

    My dad worked every afternoon on the construction and stayed through the evening, well past it got dark, for five days straight.

    Dad was on his way to leaving when a voice from my conscience rang out.

    Value your hugs, Jef. They're important.

    "Wait, Dad," I called over the crickets chirping in the night air.

    He turned around before hopping in his pickup.

    I stretched my arms out, "Drive safe," and gave him a hug.

    "Thank ya, Jef," my dad pat me on the back, "Don't go playin' with fire while I'm gone."

A week into the rebuild, and Dad and his friends were already working on the foundation for the new den. Dad was on a beam, hammering away. Mom was grilling and baking for the guys. Peter was mowing the lawn. And I was using my bare hands to repot and replant new flowers, since the old troughs and pots of tulips (and a slew of other flowers I didn't know the name of) got roasted. Not the manliest job, but it was all I could really do using my burnt hand without irritating it. In fact scooping the cool soil out of bags and stuffing it in pots felt soothing on my right hand's burns.

"Honestly Jef, I don't understand why you can't just use the garden gloves I gave you," Mom complained, "You're getting your hands all dirty."

"I know," I answered unapologetically while patting down the dirt. Even if I hadn't burnt my fingers and palm I would have deliberately opted out of wearing gardening gloves. Gloves of any sort reminded me of Lacey and her inability to touch anything.

Since my dad's friends were back and forth to help with the construction I was used to cars parking in and out of our driveway and on the side of the street. I didn't question any of the vehicles coming to and fro. For that very reason I nearly missed the one vehicle that I should have made note of.

A silver Volvo pulled up to the curb in front of my house.

I knew that silver Volvo.

The door to the driver's seat opened and...

Oh my God.

It was Lacey.

As soon as I saw her I threw the fistful of dirt at the ground and sprinted her way. Lacey advanced to speed walking. As I arched down, she got on her tip toes, and we collided into a hug in the middle of the lawn.

Her arms were wrapped so tight around my neck, tighter than I think I'd ever felt before. "I heard about the fire," she said. "I came because, because, well, I've been, I," I could see her stumbling on a medley of thoughts. Lacey paused, slowly shut her eyes, took a deep breath, then started from the beginning. "My mom told me how you came by the other day. Before I caught you off guard at your Frisbee tournament, and I just wanted to say I'm sorry. I had no idea you talked to her. And I gave you a hard time and-"

"Lacey it's okay," I breathed out without hesitation.

"No," she shook her head, "It's not. I, I've been going about this wrong. And I've realized that because, well, you see, at the treatment center I learned that before really addressing my OCD I have to go down deep and address a lot of the feelings and thoughts I have about life and relationships in general. So I did. And I realized that part of the reason I couldn't let go of my anger at you for making that research binder was because my OCD latched onto that incident and replayed it. What you did was forgivable. My obsessive compulsive disorder just did what it did best: it tried to protect me from something it mislabeled as dangerous. It lied to me. Again. And in trying to separate the truth from the lies I've done a lot of thinking. A lot of thinking. And I'm thinking that the universe has been deeply kind to have blessed me with meeting you."

Good God that was not what I was expecting.

"My life is completely different than it was before I met you. I didn't have a life before. I buried myself alive. But you dug. My God, you dug down deep. You dug deeper than anybody had dug before, and you found me. Normal people don't do that Jef. Normal, *rational* people don't do that. When it came to guys I've trained myself to believe that they wouldn't be interested in me on the inside, but would only be interested in me on the outside because I was a girl. And then I met you and you were interested in me for my mind, and isn't that exactly what I wanted? So what if you started out only caring about my brain before you cared about me? Every story has to start somewhere. And honestly, the fact that you had an interest in my sickness was a blessing. It's what brought us together. And maybe... maybe that's the avail to this whole shit storm of a mental illness. Because it brought me my best friend and the guy I love more than anybody else."

I was speechless.

"I'm talking about you."

"I know," I managed to find my voice.

Lacey's incredibly emotive brown eyes delved into me. I could tell she wanted to say more, but was struggling. Lovingly I stared into her, in my own speechless stupor, trying to send her the mental strength to proceed.

The supportive vibes must have been reciprocated from my brain to hers, because after a quick flinch of a muscle in her neck Lacey found the ability to talk. "I guess what I'm trying to say is that the reason why I came here is to tell you that I want to be able to go bowling with you. I want to be able to go to your Frisbee golf tournaments. I want to be able to take care of you when you have a cold, the way I know you would if I were sick. You know, physically sick."

"I would take care of you in mental sickness too," I barely sputtered out in a fragile whisper.

Lacey shyly laughed and looked to her feet. "I'm actually doing a tad better," she credited herself.

I couldn't have been happier to hear that. Not just the content of what she said, but the fact that she said it. Because, finally, she was boasting about her improvements rather than sulking about her flaws.

"I know you're doing better," I grinned, "You came to a place that was on fire and weren't afraid you'd somehow wind up losing your own house or possessions?"

"I was more afraid of losing you," she responded with a delicate softness.

That comment made me feel lighter than air.

Lacey, in the midst of nervously picking a hangnail, glanced up from her hand and spoke up louder. "Listen, I've also been thinking a lot about the night I found your research on me and then got in the car accident... and I realized I overreacted. I think I used your research packet as a scapegoat, a reason to get mad at you and then run off. Because I was scared."

"Of what? Of me?" I asked sheepishly.

"I think I was scared because, well, being in love was so new to me. I was trying to adjust to the feeling of falling in love, not *obsessing*, but *falling in love*. And to fall in love with a real person, not some sort of character I made up in my head. That set off all sorts of alarms. It was so exciting but also so terrifying. It was a change. And we both know I don't do well with change."

I breathed out a chuckle and bowed my head forward, "I know."

Lacey continued with her heartfelt confession. "And I think you have the right to know that the reason I was scared, really scared, was because, oh I don't know. It was emotionally overwhelming. You conquered your fear of crowds. I was so high but at the same time I was so anxious because I swear I could feel the germs all over me just by looking at another person's bed. And, I don't know, even though the plan was innocent lounging and watching Netflix I just- I don't know, I panicked. Something about it just being me and you, the most perfect person I could be with-"

A spurt of laughter ejected from my throat, "Er, sorry," I could hear myself interrupting, "I'm not used to being called perfect."

Lacey giggled her goofy giggle and covered her face, embarrassed. I was surprised to see her touching her face with her bare hand, uncovered by a sleeve. And it wasn't the back of her hand. It was the front.

"Jef, I hate that I've caused you pain. If I could take all your pain and put it in myself I would, without question. I love you. I love you in a way that I had no idea I was capable of feeling. And I'd rather suffer by myself than make you suffer by being with you."

I was speechless. "Lace, I..." I didn't know how to speak, "You don't have to choose between suffering by yourself or suffering with me. By suffering by yourself you're not alleviating any of my pain. It hurts me to know you're hurting too."

"I'm still mentally ill though, Jef. That hasn't changed."

"I don't care that you're mentally ill as long as you're at least trying to manage it. Whether you're sick or not doesn't change how I feel about you. I want to be with you."

Lacey painstakingly sighed and resorted to scratch at her nail beds. "But-"

"No," I stopped her before she could try and push me away again. "You don't need to say anything. You've said enough. Now it's my turn," I took a deep breath and, without a second thought, purged my heart out.

"I like to think I know everything, but when it came to you I had no clue what I was dealing with. Since the moment I read that poem to the moment we first kissed, all the way to the moment we broke up, you always kept me on my toes. Because you weren't what I expected, at all. When I started that OCD binder I didn't know I was going to fall in love with you. I just thought that the more I made sense of you, the less interested I'd become. But it turned out the more I understood you... the more and more I wanted anything and everything to do with you. And before I knew it I was falling hard for you. And I- I- I *love* you Lacey. And I'll love you when you do that thing where you blow the hair out of your eyes instead of moving it with your hands. I'll love you when you wear socks that don't match, or socks that do match! I don't care! I just want you well so that you can be happy. So that you can see past all the irrational bullshit, trivial fears, blaring sirens, and vibrant danger signs. And not just see, but truly believe, that you have a very important life worth living." Before Lacey could respond I tacked on an extra apology, "And I'm really sorry if that sounded like a monologue from a chick flick."

With teary eyes Lacey let out a gasp of laughter, and seeing her laugh made me so happy that I wound up laughing too.

There was a music to both of our laughter. Lacey's modest giggle harmonized perfectly with my breathy chuckle. I hadn't realized until now how intensely I missed the cheery symphony of us laughing together.

As the beautiful sounds from her mouth diffused her smile remained in front of me. And seeing that sight of Lacey made me long for her, in her entirety, to remain in front of me. I couldn't stop myself from asking the question that I was dying to ask.

"Do you want to be with me?" I spoke softly, surprised by how shy I suddenly became.

She nodded rapidly while a tear rolled down her cheek, "Yes!"

At the exact same time we both lunged at each other and squeezed each other in a hug so tight I think my heartbeat regulated itself to match hers.

After, I don't know, three straight minutes of hugging, we pulled out of the embrace. "Aren't those your favorite? Being the most gothic of flowers and all."

"Oh my God, yes!" Lacey eagerly wrapped her arm around my elbow and I led her to the space where I had been potting plants.

Lacey knelt onto the grass and I squatted down, showing her each flower. As I pointed out each flower Lacey mindlessly picked at her hangnails. It wasn't until her fingers started bleeding that I spoke up.

"Lace, you should be careful," I nodded to her fidgeting fingers.

"Hm?" she glanced up at me, smiling. I nodded down at her hands again, motivating her pupils to trail down to the blood dripping from her fingertips. Immediately she realized what she had done. "Oh, shoot!"

"Lemme get you a Band Aid," I started to stand up, but as I stared at Lacey's bloody hands I got this really eerie sense that I had lived this moment before. That eerie sense washed over me and a mesmerizing force drew me back down to my crouch on the ground.

There was a spell that had my eyes gripped to Lacey's bloody hands. Right in the middle of that spell, though, something else indescribable compelled me to transfer my focus onto my own dirt covered hands.

Why did I feel a wave of déjà vu washing over me?

My stare juggled between our differing hands while I rummaged through every nook and cranny of my conscience for an explanation to that déjà vu. Back and forth my stare went until finally I realized why this scene was so familiar.

Without a single thought I acted on instinct, picking the ripe stem of a rose from the pot before me, and I held it in front of Lacey.

Suddenly she gasped, realizing what I had just realized. In a matter of seconds tears filled her eyes. She raised her blood stained hand out to receive the flower. It was just like the picture Lacey had painted.

"Foreshadowing," I uttered.

Lacey let out a laugh as a simultaneous tear rolled from her left eye.

Ever so gently I placed the rose in her grasp, where it belonged.

The stars in her reality crossed with mine. She created this moment inside her mind, from scratch. I created this moment outside in reality, from her mind. Together, we fused two dimensions. And it was remarkable. In that moment, I was the connection that Lacey lost in Tara. I was the connection between Lacey's mental world and this world.

Chapter 65

Suddenly a stream of vehicles pulled up on the side of the road. I recognized Gabe's SUV. And Natalie's quirky pink buggy. And Carson's maroon sports car.

Gabe, Beth, Carson, Natalie, Zeke, Kenny. They all exited different automobiles with supplies in their hands.

"What's this?" I laughed.

"Free labor!" Zeke answered with the boards over his shoulder.

Lacey sniffled away her last tear. "I forgot to tell you... I didn't just come to try and win you back. I also called them to help with the home repair."

"You're kidding," I was smiling ear to ear.

"Hey!" Gabe greeted me with a punch in the arm, "If you need to just take a break from being a crazy good brother you call me! I'm happy to chill with Peter while you go out. You hear me?"

"Alright man," I reciprocated his fist bump.

Natalie walked by while holding a cardboard box of vases and other decorations she must have gotten half off at her work. "Your friends are here for you, Jef," she smiled at Lacey, "Especially her."

I smiled at Lacey and placed my hand on her shoulder, "Of course. She's my best friend."

My mom and Lacey nagged me to cover my burnt hand with gauze, so I did. That was very telling of Lacey, actually. She used to tell me she was afraid of ever needing a cast, especially on her hands, because she *needed* to be able to wash her hands. She swore if a doctor ever told her she needed a cast that she'd flat out refuse or rip it off no matter the pain, and I knew beyond a doubt that she really would.

Lacey and I agreed that we had to make a game plan if we wanted our relationship to work this time around.

We brainstormed in my room.

"We can't lie to each other," Lacey announced, standing firmly in the middle of my room while I spun myself in my desk chair.

"Agreed," I said in my dizziness.

"I mean *no* lying whatsoever. You, Jef, under no circumstances are to try and spare my feelings. You need to be honest. If I'm frustrating you with my OCD you need to say something. And I need to be honest in my own way, I can't be afraid. I can't be afraid of telling you if I'm anxious or uncomfortable. Because if I don't speak up about being nervous or uncomfortable I'm gonna bottle it in then blow up at you like I did with the research binder."

"We sure as hell don't want that," I chimed in.

Lacey went on brainstorming. I purposely kept kicking my desk, catalyzing more rotations of the swivel chair, because I needed to blur out the sight of Lacey. I knew if I saw her clearly, standing there thinking so carefully and brainstorming, I'd be too turned on.

"We need to treat each other like equals. I'm not just your 'sick' girlfriend, and you're not my 'genius' boyfriend."

I stopped the chair from spinning with a stomp of my foot onto the carpet, then chimed in, "Like two sides of a true equation!"

"Really? Pick the one subject I hate the most to make an analogy?" she joked.

"When you have variables and integers and whatever else on both sides of an equal sign, they need to amount to the same value. Me and you," swiftly I corrected my grammar before Lacey could, "*You and I* need to do that. We need to make sure we both value each other the same amount. It can't just be me always accommodating you, or you always accommodating me. That's just how it is. When one side of the equation is equivalent to the other, then it's true. There's a balance. In scientific words, an equilibrium. And it's fair."

"You're right, I know you're right," she nodded hastily while hugging her arms to her chest. "That's totally viable."

"Great," I spit out and immediately resorted back to swiveling round and round in my desk chair before I could register the sight of Lacey Parker.

She was still in full throttle brainstorm mode. "We have to work together," she declared. "In every way."

"I couldn't agree more," I vowed as my corneas blended everything on the wall into a murky gradient crimsons, greens, browns, and navies.

"Okay," Lacey sighed, then grabbed the head of my chair so that I was no longer spinning, "I had a thought."

I don't know if it was the chair revolutions or nervousness, but suddenly I felt nauseated. "Yeah?"

"I was hoping you would come with me to outpatient therapy every now and then. You know, to see what I'm learning."

"Oh, God, yeah," I exhaled a relieved breath, insurmountably favorable of that idea. "I can do that. I'd prefer that, actually."

"Good," Lacey let out a grateful sigh, then shifted her focus from intangible thoughts to my palpable presence. She nodded to my lap, "Can I sit?"

"Please…"

Lacey slid onto me and we didn't waste any time to lock lips.

I think I got a little too excited by the touch of her skin. The scorched flesh under my gauzed hand made itself evident when I clasped her waist. In my elation I forgot I needed to be gentle with my right hand.

An "ow" accidentally slipped out of my mouth, interrupting a kiss.
Lacey pulled back and knowingly transferred her pupils to my bandaged hand.

"Ooooh," she wrinkled her nose and winced like she could feel my pain. "It still hurts really bad, doesn't it?"

"It's gotten better…" I exaggerated while relaxing my uninjured hand from her shoulder blade to her lower back.

"Does it hurt every time you touch something?"
My voice trailed up in pitch as I played down the pain.
"Not so much."
"Alright," Lacey sighed empathetically.

Chapter 66

Now that there was no room for lies in Lacey and my relationship I told her, though it was extremely difficult, that my Mom had purposefully placed the research binder in my bed to break us up.

Lacey didn't seem as upset as I was, though.

"Oh shit," Lacey huffed.

"What?"

"I just realized… since your mom read that binder she knows everything about me. Like, *everything*."

I cringed, "Yeah try not to think about it."

At the exact same time Lacey and I locked eyes, mutually realizing the fault in my suggestion seeing that Lacey had a disorder that prevented her from warding thoughts away, and we both burst out laughing.

Lacey scooted off of me, and I was okay with it. With Mom at the forefront of my mind the romantic mood was ruined.

Lacey sat upright. "You should tell your mom."

A snide response emerged from my newfound scowl. "Tell my mom what?"

"That I'm being treated for my OCD. It might give her some relief."

"This isn't about my mom," I groaned, hating that there was no longer a distinct separation between my home life and my outside-of-home life. "Stop worrying about my mom. Besides, you should be angry with her."

"Why should I?"

"Because! She planted the research binder in my bed so that you'd find it and break up with me! How are you not furious with her?"

"Jef, your mom was just doing what any caring parent would do. She was trying to protect you. I guarantee I would have done the same thing if my child was in your position."

I sighed. It would almost be easier if Lacey was on my side with this.

"You're really not mad?" I asked one last time before embarking on the tumultuous journey of forgiveness.

"Just embarrassed," Lacey insisted. "But I'm over it. Well, as over it as a person who has difficulty forgetting things can be."

"So not that over it," I assumed with a semi-humored laugh.

"No," Lacey agreed and laughed with me, then stiffened up, "But really, Jef. I mean it. Tell her."

Chapter 67

"I have to apologize in advance," Lacey said as we walked down the hallway of the treatment center where her OCD outpatient therapy was hosted. "I'm not going to be able to kiss you tonight. The germs. They feel like a thick humidity in this place. I just can't do it."

"No I get it," I nodded compliantly while pulling, with my left hand, on the door handle of the room we'd be congregating in for group therapy.

Inside that inconveniently windowless room was a slew of demographics. Older woman who could have been my mom's age. Wrinkly old guy on the verge of balding. Young white man. Young black man. A little girl with her mom. Identical twin boys. A long bearded, leather jacket wearing, tattooed biker who was paragon of what you'd expect to see at a truck stop. A guy who I swear was James Franco's doppelganger (that one freaked me out a bit). And a teenage girl of some oriental descent.

I lowered my voice to a whisper, feeling like all these people were listening, and finished responding to Lacey's apology. "I can't say I like it, but I get it."

During the course of the group therapy each OCD victim went around in a clockwise circle about why they were here. I ignored everybody, except for Lacey. I didn't care about these other people.

"I had to get help. I had no choice. I wasn't doing things because I wanted to, I was doing things because the panic stricken voices in my head were telling me to at a deafeningly loud level. Every little action that I performed was really just an obsession-driven compulsion. Even the most seemingly random actions that nobody would think twice about like stepping into a room at a certain time of day or how many times I touched something with my index finger before leaving the object alone, was ruled by OCD. What I ate, when I ate it, what TV channel I put on, when I allowed myself to shut the TV off, what songs I listened to, and the most tragic of all, what I allowed myself to write, or more importantly, not write. I wasn't Lacey. I was basically some mega-computer with a limited set of rules responsible for what I could and couldn't do. I had literally gotten to a point where I didn't recognize myself anymore."

Having been touched by Lacey's honest contribution to the group therapy, I put aside my self-righteous pride and decided to pay attention to the remainder of patients' reasoning for seeking outpatient help with an open mind.

That didn't last long though.

When the James Franco's look-alike (who went by the name, Josh) opened his mouth I immediately reverted back to being overly-judgmental.

"If anything I'd say we're the blessed folks and it's your," Josh's dark eyes landed directly on mine, "*type* that is crazy."

"My *type*?" I pointed towards the sternum that caged my thudding heart. "What's that supposed to-"

"Normal," Lacey leaned my way and clarified out of the corner of her mouth in no more than a whisper.

Nervously, I jumped into defensive mode with a flurry of awkward hand gestures. "Oh no, trust me, I'm- I am far from normal. I-I memorize physics formulas for fun, I do my homework the night it's assigned, I love school, I-I-I hate parties and being drunk just doesn't appeal to me…"

Josh's intense glare caused me to shut up before I embarrassed myself any more than I already had.

Feeling ostracized as the 'normal' guy who didn't belong, I lodged my hands in my jeans pockets (God forbid more awkward hand gestures from me) and kept my input to a bare minimum for the remainder of the group session. And when I say bare minimum, I mean I didn't so much as make a sound when I breathed. And honestly, I regret that. It was somewhat emasculating to let the intimidation of this stranger, Josh, get to me so much to the point where I wasn't acting like myself. Lacey and I both knew I had a lot of comments, some snarky, some enlightening, brewing behind my lips. I just, I wasn't myself. And the one person who could tell that I was acting a little off was the one person who mattered, Lacey. She invited me to her OCD outpatient group because somewhere in her she felt like she needed me here, and what did I do? Nothing. I contributed nothing. We had just gotten back together, having vowed to be there for each other through the struggle and strife of her disorder, and I blew it by acting like a silent moron.

 I should've spoke up. I really should've.

 When the session was over I wasn't as relieved as I felt like I should have been. I couldn't get over my awkwardness during the group therapy and the way that smug-nosed Josh glared at me.

 While making our way through the near-empty parking lot I kept my hands in my pants pockets and watched my sneakers slosh through the melting snow.

 "Thanks for coming, Jef."

 "No problem," I mumbled ambivalently.

 Unexpectedly Lacey stopped in her tracks and halted me by holding my inner elbow into stillness. "You know, that was pretty adorable in there… the way you tried to pass off being an intelligent and self-disciplined student as freakish qualities."

 Ugh.

 I wasn't quite understanding the connection Lacey was making between my embarrassing tirade and the "adorable" adjective. "What- how- why would you think that?"

 "'I love school, I hate parties'- you tried to justify the traits that make you perfect as abnormalities."

 As if I wasn't having a hard enough time registering Lacey's perception of me, now she was tacking on the word "perfect"? That was beyond weird.

 "I, I don't, I've never actually seen those things as, as, as making me anywhere near 'perfect'," I stammered while my hands begged to break free from their denim jail cells.

 Lacey's hair flickered to a reddish brown tint under the moonlight as she cocked her head sideways. "Seriously?"

"Yeah," I laughed. "Besides, that guy called me 'normal', not 'perfect'."

Lacey raised her eyebrows approvingly, "True," she paused to think carefully. "I guess I have a tendency to believe normal people have it all."

"They don't," I quickly shut down.

Lacey shrugged.

All I could think of was how fucked up that Josh guy had it.

"Lacey," I spoke up, careful to censor the words looming on my tongue, "This whole 'crazy/normal' thing, it's a load of nonsense."

"You think?"

"Yeah," I laughed half-heartedly, "I guess if you're gonna live the rest of your life sporting the 'crazy' title you're bound to feel like the majority of the population has an advantage over you in every conceivable way."

My voice box must have been aching to get some exercise after it's hiatus in that group therapy session, because I couldn't seem to stop myself from ranting onward (and make no mistake, the hand gestures came out).

"That little support group back there... I didn't know it until tonight but I'm really not a fan of the whole 'group therapy' thing. Surrounding yourself with other crazy people just brings you down, it puts you in a rut. It's kind of like that crowd mentality you learn about in social psychology classes where a select few people perform an action and the rest of the crowd absentmindedly follows. That's what it's like! When one person talks about how awful their OCD is, what do you get? Another person talking about how awful *their* OCD is! And then one bad mood turns into two bad moods! That's what it's like, Lacey! You take a mentally ill person and you put them in a room with a bunch of other mentally ill people and everybody gets this warped, I don't know, 'club complex' where you each act like you're the 'chosen one' who was invited into some exclusive club you like to call 'crazy people'. And that's warped on a whole new level! All I saw today was a group of crazy people trying to rationalize all of their misguided behaviors by talking to other people prone to more misguided behaviors, which is downright comical because none of you have brains that are rational in the first place, and it all becomes sick minds egging on sick minds. And all that does is put you in a more delusional mindset! It goes back to the most basic of math: if you add a negative to another negative, you get more negative! A negative mind is bad enough, a group-full of negative minds is worse! I'm sorry, I don't make the rules, that's just how mathematics works. And I don't blame you for finding solace in it, Lacey, I really don't, but it's a big heaping load of delusions justified by more delusions. And it's so easy to fall into. Hell, even I fell into it today! That has got to be why I tried to relate myself to the other patients. Because the vulnerable part of my psyche wanted so badly to feel included. I'm telling you, it's that screwy 'club complex'! Listen, I'm not entirely sure what the thesis is that I'm trying to get at here, but if I had to guess it'd be that mental ailments cannot and should not always be treated like physical ailments. Support groups should be reserved for people with cancer or an amputated leg. Those, I can understand. Those inspire people. But support groups for people with obsessive compulsive disorder or schizophrenia or anorexia or whatever the heck other kind of mental illness, do not, at least from the perspective I got here tonight, support anybody. They just support the disorder. They strengthen the unreasonable thoughts you already have. They catalyze more demented ideas of how to miscalculate and misconstrue the world around you, and above all else they trick vulnerable people like Josh into thinking they're on the inside of some elite club when really you're all a bunch of seriously flawed individuals who were left outside of the real, happier, and far more coveted conglomeration of people and you all deserve so much better than you were given."

    When I had finally met the end of my unfiltered rant I took a deep breath. In that instant of more oxygen hitting my brain I realized what a self-righteous prick I must have just sounded like.

    "I'm sorry Lace. I can't pretend to like that group therapy scene. It goes against every bit of information my brain has ever filed away. I'm sorry."

Bracing myself for the storm of anger I must have brought on myself, I squeezed my eyes shut.

    Suddenly the giddy laugh I knew so well entered my eardrums.

    I opened one eye and let my pitch drop. "Huh?"

Lacey, who I swear had a twinkling star in each eye, shook her head and continued to smile. "I always knew, since the first moment I heard you talk, that you were a genius."

"That can't be true because I'm thoroughly confused right now."

Lacey went on in her smitten mood, "You got all of that from a man calling you normal?"

Shocked at how much this didn't feel like a trap, I half-confidently peeped out, "Yes."

Lacey took her hands out of the pockets of her pink jacket, reached up, and clasped my face in her hands. With love-struck eyes she ogled up at me.

"I love your brain," she remarked and, without a smidge of hesitation, kissed me on the lips.

Chapter 68

After my little outburst, scratch that, *giant* outburst about Lacey's group therapy her and her mom looked into finding a therapist who did one-on-one therapy.

Lacey went to the first appointment without me, which I'm glad because I didn't want to smother her. This was her disorder, not mine. I wasn't her boyfriend to control her. I was her boyfriend to support her.

I did go to Lacey's second appointment though.

Lacey and I went to the front desk, where Lacey greeted the receptionist that she had come to know. "Hey Carol."

"Miss Parker," the older woman with her purple lipstick smiled up at Lacey and I. "Here to see Colleen again?"

"I sure am. I brought my…" Lacey turned to me as if she forgot who I was, but continued to smile almost guiltily, "…boyfriend." A short trail of giggling followed the "boyfriend" title, as if she were overcome by the giddiness of a new relationship. I guess this really was like a new beginning for the both of us.

I smiled down at Lacey, wanting to laugh at her shy awkwardness, but I held back.

The receptionist received Lacey's money ($35 she'd never get back), and stuffed it in the cash register while licking her fingers to separate each germ ridden dollar. Even that grossed me out.

"Colleen will be right out when she's done with Miss Taylor's session. Take a seat."

Lacey hesitantly lowered her butt onto the very edge of the waiting room couch. I could tell she was horribly uncomfortable. "You gonna be alright?"

Lacey squirmed a little bit and tried to fight through the fear with a faux tone of confidence. "I'm fine."

About a minute went by with Lacey shuffling through her purse to find something. "Darnit," she whispered.

"What?"

"I ran out of hand sanitizer and I just touched money," she fretted and stretched her neck to catch a glimpse of the secretary's desk, "I don't think she has any hand sanitizer either."

"Miss Parker?" the wrinkly old receptionist interrupted Lacey's panic and walked around to the front of her desk.

"Yeah?" Lacey reacted with round eyes, as if she got caught doing something wrong.

The woman smoothed out her pencil skirt and went on, "I need to take a trip to the ladies room, do you mind watching Miss Taylor's daughter?" she gestured to a little girl wearing a neon pink backpack who was playing with what must have been donated toys in the corner of the waiting room.

"Oh, yeah, that's fine," Lacey answered.

When the click of the older woman's heels vanished out of the room Lacey whispered and nodded towards the young girl, "Do you think she has hand sanitizer in that backpack?"

"If she's playing with old used toys she should," I grimaced.

"I'm gonna ask."

"Are you-"

"Excuse me," Lacey stood up and walked towards the child, so I followed. At once the child flickered her baby blues upwards at Lacey, then me, then back at Lacey.

I just smiled a fake smile. I was already bad with little kids. I didn't know how to talk to them. Actually I knew how to talk to them, I just didn't like doing it. I hated dumbing myself down for their miniscule brains.

Lacey proceeded to ask, "Would you happen to have any hand sanitizer in your bag?"

Right away the girl's eyebrows furrowed in and she sassily snipped, "No. I'm not a weirdo," then she went back to playing with the toys on the floor.

"Hey!" I overreacted to the kid's snarky comment. Good thing the receptionist wasn't here.

Lacey disparagingly clung her hands to my shoulder, "Jef, it's okay-"

"Watch it kid!" I pointed my finger at the young girl. Then I pointed to Lacey while wrapping my other hand around her waist, "Don't call her a 'weirdo'. There's nothing wrong with her, okay?"

"Then why is she in therapy?" The little brat had a smirk on her face that made me want to scream at her again.

"Because she's *different*," I spit out.

"Is that why my mom's in therapy too?"

I was about to tell her no, that her mom was in therapy because clearly she was horrible at raising a well-mannered child, but the sound of an intuitive Lacey saying, "Jef…" made me rethink my response.

"You know what," I waved my hand to the toys scattered amongst the waiting room rug, "Just go back to playing with your figurines…"

"They're called dolls," the girl corrected with a sassy flair.

"Fine," my teeth clamped together as I tried to hold back from snapping again, "Go back to playing with your dolls."

With an angry pout the little girl returned to the toys.

Chapter 69

"Is it okay for him to be here?" The OCD specialist, Colleen, glanced up at me from her paisley rimmed reading glasses.

"Yes," Lacey vouched for me. I awkwardly flashed my open palm in an 'I'm-right-here' gesture to the OCD specialist sitting in her swivel chair on the other side of the vernacular designed carpet.

Colleen went onward, extracting a folder from the filing cabinet beside her desk and pulling a packet of marked up papers out. On top of the first sheet read, "OCD Evaluation Test".

"I have to be honest with you," Colleen shook her head, "In my 25 years of OCD coaching, this is the highest score I've ever seen."

"Oh," Lacey shyly shrunk deeper in the couch cushion, which was surprising since I knew how much she hated sitting on public couches (I guess cushions felt more contaminated to her).

Upon such a bold claim, Colleen didn't waste any precious time and began to read through the evaluation.

"Miss Parker, your target behaviors are a fear of being responsible for something terrible happening, contamination fears, a fear of losing or forgetting important information, fear of violent or horrific images, concern with sacrilege and blasphemy, concern with symmetry and exactness, ideas associated with numbers, concern with getting a physical illness or disease, washing hands excessively, excessive showering, cleaning household items excessively, preventing or removing contact with perceived contaminants…" the therapist flipped the page and read on "… mental rituals to prevent harm, putting things in order until it 'feels right', fear of saying certain words, checking behaviors, rereading or rewriting, repeating routine activities, counting compulsions, hoarding or collecting, seeking reassurance, and resistance to sit in certain chairs."

    I, for one, didn't know what to say. I knew all of this. I had seen it firsthand. But hearing the surplus of irrational behaviors listed like that, by a professional and not in my mediocre notes, only reassured how necessary it was for me to draw a line with Lacey and force her to go seek out some treatment. It made me feel a lot better about the tough love I had to give her.

    "So… what do we do?" I asked Colleen.

    "We tackle each behavior one at a time through a variety of therapies. I specialize in Cognitive Behavioral Therapy and Exposure Response Prevention therapy… until Miss Parker is able to suffocate the OCD."

    "What about medication?" I made sure to ask.

    Colleen's blue eyes flickered at Lacey for a split second. "Miss Parker and I talked about this in her previous session, and she's expressed some concerns with experimenting through medicines, so we're going to give these therapy techniques a try before jumping onto the pill bandwagon."

    I tried not to look too disappointed. Lacey was already making such a stride by seeing an OCD therapist, I didn't have the right to complain. Having no choice but to accept Lacey's wishes, I threw that gauze wrapped hand out compliantly, "Alright."

    "Now, since this is only our second time meeting, Miss Parker, and I'm still getting to know you, and," she rotated to me, "your boyfriend, I'd like to do some talk therapy. Are you okay with that?"

    "Yes," Lacey nodded.

    "Wonderful," the OCD specialist returned her stare to me. "Now, Jef Sterling is it?"

    "Yeah."

    "Can you tell Lacey what you think about all of this? About her condition with obsessive compulsive disorder?"

"It just sucks, you know? Because it's not like some separate entity she can just avoid like alcohol. It's interwoven in her mind and it has her so mixed up."

"Tell her," Colleen advised.

I turned to Lacey and repeated myself with a bluntness that was almost humorous. "I hate your OCD. I hate that it's some intangible disease I can't just rip out of you."

"I know," Lacey bowed her head sheepishly.

Colleen intervened, "Mr. Sterling, do you think that might have something to do with why you've been getting in physical altercations?"

"Maybe. Wait, what?" I faltered, not sure if I was more taken aback by her lack of ignorance or the unexpectedness of her question.

Lacey intervened, "I told her about the fight you had with Gabe."

I could feel the anger making the jowl portion of my face tense. I refrained from saying any more than the bare minimum in answering her question. "Yeah, I suppose."

For the latter of the session Lacey and I shared some of the key problematic OCD moments of the past few months to Colleen. I was less open than Lacey. It made me uncomfortable, to say the least, to expose so much of my life to this stranger. Lacey significantly less uncomfortable, probably because this was the chance she had coveted for, the chance for her to spill out all her feelings and thoughts and embrace her narcissism.

At the end of the session Colleen handed both Lacey and I a few packets.

I quickly scanned through all the papers in the passenger seat of Lacey's car. One packet was on "Cognitive Behavioral Therapy", one on "Systematic Desensitization Therapy", one on "Exposure Response Prevention Therapy", one on "Types of Faulty Thinking", one on "Mindfulness", and one on "Rational Emotive Behavior". I made a point of asking about Colleen's credentials, which she answered by handing me her business card and an introductory sheet of paper explaining her degree and what she does.

The packet that stood out most to me was the "Types of Faulty Thinking in People with OCD" that had the phrase "Fear of Positive Experiences" printed on top.

I read on.

"Some people with OCD express concerns that they do not deserve or will not be able to sustain positive experiences."

I showed Lacey. "Jesus Christ! That is you! That is literally you!"

"Yeah," she brushed off and her eyes trailed away from me, almost like she was trying to avoid eye contact. In her diverted glancing she stumbled upon the packet sitting on the center console.

"Guess you're not the only person who can excel on a test." Lacey playfully remarked, briefly taking a hand off of the wheel and stabbing her index finger down on the OCD evaluation packet between us.

I plucked the packet from under her finger. I went on to flip through it, still overwhelmed by the lengthy list of target behaviors my obsessive compulsive girlfriend exhibited. "Are you proud of that?"

Lacey's pitch lowered, "No. I'm just trying to make light of a bad situation."

I nodded, reading through every high score recorded on each page in bright red ink, "That's probably for the best."

Chapter 70

Lacey carefully unraveled the strip of gauze.

The first thing that has touched this hand in weeks was her.

Gently, she rubbed my hand.

"How does that feel?"

"It feels really good," I said.

She started to get up.

"Wait," I frenetically clasped her arm with my healing hand. I sounded needy, but I didn't care.

Lacey lowered back down, into the cushion, and hugged my hand to her chest while gently stroking the scar tissue.

"Cognitive therapy is designed to test beliefs with evidence through critical and constructive thinking. That means opening our mind to new interpretations, recognizing biased thoughts, practicing mindfulness," Colleen explained.

"I feel like mindfulness is what got me in this position," Lacey replied. "I'm mindful of every little thing, like germs, and I can't stop being mindful of them."

"Mindfulness isn't just about being aware of your feelings or thoughts. It's about accepting your feelings or thoughts, especially the unwanted ones."

Colleen proceeded to explain the first approach to treating Lacey's OCD without medication.

She showed us a pretty simple diagram. The drawing was a circle of three labeled arrows. The arrow labeled "Behavior" led to "Thoughts" which led to "Emotions (Anger, Fear, Guilt)".

If you ask me, it was almost too simple. Seriously, did you really need a PhD to draw a three arrowed diagram?

"That's it?" I scoffed in my usual snarky way. "It must have taken a brilliant group of scholars to come up with that incredibly basic model."

Usually I wouldn't be so forwardly facetious to a stranger, but this stranger wasn't handling a dog's ripped tendon or fixing a bird's injured wing. This was a human mind we're talking about. *Lacey's* mind. And I suppose I felt protective.

Colleen opted not to respond to me, shifting her focus to Lacey.

She laid down the goal of today's therapy session, "We're going to challenge your faulty thinking with the following questions…" she uncapped a dry erase marker and wrote the questions on the whiteboard adjacent to Lacey and my seat on the couch.

Is a thought confused with a fact?
Are my interpretations realistic?
What would be a more rational way of looking at it?
What is the evidence for and against my interpretation?

Then Colleen directed a request towards me. "What's an example of one of Lacey's obsessive compulsive behaviors?"

I thought on my feet, "She walks in every room with her right foot first."

"Okay, good," she turned to Lacey, "Now what is the thought you have when you are compelled to walk in a room right-foot-first?"

"Um," Lacey's voice hit a higher pitch, "Something bad will happen to me while I'm in that room."

"Be more specific, Lacey."

Lacey shrugged, "But the consequences depend on what room and what time of the day-"

"Bedroom at night," I shot out the specificity before Colleen could, then I took a confident swig from my water bottle.

"Well, I have to make the first step into my bedroom with my right foot because if I don't then I might die in my sleep when I go to bed."

"Holy shit," I nearly choked on my water. I was not expecting it to be that dark.

"Okay," Colleen flashed me a glare then, "now what if I asked you to ask yourself this," the therapist pointed to the question scrawled messily on the whiteboard that read, "what is a more rational way of looking at it?"

"What would you say to that, Miss Parker?"

Lacey sighed, "I guess 'Just because I walk in my bedroom with my left foot first before I go to bed, doesn't mean I'll die that night'."

"Cheery," I muttered.

Lacey glanced at me, "What did you-"

"Nothing."

"Good. Now let's try another one. What about," Colleen leaned over her desk to reference the OCD evaluation packet that Lacey had filled out. "What if you felt the necessity to change the volume on your radio dial? What thought would run through your mind?"

"What number is it at?" Lacey asked.

I swear for a split second I could see exasperation behind Colleen's blue eyes. I don't think she was used to her OCD patients having such specific thoughts and compulsions that were tailored for particular scenarios right down to the last detail.

"Thirteen," she chose.

"Thirteen," Lacey repeated under her breath with a nod as her large eyes wandered to the ceiling of the room. Her stare wasn't in the room, though. Her stare was lost high up in the most ridiculous towers of her irrational mind. "Well thirteen isn't so bad but the digits are one and three, and one plus three equals four, and four reminds me of the term 'forever' which is such a terrifying concept cause. Who wants to live forever? So I guess I'd have to change the volume to... nine. Nine is a safe number."

In my observational role I glanced back and forth between Lacey and Collen and I have to say, it was hard not to laugh. Colleen's narrowing eyes were exponentially more tired than before, and Lacey's massive eyes were so awake and focused on her thought. Seeing her like that, thinking so carefully and strategically, even if irrationally, and then relaying those unconventional thoughts to a trained professional whom she seemed to be dumbfounding was insanely amusing. I couldn't stand it. I had to cover my smile.

Colleen's posture weakened. She took a deep breath, found the strength to proceed, and asked the follow up question, "And what if I asked you to look at the situation more rationally? How would you correct that thought?"

"Well, I guess I'd say that I shouldn't change the volume because if I lower the dial off of a number that represents 'living forever' that could translate as me taking time off my total life span."

Colleen speedily caught the fault in Lacey's thought renovation. "Not so fast. You're replacing an OCD thought with another OCD thought."

Dammit! I wanted to point that out. Colleen beat me to it.

"How about we try a different question," Colleen returned to the whiteboard, this time pointing her index finger at the chicken scratch she called handwriting that said "Is your thought confused with a fact?"

"Wait wait wait, hold up," I stepped in in my usual snarky way, "If I may? I think I've got this."

Colleen's eyebrows raised. That didn't hold me back though.

"A thought and a fact are interchangeable, aren't they? A thought is a piece of information in your mind and a fact is a piece of information outside of your mind. Yes, by definition a fact is indisputable and a thought can be disputed- but who made that a rule? Somebody's *mind*. It's just not a fair question to pose. But hey, I'm just reiterating my own *thoughts*, here."

Colleen was now shooting daggers at me with her pupils.

Now Lacey joined with the glaring.

Lacey stormed out of that building with more agitation in her stomps than I'd ever seen before.

"Lacey wait..." I hurried after her down the narrow pathway.

Hastily she twisted around, so abruptly that I almost bumped into her. "You know, Jef, I love you but your behavior is really confusing!"

Distraught, I resorted to readjusting the beanie on my head, rubbing it back and forth. "I know, I know."

"No! Apparently you don't!" Lacey reprimanded while throwing her hands in the air. Her flailing hands were almost as animated as mine got when, well, always. "Did you forget that you're the one who told me to seek out a professional who did one-on-one therapy, not group therapy? So I did. And you sat in there heckling her about her credentials and then brooding every time she tries to teach me something about my brain."

"Well I'm sorry but I don't care for watching somebody *else* nitpick your brain."

"Oh my God," I realized my selfish vice and, at once, dropped my butt onto the short brick wall that ran along the narrow pathway. Distraught, I held my head in my hands. "I'm jealous of your therapist for getting to nitpick your brain..."

With her arms crossed Lacey nodded as if this was something she realized a long time ago. "Yes, and do you know why that is?"

"Because I'm a selfish asshole?" I scowled, morphing my original sheepish voice into a disgusted voice.

"No," Lacey laughed for a short breath and perched herself next to me on the cold brick wall. "Because people like you see the human mind with an intimate lens. To you Jef, the brain, I guess my brain, is..."

"Attractive," I finished.

Lacey hunched forward and blushed, "I was gonna say 'endearing' to spare us both the awkwardness but... yes... 'attractive'."

"Oh, pfft," I popped a shoulder up, "Haven't you learned by now that you can't avoid awkwardness when I'm involved in the conversation?"

Lacey flashed me an eye roll. "If it's any consolation, Jef, I prefer you nitpicking my brain over Colleen. You actually do it because you're interested in me. She could care less. She gets paid to nitpick my brain for, what, three hours a week?"

"That's true, I do it way more than that and I do it for free!"

Both Lacey and I united in laughter.

Once my laugh diffused into the early April air along with Lacey's laugh I made sure to let her know that there was still a serious side to me that heard her. "No but actually, Lace... it's astonishing how rewarding nitpicking your brain is for me."

Lacey smiled. "It is for me too."

Chapter 71

The second week of Lacey's one-on-one therapy we practiced Exposure Response Prevention therapy.

Exposure Response Prevention therapy, or ERP, was an exercise in which the OCD patient was to expose herself to something that triggered them, like putting a jar in a cabinet without the label looking outward. Putting a jar down un-ritualistically was the exposure. Then the patient was to resist the ritual, otherwise known as compulsion, which their OCD was demanding them to perform. In this case, the patient might want to turn the jar to be facing outward, but they would resist the urge to do so. That's when the anxiety was expected to kick in. The uncomfortable patient would have to suffer through the anxiety, no matter how long it takes, until the anxiety finally decreases and the patient coasts.

"What's my role?" I asked Colleen after she explained the ERP process.

"Behavioral coaching. If you see Miss Parker begin to perform a ritual, you intervene as briefly as possible."

"So I like… distract her?"

"Not exactly. You want to make yourself as small of a stimulus as possible. We don't want you getting tangled in the mix as another variable."

"Like a confounding variable," I nodded, thinking of ERP like it were a controlled sociology experiment.

"Yes, Mr. Sterling. Like a confounding variable," Colleen proceeded to explain my duty as a behavioral coach, "I want you to push her whether or not she's uncomfortable. Now that's not to go and say that I want you pressuring her to do other things and justify it because she's uncomfortable and indifferent."

"Oh, of course not." I was offended she actually felt the necessity to specify. Did I come off as some inconsiderate testosterone-driven jerk? Then again I didn't make the best impression during the CBT practices.

"But remember, Mr. Sterling, if Miss Parker starts to show signs of developing a full-fledged panic attack you have permission to seize the exercise."

Nervously, I gulped down the queasiness that stirred my stomach from just imagining Lacey having a panic attack.

Since Lacey's parents were paying for office appointments, not at home visits, Colleen had Lacey do as much ERP exercises as possible during the office sessions. I'd stand by and watch, taking notes of Colleen's actions knowing I'd have to take on the role of behavioral coach once we were in Lacey's home setting.

Colleen had Lacey touch contaminated door knobs or handles (like the door outside the building, restroom doors, and the office door). She also had Lacey touch pieces of garbage from her trash bin. She'd have Lacey say certain taboo words like "cancer".

I liked the ERP therapy. Of course, Lacey despised it. It caused her far more anxiety than cognitive therapy did since it was, quite literally, hands-on.

For the most part exposure response prevention therapy was working. But when it came to Lacey's particular OCD germ fear, Lace seemed to be running into a brick wall.

She went through an exercise of touching a doorknob at the very beginning of therapy and resisting the urge to wash her hands with soap, water, hand sanitizer, or sterilizing wipes for the entire session. As expected, she felt anxious, but that anxiety was supposed to diminish the longer Lacey postponed sanitizing her hands. It didn't, though.

Lacey was never able to lose the ambiguous "germ feeling" until she finally washed her hands with soap and water in the restroom of the treatment center. That "coasting" feeling that was supposed to eventually result from resisting the ritual didn't come during the entire therapy session. A full hour, and Lacey claimed to have felt splotches of germs on her hands the whole time. And honestly, I don't think two hours, three hours, even ten hours would have made a difference. I think Lacey still would have felt the germ spots on her hands with a feeling just as ripe as when she first perceived them to be contaminated.

Colleen brushed off Lacey's incapability to coast through the contamination feeling on her unwashed hands.

"We'll try again next session. It just takes practice, and a lot of repetition, to suffocate anxiety," she said with a generic confidence that made her seem ignorant, like she had no idea what a stubborn disorder Lacey was up against.

It was my role, along with the rest of her family, to supervise Lacey during Exposure Response Prevention Therapy in the home.

In many ways I was ready for this role. I didn't want to enable Lacey. I was done enabling her. I needed to push her out of her comfort zone.

On the contrary, I also dreaded taking on that role, because that put a lot of pressure on me. Pressure on me not to cave in and let Lacey wash her hands or do anything she's compelled to do in order to alleviate her anxiety. I knew it was going to be hard, because I never wanted to put Lacey in a position where she was uncomfortable. As her boyfriend and best friend I had my mind trained to be that way. So when the therapist told me I had to make her do things despite the fact that I was enforcing discomfort upon her… that was tough. That was tough to do to her, and tough to witness.

I had Lacey walk in each room of her house left-foot-first. I had Lacey touch certain drawers with her whole hand and not just her index finger. I had Lacey put a jar of peanuts in the cabinet while resisting the urge to make sure the front of the label was facing outward. Lacey struggled momentarily with that one. She had to talk herself through the anxiety, by explaining how if she leaves the jar alone then the next person to get a peanut might "choke and die" on the food.

"Nothing bad is going to happen if you leave it the way it is," I insisted with the utmost confidence.

"But-"

"You have to trust me."

In addition to the jar adjustment compulsion I also had Lacey address target behaviors like handling the remote control or sitting in different chairs throughout her house. The chairs compulsion was the killer.

Lacey hated not being able to wash her hands, but she knew she could eventually, so she suffered *with* the "germ feeling" (not *through* it, *with* it. Like I said, the ambiguous feeling still wouldn't go away with time, it only went away when Lacey washed her hands, but at least she was going longer periods of time tolerating the "germ feeling" and postponing hand washing.) But sitting in different chairs nearly destroyed her because she was doing something called "cross-contaminating". I remember Lacey first mentioning her avoidance to cross-contaminate when I went to her house and she knelt on her seat rather than sat on her butt because she felt that her butt, which was sitting on seats at school prior, would spread those "school germs" onto her seat.

Lacey was in a wretched mood when I had her sit on couches and in chairs that she didn't usually sit in, but when I suggested she sit on "her chair" in the family room, you know, her usual chair, after sitting on the couch, she flipped out. That's where she drew the line. And that's when we had our first big Exposure Response Prevention blowup.

She folded her arms defiantly. "No way. I'm not sitting there."

"It's no different than sitting in any of the other seats," I stated.

"Yes it is."

"Lacey I promise it-"

"No!" her voice was raised, but it was still at a low enough volume that she maintained the illusion of composure.

With a heavy sigh I rubbed my throbbing head. It had been such a long day. I figured this method of treatment would be exhausting for Lacey, not for me. But it was. I was absolutely fatigued and in no mood to argue with her irrational brain. But I had to push her. But when I pushed her I knew it made her uncomfortable and upset with me. But I had to do it. I'd rather her hate me than be a slave to her mental disorder.

"Lacey, I swear on my life, you'll be better off if you just sit in the damn-"

"No! I'm done!" she screamed at an unapologetically high volume. "Do you hear me Jef? I'm fucking done!"

Lacey's mom hurried in the room with a horrified look on her face, "Lacey! Don't yell at Jef like that!"

Lacey didn't seem to hear her mom. She was too caught up in her delusion-based verbal rampage. "I am done! I'm *so* fuckin' done! You're the crazy one if you think for one fraction of a second that I'm gonna cross-contaminate that chair! That is the ONLY chair I don't feel the 'germ feeling' in! That's the only chair where I feel free! I'm not going to sit in it and tarnish it!"

"Lacey!" Mrs. Parker hollered.

Without an angst-filled farewell or a command to leave her house, Lacey stormed upstairs and into the bathroom.

Her mom was livid and mortified. "Lacey you get back down here and apologize!"

"It's fine," I tried to convince her mother on my way up the staircase, after Lacey.

I remembered what I read in Lacey's car when I was reviewing all the handouts Colleen gave me after first meeting her, from the ERP packet. It said that the goal was not to give the subject a panic attack.

I stepped into the bathroom, where Lacey was in the middle of splashing her face with water.

"I quit, Jef! I fucking quit!" Lacey declared as she poured what my guess was makeup remover onto a tissue and wiped away her thick black eye makeup, leaving no more than a smudge below each eyeball.

"Okay, fine Lacey," I said, but Lacey didn't pick up on my compliance and continued with the f-bomb tirade.

"This is fucking hopeless! It's hopeless! I can't contaminate my chair! I won't fucking do it! I just can't! I don't want to feel those germs on me every fucking time I sit in that stupid fucking seat only to subsequently contaminate my clean bed and my bedroom desk chair and-"

I listened as the once eloquent Lacey got carried away in a pitiful potty-mouth list all of the places she would infect with the "germ feeling" if she sat in her sacred chair. As I listened to Lacey's reasoning, even though it was irrational, an epiphany sparked within me. There was a pattern to her cross-contaminating germ anxiety. She wasn't *just* anxious about contaminating the chair, in the moment of sitting in it. She was anxious about feeling that contamination *later*, in the future, when she sat in the chair then supposedly sat in her bed on her clean sheets then on her clean quilt and etcetera. It was a complex and ever so layered anxiety about anxiety. She was literally anxious about being anxious.

"Okay," I held up both palms in surrender and tried to talk over Lacey's tangent, "We can be done!"

"I refuse to make one of the only comfortable places in my house- no, in the world- germy and," she suddenly realized I was on her side and dropped her mascara-smeared tissue onto the counter, "do you mean that? I don't have to continue with the ERP?"

"No, you don't," I sighed, my mind focused on how much it might help if Lacey would stop thinking ahead, into the future, and live in the moment. So in my most soothing tone I tried to bring her back to the now. "Right now, you're done. You've clearly reached your limit for today. Just... relax. It's over."

Lacey's naked eyes were still big and full of surprise. "Okay..."

When the next ERP session rolled around and, sure enough, Lacey spent another hour of sitting and touching things accompanied by the "germ feeling". And once again, she couldn't sit in her special clean family room chair.

Third ERP session came and yes, so did the "germ feeling".

Next session with Colleen she told us to just keep pushing, keep trying, to conquer that feeling. She was convinced that Lacey would coast from the feeling of being contaminated and no longer have the sensation of germs staining her skin.

The fourth ERP session arrived, and once again, Lacey felt the "germ feeling".

Fifth? You bet it, "germ feeling".

Sixth ERP session? What do you know, "germ feeling".

Seventh? "Germ feeling".

Nothing could desensitize Lacey the mysterious "germ feeling". No amount of graduated exposure made that feeling disappear.

At that point Colleen finally admitted in Lacey's next meeting with her that the "germ feeling" seemed like a complete mystery. Surprisingly, though, I was more mad by that confession than I was relieved. Wasn't she supposed to be the professional OCD specialist, here? Wasn't she supposed to fix Lacey?

Feeling the necessity to take matters into my own hands, I dedicated the next few sessions to cracking the contamination code with more heightened observation.

About two weeks of exposure response therapy had gone by and the amount of time Lacey spent performing ritualistic behaviors surrounding checking things, repeating things, and rearranging things had significantly lessened. But alas, the germ fear was no different. For selfish reasons that was the one problem I wanted fixed, above all else. Needless to say I was feeling discouraged.

Come to think of it, nobody, no doctor, no pamphlet, ever talked about a feeling, an actual physical feeling. They just talked about emotional feelings that transpired.

I don't think Colleen understood what Lacey meant when she said "germ feeling". And the fact that an OCD coach, an expert in obsessive compulsive disorder, did not understand that feeling and still told Lacey Parker that she was the most severe case she had ever encountered was a whole new level of eluding.

So I took it upon myself to solve the "germ feeling" enigma. I wanted to get to the bottom of this OCD. To finally answer Lacey's question that lingered at the bottom of her fateful poem that incited our entire relationship.

Is there any reasoning with this brain
when there is no sense of reason in this brain?
I can feel myself try to justify
all of the obsessions and compulsions
playing over like mental malfunctions
I can feel the hope that a new day will show
All I have ached to maintain
will finally be explained.

"He won't stop poking me!" Peter barked out after agitatedly whirling around and swiping the thin air with an oafishly bent hand.

"Pete, nobody's there," I declared for what felt like the hundredth time. At that point I didn't even bother to glance up from the "Exposure Response Prevention Therapy" packet I had been perusing.

"Yes he is Jef! I can feel Henry poking my shoulder!"

"Peter, there is nobody there. Your central nervous system is probably misinterpreting false sensory signals from false stimulus. You can't feel something that isn't actually touching you…"

Then it hit me.

The "germ feeling" Lacey had was crossing over the OCD line and veering into schizophrenic territory. Schizophrenia was a mental disease that caused hallucinations, and after scouring the glossary of my psychology textbook I found that a hallucination was defined as "a sensory experience of something that does not exist outside of the mind".

No, Lacey could not see or hear a person who wasn't real like Peter occasionally could with his imaginary friend, Henry, but Lacey was, to the touch, feeling an entity that wasn't real. She didn't have the conventional hallucination regarding senses like sight or sound. Instead, she had a hallucination of touch. And touch was certainly a sense.

At the next appointment with Colleen I relayed what I had discovered with her.

"Lacey hallucinates the feeling of germs in an eerily similar way that a schizophrenic hallucinates a vision or a sound," I shared. "I don't think it's something that can be taught away, I really think it's something that only medication can get rid of."

Lacey, having no idea about my germ hallucination discovery, was taken off guard when I mentioned it to Colleen.

"No it isn't Jef. I'm fine. The way I feel when I touch germs isn't that big of a deal."

It pained me to hear Lacey. I knew how intensely Lacey didn't want to be medicated, but I knew it was for the best. What was I supposed to do? I was here to help her, not hurt her, even if it made me feel like a traitor.

"You know what," Colleen interrupted, "I'm afraid Jef is right."

Suddenly Lacey flushed to a pale hue. Ever so delicately her shimmering rouge lips parted. The voice that came out of her trailed off skeptically. "What are you saying?"

Colleen frowned, "I'm saying you need to be on medication."

Chapter 72

Lacey couldn't have marched out of that building any faster.

"Lace," I didn't yell her name with full force, knowing I needed to save my voice for whatever verbal quarrel her quick tongue had prepared. I also didn't bother to run after her. I kept a steady pace, walking behind her petite figure as it stormed through the parking lot. Even though she wasn't facing me, I threw my arms out to signal my lack of options and disclaimed, "Lacey, you know I had to say something."

Lacey made it to her car but she still wouldn't turn around to respond. I watched her from behind as she struggled to grab the car keys out of her faux snakeskin purse.

"Lace..."
She grunted something to herself as she pounded her thumb onto the "Unlock" button of the battery operated keys.

Through my speed walking I made it to her side at the same time the car beeped and flashed.

"What was I supposed to do?"

I tried to stay cool. "I was just doing my job in there."

"What? To betray me?" she retaliated as she ripped the car door open.

"No," I pushed the door shut before she could get in, "my job is to make sure you're honest with your OCD coach. And I know you and you're anything but a liar, but calling your germ fear not 'that big of a deal' is the most blatant lying I've ever heard!"

Calling Lacey out for lying was beyond weird. She was always honest. Always. That honesty, I'd argue, was one of the strongest personality traits of hers. She believed in honesty to an extent where it was almost spiritual. And it was her high regard of honesty that made it significantly more telling about the power of her OCD, since it could compromise one of her most valued virtues. This anger she had towards me, it wasn't her, but her disease.

"You know how I feel about medicine!" she argued.

"This isn't about your feelings, this is about your thoughts."

"It's my brain, Jef! My brain! And I know what's best for it, not you!"

I could tell she didn't believe her own words.

"Lace..." my voice trailed off with doubt as I tried to reel her back in from her deluded rage.

Lacey kept with her tangent, though. "That was not okay for you to say! You don't decide whether or not I get medicated!"

"Lacey..."

"You're supposed to support me, not control me!"

"Lace!" I finally grabbed her by the shoulders.

"WHAT?"

I could feel her body trembling in my hands, even the right one wrapped with gauze. Lacey's chest was pumping up and down violently, trying to compensate all the air she didn't inhale in her misguided tirade.

"Look at me," I spoke quietly, as to calm her.

Her brown eyes fixed themselves on mine. With each breath the film of rage in her stare dissolved, leaving behind a vulnerable pair of eyes marked by fear.

"I'm not the bad guy," I whispered, "I'm here to help you."

Lacey's mouth shut itself, causing her shaky breaths to temporarily seize.

"I'm here to help you," I repeated, attempting to take advantage of her OCD mind so it would get stuck on *that* thought.

"I wouldn't be pushing for you to take medication if I didn't think it would help you."

Slowly Lacey's tight lips segregated, "What If I can't write?"

"You'll be able to write," I shut down confidently, still not breaking the stare I had on her.

"But what if it strips me of my creativity?"

"It won't," I said mindlessly.

Lacey picked up on my blind thought and said "Are you sure?"

Are you sure?

She had asked that so many times before. It was actually a cognitive symptom attributed to her obsessive compulsive disorder. I remember reading that in the packet Colleen gave us called "Types of Faulty Thinking In People With OCD".

"Desire for Certainty" was the type of thought process Lacey was currently exhibiting by asking me if I was sure that medication wouldn't negatively affect her creativity.

Lacey wouldn't let up in her quest for reassurance. "But how do you know it won't? How do you know, Jef? And don't say you read it on the web. Anybody can post anything out there."

She had a point. I didn't know how medicine would affect her creativity. From what I remember from when Peter was little and first trying to find a medication that suited him, he had to try a couple of different brands before finally settling on the right fit. In many ways it was an experiment.

Now I was questioning myself.

Feeling weaker, I lowered my hands off of the pleather caps of her shoulders.

My eyes shifted to the floor, then back up at Lacey's face. Her scared eyes imitated the scared eyes of the doe I had seen in the woods back in September, when I first met Lacey. I couldn't lie to those innocent eyes, and for the first time ever I actually felt compelled to admit my ignorance.

So, willingly, I admitted, "You're right. I don't know."

To my surprise, that confession felt good. I was relieved. Very relieved. And telling Lacey that I didn't know something made the mental equation that was our relationship a little more even. On her side of the equal sign she had been trying so hard to fight her OCD. Now, on my side, I put in the effort as well by trying to change my flawed know-it-all mindset. If she was gonna change her stubborn ways I might as well too.

Lacey's mind, finally having to face the serious decision of whether or not she was going to take medication, was racing with all sorts of "what ifs". And Lacey didn't hesitate to verbalize them to me. And I tried my best to answer her as honestly as possible, meaning a lot of my rejoinders were "I don't know".

"What if I get drowsy?" "What if I develop insomnia?" "What if it gives me headaches?" "What if it lowers my blood pressure?"

Then finally came the most thought provoking question of all.

"What if, without OCD, there's nothing interesting about me?"

This time, my answer wasn't "I don't know". Because this time I realized what Lacey's real problem with the idea of medication was. She was afraid of getting better. And why was that? Because Lacey had been wrapping her identity around her sickness since she self-diagnosed herself in seventh grade.

"This isn't about side effects, is it?"

Suddenly tears built up over Lacey's bloodshot eyes and she immediately plugged her running nose with the back of her hand.

I enveloped the silently crying girl in a hug. She submissively fell into me. Rubbing the pleather on her back, I tried to talk soothingly. "Is it possible that the reason you don't want to take medication is because you don't want it to work?"

Lacey didn't answer.

"Lace," I lowered my voice and leaned out of the hug to catch a glimpse at her.

Suddenly I got a lump in my throat.

She was in a worse emotional state than I anticipated.

Her face was red, her eyes were wet, and her stare was dead. It almost looked like she couldn't hear me over the deafening sound of her thoughts. "Lace?"

Her dead eyes sluggishly trailed up and fixed on mine and a monotone whisper came out, "Yes?"

"Why don't you want to accept yourself as more than a sickness?"

Ever so delicately and quietly she laid down the truth with her articulate tongue. "Not all stories should have happy endings, Jef. OCD is what my life's story has become about. And I don't think this kind of story deserves a happy ending."

I completely let go of Lacey and tried to stay composed while retaliating, "Why the hell not?"

Her shoulders bobbed up with ambivalence, "I'm not the kind of character that deserves a happy ending."

That's it. Fuck being composed.

"What has gotten into you!" I snapped. Seriously, what had gotten into her?

Lacey's shoulders bobbed again. Red eyes aimed down on the asphalt of the parking lot, dead as ever.

Silence overtook me as a self-taught mental scan ran through my brain, sifting through mental stacks and stacks of retained information. Going through filing cabinets. Then narrowing to folders. Then...

Bingo.

The applicable piece of information also came from the "Types Of Faulty Thinking In People With OCD" packet. It was known as the Fear of Positive Experiences. I had actually pointed out how much that sounded like Lacey in her car when I first scanned the OCD packets.

Some people with OCD express concerns that they do not deserve or will not be able to sustain positive experiences.

That was the disorder talking, not Lacey.

I tried to cool down so that I wasn't yelling at her. Replanting my feet in the pavement, I stood up straight and tried to reason with her as confidently as possible. "Let me ask you something. What horrible, unforgiveable thing have you, Lacey Parker, done in your life that's so bad, so bad you don't deserve to be happy?" The harder I stared into her dead eyes, the more glazed mine became. "What are you so mad at your *self* for? Think, really think, Lacey. Your *self*, not your illness, your *self*."

She threw her arms out, exasperatedly, "That's just it, Jef. I can't tell the difference between the two anymore! I don't know where this mental disease ends and where I begin. And you know whose fault that is?"

"We both answered at the same time.
"Not yours!"
"Mine!"

Lacey trumped my voice with her impassioned volume. "It's my fault, Jef! Once upon a time I had a mind separate from the OCD and the depression, back when I was a little girl playing dolls with my sister or sledding down the hill in my backyard with my cousins, but then puberty hit and the disease got worse, and you know who let them get worse? You know who chose to identify with melancholy and being an outcast rather than fight those self-sabotaging thoughts? You know who chose to keep searching for videos of their celebrity crush and fantasize about a life with him rather than ban themselves from the damn computer? You know who chose to push away their friends so that they could spend afternoons after school bathing the day away and then sitting on that one 'clean' couch in the house writing about a life that could have been? Me! It was my doing!" The end of Lacey's spiel was marked by the up and down bob of her small shoulder frame as her frail body was left heaving for air.

Lacey could go on and list every single mistake she made all she wanted and it still wouldn't change my mind. As far as I was concerned, obsessive compulsive disorder strategically fooled her into thinking she was voluntarily making all of those "choices". That didn't cut it for me though. I knew Lacey, and I saw the pain in her brown eyes more times than I ever wanted to admit, and that type of pain doesn't come from a person in control, but a person being yanked through life like a marionette. And looking in Lacey's dead eyes now, I knew beyond a doubt that she was no more than a victim of another one of this mental disorder's trickery. Before Lacey could push me away I clasped my hands on her shoulders again and craned my neck forward so that I was talking at her short level. "You didn't know any better." Juggling my objectives I made it my intermediate task to send Lacey a calm stare that would ease her into believing my words while simultaneously glaring away the grim reaper-like parasite thriving off of her pupils.

I could feel Lacey's tight posture loosen underneath my palms. Indifference to her former claim caused her massive eyes to lower to the ground while flickering between thoughts. "But..."

I didn't realize I was holding my breath with anticipation until I began to feel lightheaded. Literally, my role flipped from bolstering Lacey upright with my grasp to faintly leaning on her for support.

In the spur of the moment Lacey gasped, "No." She took advantage of my weakness and hastily reached up, transferring me out of contact by lowering my arms by the wrists. Just as she had done physically she verbally made an attempt to push me away, "I could have fought, Jef. I could have battled my obsessions. Instead I fueled them!"

"Please!" I scoffed. While the blood rushed back to my head I failed to censor my response and carelessly blurted out. "You didn't stand a chance!"

Suddenly Lacey fell into utter silence.

"Oh, God," I revoked in my subsequent panic.

Intensely scared to look in Lacey's eyes, afraid by how much less alive they must have looked compared to their already corpse-like visage, I spastically flinched my head down, hunched over in actual physical pain, while clasping my knee caps.

Don't throw up, Jef. Don't throw up.

Desperate to make amends I apologized, "Oh my God, I'm sorry... that was mean. That was..."

"Do you really think I didn't stand a chance against OCD?" Lacey's response came out with a squeak.

I couldn't lie to her. I squeezed my eyes shut and shook my head to the ground. "Yes," I answered with painstaking resentment between my gritting teeth.

My stomach was spinning in circles. My God Jef, don't throw up. Don't throw up. Don't-

"Thank you," Lacey sighed with a gratitude that threw me for such a loop I found myself, though still hunched over, glancing up to see her eyes. They were anything but dead.

"What?" my breath barely made a sound.

Suddenly the strength returned to my buckled knees and my vertebrate stacked atop each other until I was standing up straight, six feet and two inches.

Lacey didn't have to explain herself. One look in her eyes and I realized the effect of my comment. If Lacey had never stood a chance against the onset of her OCD then that meant she didn't have to resent herself for it. And it was my brutally honest and accidental comment which reassured her of that.

Then Lacey said something I never expected to hear her say.

"Alright. I'll try medicine."

Chapter 73

During the next Colleen session I attended with Lacey, Lacey informed Colleen that she was finally ready to try medication. The OCD coach handed Lacey a card for a psychiatrist, Dr. Betsy Ellington, and personally called Ellington to make Lacey an appointment. Colleen agreed to relay her notes of Lacey's OCD to Ellington before Lacey's first consultation. There, Lacey would be prescribed the appropriate medication to fight obsessive compulsive disorder.

After brief introductions Dr. Ellington took a seat behind her desk and explained the medical side of obsessive compulsive disorder.

"There is no known antidote for OCD. This disease can't be cured, but it can be controlled with the right therapy and biochemical modifications, and one can lead a very successful and fulfilling life."

"Uplifting," Lacey's wry tongue responded facetiously.

"You will never be completely free of this mental disorder, Lacey, but studies in the medical community have shown that selective serotonin reuptake inhibitors like Fluoxetine can bring patients like you one step closer to freedom."

Without meaning to (I assume), Lacey's face contorted into a grimace. It was such a micro-movement, but I definitely saw it.

At first my brain wasn't sure where Lacey's indifference was coming from. Then I replayed Dr. Ellington's statement through my mind one more time.

Freedom.

The word "freedom" set off all sorts of bells and whistles inside my brain, reminding me of the nature verses nurture discussion I had with Lacey. She had basically admitted an aversion to the well-known philosopher, Locke, and his theory supporting nurture over nature because it favored the freedom of the human mind over set in stone characteristics (from birth) of the human mind.

I guess I just value my legacy over freedom.

"We do have ample options when it comes to different medicines that can tweak the chemical imbalance in your brain, Lacey," Dr. Ellington explained.

Lacey was flushed. Scared, I think.

"I don't want to take an antipsychotic like people with schizophrenia," she immediately addressed since I put that idea in her head during the last visit with Colleen, where I compared Lacey's touch hallucinations to my brother's vision and sound hallucinations.

"After speaking with Colleen on the phone and reviewing the notes she has given me regarding your obsessive compulsive disorder behaviors I've decided on putting off the option of taking an antipsychotic, for now at least. I think we need to give antidepressants a try first since you've never taken any medication before. And I must say, I'm surprised you've gone as long as you have without medication. Not many people could do that."

"Yeah," Lacey laughed shyly.

Immediately Dr. Ellington's comment threw me in a panic. It sounded way too much like a compliment, which reminded me of Josh from group therapy's "we're the blessed folks" boasting. And Lacey couldn't afford to think that way. Her mind was finally starting to accept the idea of going on medicine for her disorder. The last thing she needed was to backtrack and doubt her newfound acceptance.

I took the floor before Dr. Ellington could charm Lacey out of this decision. "What kind of medication do you give somebody with OCD?"

"Well," Dr. Ellington sighed, "A lot of medications that I used to work very closely with have been taken off the U.S. market so we're down to a less ample array of options. Most often I prescribe Paroxetine, Escitalopram, Citalopram, or Fluoxetine to my patients suffering from obsessive compulsive disorder. I like to start people off with a basic antidepressant, Fluoxetine, and then turn to other drugs, either replacing or combining with the Fluoxetine if necessary."

"What exactly is Fluoxetine?" Lacey questioned the psychiatrist.

"Fluoxetine is a selective serotonin reuptake inhibitor."

"An 'SSRI'," I clarified.

Dr. Ellington flicked me a nod of the head, "Very good! Are you a pharmaceutical student?"

"Oh, no," I snickered uncomfortably, "I just did some research before we came here."

"Ah," the psychiatrist smiled, then speedily started to explain how an SSRI worked. I wouldn't be surprised if she was so quick to explain because she had an inkling about my habit of educating people when it wasn't my place. After all, she did specialize in reading the human psyche of everybody that came in her office.

"SSRIs impact the chemicals that the neurons in the brain use to communicate to other neurons in the brain. These chemical messengers are known as neurotransmitters. Serotonin is one neurotransmitter that is released by neurons in the brain and is the one that Fluoxetine affects. Serotonin either attaches to the receptors on nearby neurons or gets sucked back up by the neurons which produced it. This is known as the reuptake process. Fluoxetine prohibits the reuptake of serotonin so that there is an increase of free serotonin in the brain."

As I sat there, scratching the prickles on my chin, I glanced back and forth between Dr. Ellington and Lacey. I tried to read what Lacey must have been thinking. She looked very attentive, sitting there with her legs crossed, shimmering pink lips poised and shut, alert eyes glued to the psychiatrist, silently listening. I could tell she was trying really hard to understand this chemistry lesson which must have been like a foreign language to her.

"Antidepressants commonly work by preventing reabsorption of neurotransmitters like serotonin, and as a result there is an increase of serotonin levels in the brain. Serotonin affects neurons that are responsible for our mood, our appetite, and how we perceive our senses-"

"That!" Lacey interrupted the professional. "I want that."

"The only side effects you should look out for are headaches, dry mouth, gastrointestinal issues…"

As the psychiatrist spieled on I tried to perform the difficult task of grabbing her attention while sneaking by Lacey. I locked eyes with the woman and rapidly shook my head, trying to signal that it was not a good idea to give Lacey any more reason not to take the drug.

"Do you have a problem, Mr. Sterling?" the psychiatrist asked.

Wow. Way to call me out.

"I, uh," instead of lie I renounced my discrepancy and forwardly said what was on my mind, "Maybe you shouldn't give the obsessive person in the room more phobias to latch onto."

"So," Lacey raised her voice over mine, "Is Fluoxetine what you're going to prescribe me?"

"I think that's a safe place to start. Usually I prescribe 10mg a day for starters, but seeing that your case is very severe I think we're gonna increase it to 20mg a day. You might feel relief on the Fluoxetine right away, or you might have to do some trial and error with different medicines."

"Wait-" I threw my arm out in an attempt to shield Lacey from hearing the side effects for fear that she'd arouse them through hypochondria. "Maybe you shouldn't ask that…"

Lacey turned to me. "I have to know, Jef." She then turned back to Dr. Ellington. "What are the side effects?"

Dr. Ellington had no choice but to tell Lacey, seeing that she was her psychiatrist, not mine.

"The most common side effects I've found are drowsiness, vivid dreams, nausea-"

"Nausea?" I interrupted in a panic stricken tone. Being somebody who had a nervous stomach, that side effect struck a chord with me. Nausea was miserable. I didn't want Lacey experiencing that.

Suddenly I felt a cold hand wrap around mine. Alarmed, I jerked my eyes up to see Lacey, regardless of her uneasiness towards the medication discussion, staring at me with warm eyes. I think grateful for my accidental portrayal of empathetic concern.

Lacey's pink lips forced themselves into a gentle smile. She recognized that I, as much as I hate to admit it, needed comforting in that moment.

Though my stare was probably distraught I flashed her a sincere smile in return.

My mouth was composed and my eyes were distraught.

Lacey's mouth was distraught and her eyes were composed.

We were both a little content and a little worried. But it was okay. We were equal. Balanced. And we could lean on each other without tipping the other one over.

I was there when Lacey first gulped down her 20 mg pills of Fluoxetine. She wanted me by her side just in case she had a panic attack.

Nervously she stared into the orange bottle. "I can't believe I'm about to put this in my body."

"Think of that pill like a vitamin supplement. As if you had a vitamin deficiency. If you were short of Vitamin B12 in your system, then you'd take a Vitamin B12 supplement. You're short of a chemical in the brain, and this is gonna give you that chemical."

Before a second guess could enter her mind, Lacey poured a few pills into the white bottle cap, extended her tongue out, managed to no-handedly stick one 20 mg pill on her saliva coated tongue which retracted back into her mouth, then gulped down the capsule without anything to drink.

The moment of breath after Lacey threw her head back to swallow made my entire body feel lighter, like the stress was just vacuumed out of me.

Now we just had to wait and see.

Chapter 74

5:00 PM on a Friday night Lacey burst through my doorway. It took me a few seconds to realize why Lacey looked slightly different. She had her hair completely down, as usually, but in the past she would leave it in her face rather than put it behind her hair because she never wanted to touch her head or scalp with dirty hands. I watched as Lacey went from opening the door to swiping a loose strand of hair behind her ear without the tedious interruption of washing her hands.

It only took Lacey two seconds to realize she had forgotten to perform the ritual.

"Wait," her face flushed to a pallid paste. "I forgot to clip my hair back and-"

"It looks good," I interrupted.

With Lacey's stunted mind struggling to catch up to her actions she only allowed a brief second to acknowledge my compliment. "Thanks… but… I was supposed to freak out…" Lacey recognized after mere seconds delay. The delay was so short, but so substantial. "I should go wash my hands…"

"Says who?" I spoke up at a high pitch, afraid she'd give in.

Lacey paused, stuck in thought. No, she paused in lack of thought.

"I guess I could let it slide. It's already too late, right?"

On the positive, Lacey was actually snuggling up to me. My smitten heart was fluttering because I wasn't used to having her so close. I was a little self-conscious that Lace could feel my pitter-pattering heart since her head was using my chest as a pillow, but that insecurity quickly vanished once I realized she had almost instantly fallen asleep. That leads me to the negative, Lacey was incredibly drowsy ever since she started the Fluoxetine. It was only 5:33 and she was sound asleep.

"Lace," I whispered.

She only stirred a little.

"Lacey!"

"Huh?" Lacey moaned sloppily.

During the first follow-up appointment with Dr. Ellington, scheduled three weeks after Lacey started taking Fluoxetine, Lacey vented to the professional about her drowsiness. And I certainly vouched for that.

"Any other side effects?" the clipboard wielding psychiatrist asked Lacey.

"I can't even begin to explain how nauseous I've been feeling."

"Mmmm," Dr. Ellington moaned while jotting something down with her expensive-looking argyle printed bronze and gold pen. "Unfortunately this can happen. There can be a lot of trial and error when finding the right medication for a mental disorder."

"Yay," I sarcastically grunted.

"I think I'd like you to try Escitalopram. I'll write up a prescription for the 10mg capsules. The starting dose for treating adults and adolescents is 10mg once on a daily basis. Usually that gets bumped up to 20mg after a week."

"That seems kind of quick," Lacey feared.

"Actually, it's perfectly normal for Escitalopram to be increased after the first week because the benefit of the medication typically isn't seen until four weeks have passed."

I forced myself not to make another sarcastic comment under my breath.

In quick cursive Dr. Ellington scribbled down the prescription. "Oh, and no alcohol on this," the professional advised as she clicked her metallic argyle pen shut.

Lacey received the prescription, with a semi-proud grin, "That won't be a problem."

It didn't surprise me how expensive the medication was. Peter's schizophrenia meds was costly. Being mentally ill was damn expensive.

Chapter 75

The day that I noticed Lacey was, should I say, *advancing*, was when we decided to watch a movie. We didn't watch the movie, though. No, that wasn't because Lacey was in a promiscuous mood. She was curious about something else. Lacey couldn't take her eyes off of the bookshelf in my living room. For a span of three hours Lacey plucked book after book from the shelf. I had never seen her show an interest in books before, not on her own at least. She flipped through the pages and read the summaries on the backs of each book. What was interesting, to me, though, was how she only showed an interest in the textbooks or educational books. *The Ending of Time* by J. Krishnamurti and David Bohm. *The Fabric of the Cosmos* by Brian Greene. *Relativity and Quantum Physics for Beginners* by Steven L. Manly.

When Lacey was flipping through one of my favorite books, *In Search of Schrödinger's Cat : Quantum Physics and Reality* by John Gribbin, she paused on a random page, narrowed her eyes, and read out loud, "'In the quantum world, what you see is what you get, and nothing is real; the best you can hope for is a set of delusions that agree with one another.'" There was a brief moment of silence between us. "Hm," she eventually hummed. With a bit of hesitance her lips split apart. "Could I… could I borrow this, Jef?"

"Of course!" I answered without a split second to spare.

"Are you sure?"

"Take it!" I tore her tote bag off of the coffee table and opened it up wide, like it was a basket for her to toss a basketball in.

"Okay, okay," she chuckled and carefully placed the book inside, treating it like a delicate treasure.

Another major sign that Lacey was feeling better was that she was staying out later, without letting that tiresome shower routine stop her from going out. That was more than obvious when she agreed to hang out with Peter at my house until I got home from work around 10:00 PM.

Lacey told me that she was still going to shower, but she wasn't as upset about it. She still had the germ feeling. In fact, she still had most of her OCD quirks. But she was happy. She was in a good mood. She was making jokes. She was singing along to the music playing. She was touching things, including me. And even though I knew it bothered her, she was okay with it. She knew she could shower later. In that moment, she was touching me, she was happy, and it didn't affect her *now*. She would deal with the germs when she was good and ready to deal with them.

After a long night of work, when I walked into the house, I didn't see Lacey or Peter.

"Pete? Lace?"

"We're up here!" Lacey called in response, and I followed her voice to Peter's bedroom.

I stepped in Peter's room to see Peter half-asleep in bed and Lacey, sitting crisscross on the floor, with one of my binders in her lap and a good eight others splayed out on the rug.

"What are you doing?" I asked, awestruck.

"Oh, Peter wanted to go to bed. I felt like doing something productive with my time so I started reading some of your research binders. I hope you don't mind."

"No, uh, no," I mumbled, flabbergasted by her newfound interest.

"I'm reading about all sorts of stuff! Jef, did you know that prejudice against other cultures might be a result of evolution; our ancestors learned to fear other ethnicities because they perceived them as a threat? What am I saying, of course you know that! You wrote this!"

"Lacey, what are you doing?" I asked a second time.

"I told you, I'm reading. Learning. Filling my brain with as much knowledge as I can. I can't write about depression and pain forever, right?"

No words came out of my elated throat.

I was too beside myself.

"I don't feel like leaving myself in the dark anymore. I'm ready to turn the lightbulb on and learn. To be enlightened. To take cleaner notes about psychology and theoretical physics, like you do. I- I- I want to be part of the world I'm living in. And I know I can't if I leave my mind in the dark," Lacey babbled on while skimming my handwritten notes with the aid of her perusing forefinger gliding across the page.

"Which binder is that?" I finally talked and lowered myself to sit down across from her.

"Hm?" she glanced up with her dollish round eyes, "Oh, right now I'm looking through some sociology notes. But I've gotta say, that's not even the most interesting stuff you've researched about. I'm obsessed with your binder all about quantum mechanics." Lacey reached across the floor, retrieved my thick quantum physics binder, and begin flipping through it. "This stuff is fascinating! Like how quantum physics doesn't tell you where exactly a particle is, but the probability of where a particle is, meaning there's no certainty to the tiny things that make up our universe. Yet to larger particle objects like you and me can be measured and determined. Oh, and then I love how the notion of uncertainty and probability in the quantum world brings about concepts like this," Lacey flung her hand a couple of pages ahead, "the many-worlds interpretation! Ah, it's so cool! It says that the universe splits into parallel universes to accommodate every single quantum possibility! Every possibility, Jef! That means there are infinite universes! I had always heard about parallel universes, but it always went over my head. I actually understand where that theory comes from now! Oh my God and there's this idea of antimatter you wrote down," once again Lacey flipped through the loose leaf pages of notes in the binder and reiterated what I had written a mere two years ago, "a vacuum in space, you know, pure nothingness, actually possesses a mass because of energy-mass equivalence. And that mass brings about the whole idea of particles and antiparticles! It's just so incredible how reality can be so... so... insane! Who needs a mental disorder for inspiration when there's nothing more mind-boggling than the universe and every little particle in it? I've gotta say, it's pretty flattering that you would put my mind on the same caliber as this kind of stuff and even think to make a binder about me."

I couldn't have been more stunned to hear Lacey say that. And in my wondrous befuddlement I stammered through a relentless smile while she continued to ogle at the scientific notes underneath her nose. "But I... but you, I... I thought you didn't like being studied like a science experiment."

Lacey flicked her head in my direction and, with lips arched into a beautifully genuine grin, her eyes twinkled with the utmost clarity. She beamed, "I was never really your science experiment. I was your muse."

I smirked. Typical Lacey Parker to twist my methodical left-brained action with her eccentric right-brained romanticism.

"I can't believe this," I gaped at her. This medicine was accessing a potential that I never, in my wildest dreams, imagined Lacey would be able to get in touch with.

Lacey cocked her head to the side and shrugged compliantly, "Well, you know, I don't want to be an idle member of the human race anymore."

"You never were."

Before letting flattery overtake the conversation, Lacey gently closed the quantum physics binder in her lap shut and made a bold proclamation, "I don't know why but for some reason, now more than ever, I want to be well-rounded. To know a little bit about anything and everything. To be able to contribute in an intelligent conversation when you reference ancient philosophers or have something factual to say when you start with your aerodynamic Frisbee lessons," Lacey's stare lowered to her mismatched socks, reverting to the kind of apologetic shyness you'd expect from a child, "I know it sounds kind of weird coming out of my mouth but... I... I..."

"Yeah?" I urged.

With a deep breath she spit it out. "I finally understand why you love learning so much. Why it genuinely makes you feel like a better version of yourself. I was so caught up inside my own head that I couldn't fathom why somebody would feel like a better version of themselves by stepping outside of themselves. That seemed like a contradiction to somebody as self-absorbed and obsessive as me. Because I felt like a better version of myself when I lived from the inside out, taking thoughts from in this brain and putting them out on paper, through the aesthetics of writing. But now that I'm seeing clearer, I get it. I get why taking information from the outside and processing it inside your mind can make you feel better, more whole, excited even. To learn something, to stretch your mind over its horizons and explore thoughts you've never explored before, it's like you're discovering the endless potential of your mind, uncovering another facet you didn't even know you had. And it's so reassuring and invigorating and rewarding because learning something new makes you realize that you had potential all along, but you're just accessing it now with the help of outside knowledge from the external world. It's beautiful. And if it takes medication to help me realize that, then so be it. I- I," Lacey started to cry, "This was the right choice. Going on medicine. It was the right choice. I know it was. I have more to offer the world now that I'm interested in things outside of my own head, which is incredibly ironic, because I thought going on medicine would stifle my impact on the world, but turns out my mind on medicine is actually enabling my impact. I've never felt more inspired than I do now. And it can only get better from here."

    When I first made those binders I had no idea they would help rehabilitate a narcissistic introvert back into society. A storm of neurotransmitter molecules must have been exciting the neurons in my brain because I was higher than I could ever describe.

    All along I had done one of my favorite things, teaching, for one of my favorite people, Lacey.

Chapter 76

Lacey and I just finished watching the movie *A Beautiful Mind*. I was ecstatic that she didn't fall asleep during the movie. It was quite a testament to her new medication.
Completely out of surprise, Lacey pecked me on the cheek at the end of the movie.

"I'm sorry, I couldn't help it."

"Oh," in my flustered state I cracked a smile, "Okay…"

Slowly but surely I was adapting to Lacey's mindlessly impulsive and less methodical compulsive behaviors.

"Oh my God," her face went red and she backed up, "Was that totally out of line? Was that, like, completely rude? Are you annoyed?"

"No- stop," I laughed at her anxious banter, something I knew all too much about, and pulled her back into my personal bubble, "You're fine. Stop worrying."

Lacey lowered back down. After a few seconds she poked my cleanly shaven jawline.

"Smooth," she laughed.

"You are very touchy feely today," I realized.

"Oh, sorry," she retracted her hand and shrunk lower on my chest.

"No, I'm not complaining," I laughed. "It's nice."

She smiled up at me, then snuggled deeper in my chest.

Loving the moment, and greedy for more moments like this, I thought of how much I wished Lacey and I could just move into an apartment together next year while I commuted to a university. We could never do that, though, if she had to sleep in a separate bed or never touch me after a shower and blah blah blah.

As Lacey nuzzled against me I blurted out my dissatisfaction.

"Are you going to shower as soon as you get home?"

Lacey leaned off of me, "You know I have to."

I sighed, "Why isn't this 'germ feeling' going away? It's a form of a hallucination. I know it is. I really thought I figured it out this time. I don't get it. You're taking medicine…"

"It is what it is, Jef. At least I'm in a better mood. Doesn't that count for something?"

"Of course it does," I agreed. "But I still want to understand your OCD."

"What do you wanna do, interview me?" Lacey laughed.

I paused.

That sounded like a good idea.

"Seriously?" she lowered her voice.

"Maybe it would help."

She egged onward, "You really wanna get to the bottom of this mental disorder? No matter how dark it might be down there?"

"Yes," I said with resilient sincerity. "Yes, I do!"

"Fine. Let's do this," Lacey maneuvered herself off the couch.

I was a bit flustered. "Where are you going?"

"Outside. Bring a notebook. We can at least get some fresh air while we do this."

Thank God the weather was warmer.

Lacey and I sat in the grass in her backyard. The weather was beautiful and it was a more cheerful environment to be in while I picked her brain for answers to her mental disorder. This time, I had a notebook in my lap. I was prepared to record our conversation on paper so that I could look back at it later.

I replayed the scene of Lacey flinching at the leaf that fell from the tree on our nature walk I remembered the extremely odd information she told me about how she isn't afraid of touching things from nature unless a person had touched them prior. So, for the most part, Lacey felt manmade objects or objects potentially handled by man were dangerous germ ridden entities that needed to be evaded at all costs. If I had to make a hypothesis out of that information I'd say there must be some psychological fear of people, or at least a fear of contact with people, built in Lacey's maze of a mind.

I began, releasing my question with the wind. "So… do you feel the germs on you right now?"

Lacey ran her freshly washed hand through her hair, flipping it so that her natural part was disguised by a fuller body of hair. "No. My hands are clean. The grass is clean, at least in my opinion. This- this is good. This is safe. Its people germs that are horribly dangerous. If I touch a germ that had previously touched a person then it's all over."

People.

People were closer to the root of the touching fear. Interesting…

I felt like I was onto something, so I directed the conversation onward with a follow-up question.

"What's so bad about people?"

Lacey's shoulders moved up and down, "I'm not sure. They're just, I don't know."

I could tell she was thoroughly perplexed. I was too, but I tried not to show it. I needed to be her rock right now. So, like any good rock, I presumed a stoic disposition and reworded the question. "Why is touching something that touched another person so dangerous?"

"Because," Lacey reacted adamantly in contrast to her lingering confusion, "People are covered in germs."

I didn't break my role as interviewer. "What if you could somehow know, for a fact, that the person hadn't touched any germs before touching you? Say it was possible for you to *know* that the skin on their hand was 100% clean, germ-free, and say that hand touched your hand. Then would it still make you anxious if they touched you?"

"Yes," Lacey spit out, not a moment of hesitation between the end of my question and the beginning of her answer. What was odder than her speedy response was the humored tone behind it. For whatever reason Lacey seemed to find it somewhat silly to even consider the hypothetical touch of a clean human hand as anything short of dangerous.

"Hm," I leaned back, intrigued. What could that possibly mean? "So it's not solely about germs, is it?"

"I don't know," climbed a grumble out of Lacey's throat as she folded her arms over her chest and picked her legs up off the grass so that her knees pressed against her crossed arms. "I guess 'germs' is just a label I gave that indescribable feeling of contamination from another person. That mysterious but real, physical feeling... that physical feeling that nobody else seems to be able to feel except for me."

My brain was hard at work trying to decipher the elusive information spewing from Lacey's honest mouth.

Lacey continued spilling her thoughts, "But that's not to say I don't want other people in my life. I do! But I want the *right* people. I never want to be touched by the wrong people. People who enhance my own personality. Like a friend or a family member or," her eyes flashed to me, "a lover."

I tried really hard not to turn red, but I could feel my shy face burning up.

"Am I scared of intimacy? Yeah, of course! But not if it's the right person, like you, Jef."

My eyes transferred to the ground and, speechless, I covered my mouth with clasped hands. I didn't foresee the conversation going this way, into personal territory, and it threw me a little. So I attempted, with all my might, to reclaim my control as an impartial interviewer by swaying the Lacey's spiel a few steps back.

"Hold up. You said you didn't want to be touched by the 'wrong people'. What constitutes a person as 'wrong'?"

"I don't know. I guess I'd consider somebody the 'wrong' person if they didn't care about me."

"False," I shut down, "Your parents care about you, don't they? Your entire extended family cares about you. I care about you. But you still feel contaminated when we touch you, right?"

"Oh yeah," Lacey crinkled her nose and squinted aimlessly into the swaying grass blades. "I guess it's not so much people who don't care about me... but people who don't understand me. I don't want to be touched by people who don't understand me perfectly."

I chuckled a little, "Well that's a real recipe for loneliness, Lace. *You* don't even understand you."

Lacey's annoyed pupils were sharpened darts, tiny and precise in rich pools of hazel under the brightness of the sunlight, aimed directly at me. It must have been irritating for her to listen to me correct her wording.

Exasperatedly, Lacey's chest raised then deflated as she took a deep breath. "Okay," once again she tried to rephrase her answer, "By 'people who don't understand me' I mean people who don't know what it's like to be me in my head from my point of view, having my very thoughts. Verbatim. Or feelings. People who can't feel what I feel. I'm scared of being touched by people who don't know what it's like to be me, firsthand."

"So you're scared of being touched by somebody who isn't you," I declared, then skimmed the notes in front of me. "You're literally afraid of being touched by anybody in the entire universe. Regardless if they're completely clean and germ-free. Regardless if you want them involved in your life as a friend, a family member, a partner. Regardless if they care about you. Regardless if they understand you from a secondhand point of view. Regardless if they love you."

"Well, yeah..." Lacey's inflection trailed off with uneasiness.

I continued to dissect her statements out loud. "So other people are scary. Clean, understanding, loving people are still scary. It's the fact that they're not you that scares you. Why are other people scary?"

"Oh God. I don't know," Lacey exhaled, "I have no freakin' idea what goes on in another person's head and I don't want," Lacey paused to regroup so that she could hold back any sign of vulnerability in her poignant voice, "I don't want somebody else's existence to infect me. I don't want their being mixing into my being and I can't let another identity touch me, I won't let another identity touch me, because if I do... if I do then that lessens who I am. It takes away from my individuality."

A miraculous epiphany was unfolding out of Lacey's stammering mouth and into my ears. I could feel it. I couldn't understand it, yet, but I could feel it. The epiphany was so close I could almost touch it. So I forced Lacey to ramble on, even if she thought she said it all and had nothing left to say. Because I knew, beyond a doubt, that we were onto something. I believed that thanks to Lacey during one of our earliest tutoring sessions, when she said there was a story inside each and every one of us, whether we knew it or not, it wanted to be told. You just had to find it. And I was going to find that mysterious story hiding inside of Lacey Parker. I swear, I was going to find it.

"I am *me*. I am supposed to be entirely *me*. And I don't want other people coming inside, tapping into who I am, infecting who I am, and redefining who I am. I- I don't want that! I can't have that. If I want to remain *me*, safe and purely *me*, then I can't allow myself to be touched by other identities."

I retraced the trail that the conversation had taken.

Germs pointed the finger to *people*.

People pointed the finger to *intimacy*.

And *intimacy* pointed the finger to *touching*.

And then it hit me. After all the struggle and strife of trying to understand the greatest mystery my brain had ever stumbled upon, I saw a glimmer of an explanation.

"Lace... I don't think you're scared so much of germs or people or intimacy or touching. I think all of those fears are just projections of your ultimate fear... a fear of not having a significant identity in this inconceivably massive world."

"Oh my God," Lacey gasped.

Chapter 77

"Alright," I pushed the laptop off of my lap and onto the floor without even closing the internet window regarding the anatomy of touch. I hadn't told Lacey that I became sidetracked from typing a psychology essay regarding human perception.

On eager feet I paced to the whiteboard mounted on my bedroom wall. In my eagerness I mindlessly ripped off the cap of the Expo marker with my teeth.

Lacey mocked me with a faux cringe, "Are you about to teach me calculus, or…?" She hopped off of my bedside, then sat herself on the floor in front of me. Her posture was attentive, upright with shoulders back, and hands in her lap. Like a conscientious student.

"This is what I got. The parietal lobe of the brain contains the somatosensory cortex…" I scribbled a mediocre brain onto the whiteboard, filling in the area of focus with squiggles that squeaked with every angle.

"This part of the brain is responsible for processing any sensory input, dominant or latent, from the skin."

The tense fissures on Lacey's forehead marked her deep thinking in a treasure trove of vocabulary definitions and Latin derivatives. "Latent. Latent meaning hidden… untapped… subconscious…"

"Subliminal input," I verified in elation then immersed myself back into the whiteboard.

"The skin can perceive any type of touch. Temperature, pain, and pressure. Now correct me if I'm wrong, Lace, but these 'voices' lingering on your skin, this is feeling of pressure, right?"

"You would be correct," Lacey let out a coy laugh and leaned forward into her contorted crisscrossed position, wringing each ankle, as if settling into a yoga pose. I couldn't help but notice the illuminated skin upon her sternum as she bent forward. A flush of pins-and-needles swept down my torso. I wasn't used to seeing this woman, usually so stiff, now nimble. Was this conversation relaxing Lacey? Like when I summarized science textbooks for her in the library? Was Lacey even aware of the drastic difference her subtle shift in posture had made?

"Uh, so the skin. Um," I fidgeted with the hair above my brainstem, shook off the tension in my bones, then refocused, "Er- skin. Right, pressure. So…"

I drew a rectangle divided by three horizontal lines, labeling each substrate as a skin layer.

"This top layer of skin is the 'epidermis', made of entirely dead skin cells and touch receptors. This second layer is the 'dermis', where you find hair follicles, oil glands, sweat glands, nerve endings, and, lo and behold, more touch receptors. The bottom layer, the 'subcutaneous tissue', attaches to muscles and tendons. We don't need to worry about that bottom layer. The touch receptors coating the epidermis and dermis skin layers 'feel things' by adapting to change in stimulus. Any touch, hot, cold, vibration, or mere pressure is none other than a sensation perceived through adaptation. Now, this is where it gets interesting. A touch receptor is either rapidly adapting or slowly adapting. Rapidly adapting touch receptors can sense when a touch begins and ends, whereas slowly adapting touch receptors only sense the continuous pressure in between. You, Lacey, feel pressure the split second it begins to touch, but never seem to feel it end."

"Unless I wash it off with soap," Lacey added.

"Right, right- well actually no, not right," I diffused the notion with the wave of a hand, "washing a touch off is a completely illusory experience."

"Oh thanks," Lacey snorted at the blunt rebuttal.

Before I let Lacey and her adorable manner distract me, I forced my eyes back on the whiteboard.

"Of the four touch receptors, the only one we need to focus on are the ones dedicated to perceiving pressure or texture, the mechanoreceptors. When your mechanoreceptors are stimulated they transmit a message to the brain from neuron to neuron, brain cell to brain cell."

"So are you implying that my mechanoreceptors are broken? They send messages when there's no-"

"Stimulus," I completed. "And I'm not sure. It could be that the sensory receptors are going haywire, or the neurons leading up to the brain, or the brain itself. Stimulus, like pressure, is outside energy and information about the world that gets transformed into electrical impulses. Those electrical impulses are then handled by sensory nerves, which are basically the mailmen carrying information from the sense organs, along nerves of the peripheral nervous system, to their destination in the brain. There, inside the brain, is where our senses get analyzed and you're able to comprehend information like hues in your field of vision or the sensations of warmth on your skin. Obviously you aren't conscious of every little sense around you, otherwise you'd be somewhat of a superhuman. You don't really see every little image in your peripheral setting at once or feel every thread of your clothing on every square inch of your body and every other sensation both inside and outside your body. That's why the nervous system does this amazing thing where it determines which electrical impulses of stimuli are the most important. It chooses just how aware or unaware you should be of each piece of information. Now my thought is that, for whatever reason, your brain has conditioned itself to be hyperaware of every infinitesimal touch on the skin. That would adequately explain your intense fatigue after doing the most simple of tasks. Touch, when sensed by your brain, is on a whole new caliber of awareness! A caliber based on fear and anxiety and, again, for whatever reason fear and anxiety get more attention in your OCD brain than the non-OCD brain. And that brings me to my next point!"

Quickly I drew a diagram of the human brain's limbic system.

"The limbic system is responsible for emotions. A key structure in the limbic system is the amygdala. The amygdala evaluates sensory information, but what separates it from the cerebrum is that the amygdala determines the emotional importance and reactions to that sensory information. It's what assesses danger and threats. The amygdala is what evaluates emotions like fear and anger, both emotions you're overcome by when you feel that contaminated 'germ feeling' on your skin. And when the amygdala feels endangered it alerts the cerebral cortex, the place I mentioned earlier that is extremely significant in processing touch and the cerebral cortex determines whether or not the fear alert is valid. It does the reasoning. People with damage to the amygdala struggle with recognizing fear and people with damage to the cerebral cortex have difficulty turning off fear reactions, or as you like to call them, 'blaring sirens' and 'vibrant danger signs'. Now, I don't think you have brain damage Lacey, but I do think it's possible you have an inborn deformity that didn't affect you full force until your brain pruned during puberty, explaining your sudden ability to feel germs. Your emotional complexity and how in touch you are with emotions suggest that parts of your brain like the amygdala, hypothalamus are overactive."

"That's incredible Jef," Lacey said in dumbstruck bewilderment. "You should be more than satisfied with that conclusion."

"I'm not," I countered bluntly. "All this nervous system stuff would solve *how*. That's half of the puzzle. Now I just need to understand *why* you have these unheard of germ feelings. Why touch is registered at a higher alertness in your brain. Why-" right as my nervously shifting stare fixated back on Lacey's wide and curious eyes I realized that all this research left me with more questions, and no set-in-stone conclusion for her. The back of my burnt out cranium knocked against the white board of tile and I sunk down to the floor, "And I still don't have an answer for you."

"Well it's a theory Jef," Lacey crawled across the carpeted floor then plopped her little figure in front of me. "That's one step closer to figuring out my OCD. Right? That's the first step of the scientific method, isn't it?"

My glazing eyes cleared as the smirk crept on my face, "Yes," I reached out an open palm, silently asking Lacey for the okay to touch her hand. She smiled and complied by joining her hand with mine, then, totally uncharacteristically, fell forward to nuzzle her head into my chest.

I'm sure Lacey felt my racing heart slamming against her eardrum.

Ten or twenty or maybe thirty minutes passed of pure silence. Nothing but close proximity between Lacey and I.
"Jef," I felt the heat of her breath as she muttered into my sternum. "You're gonna drive yourself crazy speculating about my OCD."

"I don't understand why I can't understand it, Lace. I can wrap my brain around esoteric subjects like quantum mechanics with concepts as baffling as wave-particle dualty or as mind-bending as the uncertainty principle, but I can't wrap my brain around this, around you and your mental illness."

Lacey's brown eyes lowered. She thought for a moment. Then her eyes locked back onto mine.

"Theories. They need empirical evidence to be proven, right?"

"Well yes."

With the crack of her joints, Lacey stood up and reached out an open palm, beseeching for my hand.

I was confused, "What?"

"You've got more than enough evidence. Let's go through that research binder."

Chapter 78

The other half of this conundrum, the half about *why* Lacey's OCD functions in the way that it does, isn't centered on physiological studies about the nervous system. It's intuitive and personality based, it requires introspection that I couldn't begin to understand on Lacey's behalf, and nobody is more in touch with their emotions and personality than Lacey.
Lacey flipped through the "Obsessive Compulsive Disorder & Lacey Parker Proverb" binder.

"So," she started and pointed at some paragraph. "Where to begin?"

I wasn't looking at the binder though. I was looking at her. Lacey and her focused stare down on the information in front of her. It made me all too happy to see her embracing the research rather than fearing it.

"Jef?"

I snapped out of my love-struck spell at the sound of her saying my name.

"Well," I picked up my "Obsessive Compulsive Disorder & Lacey Parker Proverb" binder, "I have been recording all of the profound and dramatic things you say in this binder. If we meticulously rake out certain quotes, then maybe we can find a pattern behind your virtues, morals, and yes, thoughts. And the most elusive quotes you can further explain to me."

Lacey nestled up beside me and peeped a simple, "Okay."

We rummaged through the binder and read every intricate detail. Every little note I had ever collected. I reread quotes I had memorized Lacey saying long ago and written them on my whiteboard. I worked like a manic workaholic.

"This notebook is a key to another world. I live in a mental landscape. A realm of daydreams. I use my mental illness and melancholy to create other worlds, alternate universes, make-believe dimensions, whatever you wanna call it. In those other worlds I thrive. And thanks to this notebook I can record what I see, think, and feel in those worlds. Those worlds are special places, and it would be a sin not to write about them."

"OCD brings out emotions and an extreme thought process that I can incorporate in my daydreams. The pain, the darkness, it fuels me to write. This mental illness, my demise, is the birth of my art."

"I get so overwhelmed by my own thoughts and emotions that I feel like I have to choose between me and other people because I have no capacity for both. And I always choose me. I have to. I don't know why, but I have to."

"I don't get the germ feeling when anything from nature touches me, like leaves, grass, pine needles… I feel nothing. No anxiety is triggered. Now if I saw a person touch that leaf before it touched me then I'd get that germ feeling. Or if that leaf was in a place that most likely got touched by a human being then I'd feel a horribly nerve wrecking stain on my hand. But it came from the top of that tree, and I know a human didn't touch that single leaf before it fell."

"If my mind wasn't made to be this way, at birth, then that's like saying I'm not and never was an individual."

"Sentences and idealized conversations in hypothetical scenarios are swirling around my brain and I need to get them out on paper or else… it all feels like a waste. The thoughts. The emotions. The experiences, real and make-believe. All of it seems like a waste. I, I seem like a waste."

"Maybe life scares me."

I stood back from the board.

There were so many components. So many potential suspects. Personality traits, mental sickness, phobias, and a world of other characteristics. There was narcissism. There was a fear of intimacy. There was martyrdom.

"This is fascinating, it really is. You, you are fascinating. *You* are a marvel."

"Aw, you're too kind," Lacey laughed modestly.

The mystery that was Lacey's brain was starting to make a little more sense. Was her obsessive compulsive disorder rooted from an identity crisis? Was all this darkness and martyrdom she felt obligated to serve (with every fiber of her being) a way to maintain individuality with the utmost uniqueness?

"I'm noticing there's a recurring theme in a lot of the things you say."

"Really?"

"Yeah. Like- like- like a pattern or a, uh…"

"A common denominator?"

"Well, that's math, but I guess in a metaphorical sense, yes. A common denominator."

"Wow, look at us!" Lacey whacked me in the upper arm, "You talkin' themes and metaphors and me talking math!"

I could feel a dimple dent my cheek as I flashed her a smirk. She was still as cute as ever when she tried to make mathematical references.

Retracing my thoughts, I went back to announcing the observation presented through the whiteboard.

"Lacey, if there's one thing you've made clear, ever since we met, it's that you don't want to be ordinary. And you renounced from ordinary ways of living when you succumbed to an extreme mental disorder that made it near-impossible to touch or be touched without experiencing incredible discomfort."

"True." Lacey agreed.

"Hear me out. When I asked you to describe yourself you said 'sick'. Sick! Don't you see? The OCD is connected with your identity. And deep down you don't wanna get rid of it, 'cause getting rid of the OCD would be like getting rid of something you've made a fundamental part of your identity.

"Is it possible that you felt so uncomfortable being physically close to somebody because intimacy in any form contradicts this lonely persona you've cultivated? And is it possible that the obsessive compulsive disorder is intertwined in that identity crisis phenomena? That your brain has fabricated some very real 'germ feeling' whenever you touch anything that might have been touched by somebody else because in this very complex metaphorical way physical contamination reflects the internal contamination of your individuality. And it drives you mad that something outside of yourself has touched you. Like any piece of this world is an infection to your make-believe world. So, your brain created this disorder to single you out, to seclude you from the rest of society, mistaking loneliness for individuality? Your brain in its misconstrued way thinks it's protecting you. That's gotta be the reason why you hear all those sirens and see all those danger signs. Those are things built to protect a person from danger. And your greatest idea of danger is losing yourself. When you touch somebody or something that somebody else touched you are coming into contact with the life in this world, which the sick part of your mind misinterprets as somehow diminishing your life. And somebody with a narcissistic personality can't stand the idea that your identity might be less significant in the big scheme of the world as a whole. Hence why you overindulge in an alternate fantasy world, because there you are significant. In your writing, in your mind, in your imagination, your identity is preserved.

  You can't deny, Lace, that there are uncanny parallels between your artistic personality and your obsessive compulsive disorder. Both thrive in your loneliness. Both dwell on your negative feelings. Fear drives OCD and sadness drives your art."

  "So are you saying that my identity, or illusion of an identity, is no less a disease than my obsessive compulsive disorder?" She looked queasy while grasping this new concept, "Is my entire being just a disease? Just some flawed mistake that found its way into the human race?"

  "No, not flawed," I corrected, "Wildly different, eccentric, advanced to a detrimental degree, but anything but flawed. I think you value what you feel internally because you fear what you feel externally. A touch on your skin is a contamination, but a touch on your heart is a revelation. It's almost like coming into contact with anything in the world is a violation. But when you come into contact with any emotion in your mental landscape it's is a treasure. And you want to hold onto your feelings, that treasure, so you take your key," I pointed to her notebook, "and you lock it away- AKA write about it. You're keeping a record of your feelings. And it isn't until you record them that you feel free to let them go. That creative process is eerily similar to your OCD."

  I grabbed a whiteboard marker and made a chart, "Creativity" on the left and "OCD" on the right. With the marker in hand I explained, "First you feel something. Left- emotion. Right-germ. Next you manipulate that feeling. Left- write. Right- wash your hands. Then at the end you finally feel safe to let go. I think it's incredible. Staggering. The place where you access your creativity is also the place where you access your irrational thoughts. Which makes sense, because artists usually have a few screws loose. And it's exactly what you described your mental world as. The place with decaying trees and marvelous castles. It's beautiful, and it's dark.

You're writing a story. It's almost like a creative ruse where you log your emotional history through plots that are directly proportional with your life experiences."

"Every revelation, every milestone, gets written on some loose leaf sheet or lacerated piece of paper. Almost like, like, an obsession in itself. Even your greatest quality, this God given talent of written word, has an obsessive compulsive component to it.

"You place all of your value, as a human being, on your thoughts. Your thoughts towards experiences, your thoughts towards fictitious scenes and stories you've fabricated in your mind, your feelings about anything and everything. And that must be why you obsessively record all of it on paper. You're like the masterpiece of your thoughts and, at the same time, your thoughts are the masterpiece of you. You are your greatest masterpiece, and that can be tied back to the narcissism that you experience. It's no wonder you try and protect yourself from every little germ or general intimacy or threat to your individuality.

"It's no wonder you want to be a professional writer. You were born to be one. Some people contribute manual labor to society, and some people contribute scientific discoveries, but you contribute your imagination and your creativity and your feelings and your thoughts and your struggles and every little thing that your brain has to offer. You contribute you. And don't you see? That's all you've ever wanted. For you, *yourself*, to touch the world."

    I shook my head, in pure awe of Lacey, the marvel I stumbled upon. She took away my breath in the most beautiful way.

    "I know for a fact that you've touched me, and someday you're going to touch a whole lot of other people. The people in this world are so lucky. *I* am so lucky. I feel like I've made the greatest scientific discovery I could have made in studying your brain, Lacey."

Chapter 79

Proudly I stabbed the whiteboard at the end of my spiel then threw the marker to the floor.

"Ha! Let's see a therapist do that!" I joked, then smirked and leaned over, "Pay up."

Lacey just stared at me. In awe. Or was it fear? Or anger?

I took an extra pause to try and decode Lacey's large eyes locking onto me. They were so serious. Like she was ready to beat me up.

Oh shit, she was angry with me, wasn't she?

My smirk tightened a little as I froze. "Are you about to jump me for my lunch money or something?"

That assumption wasn't too far off. She was about to jump me, but for a different reason.

"I love you!" Lacey exclaimed then pounced onto me.

"Oof!" I nearly fell over.

Before I knew it, we were tangled in affection.

"I love you," Lacey pulled out and gasped, "I love you more than I could ever describe."

"I love you too," I responded as quickly as possible so I could get back to massaging my lips onto hers.

But Lacey couldn't stop herself. She interrupted peck after peck with a failed attempt to verbalize her feelings, "I'm so, I, I don't know how, I just, just-"

"Oh my God," I couldn't help but laugh with my now scrunching nose adjoining hers. "Lace, you don't always have to be so wordy."

"I don't? I don't know how to express myself. What am I supposed to do when I can't say how I feel? Am I supposed to just, just," suddenly she yanked me close by the shirt and melded a kiss onto my mouth. After a slow exhale she found her vocal chords, "I guess that's what makes touching so special."

She wiped away stray locks of hair with her fingertips, not the back of her hands.

Just to see her do the simplest of actions was blowing my mind.

For her, this was unhinged. And, miraculously, it wasn't causing her any noticeable stress.

I could feel that the strength of her happiness, the happiness that I elicited forth, was stronger than any fallacy her mind could fabricate. The power of my touch, that sensory stimulus, was enough to surmount above all the irrational nonsense. I, in my rawest state, was able to demote what were once warped beliefs down to trivial thoughts.

I couldn't have felt more relevant in her life than I was now, in this interpersonal act.

"I want to give you an answer Lacey. You know me, I love answers. But with this, I don't have one." I confessed on our walk along the forest trail.

Lacey nodded, "I know."

I shook my head and let my arms drop to my sides, still in disbelief. "I'm sorry."

She cradled my jaw in her hands, "Don't be."

I was a little overcome by surprise. "Aren't you disappointed? I don't have an answer to why you have OCD. It's just... just... a theory."

"Jef," Lacey laughed, and to my surprise a film of tears lined her doe eyes. "I'm going to tell you something, and I want you to listen very carefully."

"What?" I begged in desperation, anticipating the warm solace of a new Lacey proverb.

She took a deep breath, then recited with a debonair candidness, "'To know that we know what we know, and to know that we do not know what we do not know, that is true knowledge.'"

Somehow, the warm solace emanating off of this statement struck me frozen.

"Copernicus," I realized as an awe-induced chill cast through my body, "you just quoted Copernicus."

"Yes," she nodded giddily.

The corner of my lip curled and a laugh tumbled out. It may have seemed like nothing to the average person, but to us, to Lacey and I, we both knew what a major feat it was for her to step outside of her self-centered mindset and use somebody else's words for a change.

With arms speckled in goosebumps, I furled Lacey into a hug, and she didn't flinch.

Overwhelming emotion caused a humble crack of the throat as I professed my feelings for Lacey, "I love you."

"I love you too. So much," Lacey promised.

I printed a kiss on Lacey Parker's forehead, right in front of her beautiful brain, making an impression on the outside of her mind to correlate with the impression that was inevitably stored inside of her mind.

Made in the USA
Middletown, DE
09 December 2018